RATIONAL CREATURES

ELIZABETH ADAMS   NICOLE CLARKSTON

KAREN M COX   J. MARIE CROFT   AMY D'ORAZIO

JENETTA JAMES   JESSIE LEWIS   LONA MANNING

KARALYNNE MACKRORY   CHRISTINA MORLAND

BEAU NORTH   SOPHIA ROSE   ANNGELA SCHROEDER

JOANA STARNES   BROOKE WEST   CAITLIN WILLIAMS

EDITED BY CHRISTINA BOYD

RATIONAL CREATURES

Library of Congress Control Number: 2018954620

ISBN: 978-0-9986540-6-5

Cover design by Shari Ryan of MadHat Books

Cover image by Eduard Friedrich Leybold, *Portrait of a Young Lady in a Red Dress with a Paisley Shawl*, 1824 (public domain)

Layout by Beau North

PRAISE FOR THE AUTHORS

RATIONAL CREATURES

"Jane Austen's heroines are reimagined in these pages: obstinate, head-strong girls, and women of spirit. We discover them anew, bright and sparkling, and above all, Rational Creatures." —Gillian Dow, Chawton House

"These are thoughtful women—rational women—with a quiet strength. Their stories feel both extraordinarily timely and quintessentially of the period. A perfect collection for lovers of Regency romance as well as those seeking historically accurate examples of feminine dignity and self-respect. Highly recommended." —Bestselling author & historian Mimi Matthews

"Reading Rational Creatures is like slipping in to the missing pages of Austen's novels." —Drunk Austen

"An excessively diverting bespoke short story anthology inspired by Jane Austen's socially and romantically challenged female characters, who after 200 years continue to reveal to us why being in love is not exclusive of being a rational creature."—Laurel Ann Nattress, editor of *Jane Austen Made Me Do It*

ELIZABETH ADAMS
Green Card, "You know the characters are interesting and well-crafted when four hundred pages doesn't feel like enough." —Austenesque Reviews

On Equal Ground, "This book marks her literary signature, she is not afraid to risk controversial stories and executes them beautifully!"—From Pemberley to Milton

The 26th of November, "I had a smile on my face the whole time I was reading this book. I sighed wistfully after finishing it and went back to my favorite scenes to enjoy it again." —Of Pens and Pages

CHRISTINA BOYD
The Darcy Monologues, "Think of *The Darcy Monologues* as your JAFF gateway drug. Don't worry, experts agree: it lowers anxiety, increases imagination, and is very good for health." —Period Drama Madness

Dangerous to Know: Jane Austen's Rakes & Gentlemen Rogues, "Each tells a story that was left out of Austen's original works. They manage to tell each in such a way it feels authentic to her vision and style." —Silver Petticoat Review

NICOLE CLARKSTON
These Dreams, "…engaged and enthralled throughout this story as she shifts from various settings to different characters, all the while weaving terrific intrigue and mystery…" —Just Jane 1813

No Such Thing as Luck, "Nicole Clarkston's John Thornton is romantic, strong and wonderful, as well as the brilliant mill owner admired by all. I fell in love with him again." —More Agreeable Engaged

London Holiday, "Nicole Clarkston did it again…an effortless masterpiece that reveals how comfortable she is bringing Darcy and Elizabeth to life." —From Pemberley to Milton

KAREN M COX

1932, "A sexy and exciting story, *1932* is a truly fresh take on this timeless tale." —Bustle

Son of a Preacher Man, originally published as *At the Edge of the Sea,* "…intoxicating and heartfelt romance…Readers will be entertained and inspired by this winning tale." —Publishers Weekly

I Could Write a Book, "…with eloquent style, grace, and insight Karen Cox has proven, once again, she can indeed 'write a book!'" —Austenesque Reviews

J. MARIE CROFT

Love at First Slight, "There was not a single thing I did not like about this novel. The author's sharp wit could rival that of Jane Austen…a pure delight to read." —Addicted to Austen

A Little Whimsical in His Civilities, "If there's an Austen hero that deserves a good chuckle at himself, I can think of none other more deserving than the proud and staid Mr. Darcy. Ms. Croft helps him loosen up his cravat in a manner that is playful, poetic and utterly romantic." —Just Jane 1813

Darcy Takes the Plunge, "Warning: one must be in the mood for humor to enjoy this book!" —Leatherbound Reviews

AMY D'ORAZIO

The Best Part of Love, "…reels with intense drama and is so emotionally charged." —Readers' Favorite

A Short Period of Exquisite Felicity, "…a rollercoaster ride of emotions— angst, heartbreak, anger, then awe, shock, and love." —Of Pens and Pages

JENETTA JAMES
Suddenly Mrs. Darcy "…a touching, sometimes dark, often playfully sexy interpretation of what might have been…" —Jane Austen's Regency World Magazine

The Elizabeth Papers, "…a novel that will appeal to fans of Jane Austen and romantic mysteries." —Publishers Weekly

Lovers Knot, "He [Darcy} fumbles, he fools himself, but he knows his own heart, and is rendered fully, beautifully three-dimensional under Ms. James's careful pen." —Beau North, three-time IPPY medalist

JESSIE LEWIS
Mistaken, "…intense feeling, dramatic consequences, surprising character evolutions, and an exceptionally ardent romance!" —Austenesque Reviews

LONA MANNING
A Contrary Wind: A Variation on Mansfield Park, "Many try to emulate Austen; not all succeed. Here, Manning triumphs." —Blue Ink Review Starred Review

A Marriage of Attachment, "…wealth of historical events woven into this finely-tuned story line are seamless and enlightening." —Carole of Canada, Goodreads

KARALYNNE MACKRORY
Bluebells in the Mourning, "…her interpretation of the characters was just about perfect." —Indie Jane

Haunting Mr. Darcy, "Mackrory's lilting prose is pleasantly reminiscent of Austen's, and readers will enjoy the unique twist to the familiar tale." —Publishers Weekly

Yours Forevermore, Darcy, "As far as Regency Adaptations that stay true to the original, this one is my favorite!!" —Margie's Must Reads

CHRISTINA MORLAND
This Disconcerting Happiness: A Pride and Prejudice Variation, "Their love affair is a thing of beauty, I sometimes felt I was intruding—but I would have loved to intrude for another 500 pages!" —Top 1000 Amazon Reviewer

A Remedy Against Sin: A Pride and Prejudice Variation, "One of my favourite novels!" —Of Pens and Pages

BEAU NORTH
Longbourn's Songbird, "North gives a voice to a whole new demographic of characters and expertly navigates the social confines of conservative Southern expectations of the times." —San Francisco Book Review

Modern Love, "...a love story that cuts through to the heart of what we're looking for as we futilely swipe right—someone who knows us, all the parts of us, and loves us all the more for it." —Maureen Lee Lenker, Entertainment Weekly

The Many Lives of Fitzwilliam Darcy, ""Readers, especially readers who already love Pride and Prejudice and all things related to Elizabeth and Mr. Darcy, will enjoy this fun take on the classic story." - San Francisco Book Review

SOPHIA ROSE
Sun-kissed: Effusions of Summer (Second Chances), "A truly beautiful and compelling romance!" —Austenesque Reviews

ANNGELA SCHROEDER
The Goodness of Men, "Schroeder did an excellent job writing very tender, touching scenes between Elizabeth and Darcy (swoon!), and she added more depth to Darcy's backstory and the events that shaped him as the master of Pemberley." —Diary of an Eccentric

A Lie Universally Hidden, "Ms. Schroeder definitely knows how to pen some romantic and eloquent passages full of ardent yearning and devotion! *sigh*" —Austenesque Reviews

The Quest for Camelot, "This well researched book draws the reader into a story that immediately grabs the reader's interest so that one can't put it down until the end. And what an ending it is—full of surprises and romance." —Dr. Marty Turner, Amazon

JOANA STARNES

The Falmouth Connection, "Joana Starnes writes with great verve and affection about the familiar characters—and an intriguing cast of unfamiliar ones." —Jane Austen's Regency World Magazine

The Unthinkable Triangle, "…full of feeling…a book full of soul." —From Pemberley to Milton

Mr. Bennet's Dutiful Daughter, "'She did it again,' I told myself as I savored the feelings whirling around inside of me." —Just Jane 1813

BROOKE WEST

The Many Lives of Fitzwilliam Darcy, "…well-written prose with perfect balance between heart-breaking intense scenes and humorous passages…" —From Pemberley to Milton

CAITLIN WILLIAMS

Ardently, "To say I was swept away into the storyline may be an understatement." —Just Jane 1813

The Coming of Age of Elizabeth Bennet, "This is a story to be completely and emotionally wrapped up in and consumed with!" —Austenesque Reviews

The Events at Branxbourne, "The evocative writing is of the highest quality and draws you in incompletely…flat out excellent." — Goodreads Review

FOREWORD BY DEVONEY LOOSER

"But I hate to hear you talking so, like a fine gentleman, and as if women were all fine ladies, instead of rational creatures. We none of us expect to be in smooth water all our days." —Sophia Croft to her brother, Frederick Wentworth, *Persuasion* (1818)

If you admire Jane Austen's heroines, it is probably about more than celebrating their beauty, strength, and generosity. You no doubt take pleasure, as I do, in their powers of reason. Austen's heroines are not mere duplicates of each other, of course. They don't all think alike. *Mansfield Park*'s Fanny Price shrinks from notice, while *Pride and Prejudice*'s Elizabeth Bennet is all impertinence.

"I thank you again and again for the honour you have done me in your proposals, but to accept them is absolutely impossible. My feelings in every respect forbid it. Can I speak plainer? Do not consider me now as an elegant female intending to plague you, but as a rational creature speaking the truth from her heart." — Elizabeth Bennet to Mr. Collins, *Pride and Prejudice* (1813)

Yet each character is drawn with a liveliness of mind that leads to her greater fulfillment and, ultimately, to the promise of domestic happiness.

In Austen's fictional world, a single woman in possession of a good intellect, must be in want of a man who recognizes its value.

It is remarkable that readers today, two hundred years on, still turn to Austen to explore what makes a well-examined life, to reflect on the world's unfairness, and to laugh at its trivial absurdities. We may mull over ways to avoid what Mr. Bennet calls the danger of an unequal marriage. We seek Austenian combinations of inventiveness, wisdom, and entertainment. That's where this book comes in. In its pages, the best of today's Austen-inspired authors use their significant creative powers to explore new angles of love and loss, captivity and emancipation. These stories reimagine both beloved female characters, like *Pride and Prejudice*'s Elizabeth Bennet, and loathed ones, such as *Persuasion*'s Penelope Clay. The results are comical, disturbing, and moving.

Would Austen approve of this book? We might as well ask, "Would she approve of any fanfiction published by non-relatives, dating back to Sybil Brinton's *Old Friends and New Fancies* (1913)?" Perhaps the better question is, "Do we approve?" To that, my answer is, what's not to love? These stories invigorate my readings of the Austenian originals, as I believe they will yours. Plus, I just can't help but imagine that one of my favorite heroines, *Northanger Abbey*'s naïve, quixotic Catherine Morland, would approve of this book, whether in her enlightened and unenlightened state. That's because these stories include the occasional, delicious very shocking somethings. More importantly, they feature no popes, kings, wars, or pestilences to torment you. In this book's pages, there are Regency women galore, with just the requisite handful of men who are all so good for nothing. Still, I'll hold my tongue from here, because I want you to be able to discover these fabulous stories on your own, without plot spoilers.

That said, it's only fair to give you a glimpse of the kinds of thought-provoking fun that you're in for in this book. First there's *Sense and Sensibility*'s Elinor Dashwood, in what might be called a portrait of the artist as a young woman (Morland). Ever wondered how *Pride and Prejudice*'s Charlotte Collins manages her new husband or what books she'll be reading along the way to stay sane? (Starnes). In other stories, *Emma*'s Emma Woodhouse finds herself suffering from restlessness after ten years of marriage (Schroeder), and Miss Bates turns out to have a surprising romantic history (Croft). *Mansfield Park*'s Fanny Price Bertram awakens to women's rights (West), while Mary Crawford comes face-to-face with the sordid choices of her admiral-uncle (James). *Persuasion*'s Sophia Croft endures hardship on shore (Mackrory), and *Northanger Abbey*'s Catherine Morland learns the pleasures of instruction (Rose). These, along with the book's other superb stories, invite us to consider how educated women of two centuries ago might have navigated social limits and constraints, whether in smoother waters or rougher ones. (That's just like Austen's fiction itself, of course.) Women must have responded to such fetters in a range of ways, with grace and good humor, as well as deceit and clever cunning. These stories trouble through those complexities. They bring into focus the fact that although there are inevitably people who do tend to plague us, others are capable of sharing profound truths.

The name of one profound eighteenth-century truth-teller recurs in these stories: feminist philosopher Mary Wollstonecraft (1759-1797). I'm not at all surprised to see her here, because she's widely admitted, and admired, as a precursor to Austen, especially in their respective portrayals of middle-class women's lot. (Wollstonecraft is perhaps most famous today for having died after complications from delivering the baby who would become Mary Wollstonecraft Shelley, author of *Frankenstein* [1818].) Wollstonecraft's *A Vindication of the Rights of Woman* (1792) was a revolutionary call to action that appeared just as Austen was coming of age. That *A Vindication* influenced Austen seems to me beyond a doubt. *How* it influenced her is a far more controversial question.

It would be a great venture to read this book's stories alongside Wollstonecraft's treatise and one or more of Austen's novels—chapter for chapter for chapter. That's because all three repeatedly invoke the phrase "rational creatures" in advocating for the betterment of women's lives. In one section of the *Vindication*, Wollstonecraft writes that she's disgusted with how her culture keeps women down. She sees females being most valued by power-hungry men, who encourage them to serve as weak, ignorant, pretty playthings. It's a perpetuating cycle, because men, Wollstonecraft writes, "have increased that inferiority till women are almost sunk below the standard of rational creatures." She concludes, "I think the female world oppressed." We might say that, across this volume's dazzling stories—and alongside the beyond-compare Austen herself—it's a belief that must seem eminently rational. Fortunately, then, as now, such a cultural diagnosis precludes neither hope nor joy. Much of both lies ahead of you in the pages of this fine book, awaiting discovery by today's rational creatures, some of whom are also proud to call ourselves Janeites.

DEVONEY LOOSER is an internationally recognized critic and expert in British women's writings, the history of the novel, and Jane Austen. She was recently awarded a National Endowment for the Humanities Public Scholar grant as well as 2018 Guggenheim Fellowship for her book project on the once-celebrated, now-forgotten sister novelists, Jane and Anna Marie Porter. She is a Foundation Professor of English at Arizona State University and is the author or editor of six books including *The Making of Jane Austen* and the new Deluxe Classics edition of *Sense and Sensibility*. Her essays have appeared in the *New York Times*, *The Atlantic*, and *Salon*, and she has been interviewed about Jane Austen on CNN and quoted in the *New York Times*, *USA Today*, and the *Wall Street Journal*. Also, Looser is renowned as "Stone Cold Jane Austen" in the roller derby world.

For Miss Austen...

TABLE OF CONTENTS

WITH MATURE CONTENT RATING

DEDICATION

FOREWORD BY DEVONEY LOOSER

Hetty Bates

(1) NONE: AFFECTION AND POSSIBLE KISSING

(2) MILD: KISSING

(3) MODERATE: SOME SEXUAL REFERENCES BUT NOT EXPLICIT

(4) MATURE: SOME NUDITY AND SOME PROVOCATIVE SEX

(5) EROTIC ROMANCE: EXPLICIT, ABUNDANCE OF SEX

N.B. For authenticity, each author has written in the style and spelling pertaining to their story setting and era or proclivity to their prose. In the spirit of the collective and to be consistent throughout, this anthology adheres to US style and punctuation. Additionally, as a work inspired by Jane Austen's masterpieces, her own words and phrases may be found herein.

SELF-COMPOSED

CHRISTINA MORLAND

ELINOR DASHWOOD

After losing her father, home, and the gentleman she loves, Miss Dashwood's altruism is nothing short of heroic. A model of decorum and grace, she appears cool while everyone and everything around her seems to be at sixes and sevens. Even as her heart yearns for what is now out of reach, this rational creature remains true to her principles by relying just as much on her artistic sensibility as her levelheaded good sense. *"I will be mistress of myself."* —**Chapter XLVIII**, *Sense and Sensibility.*

SELF-COMPOSED

NORLAND, SUSSEX, AUGUST 1797

Falling in love, she supposed, was not unlike sketching a nose. Others made it seem simple enough, yet when one tried for oneself, it came out all wrong—a smudge at the center of things, impossible to erase no matter how hard one rubbed.

"Surely," said the man in her sketch, "the drawing cannot be *that* bad."

She jumped at the sound of his voice, dropping her India rubber and nearly knocking over a pot of ink. At least she had managed to keep herself from looking up at him. Had their eyes met, he would have seen in her expression all the feeling she had been trying to channel into the portrait. How mortifying, knowing he stood just inches behind her, peering over her shoulder to stare down at himself!

Then again, perhaps the misshapen nose had fooled him.

"Is that...?" he began, and she shoved the sketch beneath a pile of completed landscapes.

Rising from the desk, she took a slow, deep breath. ("The best cure for any ill!" Henry Dashwood had liked to say, before death had taught him otherwise.) Catching the scent of fresh pencil shavings, Elinor closed her eyes and envisioned blank paper, flat and crisp; she imagined lines and circles with no clear end or beginning; she thought of her steady hands, of straight edges, of ink as smooth and black as night. As each image formed and dissolved in her mind's eye, her heartbeat slowed to its regular, dependable rhythm. Only then did she turn to face him.

There was a curve to his nose she had not noticed before.

"Forgive me for startling you, Miss Dashwood," he said, bowing and turning away in one fluid movement. Another man might have stumbled, but Edward Ferrars retreated with an odd, unexpected grace.

He ought to have been as awkward in motion as he was in speech. She recalled his reading of Cowper several nights earlier. His voice had tripped over words that should have flowed from his tongue, at least according to Marianne. But then she, that most observant of sisters, had not seen what Elinor had: Edward's fingers, stroking each page of the book, as if they felt all that his voice had been unable to convey.

She watched him go with equal parts relief and regret. Since when had he become Edward in her thoughts?

He halted abruptly, almost as if he had heard her think his name. She waited for him to move, to speak, to open the door and leave. Instead, seconds ticked past on the mantelpiece clock, and she found herself wondering if she could draw this other side of him—long spine and broad shoulders, with hair that curled slightly at the base of his neck.

Then he turned to face her. She had not captured his eyes properly, either; they were larger than she had made them in the drawing, with crinkles that appeared in the corners when he smiled, as he did just then.

"I seemed to have forgotten," he said, "my purpose in coming to the library."

Offering a hesitant smile of her own, she wondered how he saw her. Did he, too, wish to trace the lines of her jaw? Could he have been memorizing the shape of her mouth? It struck her then: she could not have sketched her own face half so well as she had drawn his. She did not know if her eyes crinkled when she smiled, or if her nose possessed that same graceful curve along the bridge. When she sat before a mirror, it was only to check the pins in her hair or to ensure she had not rubbed ink onto her cheek by mistake.

How, in a matter of months, had she come to know his face better than her own?

Another deep breath, and then, in a voice as steady as her hands: "I suppose you came to the library for the usual reason."

He raised one eyebrow. "To avoid the company of others?"

She laughed before she could help herself. He was as witty as he was graceful, a fact no one else in the household, himself least of all, seemed to recognize. She wished that she, too, had remained ignorant of this truth.

"If that is your idea of how to make use of a library," she said, turning back to the desk and gathering her pencils, "then I will leave you in peace."

"No!"

The word shot through her, a frisson of hope and desire that took her breath away.

Breathe, Elinor.

"That is, please," he said, "do not...you must not leave."

She heard footsteps and knew, without looking, that he had come to stand beside her.

"The aspect from this window—it is, it is..." He sighed, and she allowed herself a quick glimpse at him. She judged his shoulder to be but six inches from her own, and his long fingers grasped the back of the chair she had only just vacated. He stared out the window, his face a ghostly reflection in the glass.

"It is lovely, the view," he said.

She did not need to follow his gaze to know what he saw: the line of silver beeches that separated the park from the pastures beyond. They were indeed lovely, those ancient trees with their wide white trunks and multitude of thick branches. In this rain, they also appeared muddy and tired—sentinels near the end of their watch, ready to be relieved of duty. Somehow, the verdant summer foliage, which on every other tree brought zest and vigor, made the beech appear a little less noble in Elinor's eyes. She preferred them in early spring, when they stood bare to the world, grasping for the weak March sun.

She would never see them like that again.

"I should have drawn them," she murmured, realizing only when he turned to look at her that she had spoken aloud. Blushing, she returned to gathering her things. "The library is yours, Mr. Ferrars."

"No, no, you must not go, I..." He leaned forward, reaching out with his hand, as if he would touch her.

Her heart beat furiously and, though she urged herself to be steady, to think of lines and edges and all the straight and reasonable shapes in her life, her mind kept coming back to the same wild hope: *he wishes to declare himself.*

But he dropped his hand, stepped back, and said, "You must not leave on my account. I am the one who has intruded upon your work."

"I would hardly call it work." She offered a wan smile. "Work is what Thomas does when he chops the firewood, or Mary when she washes the linens."

"Ah, so you believe physical labor alone qualifies as work?" He cocked his head to one side, a movement he performed whenever he wished to engage her in debate or discussion. She had come to think it of as the "Elinor tilt".

He had developed movements for all the family: there was the "John Dashwood head nod" (up and down in time with the monotony of her brother's platitudes) and the "Margaret eyebrow waggle" (he never failed to make her youngest sister laugh); with Marianne, he propped his chin on his thumb so that the rest of his fingers covered his lips ("He listens with such seriousness!" Marianne had exclaimed, but Elinor suspected he was in fact hiding a smile); and, in the presence of Elinor's mother, he clasped his hands behind his back (a schoolboy, hoping to impress). Oh, and one must not forget the "Fanny Dashwood shoulder slump" (no explanation required).

She had not, at first, known what to think of the "Elinor tilt", but after months together at Norland, she had come to love that gesture. Why he did it, or if he even realized he was doing it, she could not say. But she thought he was trying to tell her, with that one small motion: *When you speak, I listen.*

So she spoke, this time aiming for a laugh: "If I defined work as something more than hard labor, you and I might be accused of serving some useful purpose in the world."

Her aim was poor indeed. His face fell, and she cursed her carelessness. If there was one subject to make him despondent, it was his lack of independence. "I feel"—he had admitted to her once, picking up one of his sister's knickknacks from the mantelpiece—"about as useful as this ridiculous bauble."

"Of course there may be other kinds of work," she said in a rush, as if the rapidity of her speech might make up for her error. "My father did a great deal of work at this desk, writing letters and keeping the ledgers."

"This desk was your father's?" Edward asked, his voice so gentle she found herself blinking back unexpected tears.

She stared resolutely at the wooden tabletop, smooth and shiny except for one barely noticeable scar. How her heart had pounded that night she had come into the library to find her father asleep at his desk, a candle tipped on its side, the flame hopping from wick to paper, paper to wood. The fire had been small enough that she had doused most of it with her father's half-finished cup of tea, but one stubborn spark had continued to smolder. In thoughtless desperation, she had slammed her thumb upon it and pressed until tears came to her eyes. Her thumb, oddly enough, had not been scarred; only the wood had been marked.

"So steady!" her father had exclaimed, taking her uninjured hand into his. And it was true; though his hands had trembled, hers had been as still as stone.

"Yes," she said to Edward now. "It is...was my father's desk." He had often called it *their* desk, even after he had purchased Elinor a drawing table of her own. But the light in the library was the best in the house, and so she had always been welcome to draw here.

She cleared her throat and forced a smile. "And now, if you will excuse me, I will—"

"But I thought..." Edward shook his head. "Fanny said this piece was to stay with the house."

"So it will." She reached for the pile of sketches. "In fact, I am here now only to remove my things."

"No, you came here to draw. I saw you drawing when I entered."

She laughed softly. "You are not the only one, Mr. Ferrars, who may forget his purpose when entering a room. I came across a piece of blank paper and could not resist sitting down to fill up the page."

"May I see your work? And yes, I have determined that it is indeed work—manual labor in its purest and best form."

He smiled at her, and she handed over the pages without stopping to consider. Then, a moment too late, she remembered. What would he think when he came to that unfinished portrait of himself? She could not claim she drew him because she often drew people; there were no other portraits in the stack. She was a landscape artist, depicting inanimate objects and faraway places. She captured life from a distance.

But then she'd had the idea that drawing him might help her put life in its proper perspective; if she could draw his portrait, if she could but capture the details of his face, she might finally accept the situation as it really was. And it was all but hopeless, for she had heard enough of Fanny's snide remarks to guess that Mrs. Ferrars would never approve of Elinor Dashwood as the wife of her eldest son.

Marianne would have scolded her for coming to this conclusion. "How can you care—either of you!—what Mrs. Ferrars thinks? Who is Mrs. Ferrars? She is nothing if you love each other, Elinor!"

She was nothing at all—only the person entrusted with the entirety of Edward's fortune. Mrs. Ferrars alone would decide her son's wife, and Elinor would never be her choice.

But he was *Elinor's* choice. Oh, if only the world were upside down, and *she* might be the one to decide their future! She would have handed him her drawings and said, "Here, Edward, this is who I am," and he would have flipped through the pages, just as he was doing now, stopping here and there to admire the perfect symmetry of her landscapes. And then, when he reached his own portrait, he would look up at her and know exactly how she felt.

Elinor, he would say. *Elinor, Elinor, Elinor.*

It took her a moment to realize he was staring at her now. He has found it, she thought, not daring (not wanting) to break the intensity of his gaze. Could he see, in that drawing and in her face, all she wanted of him? What would he do if she were to reach out and touch him—to feel for herself the line of his jaw, the arch of his brow, the fullness of his bottom lip?

Clearing his throat, he glanced away, and only then did she see the flush creeping up his neck and into his cheeks.

"This one," he said, holding out the drawing, and she had to take two long breaths to steady herself this time.

It was not the portrait, after all. He had chosen her illustration of a dilapidated house. It was not one of those fashionable ruins, with roses and ivy growing in the cracks and crevices. No, this was a square, two-story edifice, the shutters hanging at odd angles and the roof sagging as if it were only moments from collapsing in on itself. Though she had drawn stately trees, rolling hills and even a hint of the sea in the background, the drawing as a whole gave the appearance of drab reality.

"What an...intriguing sketch."

She managed a soft laugh. "It is not very picturesque, is it?"

He laughed, too. "No, not at all. I feel almost sorry for the house, but at least the scenery around the place is welcoming. Where is this meant to be?"

"Devonshire."

He looked up sharply. "Devonshire? That is where you...it is all settled, then? Your removal?"

"Yes."

"Devonshire is very far from Sussex," he said softly.

"Two days' travel, I am told. Have you been?"

"Yes." He pinched the bridge of his nose. "Yes, I have been to Devonshire— at Longstaple, near Plymouth."

"And what did you think? I have heard it described as pretty."

"Pretty!" He gave a cheerless laugh. "Yes, very pretty."

He looked so miserable in that instant that she forgot all her embarrassment, all her pent-up desire, and smiled, as one friend smiles at another. "You sound as if you blame Devonshire for its beauty."

"I did not say beauty." His voice was clipped—no, angry. "There is a difference, you know, between beauty and mere prettiness."

Now she was tilting her head at him, and his expression softened, as if he recognized the gesture.

"Forgive me, Miss Dashwood. I was in Devonshire at such an age when

I did not yet know the difference. I doubt you would ever make such a mistake."

She did not know how to respond to such a statement, and silence fell between them. It would have been the proper moment to take her leave, yet even sensible Elinor could not deny herself these last minutes alone with him. She would depart Norland in a matter of days, headed for this pretty and beautiful place that held nothing but uncertainty for her.

"And when were you last in Devonshire?" he asked after the silence had grown too long to be ignored.

"I have never been."

"Then this drawing—how did you compose it? Is it a copy of another's work?"

"No, it is my own. The house is meant to be Barton Cottage. Our cousin, Sir John, described the place in his letter to my mother, and I thought I would attempt a rendering."

He glanced between her and the sketch. "This is where you are meant to live? But it is in complete disrepair!"

She laughed. "Do not fear. Sir John has assured us that the house is structurally sound. This picture, Mr. Ferrars, comes solely from my imagination. I decided to draw the most wretched house I could, supposing I should then be quite pleased with the actual Barton Cottage."

He tried for a smile, but his lips faltered. "It is not fair." With a vigorous shake of his head, he exclaimed, "It is not fair, nor is it right!"

"Mr. Ferrars," she said softly. "Please do not be distressed for my sake."

"Perhaps it is not for your sake." His eyes closed briefly, and she wondered what he imagined as a way of calming himself. Whatever his method, it was faulty, for when he spoke again, his voice still shook with emotion. "How do you stand it, Miss Dashwood? How do you face the future, knowing that what is ahead of you will be so much more difficult than anything that has come before?"

"I know no such thing," she replied brusquely, "and neither do you. I cannot say what is fair, or what is right. I can only say that this is life, Mr. Ferrars, and life means change."

He gazed at her, saying nothing.

"I have no reason to despair," she continued in a gentler tone. "I have my mother, my sisters, and my own good health. I can surely wish for nothing..."

More. She had been about to say "nothing more," but she could not lie, not to herself. She could indeed wish for more—she did wish for more! She wished for her father, for Norland, for days when she did not worry about how they would make do on their reduced income. She wished for the tree outside her bedroom window and the mare she used to ride across Norland's meadows. Most of all—and she knew it was wrong to feel this way, given all she had lost—most of all, she wished for Edward, for this man with the face she had come to know better than her own.

One breath, two, three breaths, four. Black ink, blank paper, straight lines, an India rubber.

But no. Her method, too, was faulty. The smudge would not disappear.

"I *will* be content," she said, pressing her hands against her legs to keep them from shaking.

"So brave," he murmured. "Would that I had half your courage, Miss Dashwood."

He handed her the rendering of Barton Cottage and then, gently, placed the remainder of her artwork in a neat pile on the desk. Bowing and turning (all in one fluid motion), Edward Ferrars retreated, and Elinor saw, when she looked down at her sketches, that his portrait was on the top of the stack.

BARTON COTTAGE, DEVONSHIRE, OCTOBER 1797

"Elinor sat down to her drawing table as soon as he was out of the house, busily employed herself the whole day, neither sought nor avoided the mention of his name.... Without shutting herself up from her family, or leaving the house in determined solitude to avoid them, or laying awake the whole night to indulge meditation, Elinor found every day afforded her leisure enough to think of Edward..." —Chapter XIX.

∽

She found his hand surprisingly difficult to draw, almost as challenging as the nose. Hands, of course, were not generally included in portraits (or in landscapes, which is why Elinor had such trouble drawing them). Perhaps this new sketch of Edward fell into neither category. Indeed, it might not have qualified as a formal drawing at all. Margaret peeked over Elinor's shoulder to see what occupied her and asked, "Is this an exercise, like Marianne's scales or etudes, only on paper instead of piano?"

Elinor thought this a clever analogy, and told her sister so, and as Margaret (being the youngest) so rarely received attention or praise, she promptly forgot to ask why Elinor had filled almost an entire piece of paper with images of disembodied hands, and instead ran to repeat her witticism to anyone she could find.

But Margaret had not much time to glory in her verbal accomplishments, for everyone else in the household was focused on Edward's departure.

"He is leaving now," said Marianne from the doorway of the sitting room. "Will you not walk him to his horse?"

Elinor shook her head, remaining at her drawing table.

"At least bid him adieu!" cried Marianne.

"I have said goodbye to him twice already this morning: once at breakfast and once in the corridor just now. I see no reason to belabor the point."

"Oh, Elinor!" Marianne spun away, slamming the door behind her. A few moments later, Elinor saw through the front window how her sisters and mother waited in the garden as Edward mounted his horse. When he rode off, they waved and called out, but he did not look back.

She returned to her drawing. She had filled nearly every available space on the page (front and back), and because she did not wish to dedicate another sheet of paper to this "exercise," she concentrated on perfecting this final attempt. She put pencil to paper, and then—nothing. It was not the hand that was troubling her; it was the ring.

Studying the many versions of his hand, Elinor approved of the wrist and fingers—all but one of them. How ungainly the index finger appeared, and all due to that ring! It threw off the proportions; it made the entire hand appear clumsy and wrong.

Where had it come from, that gaudy gold band? He had never worn a ring at Norland, and the style—so bright and ornamental, as if it were made to call attention to the wearer—was nothing like Edward. Elinor had noticed the ring immediately upon his unexpected arrival at Barton, when he had taken her mother's hand (but not hers) in greeting. It was only later, when Marianne had exclaimed over it, that Elinor had noticed the strands of hair.

"Yes, it is my sister's hair," he had claimed, glancing at Elinor as he spoke the lie. For it must have been a lie. Yes, Fanny had once said she would give Edward a lock of her hair, but that pledge had been made in jest (or as close to a jest as Fanny could come) after Edward had teased her about how infrequently they were in each other's company. Besides, as Marianne had pointed out, the hair in the ring looked nothing like Fanny's. These strands were honey brown, not Fanny's dark ringlets. Edward might claim the setting gave the hair a different appearance, but the oval disk was transparent, and even Elinor knew enough of physics to recognize Edward's excuse for what it was.

It had to be her own hair; the color matched, and besides, he had looked at her with such mortification when speaking of the matter. He must have stolen a lock—but how? When? She had initially thought the gesture proof of his affections, but the more she considered the matter, the more it troubled her—not on moral grounds, but because the entire situation was illogical. He'd had no opportunity to steal her hair, and even if he had, why would he wear that ring (that ugly, gaudy ring!) and then spend the entirety of his visit attempting to avoid her?

No, something was wrong, and she had only to look at her sketches to see the problem: the ring ruined the hand. So she took the only action in her power: she pulled out a clean sheet of paper and drew his fingers, bare and unadorned, reaching for she knew not what.

NOVEMBER 1797

"Writing to each other," said Lucy, returning the letter into her pocket, "is the only comfort we have in such long separations.... I gave him a lock of my hair set in a *ring when he was at Longstaple last, and that was some comfort to him.... Perhaps you might notice the ring when you saw him?"*

"I did," said Elinor, with a composure of voice, under which was concealed an emotion and distress beyond anything she had ever felt before." —Chapter XXII.

The moment the Miss Steeles left the cottage, Elinor raced to her drawing table. Barely suppressing a sob, she yanked open a drawer, revealing a compartment filled to the brim with papers. Landscape, landscape, unfinished letter, landscape. Where *was* it?

Page after page, a blur, barely examined, but she had very little time before her mother and sisters returned to the sitting room, and besides, she did not need to see the details of her sketches to find what she sought. The smudge would be clear enough.

"Thank goodness they are gone!" she heard Marianne say from the corridor and knew her few moments of solitude were almost at an end. There! She had found *him*—half-finished and indelibly flawed.

Her heart pounded, but she did not take a calming breath; her eyes stung, but she refused to think of symmetrical shapes. She *wanted* to feel this unbridled, irrational fury as she stared down at her two-dimensional Edward Ferrars.

Tear it to shreds or throw it onto the fire?

Before she could decide, the door opened behind her, and she balled the portrait in her fist, each crunch and crackle a knife in her heart.

Oh, what had she done?

She sucked in a painful breath, hoping the air would clear her head. She had thought—no, she had not thought; that was precisely the problem. She had *felt* as if destroying the portrait would bring her some measure of satisfaction, but was left only with the notion that, had their positions been reversed, Lucy Steele would have acted no differently.

Before she could smooth out the portrait, before she could try and repair the damage, her mother said, "Oh, there you are, Elinor! I thought perhaps you had retired after the walk with the Miss Steeles. You look fatigued."

Managing a nod, Elinor concentrated on picking up the sketches she had thrown aside in her search for Edward; she returned them, one by one, to the drawer. The balled-up portrait would not fit; it remained on the surface, inescapable proof of her misery.

Grasping the edge of her drawing table, she leaned toward the window, wishing the weak sunlight had the power to warm her. For the first time in her life, Elinor doubted her ability to remain calm. It had taken so much of her willpower to pretend indifference during Lucy's recitation. How was she ever to keep up the charade?

Yet the world would go on. With her back to them, Elinor could hear her mother and sisters go about their daily routine: the click of her mother's needles; the clatter of shoes on the floor, kicked off, no doubt, so that Margaret might curl her stockinged feet beneath her as she read; and the scrape of the piano bench as Marianne took up her usual seat at the instrument.

"Of course she is fatigued," said Marianne, playing first a trill and then two rapid scales. "Anyone would be exhausted after having to spend a half hour in such company. I do not comprehend, Elinor, how you managed a civil word for either of them—Miss Lucy especially!"

Elinor could say nothing in response to this; she could say nothing at all. She wanted to escape but knew not how to excuse herself without bursting into tears. Though her sisters and mother would be the most sympathetic of audiences, she knew the effect such a display would have on them, and while *they* might find solace in shared grief, Elinor did not. Besides, she was now bound to keep Lucy's confidence.

Or was she?

The query was ill-formed in Elinor's mind, wrapped as it was in so many other questions: Did she owe Lucy—insincere, vindictive Lucy!— any consideration at all? Did she not deserve to share her burden with those who loved her best? How in God's name could Edward have done this to her?

These questions came and went, each dismissed almost the moment they had formed in her mind. She owed Lucy nothing, but she owed herself the respect of keeping a confidence. Never mind that Elinor had never asked for such a burden; it was now hers, and hers alone. As for

Edward, she had only to think of her own short acquaintance with Lucy Steele to feel pity for the man bound to her for life. Though Elinor knew none of the particulars, she could imagine the origins of their engagement: he, young and idle, and she, pretty and manipulative, had formed an attachment unchecked by any sensible counsel. Elinor did not think it presumptuous of her to believe that the Edward who had visited Norland last summer was a wiser man than the one who had proposed a secret engagement to Lucy four years earlier.

Of course, she did not think him blameless; indeed, she believed him to be the sole author of their shared misery. But at least she finally understood his hesitancy and changeable moods; she could at last make sense of that afternoon, during his visit to Barton, when he had come upon her drawing a new plan for the kitchen garden.

She had been outside, sitting on a low stone wall, sketchbook on her lap. He had come to sit beside her—not so close as to be improper, just close enough to see her work. Never once did he speak—no greeting, no questions, no observations about the weather. They communicated only through breathing: his, irregular and fitful, hers, consciously even. Her stomach flipped with each unsteady breath he took, but she neither paused nor faltered, finding comfort in the soft scratch of the pencil as she drew and labeled neat rows of vegetables. When a breeze swept past, ruffling her hair, she let out a soft, instinctive laugh. He inhaled sharply, and she turned to look at him. There could be no other word for the expression he wore except longing.

Their eyes met, his lips parted—but no words came forth. He stood, bowed, and fled.

Oh, how vexed she had been! Why bother to join her outside at all? He had spent so much of his short visit to Barton avoiding her presence; he might as well have let her sketch in peace!

But now she supposed (hoped, needed to believe) that he had been unable to resist those few, solitary moments together in the garden. His honor had kept him from making any promises, implicit or explicit, but he loved her, of this she was sure—no matter whose ring he wore. He was at war with himself, and she could not despise him for it. Indeed, she supposed that he had hurt himself more than he had hurt her.

With so many thoughts swirling, Elinor could offer no response to her sister's ill-mannered remarks about the Steele sisters. Fortunately, no response was required. Too busy practicing a difficult piano sonata—"I do not know why Colonel Brandon gives me such music, but I might as well make use of it"—Marianne seemed not to notice her sister's silence, and so Elinor struggled to collect herself as best she could: breathing, imagining, drawing.

Nothing in her silence seemed strange to her family; it was Elinor's habit to sketch almost immediately after returning from a walk. They supposed she had seen a late-autumn bloom or a particularly pretty view from the downs.

Yes, pretty indeed.

"We may only hope," continued Marianne, even as she played her instrument, "that the Miss Steeles will not stay long at Barton Park."

"For shame, Marianne!" said their mother, laughing at her middle daughter's impertinence. "The Miss Steeles are agreeable young ladies."

"Agreeable to Mrs. Jennings and Lady Middleton, no doubt," replied Marianne, and everyone in the room understood this to be the very worst sort of insult.

"I would have thought," said Margaret, "that Miss Steele, not Miss Lucy, would be the one you liked least. All her talk of beaux is very tiring!"

"Indeed it is," said Marianne, pausing her practice. "I do not esteem Miss Steele, by any means, but I may at least credit her with some degree of candor. I prefer her vulgar truths to her sister's varnished pretense of it."

Elinor put down her pencil and stared at Marianne.

"Well, dearest," said Marianne, eyebrows raised, "pray, do not keep silent. I know you wish to chide me for my incivility."

In fact, Elinor wished to congratulate her. Marianne had recognized what she herself had not immediately grasped. Yes, she had seen the way Lucy flattered anyone who might be of use to her, but she had not realized the extent of Lucy's duplicity until it had wounded her.

"There may be instances," said Elinor, "when it is not uncivil to speak the truth."

This reply caused the others to laugh, Marianne most of all.

"I believe we have had a corrupting influence on Elinor, Mama, if she is willing to choose sincerity over civility!"

"Or perhaps *she* is having a beneficial influence on *us*," replied her mother, smiling warmly at Elinor, who knew her thoughts exactly: they had not heard Marianne laugh with such spirit since Willoughby's departure.

Elinor turned quickly back to her sketch; she would not—could not cry in front them, not now.

"Whatever are you drawing with such ferocity?" Marianne asked, rising from the piano.

Too exhausted to hide or distract, Elinor moved aside and gave Marianne a clear view of the sketch.

"Oh, my!" she cried, picking up the drawing. "Come see, Mama. Is this not a most compelling portrait of Lucy Steele?"

"Lucy Steele!" exclaimed Margaret, propelling herself off the settee to join the others. "How could you draw Miss Lucy when you have never drawn *me*?"

"She rarely draws anyone," Marianne said, tilting her head. "Why ever *did* you draw her, Elinor?"

"Yes, I thought you were committed to landscapes," said their mother. "Ah, but it is a fine rendering of Miss Lucy, and performed so rapidly! I am impressed, my dear."

"Fine is not the word I would use," said Marianne, and Elinor nearly smiled. The portrait was quite clumsily done in some respects (the hair did not quite look like hair, and the face was too round; the nose, however, was perfect.)

"Though the portrait is not wholly correct, I *would* call it accurate," continued Marianne. "You have certainly made her appear cunning, Elinor."

"Oh, Marianne!" chided Mrs. Dashwood.

"I wonder how you do that," Margaret said, "taking lines and circles, and turning them into a recognizable face."

Elinor smiled in spite of herself. Though her chest ached, as if something sharp and heavy were permanently lodged there, she also felt stronger, surrounded and supported by three such remarkable females.

"I could teach you, Margaret, if you would promise to practice."

Margaret wrinkled her nose. "I would much rather you draw a portrait of me, Elinor."

"Not while making such faces, my dear," said Mrs. Dashwood, putting an arm about her youngest daughter's shoulders.

"Oh, please, Elinor, please sketch my portrait?"

"Perhaps," murmured Elinor, staring down at Lucy's face. It had lost much of its power, in the light of her mother and sisters' laughter. Indeed, she wondered why she had worked so furiously to depict Lucy's hard smile and narrowed eyes, when instead she might have captured the purer features of Marianne or Margaret. Yet even in this angry, crude rendition, she had made Lucy pretty. Not beautiful, perhaps, but very pretty indeed.

The memory that shot through her then—Edward, Norland's library, her father's desk, the beech trees; all those never-again desires, side by side—nearly undid her.

"You do not *have* to draw me, of course," said Margaret, crossing her arms. "Certainly not if you are going to sulk about it."

Yes, she was sulking—how could she avoid it? And yet she must not allow herself to become bitter or despondent, no matter how much right she had to those feelings. Taking one of her long, fortifying breaths, Elinor reached out and tapped her youngest sister's nose. "I should be glad to draw you, Margaret."

And she found this to be true—or true enough, especially when Margaret and Marianne began dashing about the sitting room, dragging chairs here and there to find the best light for posing. As they set up the impromptu studio, Elinor slid open the desk drawer and exchanged Lucy's face for a blank sheet of paper.

She looked up just in time to see her mother removing the ruined portrait of Edward, still crumpled into a tight ball, from the desk.

"Wait, Mama!"

Mrs. Dashwood's brows knotted in confusion. "Is this not refuse, my dear? I thought to discard it for you."

"No, I...it is not finished yet."

"But you cannot possibly draw on this paper now! It is ruined."

"Yes," said Elinor, holding out her trembling hands, "but I want to keep it."

"Well, of course, if you wish, but…"

As Elinor gently pried the portrait from her mother's hands, the edges unfurled, and the paper flattened just enough to make visible the outline of Edward's face.

"Oh, Elinor," Mrs. Dashwood murmured, her eyes bright with tears. "My dear Elinor."

"I am ready to sit for my first portrait!" Margaret announced, and Mrs. Dashwood said no more on the matter.

In an excessively cheerful tone, their mother declared Margaret to be a most elegant lady—and though that was not quite true, Marianne had made Margaret look spritely, crowning her upswept hair with a garland of dried flowers.

"Give me just a moment," said Elinor, turning back to her drawing table. She smoothed out Edward's portrait as best she could, pressing it flat enough to fit in the drawer, just next to Lucy.

"Very well, Margaret, I will begin."

And so she did, finding as she sketched that her heart was just as full as it was broken. She loved Edward as much as ever—but he was not the only person she loved.

MAY 1798

"They would soon, she supposed, be settled at Delaford. Delaford—that place in which so much conspired to give her an interest; which she wished to be acquainted with, and yet desired to avoid. She saw them in an instant in their parsonage-house; saw in Lucy, the active, contriving manager, uniting at once a desire of smart appearance, with the utmost frugality, and ashamed to be suspected of half her economical practices.... In Edward—she knew not what she saw, nor what she wished to see; happy or unhappy, nothing pleased her; she turned away her head from every sketch of him." —Chapter XLVIII.

Given all she had experienced over the past twelvemonth—her father's death, the loss of Norland, Willoughby's betrayal, and her sister's subsequent illness—hearing of Edward's marriage to Lucy, an event she had long been expecting, should not have affected Elinor's equanimity.

In Marianne's estimation, it had not.

"Did you not see, Mama, the serenity of her countenance when she heard the news? Oh, she is the noblest of sisters! I am afraid I will never possess her strength."

Marianne's voice reached her through the front window, which Elinor had thrown open in hopes of distracting herself. Surely she could not be miserable in the face of such beauty: Marianne, bonnet fluttering in the breeze; Margaret, bent over a patch of grape hyacinths; and their mother, arms full of bright and fragrant mayflowers.

What a picture they made! If only she could draw herself into the scene.

"Yes, Elinor composed herself quite admirably," replied their mother.

But, no, that was just it: Elinor had *not* composed herself.

In the past six months, she had drawn so many others: Edward, with uncertainty and desire; Lucy, in a rage; Mrs. Jennings, for a laugh; Colonel Brandon, out of pity; and, closest to her heart, Mrs. Dashwood, Margaret, and Marianne. Yet in all these drawings, Elinor was nowhere to be found; she was always outside the frame, invisible.

She closed her eyes, trying to picture her own face, but all she could see was Delaford's parsonage-house: red bricks, green vines, three chimneys, and a wooden stile separating the parsonage from the road—these were the extent of what she could recall from her one visit to Colonel Brandon's estate. Next time, there would be more to the picture: Lucy Ferrars, standing at the front door, waving, and behind her...

No! Breathe, Elinor. Think, Elinor. Draw, Elinor.

Frantic, she searched the desk for what she knew would not be there: a clean sheet of paper. She had used up her supply on other portraits, on other people, and now, when she needed to compose herself, she had nothing left.

Still, she pulled out every old sketch, desperate to find that one forgotten sheet. Instead, she found their portraits, side by side.

Her first thought was to leave them in the drawer; she could not bear to look at them, not today. Her second thought: finish what she had started with Edward's portrait and destroy them both. But the moment she touched their faces, she felt a surge of protectiveness toward these two, her first portraits. Holding them up, one in each hand, Elinor forced herself to examine them with the eye of the critic, to judge the lines and strokes instead of the people who inspired them. She had improved as a portrait artist since these early attempts; she could draw noses and hands and hair and eyes, all with bolder strokes and fewer smudges. Yet none of those other portraits, not even the depictions of Margaret, Marianne, or their mother, could inspire such a wellspring of feeling as these two. Lines and circles, yes, but love and loathing, too. Her feelings colored every view of them.

Tears falling, she shoved Edward's crumpled portrait back into the drawer. When returning Lucy's, however, she paused. The other side—it was blank! Elinor generally drew on both sides of the page; after all, they were four women living on very little income, and drawing paper was expensive.

But she had not touched Lucy's portrait since drawing it; she had not forgotten it, of course, but she had been afraid of it, as if the paper and pencil markings were infused with all the fury that had inspired the portrait. And perhaps there was truth to her fear, for tears ran hot and fast down her cheeks as she flipped the paper to its blank side. She stared at the page for a long time, trying not to see the woman on the other side.

Yet the outlines of Lucy's face seemed always visible to Elinor, even as she tried to sketch her own countenance. Draw, erase, draw again. So many smudges, made worse by the teardrops that stained the page. She wished she could draw herself without pause or reflection; she wished she could draw from instinct rather than memory or rational thought. But she had to squeeze her eyes shut and concentrate to produce anything like herself. It was work—yes, it was work—to make visible what had been hitherto indiscernible. Did her skin crinkle when she smiled? What shape was her nose? She had to press her fingers to her face, and when that did not work, take up a particularly shiny pair of scissors, angling them this way and that, to catch the slightest reflection of herself. And when finally she was done—when the face had a nose and eyes and a mouth, brows and hair and ears—she was still unfinished, incomplete.

But she could see something of herself—imperfect, but true. It had not cured her of her grief, this act of self-portraiture; no, she would always miss and mourn Edward Ferrars. But however much she might love him, she did not need him. She would live a full life as Elinor Dashwood, sister and daughter and artist. When their paths crossed next, she would meet him with more than the appearance of composure.

"Is that a rider on the road?" Margaret called from beyond the window.

Glancing up, Elinor saw that yes, indeed, a gentleman was approaching the house.

"Colonel Brandon, no doubt," said Mrs. Dashwood.

Squinting into the distance, Elinor wondered if her mother might be wrong. He was not quite tall enough; he had lighter hair. If such a thing were possible, she would have thought…

"It is Edward!" cried Margaret, and the Dashwood ladies hurried inside, throwing off their aprons and taking up their needlework.

Dizzy, disoriented, barely able to breathe, she ought to have been insensible of her surroundings. Yet even now, as her pulse pounded in her ears, she could not help but be conscious of her mother and sisters. How they stared at her! How they worried for her! She wished she could say something to reassure them, but the only words she had were for herself: *I will be calm; I will be mistress of myself.*

The door knocker sang out. *Why has he come?* Mary's voice called in greeting. *How dare he come!* The hall floorboards creaked. *He has come; it is enough.* Elinor took a slow, deep breath—*"The best cure for any ill!"*—and closed her eyes. Smudges, stains, and unfinished faces.

She might not be able to face him with perfect equanimity, but she would at least be self-composed.

But Elinor—how are her feelings to be described? From the moment of learning that Lucy was married to another, that Edward was free, to the moment of his justifying the hopes which had so instantly followed, she was everything by turns but tranquil. But when the second moment had passed, when she found every doubt, every solicitude removed, compared her situation with what so lately it had been, saw him honorably released from his former engagement, saw him instantly profiting by the release, to address herself and declare an affection as tender, as constant as she had ever supposed it to be, she was oppressed, she was overcome by her own felicity; and happily disposed as is the human mind to be easily familiarized with any change for the better, it required several hours to give sedateness to her spirits, or any degree of tranquility to her heart. —Chapter XLIX.

CHRISTINA MORLAND spent the first two decades of her life with no knowledge whatsoever of *Pride and Prejudice*—or any Jane Austen novel, for that matter. She somehow overcame this childhood adversity to become a devoted fan of Austen's works. When not writing, Morland tries to keep up with her incredibly active seven-year-old and maddeningly brilliant husband. She lives in a place not unlike Hogwarts (minus Harry, Dumbledore, magic, and Scotland), and likes to think of herself as an excellent walker. Morland is the author of two Jane Austen fanfiction novels: *A Remedy Against Sin* and *This Disconcerting Happiness*.

EVERY PAST AFFLICTION

NICOLE CLARKSTON

MARIANNE DASHWOOD

A young lady of great feeling, Marianne's high spirits and spontaneity are dramatically magnified after her father's death, loss of her childhood home, and by acting the part of a woman wildly in love. Her disappointments, pleasures, and affections have no limits—to the detriment of all in her sphere. After she has been betrayed by a practiced rake, she finds herself at death's door but has a second chance at love and becoming a rational creature. *"I wish, as well as everybody else, to be perfectly happy; but, like everybody else, it must be in my own way."* —**Chapter XVII**, *Sense and Sensibility.*

EVERY PAST AFFLICTION

Marianne's eyes still felt swollen and dry. They must have been opened for some while, but only now was she beginning to perceive light and colour. She blinked, a deed which required conscious thought, and a shape began to form. "Mama?"

Her voice was foreign to her—so hoarse and feeble—but a gasp, a choking back of tears, informed her of what her eyes still could not confirm. "Mama? Elinor?"

"Hush, my darling," her mother soothed. "You must not exert yourself. Oh, my child, I thought I had lost you!"

Marianne was still beyond sentiment. All the passion and sensibility she had always borne as her most open aspect, she was too exhausted to experience.

"Mama, we must let her sleep," she heard Elinor suggest. "That is all she wants now."

"She must take some nourishment," Mrs. Dashwood protested. "Did not the apothecary suggest it?"

The sheets were damp, her very body clammy and dull, but that horrid delirium was gone. She could hear, she could see, and she would live. "Thirsty, Mama"—she managed through her cracked lips.

"Elinor, ask the colonel to have a tray sent up. I imagine it would please him above all things to be of use, the dear man."

Marianne could see her mother clearly now, feel the comfort of her arm sliding beneath her shoulders. "The colonel?" she said thickly.

"Never mind that now, my love." Mrs. Dashwood arranged the pillow behind Marianne's shoulders, but Marianne carefully shook her head.

"Colonel Brandon?" she asked again.

Her mother's gentle laughter could be heard in her voice. "Indeed, none other. The poor man has scarcely left his post in the hall, nor ceased pacing in the drawing room since your illness set in, save to ride to Barton special to bring me to your bedside. Is that not like him? He has been so kind."

Marianne lay her head back against the pillow, too weary from battling her illness to hold it erect. Now everyone would renew their expectations of the colonel, and she would be duty bound to receive his company, if not his suit. He had none of Willoughby's passion, none of the spark and vigour she had always known would touch her heart the moment she saw the man she would love. Yet...he had uncommon goodness—or was that tale of Elinor's some spectre of her illness? No, no, she was quite sure of it. Colonel Brandon *was* the better of the two, grave and steady as he was. Was that the mark of goodness?

It was too much to think on now. Her head hurt, her stomach grumbled, and she was too weak to meditate long on any one object. As her thoughts faded, she became aware of Elinor's voice, low and sensible, detailing her wants to someone in the corridor. Another replied, and Marianne would have known that voice anywhere, for there was a deep, raw quality to the rich, cultured tones.

"You are certain she is out of danger? The fever shall not return?" Colonel Brandon was asking of Elinor.

"She has only continued to improve since directly before your arrival last night. She is now alert, and she has spoken. That is a very good sign, for the apothecary was uncertain if she would ever recover her senses after such a fever. Mama is asking for some sweet tea and perhaps some broth for her."

"I will tend to it, Miss Dashwood. Pray that Miss Marianne's strength shall soon return."

Marianne heard steps: the colonel's hasty, commanding strides in the hall and Elinor's lighter feet returning to her bed. She opened her eyes. "Has he really been there all night?"

"For days." Elinor drew up her chair and took Marianne's hand into hers. "I thought the man was set to run mad. I suppose the gentleman always has the worst of it, for he cannot wait at the bedside."

"He is not *my* gentleman," Marianne protested weakly.

Marianne was not so far beyond perception to miss her mother's and Elinor's amused expressions. "We shall see, my dear."

When Marianne next awoke, it was to vastly different sensations. The bone fatigue of her fever still lingered, but her mind felt fresh, the sheets no longer clinging to her, and she was no longer disoriented from lack of nourishment. Elinor was reading beside her, but she set her book aside when Marianne tried to sit up.

"Did you wish for some more tea, darling?"

Marianne's brow pinched. "Are you intending to mollify Colonel Brandon by granting him the quest? Shall you turn him into my personal footman?"

Elinor laughed gently. "He has retired, the poor man. I should think he would not be more than an hour or two; military men know how to sleep nearly anywhere and be alert at a moment's notice, I am told. Mama has gone to her bed as well, for she has not slept in nearly two days."

Marianne shifted, thinking that she must have been in bed a very long time herself, for no comfortable position remained to her. "And Mr. and Mrs. Palmer? I must have become a rather tiresome guest."

"They departed at once when the apothecary told us your fever was grave. Mrs. Palmer naturally feared for her child, and even Mr. Palmer was concerned enough to placate her. Mrs. Jennings would have gone with her daughter, but she preferred to stay and be of some use to you. I believe her primary object in remaining was to entertain Colonel Brandon, though aloud, of course, she protested that *he* was to remain for *her* amusement."

"It seems the colonel has attached himself in such a way that I cannot now escape his company without becoming an object of scorn."

"Marianne, I believe this is your fatigue speaking rather than your true sentiments." Elinor smoothed the counterpane and fluffed a pillow, offering her sister a teasing smile.

Marianne groaned and exerted herself to sit a little straighter. "You are correct, of course, but I am not in search of a lover, Elinor. I have only been newly restored to you, and to Mama, and all anyone can speak of is Colonel Brandon's despair. Is he the only one who might have mourned me, had I succumbed?"

"You know that to be untrue, Marianne. Colonel Brandon can expect no reward but your own regard. Is the devotion of such a man to be disdained? Can you object to the honours he has accorded you?"

"I can where it obliges me to an interest I have not felt. One cannot feign love, Elinor. As you once said, 'I esteem him,' but I am afraid it does not go beyond that. He has not that kindred soul, that sense of fellowship I crave and, good heavens, Elinor, he could be my father!"

"But he is not"—Elinor smiled again—"nor are his feelings for you paternal. Let it rest, my dear, for you are not strong enough to worry about such. Two things that Colonel Brandon knows better than any other: patience and self-denial."

"Let him become the master of them." Marianne sighed, then fell back against the pillow. As Elinor stirred herself to summon a maid, Marianne steadied her breathing. She drew slowly in, filling her lungs from the bottom, then released with the greatest care. Another attempt induced a burning sensation and, in the next instant, she was curling on her side and choking for breath as her lungs struggled to expel the last of the putrid sickness.

"Marianne!" Elinor rushed back to her side. "Try a sip of water."

But Marianne could not cease coughing, and she waved her sister back with a feeble hand.

"Marianne! Someone, help!" Elinor seemed to pray.

Whatever heavenly call her sister had sent was answered by the colonel's strong hands which bore her up, bent her forward, and began a rhythmic tapping in the middle of her back. Marianne continued to cough, each heaving breath burning less, until at last she gasped and could breathe freely. His strong arm draped behind her helpless body, drew back, and she felt herself eased back to her pillow.

"Forgive me, Miss Marianne. I heard Miss Dashwood cry out and your distress."

He bowed, shielding his eyes as he turned and retreated towards the door.

"Colonel Brandon." Marianne coughed again.

He stopped and looked over his shoulder.

"Thank you."

The succeeding days brought about a remarkable turn. Marianne felt stronger every hour, and those who had watched over her illness and known dread as their constant companions could take some measure of ease. Her appetite returned, and even her mother, who encouraged her to take all she could, betrayed some hint of astonishment at Marianne's ready obedience in doing so. By afternoon, she was out of bed, slowly pacing, her disused limbs tingling with the longing to move once more.

It was not only the recovery of her strength which impelled Marianne to abandon her peaceful repose. She was anxious in her heart, troubled at discovering in herself the one thing she could never tolerate in another: duplicity.

Certainly, she had not intended such, nor had she even been aware when the incautious words of scorn and annoyance had slipped from her tongue, but the words had been spoken, nonetheless. And not only these but a hundred previous moments stole in to taunt her. Earnestly felt at the time, now they reeked of carelessness, of idle vanity, and of self-deception. And she had acted upon those words!

Pensive, she paused at the window, unconsciously nibbling the tip of one finger as she looked out over the fields. Earlier she had seen Colonel Brandon ride out on that steady brown gelding he preferred, his greatcoat buttoned against the rain. He had gone to offer assistance to one of Mr. Palmer's tenants, a man whose wife was languishing with childbed fever, Mrs. Jennings had said. The apothecary had been called, and the husband had little heart to leave his wife's side.

Marianne lingered until the colonel's horse trotted back into view. His hat was pulled low, but his firm jaw, the set of his mouth, hinted at his satisfaction, and yet…. His concern was in every move, in the whole of his manner, though she knew him to forbear displays of feeling.

This, perhaps, served only to intensify Marianne's irritation with herself. Was Colonel Brandon any less sincere for his quieter means of expression? Were his sentiments less profound? And she, ignorant and conceited as she had been, had presumed that anyone whose behaviour did not openly reflect each facet of feelings must, of necessity, experience an inferior quality of emotion; or worse, that they must be tempering an honest conviction with prudence or deceit. Yet, to look on Colonel Brandon's shadow of a smile, to see the easy way he handled his mount or gestured to the stable boy who ran to meet him, was to understand that his satisfaction and care were as earnest as all her most effusive displays.

"Marianne, why are you out of bed?" The door creaked, and Marianne turned to see Elinor.

Marianne greeted her in genuine pleasure, then turned back to the window. "I am not entirely recovered but feel stronger."

Elinor drew near to her shoulder. "Whatever are you thinking?" There was a note of caution in her voice, as if she feared raising any subject which might cause distress and she could not depend upon Marianne to refrain from vexing herself.

"I am thinking"—Marianne sighed—"that I have scarcely known myself. That all my frankness was instead pretence, and all my honest professions stemmed rather from a mind little disposed to introspection and unwilling to be tempered." She turned to her sister. "Much as a child might persuade himself that he desires something and then works diligently to assure himself that he *must* be grieved, he *ought* to feel wronged when it is denied. Perhaps I have allowed selfish thoughts to lead my feelings far more than I care to confess."

"Marianne," cautioned Elinor, "I shall not forbid you to follow this notion, for such admonishment would be fruitless, but you are not strong—"

"I am. Or at least, I am strong enough to begin to do right. I believe I ought to begin by showing my gratitude for, if I lack the courage to do so now, I shall become afraid to do so later. Please, do not ask me to say more so soon, but will you arrange it? I should like to thank Colonel Brandon for his exertions on my behalf."

Elinor raised her eyebrows, but she kept back whatever expressions of surprise or approval she might have voiced. "I will help you dress."

Soon the entire party had returned to Barton, where Marianne could once again be at ease in her own cottage. As her strength continued to return with all the expediency and vivacity of her youth, her gnawing sense of disquiet grew. Here again, in the places she had walked with Willoughby, the very rooms where they had played and sung together, the groves where he would read to her, she had all the mortification of examining past mistakes.

Sincerity was her highest praise, passion the most laudable end. But what of good sense? Patience? These were virtues, were they not? Yet they had seemed so much at odds with her character, those very qualities that had been her greatest sources of...of pride. And pride, unchecked by reason and invested in herself rather than in another, certainly was not a virtue to attain satisfaction.

Nor was her own naïveté, and perhaps this tortured her the most. Marianne valued nothing more than indiscriminate honesty between two people, but the lessons of the world had taught her by the cruellest means possible that not all others were worthy or capable of such selflessness. If her judgment had so erred when the conviction of her heart had cried out loudly in the defence of a blackguard, how was that organ now to be trusted not to lead her astray again?

Her attitude had become so brooding, her demeanour so meditative that once while walking out with Elinor, her sister ventured to ask after her well-being. Indeed, Marianne was glad of it, for she had stumbled about her own mind, judiciously sweeping the clutter from the crowded spaces of her heart, and now one looming obstacle must be addressed. If she could know, have some assurance that her heart had not been entirely wrong, she might find relief!

This final longing she expressed to her sister and was rewarded by guarded looks, conscious sighs, and thoughtful pauses. Marianne was thus convinced that her sister was dissembling, and only the sternest command of herself kept her from falling at Elinor's feet, supplicating hands laced together in a mournful plea.

Elinor hesitated, then of a sudden revealed the events of the night when her fever had at last broken: the first caller Elinor had met in her joyful relief had been none other than Willoughby.

Elinor's revelations, given cautiously and with no little concern for Marianne's sensitive spirits, proved the answer she craved. Willoughby had, indeed, loved her! She had not been entirely wrong about him. In that most essential quality of honesty and artlessness, she had been misled, but not in his expressions of love—those looks and gentle touches, those hours spent admiring the same books or the same walks. He was a rascal, as he had so aptly confessed to Elinor, but a rascal who had loved her, in his own way.

Relief, coupled with vexation about the character of a man she had thought she had loved, warred for supremacy in her heart, but her mind, at last, was brought to order. Gladdened that her faith in Willoughby's affections had not been entirely misplaced, she permitted herself a measure of relief from the chastisement she had borne for months. She had long despaired of his honour and her judgment thereof, but in this, at least, she could take comfort. She was not so fearful now that she could be easily led astray by another, nor was she without hope for his soul. He would be punished for his sins, and it was his own conscience which would do it. But she could be free.

Marianne could breathe again. A crushing weight had flown from her heart, her steps came more easily, and the sensation of gloom which had long been her companion seemed to fall from her shoulders like an unwanted cloak.

She glanced at her sister as they walked, then her eyes drifted to the horizon. Willoughby, by his own deed and vice, was lost to her, and she would never again regret him. But her own actions, those sins against all who had loved her and, indeed, against her own well-being, had nearly cost her life and any chance of repentance.

Her resolution fixed, she would take comfort knowing at least she had been blameless compared to a scoundrel. She would measure her virtues not against a flawed example but a higher standard—and in her own sister, she possessed a perfect image of all the grace to which she might aspire. No longer was it sufficient to simply *behave* better than Willoughby. If the capacity lay within her, she would prefer to be like Elinor.

Soon after this soul-baring revelation, the ladies of the Barton Cottage had the astonished pleasure of receiving Edward Ferrars. Marianne experienced, as if it were her very own happiness at stake, all the indignation regarding his reported marriage to Lucy Steele, and subsequently all the exultation in the truth which followed. It was now for her to look on as her beloved, worthy sister found joy.

The courtship of Edward Ferrars and Elinor Dashwood was a short one but, nonetheless, required occasional chaperonage. Marianne and Margaret trailed behind the betrothed couple, collecting the summer blossoms that grew along the path, but often Colonel Brandon would join their company.

He had become a great friend of Edward's after he had taken up the living at Delaford, and it seemed to bring the colonel pleasure to see such a genial, honourable man made happy by a woman who had equally merited his regard. That his visits also served to bring him into Marianne's presence seemed an obvious inducement to his daily calls.

On this day, Marianne greeted him at the door with a welcome that was warmer than usual. The weather was exceedingly fine, and she was eager to venture forth. Indeed, only Edward's great politeness towards Mrs. Dashwood had restrained the party, for he had sat with their mother half an hour talking of his plans for fitting the parsonage to prepare for his bride.

"Elinor"—Marianne sighed, smiling indulgently—"I am afraid you will have to draw him out if we are to take our walk today."

"If you are impatient to enjoy the day," Colonel Brandon offered, "perhaps Miss Margaret might accompany you. We can catch you up, once Mr. Ferrars and Miss Dashwood are quite ready to depart."

Marianne glanced round in surprise. This was hardly the speech of a would-be lover!

"Colonel, you are too good," Mrs. Dashwood replied warmly. "It is generous indeed to propose a means of securing the pleasure of everyone save yourself, but I do not intend to keep my future son-in-law when others desire his company. Do go, Edward, and with my blessing. You have been most kind to entertain me this morning. Perhaps Margaret and I might call on Lady Middleton and her mother, for I am quite a visit in their debt."

Margaret wilted, but Marianne paid her little mind. She was studying the colonel, who had flushed. He turned then, stopping in the corridor as Edward helped Elinor with her shawl.

"I hope Miss Margaret's absence from our party does not distress you," he murmured.

"Not at all, sir, for your company shall be more than adequate compensation."

He did not appear convinced. "I am afraid I am but a poor conversationalist and cannot hope to properly take her place."

"Margaret's clever conversation is not why I take pleasure in her company. Pray, sir, do not feel as if you must keep me entertained with a constant barrage of witticisms."

He released a deep breath, smiled, and extended his hand towards the door. "Shall we?"

Edward and Elinor preferred a leisurely pace; thus, their chaperones were obliged to amble along, allowing Marianne to collect sprays of wild flowers. As she straightened, his hand caught her notice, offering a complementary assortment of buds. Marianne glanced up at the colonel's face as she accepted them; he gasped at her touch, his fingers stiffening.

His fingers felt gentle and warm...somehow familiar. Her eyes lingered on his hand long after it fell to his side, as if yearning for the steady comfort and affection she had sensed there. With some effort, she stole her eyes away to his offering of wildflowers, and she began to blend them with her own. "Thank you."

He smiled again, not the beaming, laughing countenance that she had found so attractive before, but the modest, reserved aspect of a man who sought to give pleasure and was relieved that it had been accepted. "If you like these, there is a field at Delaford which abounds in foxglove every spring. Perhaps one day our party might venture there, and you may have the pleasure of collecting them to brighten your sitting room."

"Alas"—Marianne shook her head—"those have always made me sneeze."

His face fell, the shy pleasure gone. "Forgive me, I would not wish to cause you that sort of distress."

All amusement, she said, "The blame could hardly be yours, sir! But if you are proposing another outing to Delaford, I believe Edward and my sister would both thank you very much."

"I would wish them to come as often as they like before they are settled. The parishioners look forward to knowing Mr. Ferrars. Did you..." He hesitated, glanced her way, then— "Did you think the situation agreeable to their wants when you visited last week?"

"Very much so," she avowed.

His eyebrows raised, relief lighting his eyes.

"Oh, I see your misgivings, sir," she teased. "I believe you are generous in wishing to spare my sister and my future brother any inconveniences in the size of the parsonage. But do you see how it is with them? I should think a house which boasted more than two or three rooms far too large for them, for what can be lacking when they share but one soul between them?"

A hesitant smile, almost a chuckle, tugged at the corners of his mouth. "I should ask if you are in earnest, Miss Marianne, but I know that you must be, for there is no artifice in you. You have eased my mind greatly, you must know, for if there were any dissatisfaction with the situation, I fear I would be the last to hear. May I depend upon you to advise me if there is anything that can be done to increase their comforts beyond the improvements we have already decided upon?"

"I shall indeed, sir."

They walked on a moment in silence, and each time Marianne found the courage to look at his face he seemed to flush, smile nervously, then look again at the path.

"Sir…" Marianne wetted her lips, waiting for those steady grey eyes to turn again to her. "I have a confession, and I cannot in good conscience delay the admission any longer."

He blinked, his shoulders tensing as his eyes swept her face for any signs of affliction. Marianne looked to the ground as she walked. "It regards the subject of grievances and the imposition of wrong behaviours upon others."

His eyes narrowed; he looked again to the path ahead. "Ah" was his only response.

"I want you to know—I wish for everyone to know—that my only regrets are in myself. The disappointment that would surely have followed, had events occurred which I had expected, would have been the most grievous, and I would have been no less guilty in bringing about such pain to my family than—"

"Miss Marianne," he began softly in a voice which pleaded reason, "you were innocent of any wrongdoing. It does not follow that you must now share in the guilt of another to set right past wrongs."

"Nay, sir, but you are incorrect. I have been incautious and indiscreet. I have allowed my feelings—nay, provoked them, beyond what was natural —to lead me into behaviours which I cannot now recall without remorse. Had I seen the culmination of all my desires, been granted the prayers I whispered so fervently each night, I have no doubts that I should already have begun to regret their fulfilment. How wretched might have been the second year after having my eyes so forcibly opened to my own folly? Ten years? No, I am satisfied, but my present peace of mind does not answer for the injuries I have done, the indifference and abject incivilities I bestowed upon all those who have been only gentle with me. To Elinor, first of all, but also to Mrs. Jennings, to Sir John, to Mr. and Mrs. Palmer, and to you, I must now tender my apologies—"

"No, Miss Marianne," he objected with feeling. "You must not apologise to me for any wrong, for there has been none. What have you done that I did not admire, for it revealed your pure, faithful heart and your great capacity to love? Shall I be affronted that you gifted one who was unworthy with the selfless affection which defines your character?"

"With my disregard, you should be affronted. My folly was my own to regret, but I have become ashamed of my carelessness. I have been in want of instruction and, in observing the more thoughtful manner of others, I have determined to better educate myself. I shall begin with the reading of great works rather than the romantic poetry which has been my fodder. I hope my mind shall be improved in the course of a twelve-month."

"By reading?" His brow furrowed as he walked, his eyes still trained on the ground. "I am afraid Barton Cottage boasts little in the way of a library, and Sir John's has not been kept up. Might I offer you the use of my own library at Delaford?"

As he looked up hopefully from the road, she could not help a shy smile crooking the corner of her mouth. "I was hoping to ask that very thing, Colonel. I expect we will often be in company there, as Edward and Elinor have already requested our frequent visits."

He paused his steps, a rare smile warming his face. "Then hasten the day of Miss Dashwood's marriage"—and offered a gentle bow. "You may be certain that I shall exert myself on her behalf so that all might be in readiness for her arrival."

Marianne laughed softly and found it necessary to look away. It was too difficult to meet his gaze, so tender and eloquently expressive. She was not in search of a lover and could not think upon the prospect now with any hope of rational thought.

Yet he was the choice of her family, this she knew, and his good sense and sincerity were recommended by every action, every well-chosen word, and even more by what he did not say. When Colonel Brandon spoke, his words had already been sifted and measured for their merit; when he remained quiet, she now knew his words were not restrained for dullness or lack of interest. The weight of his silence, she was beginning to discover, was far more indicative than all the fluency of Willoughby.

"I thank you, sir, for all your kindness to my sister and brother-in-law." She felt her cheeks growing warm and fidgeted with her glove as her eyes wandered over the hedge. Oh, this would not do! She had resolved that she would no longer be the silly girl, and did not Elinor encounter all with open frankness regardless of her true sentiments? She steeled her courage and looked back to him with resolve. "Colonel Brandon, might I ask one more kindness?"

His brows rose and those colourless grey eyes seemed to kindle with new interest. "Pray, ask anything you will, Miss Marianne."

She hesitated, knowing that he would rush to meet any request of hers whether it was his true wish to grant it or not. "Shall we be friends, sir?"

The lines of his lips thinned. "Friends?"

"I have not been a good friend to you"—she hastened to explain—"nor to anyone this past year. None who deserve my regard have felt it as they should, and I am determined to mend that breach. You have had every right to grow impatient with my folly, but you have not withdrawn your friendship. I hope I may prove worthy of it."

"Ah." His mouth twitched, and a genuine smile began to grow. His features thus softened, Marianne could have thought him ten years younger than his true age. Indeed, for the first time, she understood how he must have appeared to his first love—gentle and patient but firm in all his resolutions, with an agreeable countenance that drew the eye for a second look, and then a third.

In fact, the longer she looked at him, the more his looks impressed upon her that no other visage would suit him; his appearance had now become so familiar to her that she could no longer find defect. Rather, she loved to look at him, for his was the face in whose presence her heart found peace.

"Miss Marianne"—he bowed—"I covet your friendship and would wear it as an honour more dear than all the medals I ever won, for I know that it shall never tarnish."

"I have given you little cause to place such faith in me," she reminded him. "We cannot be true friends if you insist on remaining blind to my faults."

"Your faults, as you claim them to be, are in equal measure virtues. Blind to them? I could never be. Nor could I admonish you to any degree for past mistakes, for they were the product of an earnest, passionate heart and youthful innocence. I have seen the loss of such innocence, and I would not have desired it for you. Wisdom will come soon enough and too soon if you deny your true nature and determine to punish yourself for nothing more than your own feelings. Pray, do not change, Miss Marianne. I have faith in your friendship because you have ever been honest and wholly without guile."

She could not help a laugh. "Entirely! One might say a small portion of guile might have spared me a great deal of embarrassment, but I am afraid I am incapable of it."

"Then do not try to affect it. Others may do so but, in you, I am certain of a friend whose mind and heart are never concealed."

He offered her his arm and, with only a heartbeat's hesitation, she accepted it.

Elinor wed her beloved in late summer. As some accommodations were still wanting at the parsonage, Mr. and Mrs. Edward Ferrars were installed temporarily at Delaford House, and Marianne, with her mother and Margaret, were often in company there. Upon her first visit, Colonel Brandon had charged Marianne to view his library as her own and, with no further encouragement, she did precisely that.

The early September weather being too fine for one of her disposition to remain within the house, Marianne set out one afternoon to ramble about the park with a book in her hand. Even as she set her footsteps on the path to her favourite place, the pages were open before her, and she devoured Plato for the first time.

So absorbed was she that she had not heard the hoofbeats approaching from behind until they were almost upon her. She turned at the last moment and found the brown head of Colonel Brandon's gelding bobbing at her shoulder. She gasped in surprise, then laughed.

The colonel lifted his hat, then, at a smile from her, dismounted to walk beside her. "Do you never falter when reading while walking?" he asked with gentle amusement.

"Daily, sir. And what better fate, indeed, than to fall helpless in the thrall of a great book? I do not mean simply a 'good' book, where one closes the pages and is satisfied in a charming tale, but one such as this— oh, let me fall in raptures at the wit and wisdom, the eloquent turn of phrase which expresses far more than words. A book such as this measures its worth, not in hours spent in pleasure, but in minds forever enlightened and nations guided by its precepts. How could I object to a bit of grass on my skirt? It would be a punishment merely to carry such a book, an injustice to leave its pages dark for even a moment of the time I have it in my possession."

"May I?" he extended his hand.

Searching through pages which seemed familiar to him, he paused when he found one of interest, then his sombre, deep tones recited:

"Therefore, Phaedrus, I say of Love that he is the fairest and best in himself, and the cause of what is fairest and best in all other things. And there comes into my mind a line of poetry in which he is said to be the god who 'Gives peace on earth and calms the stormy deep, Who stills the winds and bids the sufferer sleep.'"

"There, do you see?" she sighed, turning her face up to the sun. "How can any not thrive on the words, enrich their souls with such wisdom?"

He turned the book over in his hands, his brow etched with thought.

"Colonel? You are not an admirer of Plato?"

"I do not admire all his precepts," he confessed. "While I grant you that he puts his thoughts forward in an elegant way, I cannot wholeheartedly agree with every one of them."

"But you read the words as if they were old friends. It is not possible that you could have brushed over them and then rejected them."

He cast her a careful look. "Many have been the days when such books, filled and brimming over with the wisdom of another age, have been my most constant companions."

Marianne's eyes drifted to the path before her. "Do you mean when you were on the battlefield?"

His lips tightened, almost an expression of pain, but softened with an attempt to dismiss some deeper feeling. "And again in England. I found little comfort or companionship elsewhere, and a young man, such as I was then, must have some employment for his mind. I had set upon a course to improve myself, seeking to partake of all the wisdom there was to be found within these pages, but, as with people, I found that the works of the great philosophers are often in discord with one another. I could not wholeheartedly endorse one without disagreeing with a second."

"You speak as if to disagree with someone would be a personal affront."

"I once thought it must be, but life has taught me otherwise. This discourse, magnificent as it is, flows directly on the heels of Plato's ardent opinion that Love does not concern itself with any deformity of form and is only inspired by beauty. With that I cannot concur, though I acknowledge Plato's superiority of thought in this instance, in Love's abiding influence in the hearts of men. Is it not possible to admire a thing—or a person—and yet not be ignorant of their faults? Or, rather, can two people of dissimilar natures not find some commonality and thrive together in harmony, though they are not alike in every way?"

Looking up to his intent expression, she was obliged to put her hand to her bonnet, as she had untied the ribbons and a light breeze threatened to carry it away. Marianne could not help but notice the admiration in his eyes as he looked at her. She was perfectly conscious that she was in remarkable looks this day and, with that awareness which all young ladies are endowed, she sensed that the afternoon sun was spilling over her shoulders in long, broken shafts. That she presented an image which he must look upon in some wonder, she could not fail to recognise. That such a picture and such an attitude might lend him encouragement she understood equally well, and the notion was not half so unsettling as it had once been.

Colonel Brandon could not, or would not, conceal that he was affected. His chest rose as he caught his breath and his lips parted slightly as if to speak, but he stood silent. He waited upon her to respond, and his eyes studied her as if for some deep hope of his own.

"I believe, Colonel," she spoke slowly, "that dissimilarity in character and feeling must be an insurmountable obstacle between two individuals."

He blinked, his disappointment sharp and clear, and looked down.

"But..." Marianne continued, drawing his eye back to her, "dissimilarity in temperament and education, why, that is scarcely to be thought of. Indeed, perhaps it is a strength which can be shared by the two in question. By one, the other may be enlivened, and by the second, the first might receive instruction. Far better to be similar in character than in temperament, for one construct is at the core of our being, constant and defined by every action and thought, while the other is merely an outward reflection and may alter with each passing mood."

A light had flashed over his countenance, as if some new desire awakened in him and he remained terrified to confess it. He drew another long breath, then slowly began to walk again. For some while, the only sound he made was the crackling of fresh autumn leaves under his boots. He seemed uncertain of his voice, but after a moment he ventured another question, one which must have been always in his thoughts.

"And what of dissimilarity in age?" he asked unsteadily. "What sort of connection can exist between two who are separated by nearly a generation? Their understanding, their experiences and expectations, must all speak against any near connection with abhorrence."

She could not dare look at him. Kicking up the withering foliage beneath her feet, Marianne was reminded how Elinor had once teased her that not everyone had her passion for dead leaves. Marianne recalled professing then how her own feelings were not always shared, not always understood....

Rousing herself, she carefully parsed her thoughts and words until she could verily sense the colonel's agitation. "Is similarity in age necessary for two people to understand each other?" she asked with care.

"The mind may be constantly refreshed, and the spirit is immortal, but what of the body? One will suffer the ravages of time long before the other and, for that other, what comfort would remain?"

"You speak, sir, as if each day is one's own. My illness, brought on by none other than my own carelessness, taught me that our days are less certain. One person may have all the comfort of a long life; the other may spend all their joys in one brilliant flash and then fade. Can you, by prudence or regret, add one moment to the span you have been given? Can I?"

He stopped again, and this time his entire being seemed to tremble. His eyes lingered on her, a long, intimate look which spoke of an ache deep within. Had she but stepped towards him, she sensed that he might have taken her in his arms on impulse.

He tore his eyes from hers after it seemed that one of them must speak and handed her the book. "Perhaps, Miss Marianne, I might introduce you to Plutarch. I believe you will enjoy the contrast with Plato."

"I am certain I would, if that is your wish, Colonel." She accepted the book but did not hold it as if she would open it again. "Sir, had you other business or are you free to walk farther with me?"

He glanced to his horse, that gentle beast which had trailed placidly behind rather than demanding constant attention as Willoughby's stallion had often done. "I am at my leisure, Miss Marianne."

Marianne accepted his arm, her cheeks warming and a new sort of pleasure bubbling from somewhere deep within. His head bowed as they walked, and she raised the book. Depending upon his guidance, she thumbed it open and read:

"And then I perceived how foolish I had been in consenting to take my turn with you in praising love, and saying that I too was a master of the art, when I really had no conception how anything ought to be praised."

She continued to read aloud, glancing up now and again to determine his feelings on each passage. As they strolled through the park, their arms linked, never once did Marianne fear that she might stumble.

The residents of Barton Cottage enjoyed Christmas at Delaford, for Mrs.

Dashwood, full of nothing but the most acute joy at her Elinor's happiness, did not miss her eldest daughter the less for it. Marianne, too, missed her sister's steady companionship and longed to be often at Delaford.

The parsonage was not large enough for them all to stay comfortably, but Colonel Brandon was only too happy to offer his own hospitality. On this morning, the day before Christmas, the gentlemen had gone off together to talk about repairs to the roof of the church.

Marianne found Elinor with Margaret in the library. The latter had been kicking her feet restlessly as she read, twirling her ringlets and looking as if she wished for some diversion.

"Margaret," Marianne informed her, "did you know the colonel's pointer had her puppies last night?"

Margaret wasted not a moment. She leaped from her chair with a cry of delight and was out of the room before another word could be spoken.

"She has grown much since autumn," Elinor observed, still laughing.

Marianne curled in the divan and tucked her feet under herself—her favourite posture when reading. "Has she? I had not noticed. I suppose in another year, or perhaps even by spring, she will be putting her hair up and wishing to attend evening events."

"She is only fourteen. But soon, she will no longer be safe from society —or Mrs. Jennings' suppositions," Elinor added with amusement. "I am not surprised you had not thought of it, for you see Margaret daily. The changes I see must not be so remarkable to you."

Marianne tilted her head, her eyes focusing on some point beyond her book. "And we have grown more intimate since you have been away. The difference in our years has seemed to narrow. You are right, Elinor. Perhaps I had not observed her growth."

"Perhaps that is not an appraisal of Margaret's growth. She is your closest companion at Barton now, is she not?"

Marianne fingered a page. "That is true. And after all that time spent in close conversation, I suppose two must become more similar. Oh, I dearly hope I have not grown as silly as a fourteen-year-old!"

Elinor laughed. "You are not silly, but your heart is lighter of late.

Whether I can attribute that to Margaret's society or some other's I cannot say, but I am comforted to see it."

Marianne did not blush as she might have done in former days when someone supplied such a vague hint. She turned her head to Elinor.

"You are indeed correct. I am content, and I am no longer troubled by regret or sorrow. I am quite pleased with my efforts to improve my mind —not with my own achievements, you must understand, but with the direction it has given my thoughts. I feel I am wiser now, and I have more the means of securing happiness."

Elinor gave up all interest in reading her own book. "And how do you mean to do that? Have you some alteration to your plans or circumstances in mind?"

"Oh! It is not so much my circumstances but in how I perceive them. I believe that has been one of the greatest fallacies I have believed, that my situation must be happy for my heart to be so. While I would not wish grief to strike our house again, I know now that I should regulate myself differently."

"You? Regulate yourself? Why, Marianne, does that notion not savour of artifice to you?"

"No, for I should be honest with myself and with those closest to me. However, I will not, by my behaviour or by dwelling upon my sorrows, provoke myself into hysterics. I believe that former attitude to be more artifice than my present one. I do not intend to conceal my feelings from the world, but I shall take care to divert my energies towards attitudes which will mend my spirits, rather than the reverse.

"Do you know, Elinor, I believe that is the secret. We may not—we *cannot*—always think upon our circumstances with satisfaction, but we need not spend all our days in despair over them. I can think of no more foolish way to waste my life than to always be caught in the throes of some agony or other. When I said that I now possess the means to happiness, this is what I meant. I have a new philosophy, dear Elinor, and I pray it will serve me well, for no life can be without trials or hardship, but I cannot improve what is beyond my control by making myself miserable over it."

Elinor looked pleased and made some pretence of opening her book again. "I daresay you have struck just the right notion, Marianne. Perhaps I might adopt your philosophy, for always concealing my feelings from those dear to me has done little to forward honest relations. Perhaps it is possible instead to make my sentiments known without allowing them to dictate my course."

"Oh, but they must!" Marianne insisted. "If your feelings will not have some part in guiding your actions, of what use are they? I only think now that they must be governed by good sense and consideration, else they might lead you too far."

"And what, my dear Marianne, do your feelings urge you to do at present?"

Marianne wrinkled her brow. "I am sure I cannot know what you mean. I intend to enjoy our Christmas holiday among good friends, and then I shall continue on as before until some alteration should occur."

"And you do not see that alteration rising before you even now?"

Marianne bent her head and toyed with the lace of her sleeve as she thought. "I know you wish me to marry the colonel. He truly is the best man I know, Elinor, but my interest in him is not in securing a husband. He is my dear friend, and I am proud to call him such. I wish for no more at present."

Elinor arched a brow, her lips curving. "You are sure?"

"Perhaps not. Do you remember what we said a moment ago about Margaret? I feel less keenly the distance between my age and the colonel's than I used to do. In my mind, I know him to be old enough to be my father, but when we are together, I see only my friend."

Elinor smiled. "Then think on that and let the rest trouble you no more. Whatever Mother's hopes and my own wishes on the matter may be, you must concern yourself only with what is right in your own heart."

Conversation idled, and each sought the quiet amusement of their book until the gentlemen's footsteps sounded at the door.

Marianne studied her sister as the gentlemen entered the room. Contentment and peace. Elinor's entire person glowed when her husband was near. Steady, reasonable, cautious Elinor. Marianne reflected wistfully that her sister's passions might run deeper and more faithful than hers ever had.

"My apologies, my dear"—Edward took his wife's hand—"I must step over to the church to see that all is arranged for the service. Will you remain here?"

Elinor glanced to her sister, and Marianne caught a hint of mirth in her expression when she answered. "No, Edward, I shall come with you. I believe my sister will be as content without my company, for she has an entire library to amuse her." Elinor rose, set her book aside, and promised to return that evening.

Marianne began to stand as well, but the colonel hastened to stay her. "Pray, wait a moment, Miss Marianne."

"Are you well today, Colonel?"

"Exceedingly. I was hoping to find an opportunity to speak with you alone. I... I have a gift for you, if you will permit me. I hope you will not think it improper to accept."

"Colonel, surely you must know that now you have piqued my curiosity, and I could no more refuse to accept your gift than I could hide my face from the sunrise and the dewy meadows on a fine morning."

He smiled at her pretty words, claimed a chair beside her, and then withdrew a slim parcel from his breast pocket. It appeared to be a small book of some sort, wrapped in simple parchment. She thanked him and unfolded the wrapping, then gasped in some surprise.

"*Childe Harold*! But how did you come by it? Hardly anyone can get it yet."

"I spoke with the author some months ago and asked if he might do me the service of obtaining a copy from his publisher."

She arched a brow. "You are friends with Lord Byron? I would not have expected it of you, sir."

"'Acquaintances' is a better word, but any patron of his art has slightly more influence upon him than a common stranger. Do you like it?"

She lifted it between her hands, her thumb stroking the binding, and beamed her most earnest, heartfelt appreciation. "I do, sir. Thank you. Are you at leisure now to read it with me?"

"I am entirely at your service." He leaned back in his chair, prepared to listen, but straightened when Marianne extended the book to him. "You wish for me to read?"

"If you will, sir."

His expression betrayed his uncertainty—he blinked rapidly, his eyes fell upon the book for a moment, and she could see his breath quicken.

"If you would prefer that I read, Colonel—"

"Not at all." He smiled and, as he did so, his look lingered on her. It seemed then that his symptoms of discomfort vanished, and his expression of pure, selfless affection caused her to shiver. No one had ever looked at her the way Colonel Brandon did, as though the whole of his delight centred in her.

Marianne felt her cheeks warming, but she could not look down as a maiden ought. Indeed, there was nothing from which she desired to look away, for there was no blemish or indecency in him. Even his countenance, once so haggard and worn in her naïve opinions, seemed only to open a window into the depths of his being. There was no mask, no flashing charm to divert the eye from what lay within, and what Marianne had begun to see was more beautiful than all her most poetic eloquence could ever express.

At last he looked down and allowed the pages to fall open to one that he must have marked for her. There was a slender length of blue ribbon tucked between the pages, and his fingers gently moved it aside to read.

> "The seal Love's dimpling finger hath impress'd
> Denotes how soft that chin which bears his touch:
> Her lips, whose kisses pout to leave their nest,
> Bid man be valiant ere he merit such:
> Her glance how wildly beautiful! how much
> Hath Phoebus woo'd in vain to spoil her cheek,
> Which glows yet smoother from his amorous clutch!
> Who round the North for paler dames would seek?
> How poor their forms appear! how languid, wan, and weak!"

He stopped, and his eyes remained fixed on the page.

"What do you think of it?" she asked softly.

He did not speak at first. She saw him swallow, his jaw worked, and he drew a long breath. "Byron is possessed of a superior gift for expression.

He writes with fluency and ease, a talent which many ought to admire. The imagery and feeling he evokes are startling in their clarity. Would that such eloquence could be employed by the humbly endowed—those with hearts more pure and more earnest than Byron's own."

"But, did you like it?"

"I must confess, Miss Marianne, that Byron is not... specifically to my taste."

"How so?"

He shifted in his chair, finally daring to meet her eyes. "The sentiments he expresses are of bewitching charm, but the soul from which they spring is that of mortal man. I struggle to believe fine, ethereal words when the frame is weak and flawed. Perhaps that is the reason my preferences tend more to the logical than the romantic. But it matters not what *I* thought of the book. I hoped instead to please you."

She remained steady, unwavering, and hesitated.

He dropped his eyes and lowered the book. "Forgive me if I have misjudged your tastes, Miss Marianne."

"You have not, sir," she murmured.

He stirred, some hopeful energy rising in his complexion. "I do not read well, with passion and fervour, as such writing deserves. I am certain that I do it no credit, but if *you* were to lend it your voice—"

"Colonel, no improvement is wanted. I can think of nothing which could please me more than your reading, for nought but your kindness and generosity inspired you to it."

Colonel Brandon blinked and swallowed. "But you did not seem to relish it as I have seen you do on prior occasions. Fear not that you might offend me with the truth, for I earnestly wish to learn what pleases you."

She reached towards him. He began to offer her the book but froze when her fingers rested, not on the pages, but on his hand.

"Colonel, if I seem not to swoon for beautiful words as I had once done, it is not for any deficiency on the part of the poet, nor is it for any lack of appreciation for your gift. It is rather that, like yourself, I have discovered something far better. Shall I worship pretty words in preference to the truth, or blind myself with what is fleeting and fail to see what endures—what is before me? I shall forever treasure this volume, not for the eloquence of the words on the page, but for the sincere feeling with which it was given."

Colonel Brandon's mouth opened as if to speak but closed helplessly without finding words. His eyes began to shine and he set the book of poetry aside. He looked at his fingers twined through hers and whispered, "Merry Christmas, Miss Marianne."

Marianne daringly raised his hand to her lips—she could do no less! "Merry Christmas, Colonel."

Marianne lingered in the drawing room at Delaford, peering out at a cold, unremitting rain that had come to wash away the new snow. All expected it to freeze again by late afternoon, making the roads impassable. Christmas was over, Boxing Day complete, and her mother had determined that they ought to return to Barton Cottage once the roads were clear. Marianne, however, felt a flutter of relief that their return would not be effected this day.

Colonel Brandon was to meet her in the library again, for she had asked him to read with her. She could find most of the books she desired easily enough on her own, but his education far exceeded hers, and she had come to delight in sitting with him by the hour as he walked through the great minds of old with her. She had expected their afternoons together to feel rather like a pupil questioning a master but, though she gained instruction and came to a deeper understanding, their conversations were far richer. They would take turns reading, then share honest opinions.

She craved the way he listened so raptly and seemed to value her deepest thoughts. In his company, she felt so much more than an eighteen-year-old girl with hardly any experience of the world. Though she knew he admired her person, his love—yes, he loved her, she could confess it now with pleasure rather than discomfort—his love for her was not merely the product of her beauty or form. In his eyes, her sentiments and opinions were treasured, worthy of esteem, and her merits measured by the same standards she would judge herself.

And she must now, after learning to cherish such intimacy, return to Barton! Marianne released a long, reluctant sigh, and her head fell against the window. The colonel had gone out two hours ago, even in this rain, to look after some crisis in the village. She had expected his return any moment, for he had promised her upon his departure that he would not be long. The minutes ticked by, however, with no sign of his return.

Perhaps he had been prevented in coming and had sought to wait out the worst of the day's rain where he could. Even as she comforted herself with this notion, an unease grew in her heart. The snow had become a thick, icy sludge on the roads and would only become more treacherous as the afternoon cooled. Surely one so steady and experienced as Colonel Brandon would take all possible precautions and would keep quite safe, but Marianne's disquiet only increased. Yet what could she do but worry?

With an impatient sigh, she moved to the pianoforte. At least in music, she could express her frustration and provide her restless energy some outlet. Page after page she flipped, her fingers soft and rigid by turns as she coaxed her own feelings from the instrument. It was when her mother's hand fell on her arm that she realised that she had been playing with passionate volume, impervious to any distraction but the hope of a figure riding up a lane. She let her hands fall, discovering only then how weary her arms were.

"Marianne! My dear, whatever is the matter? You have played this sonata three times now, and in such a way that the entire house can hear nothing else!"

"Have I?" Her eyes darted to the window before returning to her mother. "I did not intend to disturb anyone."

"Margaret is asking me what is troubling you, for she is afraid to interrupt you herself. Have you had a quarrel with someone—not the colonel, my dear!"

"Oh, no!" Marianne shook her head at the absurdity of that notion. "I believe no one could quarrel with Colonel Brandon. He is far too amiable, and he never does anything one could object to. Moreover, he is not here to quarrel with."

"Oh?" Mrs. Dashwood turned her own eyes to the window, then back to her daughter. "I did not hear that he had gone out. In this weather! The dear man is so attentive to his duties. He ought to return soon, surely."

Marianne felt her brow furrowing as she searched out the mantel clock. "He has been away nearly three hours now. He must be soaked through. The roads are dreadful and will only grow worse."

Mrs. Dashwood looked thoughtfully at her daughter.

Marianne fidgeted under her inspection. "Surely the men at the stables are keeping watch for him. He would have taken one of the grooms, would he not?"

"I am certain of it, my love," her mother assured her. "If he promised to return this afternoon, then you may be assured that he will do so."

Marianne nodded, and her fingers traced the keys. "I think I shall continue to play, Mama. It is a relief to find such a diversion."

She did so, pounding out her uncertainties, her worries, and her confusion on the hapless instrument as the mantel clock ticked. She was vaguely aware of her younger sister peering into the room now and again, but no one dared interrupt her. In the middle of her third piece, a disturbance through the window caught her eye, and she abruptly ceased playing.

It was not the colonel, as she had expected...hoped. Two riders from the stables trotted off in the distance, their figures obscured under heavy cloaks. Marianne stepped to the window in alarm, leaning into the casement with panting expectation. Where was he? What had happened! She saw two more riders galloping out in the opposite direction. A search party?

She stepped back, her skirts swirling about her as she turned away. Mr. Harris, the butler, would know! She found him outside the master's study giving directions to a footman. The butler dismissed the servant and offered her a greeting which was far more deferential than usually accorded a guest—all the servants did, as if she were the mistress of the house.

"Mr. Harris, have you any word of Colonel Brandon?"

"No, miss. We expected him back some time ago. He had not intended to go far."

"But the roads!" she protested. "Did he take no one with him?"

"No, Miss Dashwood. He did not think it necessary and wished to spare the grooms on such a wet day." Betraying some hint of feeling, the butler added in confidence, "Most masters would not think twice about a servant's comforts, miss."

"I know. But it was all for nought, for the riders have now gone out to search for him, I presume?"

"Yes, miss. They will bring word back if the master has taken shelter at an inn or a local house. Perhaps his mount threw a shoe...."

Marianne thanked him and then: "The colonel will be quite chilled when he returns. Has hot water been readied, and perhaps a fire built up in his rooms?"

"Of course, miss. Is there anything we can do for your comfort at present? Perhaps tea?"

She shook her head slightly. "No, I am quite well."

But she was not. Another miserable half hour passed, and Marianne began to think that she would wear a path in the carpet by the window. Fear such as she had never known descended round her heart. She had been often enough at Delaford now to know his ways, and to remain out contrary to his expectations—and in such weather!—bespoke only ill tidings. She worried her fingers into a knot at her stomach and forced herself to calm only when they began to ache.

What nonsense had possessed her mind? Colonel Brandon was the steadiest of men, and he had not intended to go far from his own home. Surely, if something had happened in the village, the house would have heard by now! But what of the fields and roads? Anything might have occurred... his horse slipped in the mud, an ice-laden branch falling across the road at the wrong moment, or a debilitating, overpowering chill which might have taken him from his course. A nervous tingle, almost a pain shot through her limbs as she imagined the worst. A thousand prospects troubled her—most harmless and easily explained, but not all. It was these dark possibilities which restrained each anxious breath.

"Marianne, why do you still stand at the window?" Margaret's voice broke through Marianne's haze, and she turned to see her sister tilting her head in some bewilderment.

"I was watching for Colonel Brandon. He has been out in this weather far too long. Are you not concerned for him?"

Margaret frowned. "I must be, I suppose, if you insist upon it, but no one else appears to be. Come, Marianne, will you not play at cards with me until he returns?"

"I am afraid I would not be a suitable partner," Marianne answered distractedly. "Another time, Margaret."

She turned eager eyes again to the window. Was she truly the only one fretting about his safety? And when had Colonel Brandon become so dear to her that any threat to him was naturally hers to meditate, taking upon herself alone all the trepidation which ought to be shared by ten? For so vital had he become to her happiness that nothing else was to be done, nor even thought of, until his safe return had been achieved, been seen with her own eyes. How deeply she longed to see that grey hat pulled down low, the strong line of his jaw cutting through his thick oilskin. If she could but know that he still rode erect and powerful in his saddle, that his horse even now made its faithful way back to the stables, she could be easy!

Yet, as she watched, the most dreadful shock of all followed. A lone rider appeared far up the lane, galloping for the stables. Marianne pressed her nose to the glass and could faintly hear the rider crying out for a carriage. This was all her aching spirits could withstand, and she flew again from the room in search of the butler.

"Mr. Harris! What has happened?" she demanded, with no thought for the man's station or the respect which was due him. All she could think of was the finest man she had ever known, alone and cold, quite probably injured and prone to a chilled fever such as hers...and never assured of a warm reception from her when he did return.

"I have sent a footman to the stables to learn, miss."

She fought for calm, her fingernails biting into the palms of her hands as she struggled for even speech. "I must have my cloak, for I intend to ride in the carriage."

The butler's expression altered from concern to dismay. "Miss Dashwood, pray remain here. The men will do all that can be done, and the master would not have you endanger your own safety by venturing out in this weather."

She trembled, cast her eye again to a window, and drew herself up. In this, she was assured that she was not acting on foolish impulse, but on prudence, justice, and every natural sentiment which was owed to the man she missed.

"Tell my mother I shall be quite safe in the carriage, Mr. Harris. Colonel Brandon himself could not disapprove. Please, my things, at once, and another thick rug for the carriage. I will go alone, Mr. Harris, for I must be off in a moment!"

The butler hesitated, then bowed his obedience. With a gesture, Marianne's warmest cloak was sent for, and the butler himself escorted her to the carriage as it emerged from the stables. He handed her in with a nod to the coachman, then lingered at the door before he closed it. "I give you my thanks, Miss Dashwood," he murmured. "Pray, see the master is well."

Marianne nodded, her breath catching as the door closed her in darkness. Men shouted to be off, hooves clattered in the gravel, and the wheels began to grind. She closed her eyes. No one had even told her what had happened to him! She doubted Harris had even had a chance to hear the report as he had hastened her to the carriage. She had only been grateful to catch it without causing delay, for nothing ought to keep it from its mission and the man who had become everything to her.

Marianne shivered in the carriage, more with anxiety than cold. Her gloved fingers were knotted in painful little balls and straightening them was a task which required an act of conscious will and some brisk warming. She could not be trusted for an accurate opinion of how long they had driven before she heard men calling to the carriage from somewhere ahead, but, after what seemed like an age, she heard some indication of Colonel Brandon's disposition.

"He's over here," one man called. "Hold there. We will bring him up."

As soon as the carriage lurched to a halt, Marianne's hands were on the door latch, and she leaned out, straining her eyes. Men darted away from the carriage. One groom remained, standing with Colonel Brandon's horse some fifty feet from her. The beast was balancing on three legs and covered with the icy mud, which the groom was whisking away with his bare hands to examine the horse's injury. But his rider...

A cluster of hats crested a small knoll, and then she could see him, straining to limp between two grooms with a third hovering close behind him. His right side looked to have fallen directly in the mud, and even much of his left side was splattered. His greatcoat was gone, and he looked soaked through. His face, with that straight jaw she knew so well, the clear brow and grey eyes which could belong to no other, was twisted in pain.

A cry escaped Marianne: relief, distress, joy, pity. She had feared the worst, her imagination expecting him to be carried lifeless to her. That he was on his own feet answered most of her worries, and a moment more would tell the rest. She gathered up the thick lap rug and, heedless of her own shoes, stepped down from the carriage unassisted to race to his side.

His head came up as she approached, his face aghast. "Marianne! Why are you here?"

Words were insufficient to all she would express. In the company of his men, what could she say that would not make her ridiculous? The grooms had fallen back, and Marianne could feel him trembling with cold as she settled the rug over his shoulders. Tucking it under his chin as her mother had so often done with her own cloaks, she could feel his icy flesh even through her thin gloves. Her hand fell away, and he caught it.

He stared, and only seemed to recall himself when a pain from his leg caused him to wince. Marianne withdrew again to allow his men to help him. All her blackest fears were now banished, and she could breathe. In a moment, they were both settled into the carriage. Marianne braced her own shoulders up under his arm, so that he could shift in the seat without disturbing his injured leg.

"Marianne, you ought to have stayed at the house," he protested, but his tones were anything but an admonishment. "Why would you come out in this weather?"

She stripped her gloves and wrapped her hands over his, rubbing them briskly between her own. "I feared for you."

Something kindled in his eyes, and his fingers tightened in her hand.

"Colonel, what happened?" She reached to settle another rug over him and pulled it close over his arms. "How badly are you hurt?"

He was gazing at her, so close, even his breath was warm upon her cheek. "A bad sprain and an ice water bath, nothing more. A part of the embankment at the bridge washed out," he explained. "It looked safe enough until we stepped on it, but it gave way. We suffered a dreadful fall down the embankment and into the stream, but I am afraid my poor horse may have had the worst of it."

She stiffened some in alarm. "I saw him crippled—"

"He may never fully recover. Poor old fellow, he has been a faithful creature. Perhaps a year on pasture will be just the thing and then he may do for a..." The colonel's eyes darkened strangely, and he fell silent.

"For a what? Oh, you would not make him a drayage horse!"

"No." He smiled. "I was thinking he would make a capital *child's* mount." There was a significance in his tone which was not to be missed.

Marianne was silent, then dared to meet his eyes. The look she found there, patient longing, hope and tremulous joy, stirred her to make some confession of her own. "I feared the worst might have happened to you. Oh, you cannot know all the things I imagined, waiting with no word of your welfare!"

"I believe I can imagine such distress."

The rug moved, his cold hand emerged, and his fingers laced again with hers.

The darkness enveloping them gave her courage. "I have been blind," she whispered. "And a fool. I sought what I thought was beauty and passion, and now I find that it was before me all along in the guise of truth and good sense. I have come to know it now and confess it even to myself, but it was not until today when my fears for you overcame me. I knew what it was then to think I had thrown away everything that is precious to me in pursuit of my own vanity. The thought that I might have lost you, unreasonable as it now seems, darkened all other concerns until I could only think of reaching your side, easing you in some way. Oh, Colonel, forgive a foolish creature who has only now known what it is to love!"

"Love?" His voice dropped to a whisper. "Love? Can it be possible?"

Marianne stroked the icy fingers of his hand. "You have taught me what it is, Colonel, to care more for another than I do for myself."

He raised up, drawing her shoulders under his arm and turning her more to himself. "Marianne, could I dare to hope? Could you be content with a man eighteen years your senior, who possesses neither beauty nor any grace to speak of?"

"Indeed, I shall not hear you abusing the qualities I admire, for the beauty you speak of is in a heart given freely, in honour defended at great cost, and your grace has been daily shown to me as a precious gift I do not deserve. I ought instead, Colonel, to ask whether you could reflect with satisfaction on one who has been naïve, rash, and without understanding."

He lifted his hand from hers, and the backs of his fingers brushed her cheek. "I have never admired any other more, my Marianne. Your spirit grows only more exquisite with intimacy. I shall love you to my last breath, but I would neither bind you to myself nor even do you the injustice of asking for your hand if you have the faintest doubt. You must not settle for mere contentment, Marianne, for I could never be easy knowing you might have passed over a chance to love one more suited with that exquisite passion only you possess."

"Colonel, I cannot think with felicity on my future without you at its centre."

"But our respective ages," he protested. "In ten years when I have gone grey, and the bloom of youth is still fresh upon you, will you not have cause for regret?"

Marianne captured his hand again and pressed it to her face, leaning against his palm and quoted:

> *"Let me not to the marriage of true minds*
> *Admit impediments. Love is not love*
> *Which alters when it alteration finds,*
> *Or bends with the remover to remove:*
> *O no; it is an ever-fixed mark,*
> *That looks on tempests, and is never shaken;*
> *It is the star to every wandering bark,*
> *Whose worth's unknown, although his height be taken.*

Love's not Time's fool, though rosy lips and cheeks
Within his bending sickle's compass come;
Love alters not with his brief hours and weeks,
But bears it out even to the edge of doom.
If this be error and upon me proved,
I never writ, nor no man ever loved."

"Oh, Marianne..."

He whispered no more words—no further assurances of love, no lingering objections. Instead, the steady and even-tempered man whose every move, every word or deed had always been calculated and ordered with propriety and deliberation, startled her. His hand cupped her cheek, brushed her sensitive skin so lightly that his fingers were more sensed than felt, urging her to come to him. Her eyes closed—one last sigh from her lips, and she felt him lean close.

His lips were sweet upon hers, tender and coaxing but never insistent, never asking more than she would give. In truth, she desired more; her arms had wrapped round his shoulders, under his warm rug, and it was she begging him to come closer, to hold her more tightly, and to love her more deeply.

He pulled away, breathless, resting his forehead against hers. One of his arms tightened round her waist, while his other hand still caressed the line of her jaw. Marianne pressed her lips to his cold cheek, drinking in the scents of saddle leather and his damp hair.

"I did you an injustice, my Marianne."

She shook her head gently against his. "You have done nothing of the kind, sir."

"But I have! I had always intended, if I were ever so blessed, to speak before claiming such a liberty as I have done. I wished to know, to be sure in my own conscience, that you harboured no reservations—that the strength of your feelings was comparable to my own."

"You may be easy, for I know my own heart. It has become a rational thing, governed by good sense rather than wilful inclination, but it has only grown the truer for it. What confidence, what faith could I place in my own feelings if I did not trust their object with my very life?"

"Then will you also trust in me? Will you walk beside me and lend me your faith when mine is weak? Will you bring light to cheerless rooms, rest to a weary soul, and joy to one who had once thought happiness but a distant memory? Oh, my Marianne, bless me with your hand unto the end of my days!"

She rested one hand on his chest, her eyes full and her heart overflowing. "The blessing would be mine, my love."

His chest shook beneath her hand, a jerking sob which gave way to trembles of elation. He tried to smile, to laugh out for joy, but tears filled his eyes instead. Marianne brushed her thumb over his cheek, soothing away the last of the pain and doubts which had surely been of her own making. His lips sought hers again, and this time, they gave of themselves freely and without hesitation.

NICOLE CLARKSTON is a book lover and happily married mom of three. Originally from Idaho, she now lives in Oregon with her romantic hero, several horses, and one very fat dog. She has loved crafting alternate stories and sequels since she was a child, and she is never found sitting quietly without a book or a writing project.

HAPPINESS IN MARRIAGE

AMY D'ORAZIO

ELIZABETH BENNET

Intelligent and quick-witted, the second daughter of an unremarkable country squire, Elizabeth Bennet refuses two advantageous marriage proposals, choosing love and respect over money and security. *"Do not consider me now as an elegant female intending to plague you, but as a rational creature speaking the truth from her heart."* —**Chapter XIX, *Pride and Prejudice*.** She is able to laugh at her own flaws yet is wise enough to admit when she has judged poorly. When the interfering and overbearing Lady Catherine de Bourgh declares her an "obstinate, headstrong girl," Elizabeth defends herself and is fiercely protective of those she loves... even the man she believes is lost to her forever.

HAPPINESS IN MARRIAGE

It now first struck her that she was selected from among her sisters as worthy of being the mistress of Hunsford Parsonage, and of assisting to form a quadrille table at Rosings, in the absence of more eligible visitors. The idea soon reached to conviction, as she observed his increasing civilities toward herself, and heard his frequent attempt at a compliment on her wit and vivacity; and though more astonished than gratified herself by this effect of her charms, it was not long before her mother gave her to understand that the probability of their marriage was exceedingly agreeable to her. —Chapter XVII.

SUNDAY 24 NOVEMBER 1811

"I have the most delightful notion for your hair."

"Do you?" I asked Jane with playful astonishment. "I do too. I shall plait it as I always do and then go to sleep."

"Lizzy."

"If I hear one more thing about the ball, I promise you I shall run stark, raving mad."

Jane smiled that gentle, knowing smile she always wore when she was about to vex me and said, "Very well, I shall not speak of the ball. I shall instead speak of a certain officer I think you like. I shall only ask if, upon the next occasion at which you would likely see him, you might prefer your hair arranged in a particularly becoming manner."

I sighed heavily. Since we had received Mr. Bingley's note on Friday, there had been nothing but talk of shoe roses and dance partners at Long-bourn. My sisters were nearly aloft with their delight and anticipation but, of them all, Jane—in her own way—was most eager. Given Mr. Bingley's attentions to her, Jane had every cause to expect the sort of evening which exceeded her every dream. *Happy for Jane*, I reminded myself.

"Very well," I said, seating myself at our dressing table. "Have your way with me."

Jane wasted no time, coming immediately to set about the work of unpinning my heavy mass of curls. As she set to work, I decided I should confide in her about a question which had plagued me for the past days— a question for which I had at last arrived at an answer.

"I have made a decision."

"Have you?" Jane asked. "I do hope you have decided in favour of your ivory gown because I think—"

"No, no." I laughed. "Not about my gown, although yes, I do think I shall wear the ivory. I speak of a different decision."

With a deep inhale to fortify myself, I told her, "If Mr. Collins asks me to marry him, I daresay I shall accept."

Mr. Collins had made no secret of his intention to choose a wife from among me and my sisters. As he had asked me to open the ball with him and had been paying me very particular compliments over the past few days, I believed I was the chosen sister.

Jane was using her fingers to untangle my curls; it felt heavenly but, alas, was not sufficient to soothe my anxieties. At long last, she spoke, admitting, "I have noticed his attentions to you. I think it very likely he will speak soon. But Lizzy, do you not think it would be a mistake to accept him?"

Cold nausea washed over me, but I was determined. "I think it would be a mistake to refuse him."

"No, please Lizzy, you cannot."

"I can Jane. I think I must." I sighed. My nausea had abated; I was growing accustomed to this idea. "Papa could die tomorrow, and then what would become of us? For as much as Mama's nerves do vex us all, I daresay it is she, and not our father, who has a true comprehension of our situation. If I marry Mr. Collins, we will be safe. I will have all the respectability of marriage and our home will be secured in him. I will make those things sufficient for my contentment."

Jane closed her eyes and pressed her fingers to her forehead. "I cannot permit you to sacrifice yourself in this way."

"It is for the best," I protested immediately. "It is by no means certain that I, that any of us, will ever have another offer. We are not good prospects for eligible gentlemen."

We had no fortune, our mother's family was not distinguished, and our education had been indifferent, at best. My mother had placed great faith in the beauty of her daughters to make a good match, but I had no great opinion of my beauty. I was well aware of my shortcomings.

Jane had opened her eyes by then and began drawing the brush through my hair with long, languid strokes. "I wish I could deny that, but I cannot, not if I care to be honest. For as much as people have always said that we are the jewels of Hertfordshire, no one has ever proposed to us. I am almost three-and-twenty; I have been attending balls and parties since I was sixteen. That is seven years with nothing to show for it."

I gave her reflection a reassuring smile. "The attentions of Mr. Bingley are not nothing. I daresay Mama will have two daughters settled soon."

"I think, of every lady Mr. Bingley has met in Hertfordshire, he likes me the best," said Jane with a little sigh. "In Hertfordshire. We cannot forget that this is but a small bit of Mr. Bingley's life. He may well have a girl he likes best in every county, for all I know."

"Mr. Bingley is in love with you. I am sure of it." I twisted to face her. "You have nothing to worry for. Mr. Bingley will speak very soon, I am sure of it."

"If you are so sure of it, then why will you marry a man I know you do not love? Will not my marriage to a man worth five thousand a year be sufficient to keep us all?"

She had me; I could not reply. Instead I rose, pushing past her to go to my window. After a succession of rainy days, it was at last a clear night. "Our mother found beauty sufficient to raise her own prospects. It is likely unimaginable to her that her own daughters should not do likewise."

Behind me, Jane said softly, "I wish I could be as certain as she was that beauty was sufficient to overcome any objections to a match."

"I do not think either of us should wish to follow my mother's example. Yes, she raised herself to the status of a gentlewoman, but has she true contentment? I doubt it. Not for many years now."

My parents' marriage has never been a happy one, not for as long as I could remember. My father was captivated in his youth by my mother's liveliness and beauty, and they were, alas, well and truly married when he realised such charms were not sufficient for a lifetime of happiness. Disenchantment sank into indifference and resentment; it was dreadful for the whole family, most of all for my mother, who became increasingly silly to draw his notice.

With a sigh, I returned to my seat at the dressing table, and Jane silently took up her position with the brush behind me.

"Did you ever wonder...?" I was not sure I wanted to know Jane's opinion on the question that had always niggled at my mind.

"About Papa?" Jane's eyes met mine in the dressing table looking glass.

"No." In this I was certain. No, our father's only mistress was his books, to be sure.

"Our mother?"

My steady gaze was her reply. I expected an immediate denial, perhaps some confusion and embarrassment. Instead I had a surprise. Jane blushed, very faintly, and dropped her eyes to my box of hair pins. With one hand buried in my curls, she rifled around a bit in the little box.

Once the precise pin had been located, she spoke. "Some years ago," she said and then had to clear her throat. "Probably three or four years ago, I suspected something."

I knew immediately that of which she spoke. "Right around the time she had her fortieth birthday?"

Jane nodded, her fingers busy in my hair. "It was one of the few times in our lives she was not wholly dedicated to seeing us all married."

"She was uncommonly gay in those days."

"Very much so…and Mr. Morris was often lingering about in those days."

"Mr. Morris?" I tried not to gasp. "The land agent?" Not that I took airs about such things, but I should have thought my mother would.

Jane shrugged, then rifled for more pins. "If you are not looking for a husband, then a handsome face and fine figure will do, no matter the purse attached to them."

"What do you mean, 'he lingered about'?"

"He was around quite a lot. I believe it was then that the Darlingtons left Netherfield, but surely their leaving did not require him to be so often present? Always around in the field, or the lane, here and there?"

I had no idea what to say. I had some vague recollection of that time. Mr. Morris once gave me a ribbon, a very pretty yellow ribbon that he said would be lovely in my dark hair. I thought it a bit odd at the time, but I was too pleased by the present to think overlong on it. In any case, I never would have imagined the truth of it!

"One day," said Jane, "she asked me to take a note with me when I went to visit my aunt Philips. She said that a boy would receive the note and take it up to his master's lodgings. She said I must not tell anyone about it, that it was a private business."

"What did you do?"

"I took the note," said Jane. "But my conscience would not allow it. Right before I left, when my gloves and bonnet were on and everyone was waiting for me, I ran back to the drawing room where she sat alone. She was surprised to see me, and I nearly threw the note back into her lap. I said 'Mama, what you do is your affair, but I pray that, if what you are doing will injure my father, then you should not involve me in it.'"

"And what did she say to that?"

"Nothing," said Jane. "I left the room then and went with you and my sisters to Meryton, and that was the last I ever knew of it."

I hardly knew what to say, but we were much too sober by this time, so I said, "If you mean to suggest that in marrying Mr. Collins, I was likely to find myself taking up with Mr. Morris later, then I shall have to disagree in the most violent way possible."

It worked; Jane giggled. "Of course not."

"It does seem to be the way of it though, does it not?" My mind had drifted away from my own parents onto my aunt Philips. Like Mama, Aunt Philips was once a beautiful woman; unlike Mama, she was unconcerned with raising her status.

"Does it?"

"I am thinking of Uncle and Aunt Philips," I said. "They married for a mutual fondness of parties and balls."

"And for our uncle," said Jane, "surely the prospect of succeeding in our grandfather's business was some inducement."

"Possibly. And now my aunt entertains the young people while our uncle visits Miss Watson."

"Oh Lizzy!"

"Can you deny it?" I turned to look at her. "We have both seen him coming and going from her house."

"Perhaps he has some business with her."

"Indeed he does," I agreed. "Only it has nothing to do with his business of being a solicitor."

Jane frowned at me in a disapproving way, but she could offer no denial. In any case, it did not seem to injure my aunt any, not that she showed anyone. She enjoyed heartily being in the middle of town, enjoying visitors and revelries, and hearing all the gossip before anyone else.

"But our aunt and uncle Gardiner are truly a love story," said Jane, obviously eager to be done with any unpleasant thoughts of Miss Watson and my uncle Philips. "Theirs is a marriage to which we might all aspire."

"And yet how inauspiciously it began!" I said. "A poor man who had just put all his money into a business—"

"And a very young lady whose parents did not wish her to marry!" Jane said with a little laugh. My aunt and uncle's story was well known to us: both of them too young, with no money to speak of; all their friends and relations urging them to do the very opposite of what their hearts desired.

"And look how it has all ended," Jane said enthusiastically. "Theirs is a true marriage, a marriage I might like to have for myself."

"And yet, I do not think it is their love for one another that has brought them to where they are."

"How can you speak so?"

"Because, although they do love each other, I think it more their mutual regard and respect for one another that has played to their success."

"How is mutual regard different from love?" Jane's scepticism made her heedless to the tenderness of my scalp and I gave a little yelp as she tugged at a particularly fierce knot.

"Because love might burn brighter but it will eventually dim, perhaps even disappear completely. For a marriage to succeed there must be fondness, shared interests…and above all, respect."

"Do you…?" Jane hesitated and then, overwhelmed by her natural inclination to approve of everyone, said, "Of course, as a clergyman, Mr. Collins is always due respect."

"Yes," I said, "there is that. And I think as I knew more about him that I could find more to appreciate about him and then, in time, perhaps even… grow attached to him."

Jane did not reply to this. Her mouth stayed tucked into a gentle frown while she tugged and braided and did all manner of things to my hair. When she was done, she stood back and, I had to admit, she had made a very pretty job of me.

"'Tis lovely," I said with a smile. "Thank you, Jane. My pillow will appreciate it enormously."

"Silly," she scolded me. "But we had to try it before we thought more on it. In any case, what about Mr. Wickham? I thought he had tugged at your heart a bit."

That thought made me wistful. Ah yes, Mr. Wickham, with his fine form, his handsome face, and his very agreeable manners.

"I like Mr. Wickham a great deal," I said. "Indeed I might say that—in other circumstances—I could fall in love with him. But Jane, it would never do."

"Why not?"

"Because Mr. Darcy has left him penniless," I said, immediately impassioned; such was my vexation with that odious gentleman. "Mr. Wickham has already hinted to me that I should not expect anything of him and, indeed, I know it must be true. For a man to throw in his lot with the militia speaks to straitened circumstances. We would all do best to recall that these gentlemen, while pleasing enough at a party, are not likely to afford us lives in any way equal to that which we know in our father's home."

"That is true." Jane began to undo my hair. "I should not like to see you following a soldier about the countryside, in any case. But Lizzy, you do have a heart that is made to love. I can more easily imagine you working as someone's governess than I can imagine you married to a man you cannot love."

This was a home truth. I stopped teasing and dropped my eyes to the surface of the table. There was a fine film of the scented dusting powder my sister and I both used on the surface. I dragged my finger through it, writing my name.

"I think I require too much to fall in love," I said. "I do not think any man possesses the qualities I find worthy of my whole heart."

"And what qualities are those?"

After a moment's thought, I rose and went to retrieve my journal. I was an indifferent journal-keeper at best and most often resorted to using it to remind myself to do things. But there was one page I had written once that I thought might divert my sister now.

"Hear ye, hear ye," I intoned solemnly. "Lizzy's List of the Perfect Gentleman!"

Jane laughed and sat down on her bed to listen to me. I cleared my throat in an excessively important way and then began to read.

"Tall, because I am short and I do not wish for short children. Preferably dark-haired. Intelligent and likes to read. Is good to his family and mine. Likes to walk and be out of doors. Enjoys games. Has a good sense of humour—"

"For a moment, it seemed like you described Mr. Darcy," Jane exclaimed.

"Mr. Darcy! Forgive me—did I say disagreeable when I meant to say pleasant?"

Jane laughed. "No, but the rest of it sounds very much like him."

"Hardly," I said with a sniff. "In any case, there are about ten more things on here, everything from how much we would talk every day to—"

"You and Mr. Darcy have surely not wanted for things to argue and discuss." Apparently she was intent on plaguing me.

I rolled my eyes. "My marrying Mr. Darcy—who by the by, would not even dance with me, as you seem to have forgot—is only slightly less likely than me finding any man who has all of these qualities I have listed. Any intelligent man is also going to be prudent, and no one with any prudence would marry someone as poor as I am. No, I cannot afford love; I ask only for mutual respect, and I daresay I can respect Mr. Collins enough to tolerate his fatuousness and servility. Indeed, these qualities may naturally wane with age anyway."

"If you say so, but please, Lizzy, I do implore you to consider carefully. Some sacrifices may prove not to be worthy of you."

Two days later, as I stood in the vestibule at Netherfield—our carriage having been the absolute last to be ordered from the ball—things seemed very different.

There had been much to distress me that night. Mr. Wickham failed to attend—due to Mr. Darcy. I danced with Mr. Darcy, the only local lady so distinguished, and argued with him. And I was utterly, painfully humiliated by my family. I had never seen them so ill-behaved, and worst among them was Mr. Collins.

Mr. Collins had not been respectful to me or to anyone else there. He had embarrassed me while dancing, proving lacking in even the most basic manners; he had been too familiar with Mr. Darcy against my better advice, and he rattled on when it should have been far, far better to be silent. Even now he stood, offering endless compliments while Miss Bingley and Mrs. Hurst yawned and ignored him. My cheeks burned anew just beholding him. He had no wit, no discernment, and no regard for those around him. He was a strange mix of humility and arrogance, foisting himself on the unsuspecting to ply them with his peculiar brand of unctuous conversation. I tried, valiantly, through the course of the evening to persuade myself that with time, with experience, with the gentle hand of a wife to guide him, he would improve but even my best efforts failed me completely.

I cannot, I realised. God help me, I simply cannot.

More than once did Elizabeth, in her ramble within the Park, unexpectedly meet Mr. Darcy. She felt all the perverseness of the mischance that should bring him where no one else was brought; and to prevent its ever happening again, took care to inform him at first that it was a favourite haunt of hers. How it could occur a second time, therefore, was very odd! Yet it did, and even a third. It seemed like wilful ill-nature, or a voluntary penance, for on these occasions it was not merely a few formal enquiries and an awkward pause and then away, but he actually thought it necessary to turn back and walk with her. He never said a great deal, nor did she give herself the trouble of talking or of listening much; but it struck her in the course of their third rencontre that he was asking some odd unconnected questions—about her pleasure in being at Hunsford, her love of solitary walks, and her opinion of Mr. and Mrs. Collins's happiness. —Chapter XXXIII.

WEDNESDAY 8 APRIL 1812, THE GROVE AT ROSINGS PARK

And there he is.

I had just come around a particularly pretty part of the glade, one marked by a profusion of bluebells on the edges of the path, and there I found him. It was the third time that Mr. Darcy had come upon me during my rambles, though the grove at Rosings is very large and I had warned him of my preferred paths. I thought surely I must not see him again...until there he was.

He was examining some foliage nearby him—no doubt finding fault with it as he did me. The idea of myself and the leaf of one accord made me giggle.

"Good day, Miss Bennet." He straightened immediately. "You are looking cheerful today."

"I hope," I said, "that I am always looking cheerful. Life is too short to be ill-humoured, do you not think?" *Calm girl*, I told myself. *No need to come out swinging at him.*

If he perceived any slight to his own disposition, he ignored it. "I have always admired that about you, Miss Bennet. You seem to find felicity wherever it might rest."

"I do try," I said lightly.

"May I have the honour of joining you?"

"You may," I said, managing to keep my disappointment at bay. *At least he does not speak very much. I am almost as much in solitude as I am without him.*

We wandered in silence for only a short while until he asked, "Your visit with your friends has been pleasant, I hope."

"Very much so."

We had then more silence which stretched long between us. I refused to trouble myself for it. With anyone else, I might have been compelled to introduce some subject of conversation, but Mr. Darcy had intruded on me. If he wished to importune me, then the burden of discussion must rest on his head.

"I am surprised Mrs. Collins does not join you on your walks."

"Are you?" I gave my reticule a little bouncing swing. "Then you must know very little about being the wife of a parson."

Strangely, this led to a loud guffaw, the likes of which I should never have expected from him. I turned to look at him with no little amazement.

"No," he said, still chuckling. "I confess, I know very little about being a wife of any kind, much less that of a parson."

Still astonished, I said, "Charlotte's household and her duties to the parish keep her far too busy to be out rambling about all day. In any case, she had never much fondness for the exercise."

"Perhaps that suits your preference? I have noticed, both here and in your home county, you are often alone on your walks."

Was he asking if I minded his company? It was late to enquire about that, but I would not insult him for it. "The pleasing society of a friend is always welcome, although I am equally content with the flora and fauna as my companions."

Silence again entombed us and I allowed my mind to drift, thinking of how it might have been me instead of Charlotte tending to all of those parish duties. I still, at times, had pangs of guilt, worrying over the fate of my mother and sisters, a fate I might have rescued them from—but had chosen not to.

What had persuaded me against him, more so than anything, was the other family I had to concern myself with—my future family. Did my children deserve to suffer the same variety of humiliations that my sisters and I had, courtesy of our mother? How might Mr. Collins's foolishness affect their lives? Did they not deserve a respectable, dignified father?

None of Mr. Collins's actions since the day he proposed to me—including his proposal to my friend only days after I refused him—had improved my opinion of his character. Charlotte seemed well able to tolerate him and find contentment in their situation, but I know myself well enough to comprehend that I could never do likewise. To even imagine myself a permanent resident of the parsonage house, with its indefinite bondage to Rosings Park, brings me sorrow; I could not bear to imagine my children suffering likewise.

I had refused Mr. Collins on the basis of needing to respect my life partner and needing him to respect me. Based on this visit, however, I thought to add one more requirement for a marriage partner: the ability to build a life that would be pleasing to us both.

It seemed that Mr. Darcy knew my thoughts, for he said, "Mr. and Mrs. Collins seem well settled for so short a marriage."

"I find them both very content in their situation."

"But some perhaps might not have made the like choice?"

I silently congratulated my bonnet on its usefulness; it permitted me to see Mr. Darcy peering at me whilst still seeming unaffected by his query. "Different people want different things. What is important for one might not be important for another."

"I should think everyone would wish for affection in their marriage partner, perhaps even love."

"Even if they do wish it, not everyone can afford to be imprudent," I replied airily.

"But sometimes those who cannot afford it are imprudent nevertheless."

So he knew about my refusal of Mr. Collins, did he? I was not surprised. Mr. Collins had himself made a mortifying allusion to it one evening at Rosings Park, and from it I surmised that he had told Her Ladyship all about it. It was a short jump there from Lady Catherine telling Mr. Darcy, and likely Colonel Fitzwilliam too.

Mr. Darcy was still studying me. His casual candour had stung a bit, but I would not rise to the bait. "Prudence in matters of fortune is some-times overcome by prudence in other matters. There is more than one consideration in regards to making a good marriage. For husband and wife to be happy and respectable in their union, there must be both happi-ness and respect. I fear I have seen too many marriages that lack one or both to enter wantonly into such a state."

"So you are determined to marry for love?"

"No," I said. "But nothing will induce me into matrimony save that I have sufficient respect for my husband's character and enough fondness for him to make me feel that I will grow to love him. Many marriages begin with respect and with fond regard that grows into love, I daresay."

He had turned his head from me then and seemed to be pondering my words. He likely thought me very feminine and foolish. After all, he would marry Miss de Bourgh and, from what I had seen of the matter, that would be a match rooted wholly in matters of fortune and family. Still, I did not care what he thought about it; if he chose to scorn me for refusing Mr. Collins, then so it was.

The day was too lovely for me to waste time dwelling on Mr. Darcy. I looked to the side, allowing my bonnet to obscure him while I basked in the sights and smells of spring around me. The sun where it pierced the canopy of trees was warm, and the scent of new grasses and hay was in the air. I drank it into my lungs.

"So, if a man of good character," said Mr. Darcy suddenly, "for whom you had some fondness were to propose to you, then that man might expect a favourable reply? Regardless of his fortune or situation?"

He wished to see me refute my own claims. It was a test, but I already knew how to pass it. "I have already said that fortune is not a sufficient inducement," I replied with a little smirk. "However, foolhardy is the man who will seek to marry without being sure of his own ability to support his family. Being a fool is certainly no recommendation to me, so make of that what you will, sir."

Mr. Darcy's only reply was a strange enigmatic smile and a little nod of his head. It gave me a strange sense. I wondered if he was thinking of his cousin, if perhaps the colonel had some intentions towards me? Other-wise, such a reply made no sense.

"Had they fixed on any other man it would have been nothing; but his perfect indifference, and your pointed dislike, make it so delightfully absurd! Much as I abominate writing, I would not give up Mr. Collins's correspondence for any consideration. Nay, when I read a letter of his, I cannot help giving him the preference even over Wickham, much as I value the impudence and hypocrisy of my son-in-law. And pray, Lizzy, what said Lady Catherine about this report? Did she call to refuse her consent?"

To this question his daughter replied only with a laugh; and as it had been asked without the least suspicion, she was not distressed by his repeating it. Elizabeth had never been more at a loss to make her feelings appear what they were not. It was necessary to laugh, when she would rather have cried. Her father had most cruelly mortified her, by what he said of Mr. Darcy's indifference, and she could do nothing but wonder at such a want of penetration, or fear that perhaps, instead of his seeing too little, she might have fancied too much. —
Chapter LVII.

SUNDAY 4 OCTOBER 1812, LONGBOURN

When my father had at last finished teasing me about Mr. Darcy, I left him, walking first sedately and then more quickly to my bedchamber, where I tossed myself face-down on my bed and awaited the torrent of tears which must surely come. Alas, it did not, remaining lodged in my chest, a hard, painful lump of sorrow that would not be excised.

At length, I turned over and gazed at the canopy above my head. Had I fancied too much of him? Had his love for me grown cold? And if it had not, what might Lady Catherine's violent objections against me do to him?

I rolled off the bed, finding my journal and quickly finding the pages where I had written all about the perfect gentleman, the subject of all my youthful romantic fancies. A half-smile came to my face as I read over the qualities I had prized, seeing that, yes, just as Jane had said long ago, it did indeed describe Mr. Darcy.

"A marriage for the sake of prudence, or for fondness, or respect, is all well and good," I mused aloud, "but only for those who have never been in love before. Once you have given up your heart and allowed another to take residence in yours, I daresay there is no going back."

It was the first I had admitted it, even to myself. I, Elizabeth Bennet, was in love with Mr. Darcy, painful though it was to admit it at present.

I remembered thinking, as I lay in my bed at the inn at Lambton, how altered he was. He had changed, becoming 'all ease and friendliness,' as my aunt had said it. I had wondered, as I lay there in the dark Derbyshire summer night, if it could possibly be all for me.

Love changes a person. He had changed me, to be sure. I had been overwhelmed by prejudice, swollen with immature certainty over things I had no right to be sure of, but I had learnt. I had believed I could marry prudently, then wisely, then for respect alone. But then had come our brief time at Pemberley, when Mr. Darcy had lit my fancies with hope, with dreams and possibilities of what a true union of like souls really could be.

And now he was gone again. Would he return to me? I had to believe that he would. I had to believe that his aunt would be vanquished by him as she was by me.

I cannot, I simply shall not, ponder any more on the subject. If he loves me, if he returns to Longbourn, I will leave him in no doubt of how I feel.

"But tell me, what did you come down to Netherfield for? Was it merely to ride to Longbourn and be embarrassed? or had you intended any more serious consequence?"

"My real purpose was to see you, and to judge, if I could, whether I might ever hope to make you love me." —Chapter LX.

16 DECEMBER 1812, LONGBOURN

Snow had fallen, and I thought the woods of Hertfordshire had never before looked so charming with it. I have always loved the particular hush a snowfall brings and no more so than today, as I walked with my betrothed, breathing in the clean, crisp air and enjoying the feel of being tucked against his warm side. His cheeks were faintly flushed, rendering him even more handsome than usual. I thought about telling him so but did not, for I had more important confessions to make.

"I have something to show you."

"What is it?"

"It is something I wrote when I was about eighteen," I said. "Long before ever I knew you."

From a pocket in my coat, I withdrew the page I had torn from my journal. "My perfect man" described on paper so long ago and standing before me in the flesh. He read it with an amused air, chuckling at some of it but mostly silent.

"And here, I believed you were always determined to marry for love," he said.

"No, I never said that," I replied. "I might have wished for it, but my circumstances had persuaded me differently. As soon as I was old enough to understand how the world works, I knew love was unlikely; prudence was the more probable course."

"My brave girl," he said with a little sigh. "How glad I am that you had courage sufficient to wait for me! How thankful I am that you did not give in to prudence whilst waiting for me to surrender my pretensions and love you as you deserve to be loved."

"I cannot lay claim to such courage as you will afford me," I told him. "It was something much simpler than that. You have altered me, you see. Knowing you has made me know myself better; but also it has changed what I want.

"It was scarcely above a twelve-month ago that I believed I could happily endure a marriage of prudence—I speak of Mr. Collins, of course. I truly thought I could do it until I realised I could not. I realised then I needed to respect my marriage partner and feel that he was truly superior to other men."

"And you could not do that with Collins?" Mr. Darcy asked gravely; but no, I knew his manner of teasing now and permitted myself a giggle.

"No, I am afraid I could not. So it was settled from there: I would seek a marriage partner whose character I valued, who respected me as I respected him. So I decided a husband with whom I shared mutual respect would do. This, I believed, would be enough for a happy life; and I still think, for many ladies, it is indeed."

"I daresay it is," he said. "Certainly most marriages I have ever heard of are thus. My parents began in such a way."

"Did they?"

"Their marriage was not arranged, not exactly, but my grandparents were all friends, and suggestions and implications were made that did the job from there."

"You say they began in such a way; how did it end though?"

"I believe they loved each other," he said. "Of course, a child always thinks so but, at the very least, they were very fond of one another and enjoyed spending time together."

We walked on, the sound of our steps muffled on the path which was yet carpeted with fallen leaves. Snow was gathering on the ground, making for a tricky business but, I knew if I slipped, he would be sure to catch me.

"And you," I asked, "in all your youthful fancies, did you wish to marry for love? Or were you resigned to practicality?"

"Hmm," he said, thoughtfully, "I was determined to have some heart in the matter. I daresay I thought love would come later, however, so only wanted to marry where I had fondness and regard."

"And shall you? Marry for fondness and regard?"

He knew that I was teasing him. "Indeed Miss Bennet. I have grown excessively fond of you."

I laughed but then grew serious. I had not yet told him—he knew my heart had changed and he knew how much I esteemed him, but he had not yet heard me say the words.

"No matter how I began," I said, and my voice cracked a little, "from prudence to regard, one thing I know to be true. It was you who upset everything, who changed what I knew about myself, and altered what I thought I wished for in a marriage partner."

"I did?"

"Who, having tasted of such a love as this, could ever settle for anything less? Once I knew your love, I was certain: nothing but the deepest love could induce me into matrimony."

His face had changed then.

"And I do mean to say," I continued, "that I am in love with you, Fitzwilliam Darcy. Nothing else matters to me but that. Ours is a love match, through and through."

Heartfelt delight, such as I had rarely seen, spread over his countenance. I had but a moment to think how well it became him before I was pulled into his arms. He had kissed me before but not like this. This kiss, our first kiss as true lovers, I felt into my very bones.

We kissed until the snow had gathered on the brim of his hat, until Jane and Bingley, who had walked out with us, began to call out in worried tones; we kissed until I forgot everything else but the taste of his lips and the feel of his hand pressing against my back and folding me into him.

"Lizzy? Mr. Darcy?" Jane's voice had come closer.

Reluctantly, he released me, but I had one more thing to say. "Always," I promised. "I will love you forever."

AMY D'ORAZIO is a former scientist and current stay-at-home mom who is addicted to Austen and Starbucks in equal measure. While she adores Mr. Darcy, she is married to Mr. Bingley, and their Pemberley is in Pittsburgh, Pennsylvania. She has two daughters devoted to sports with long practices, and began writing stories as a way to pass the time spent at their various gyms and studios. She firmly believes that all stories should have long looks, stolen kisses, and happily-ever-afters. Like her favorite heroine, she dearly loves a laugh and considers herself an excellent walker. She is the author of *The Best Part of Love* and *A Short Period of Exquisite Felicity*.

CHARLOTTE'S COMFORT

JOANA STARNES

CHARLOTTE LUCAS

A sensible, intelligent young woman, Charlotte Lucas is Elizabeth Bennet's most rational friend. However, after marrying the odious, obsequious Mr. Collins, one might argue the sensibility in the act. Has she empowered herself by taking her fate in to her own hands or merely affirmed Regency era women's limited choices? *"Without thinking highly either of men or of matrimony, marriage had always been her object; it was the only honourable provision for well-educated young women of small fortune, and however uncertain of giving happiness, must be their pleasantest preservative from want. This preservative she had now obtained; and at the age of twenty-seven, without having ever been handsome, she felt all the good luck of it."* **—Chapter XXII,** *Pride and Prejudice.*

CHARLOTTE'S COMFORT

FEBRUARY 1812

I am not romantic. I ask only a comfortable home. Or at least this is what I have been telling myself these seven years, ever since John Purvis returned from Bath an engaged man. Engaged to someone other than myself, needless to say.

Well, now I have the comfortable home I wished for, and comfortable it is indeed. Spacious and well-appointed. Recently refurbished, too. There is a modern-looking range in the kitchen, and the whole house has benefited from a fresh coat of paint. I like the gardens as well. There are a few beds at the front of the house and a very proper kitchen garden and a small orchard at the back. I could not have wished for more. The Hunsford parsonage pleases me very well indeed.

I do miss the lively society of Hertfordshire, truth be told. Still, I never expected this arrangement to be perfect. Nothing ever is.

I move in a very confined and unvarying circle these days. There is my husband—naturally—and his patroness, Lady Catherine de Bourgh, to whom he is indebted for all his present comforts and, by extension, so am I. Her Ladyship has but one offspring, a rather frail daughter who never says much. Miss de Bourgh's companion, a Mrs. Jenkinson, has little to say to me as well.

But Lady Catherine de Bourgh amply compensates for the other ladies' disinterest in conversation. In point of fact, I doubt she is ever silent, not even in her sleep. Her Ladyship has opinions on every topic and harbours no reservations about sharing them. So far, following her…hmm…let us say, advice, Mr. Collins and I have changed the dinner hour, the location of several paintings and ornaments, and the maid-of-all-work was dismissed, as her ways were deemed unpardonably deficient for a parson's home. I daresay that whenever Lady Catherine graces us with her presence, she only accepts refreshments so that she can inform me that my joints of meat are far too large for my small household.

Mr. Collins insists we follow Her Ladyship's advice to the letter in everything—that is to say, in everything but the size of our joints. He is most fond of his victuals, as I discovered during our brief engagement, when he had enthusiastically partaken of the fare served at my father's table.

Even now, he heaps a generous second helping of steak and ale pie upon his plate and casts me a beatific smile.

"You bake the most excellent pies, Mrs. Collins," he says, loading his fork and doing full justice to the fare with eager chomps. This does not hinder his desire for speech, apparently, for he resumes, his mouth half-full: "Your dear mama's recipe, is it not?"

I assure him he is not mistaken, and he nods with satisfaction at being proven right.

"I recognised the taste. She keeps a remarkably good table, does Lady Lucas, and I am most grateful to her for teaching you such skills. Not brought up too high, are you, my dear? How exceedingly kind of Lady Catherine to urge me to seek just such a life companion, and what a fortunate choice you turned out to be. Unlike some who should remain unnamed, whose mother deems too grand to step into the kitchen. But on this topic, we might as well be silent."

I smile and nod. We might as well be, but we never are. Rather, *he* is not. He often has something disparaging to say about the Bennets in general and Elizabeth in particular. He has never gone as far as to speak of his failed offer of marriage to my friend, but everything he has to say about his Hertfordshire relations plainly shows that his treatment at Elizabeth's hands still rankles. I expect it will continue to do so for quite some time, given his excellent opinion of himself and his prospects.

The second helping of steak and ale pie now vanished from his plate, Mr. Collins applies himself to the roast mutton with gusto, and suddenly I am reminded of Mrs. Phillips, Elizabeth's aunt.

"Keep him well-fed and he shan't trouble you much in bed," that lady had snickered under her breath towards me, halfway through my wedding breakfast, when she had doubtlessly noticed my new husband doing full justice to the fare on that occasion, too.

Yet again, I cannot help wondering if the good lady was imparting wisdom gained from her own experience or whether she was hoping, for her sister's sake, that Mr. Collins's line would not be continued. Given Mr. Phillips' portly figure, I am disposed to believe the former, but I would not put it past her to consider the latter.

Either way, some hours later when we retire for the night, I discover there is truth in Mrs. Phillips' words of wisdom. The Longbourn entail aside, I do want children—perhaps I should see to some light dinners now and then.

MARCH 1812

Easter is fast approaching and, with its coming, I have grown very busy, preparing the household for the impending arrival of our guests. Papa is expected, along with my sister Maria and my dear friend Elizabeth Bennet. I do declare Mr. Collins is as caught in the fever of preparations as myself. He keeps haranguing our poor new maid, Peggy, asking her to scrub this, polish that, or rearrange the other. I doubt he is exerting himself thus for Papa's sake. 'Tis Elizabeth he is aiming to impress.

Had I married him for love—and indeed, had I thought him capable of that noble sentiment—I would be wretched now to see him fussing so. As it is, I am not wretched in the least. If anything, I find the entire business quite diverting. Not a response befitting a good wife, so I endeavour to feel a little sorry for him and his wasted efforts. I know full well that Elizabeth shan't oblige him with a wistful glance or a sigh of regret.

~

I was right. She did not. But Eliza did forbear to smile when various features of Mr. Collins's *humble abode* were put forth for inspection and admiration, from newel posts to the shelves in the closets—the latter installed just so at Lady Catherine's express instructions.

My dear friend, bless her, made every effort to keep her countenance despite even greater provocations—namely, Lady Catherine herself. Her Ladyship was in excellent form when we were asked to dine at the Park soon after our guests' arrival. Poor Papa and Maria were rendered speechless by the magnificence of Rosings and no less by the imposing lady of the house. Elizabeth? Not at all, to be truthful. It would take a vast deal more than a grand house and an officious Lady Catherine to render my dear friend tongue-tied.

~

APRIL 1812

The parsonage has become a very cheerful place since the arrival of Maria and Elizabeth. My father has left us to make his way back to Hertfordshire. Free from the obligation to show Papa the glories of Kent, Mr. Collins has returned to his habitual pursuits—his bees, his sermon-making and his daily walks to Rosings—leaving us to amuse ourselves as we see fit.

We do. We go on short walks or potter in the garden on dry days and sit in my private parlour to sew and talk on wet ones. I had almost forgotten how pleasant this could be. I have missed the excellent company of my dear sister and my friend. We chat and laugh together as freely as ever.

'Tis but one set of topics that we address with civil reserve rather than candour, and that is my marital felicity and my husband. Oh, and Longbourn. We never, *ever*, speak of it. Instead, we speak of Meryton, and childhood romps, and our mutual acquaintances.

This morning, while the three of us were at work in the kitchen garden together, Elizabeth had just chosen to entertain us with an account of Jenny Long's encounter with an intractable sow when Mr. Collins stumbled through the garden gate, beet-red and clutching at his garb as he struggled for breath. He gestured towards me, then towards the back door. _____

"The mud, Mrs. Collins. Indoors—" He gasped.

"Mud?" I asked. "How? Pray, tell me Peggy did not walk through the house in her pattens."

Mr. Collins rolled his eyes in exasperation and spoke haltingly, his chest heaving.

"Nay-nay. You must—wipe the mud off—go in. Great honour —upon us."

It soon emerged what the great honour was: Mr. Darcy and his cousin, a Colonel Fitzwilliam, had just arrived at Rosings on their yearly visit and, finding Mr. Collins there, walked back with him to pay their respects. Inwardly, I seldom agree with Mr. Collins, yet this time I was compelled to do so. A great honour indeed, that Mr. Darcy should call upon us at the parsonage less than one hour after his arrival into Kent.

I harboured no illusions that he came on my account, or my husband's. Nay, I was quite certain that Elizabeth was the inducement. But I would not tease her on that score. Not yet. I would see first how the gentleman behaved.

～

He puzzles me, does Mr. Darcy. He hardly ever speaks to Elizabeth—not since that time at Rosings, when she was playing for the company with Colonel Fitzwilliam staunchly at her side to turn the pages, and Mr. Darcy had joined them till called to order by his aunt.

He does stare at my friend a great deal, just as he used to do in Hertfordshire, but I cannot detect visible symptoms of regard. Often, his stare seems almost a sign of absent-mindedness rather than affection. Yet he calls at the parsonage nearly every day, either alone or with his cousin.

This morning was no exception. Both gentlemen came to call, as early as ten hours in the morning!

"Heavens," Elizabeth muttered when she espied them through the window.

I suppressed a smile. Seemingly, Mr. Darcy was apt to learn from his mistakes. Twice already, he had called at a more sociable hour and missed her; Elizabeth had taken herself on one of her long walks. This morning, the gentlemen came so early that even Mr. Collins had not readied himself for his daily trek to Rosings. Thus, as soon as Peggy showed the callers in, the parlour became uncommonly crowded. Colonel Fitzwilliam was as affable as ever, and, as ever, Mr. Darcy remained silent.

He would not even sit. For his part, my husband would stop at nothing to ensure the comfort of Lady Catherine's esteemed nephews and insistently pressed Mr. Darcy to have this seat or that and answered his own questions. Would Mr. Darcy like to take the seat by the hearth? Nay, nay, he would be too warm. A chair at the table, perhaps? Nay, that one was in too much sunlight. What of the armchair by the door? Mr. Darcy would be most comfortable there—that is, if he did not object to a slight draught.

Mr. Darcy grimaced and sat. Goodness, he must have been quite keen to remain in our parlour, otherwise Mr. Collins's pestering would have driven him out, and no mistake. Yet no sooner had he taken the seat by the door than he shifted and stirred, then produced a book from under the cushion.

"That must be yours, Lizzy," Maria piped up. "You were sitting there reading before breakfast, were you not? Perhaps Mr. Darcy would be so kind as to read for us? What book is it, sir?" she asked, craning her neck to peer at the spine. "A Vindication of—?"

"Poetry," Mr. Darcy promptly cut her off, setting the book spine-down between him and the side of his armchair and darting the briefest glance towards my husband.

Maria's eyes widened.

"What a singular notion. Why should poetry require vindication?"

"Indeed, Miss Lucas," Colonel Fitzwilliam chimed in with a bright smile. "To my way of thinking, poetry speaks for itself. Take Master Shakespeare's sonnets, by way of example. *Let me not to the marriage of true minds admit impediments...*"

Mr. Darcy glared at him, I could not fail to notice, even as I pursed my lips and glared at my sister, then my friend. Maria would do well to hold her tongue. As for Elizabeth, I would greatly appreciate it if she refrained from leaving incendiary reading matter tucked under my cushions for callers to find in my husband's presence.

I have no quarrel with Miss Wollstonecraft—or was it Mrs. Godwin? There is a great deal of wisdom in the paragraphs Elizabeth and I were discussing yesterday. Indeed, if young girls are discouraged from learning useful skills that speak to the mind and are merely expected to acquire a smattering of genteel accomplishments, it is unsound to expect them to efficiently run a household once they marry and educate the babes they bring into the world.

Then there was the other passage that Elizabeth read out to me this very morning before she felt compelled to set the book aside when Maria joined us, promptly followed by Mr. Collins, who came in to inquire about his breakfast. Elizabeth found that paragraph noteworthy, and that did not surprise me, for it seemed particularly apropos to her tastes and disposition. It spoke of the woman who strengthens her body, exercises her mind, and thus becomes her husband's friend rather than his humble dependant; and if she deserves his regard by possessing such substantial qualities, she will not find it necessary to conceal her affection or to pretend to an unnatural coldness of constitution to excite her husband's passions.

That is all well and good, in theory. But I have no wish to weather the storm that would be unleashed should Mr. Collins stumble upon the self-same paragraph and learn that we were discussing exciting a husband's passions or the manner in which young women are urged to gain vacuous abilities that only make them fit for the seraglio.

I need no storms, Lizzy; I thank you just the same. Frankly, someone as astute as you should know without being told that a tranquil life with Mr. Collins hinges upon subtlety masquerading as compliance. I flatter myself that I have grown exceedingly adept at making him give voice to my views with the firm conviction that they are his own. I need no revolutionary theories and no controversy. Faced with overt opposition, that man grows as stubborn as a mule and every bit as ungovernable.

"Pray read to us, Mr. Darcy," Maria insisted, and much as I love my sister, at that point I would have dearly liked to throttle her. For once, I was indebted to my husband's determination to save Lady Catherine's nephew from every imposition for, in short order, he silenced Maria more effectively than I would have done.

When the tea was served, I must confess I grew rather cross with Mr. Darcy, too. While Elizabeth and I were filling the cups and distributing them, he took advantage of Mr. Collins's temporary distraction to open the book at the page marked with an embroidery thread and, one brow arched, he lost himself in its contents. I rather wished he did not. My husband's distraction could not last forever. But thankfully it had lasted long enough, that is to say, until Elizabeth approached Mr. Darcy with his cup of tea. Of the same mind as myself as regards keeping the writings from Mr. Collins's notice, she boldly asked:

"Might I have my volume back now, sir?"

"By all means, Miss Bennet," the gentleman courteously replied, but his lips did twitch ever so slightly.

As is often the case with Mr. Darcy, his thoughts were well-nigh impossible to ascertain, so I still have no notion what he made of Elizabeth's choice of reading matter. All I can say with confidence is that, whatever his response might have been, it was not Mr. Collins's very own brand of righteous indignation. Seemingly, Mr. Darcy could weather the passage about the woman who strengthens both her body and her mind and, rather than becoming her husband's dependant, she excites his friendship as well as his passions.

Good. I should not wish my dear Eliza to forfeit her every chance of making an excellent match simply because she has the run of Mr. Bennet's library with no restrictions whatsoever from her father in that regard—or in anything else, for that matter.

I declare that Maria must have spent far too much time with Elizabeth's sister Lydia of late. Goodness, she keeps making blunder after blunder (over and above her ill-judged insistence the other day that Mr. Darcy should read to us from Elizabeth's book.) Not in Lady Catherine's presence, thankfully, or my husband's, but, three days ago, when Mr. Darcy and his cousin called again, she let slip that Mr. Collins had offered for Elizabeth first, and was rejected!

Unlike my foolish sister, the gentlemen were too well-bred to pursue that topic. However, for the rest of the visit, Mr. Darcy had eyed Eliza in the oddest manner.

Well, no sooner had I reassured myself that Maria's blunder did no lasting harm than she blurted another. I can only imagine she was seeking to impress Colonel Fitzwilliam by appearing droll, but I have never seen such a poor attempt at drollery in anyone but Lydia Bennet.

Yesterday we were strolling along the lane: Maria, Elizabeth, me, and our ever-so-regular gentlemen callers from Rosings. For some reason, upon which I shall reflect at leisure later, the colonel chose to turn the conversation towards matrimony and the comforts of the home. Not altogether wisely, Elizabeth quipped:

"For your sake, Colonel, I hope your experience on the battlefield will stand you in good stead when you marry."

Colonel Fitzwilliam chortled. "Miss Bennet, surely you are not about to liken matrimony to a military engagement."

"It might seem a strange comparison, I grant you"—smiling, she conceded—"but sometimes it *can* be a battle of wills, can it not? It may surprise you, sir, but not every wife is a model of dutiful compliance."

The colonel might have been inclined to match her raillery like for like but, to my not insubstantial surprise, it was Mr. Darcy who replied. His sudden readiness for conversation astonished me no less than his unusual forthrightness, for what he quietly said was:

"'Tis just as well. Not every man would wish for a dutifully compliant wife."

While I could never claim to be as angelic as Jane Bennet, by nature I am not as quick to judge as Elizabeth, so I did not jump to the conclusion that Mr. Darcy meant that as a jibe at either Mr. Collins or myself. Rather, I was and still am disposed to think that his tongue ran away with him, and what he had in mind was himself and Elizabeth.

Naturally, I knew better than to let my face split into an unseemly grin. Colonel Fitzwilliam had no such scruples. He grinned ever so widely when he showed himself in agreement with his cousin with a hearty, "Hear-hear. Aye, Cousin, I say amen to that."

I have no notion where the conversation might have led had Maria been endowed with the wisdom of thinking before opening her lips. Sadly, she lacks it. She released a Lydia-like snort and blurted, "I heard it said that, although the man is the head of the household, the wife may be likened with the neck for, with a modicum of shrewdness, she can turn the head any which way she likes. Your dear mama said that, Lizzy, if I am not mistaken."

No, she was not mistaken. I have heard Mrs. Bennet say as much myself, little as it held true in her own case, for she could never alter Mr. Bennet's ways. Regardless of her views on the matter, Elizabeth turned beet-red and made no answer. It was Mr. Darcy who replied, or rather snapped:

"Oh, did she, now?"

Poor Elizabeth. I know for a fact that her warm-hearted but loose-tongued mama had caused her many a mortification. Thanks to my foolish sister, this time Mrs. Bennet could mortify Elizabeth even *in absentia*.

I was too vexed with Maria to think straight, so, when I tried to change the topic, I could offer nothing better than a comment on the width of the lane. (Goodness, I had better watch myself, by the bye. I am beginning to sound just like Mr. Collins.) Nonetheless, I had a great ally in Colonel Fitzwilliam, who employed my witless remark as an opening for a tale about narrow country roads, muddy ditches, and a mired carriage.

I cannot say that his endeavours bore fruit. To my distress, despite the rather entertaining tale, for the rest of our stroll Elizabeth remained uniformly quiet. As did Mr. Darcy.

I cannot say if Maria's careless remark had any role in the affair or whether Mr. Darcy had been swayed by weightier matters but, to my disappointment, yesterday he left Rosings a free man still. I am convinced that others share my disappointment. Mr. Collins and Lady Catherine, naturally—since both of them are expecting his betrothal to Miss de Bourgh, and I honestly cannot say which one of the two shows more vocal interest in the matter. Needless to say, I was hoping for a different union, but he did not announce himself betrothed to Elizabeth, either.

My friend would not speak of it, but she looks dreadfully out of sorts. I shall not press her to take me into her confidence on such a delicate subject. Were I still unwed, in Hertfordshire, I would have. As it is, I feel I should tread lightly. I, of all people, should not remind her of the Longbourn entail and of the fact that she would have been wise to accept Mr. Collins's offer. Still, knowing Elizabeth, I expect she would have chosen to aim high and lose rather than settle for darning Mr. Collins's shirts, planning his meals, and listening to his sermons within the confines of the church and without.

The house is very quiet now with the visitors gone from the parsonage as well as Rosings. I like the quiet, sometimes. I certainly prefer it to mindless discourse, much as the latter offers at least *some* distraction when there are basketfuls of shirts and socks to darn.

~

JUNE 1812

"Mrs. Collins, I am most seriously displeased! Nay, I am shocked and saddened to hear you have given charity and succour to Hobbs, despite Lady Catherine's express wishes. The man is late with his rent as it is. Her Ladyship is eminently in the right when she points out that charity only serves to encourage complacency and sloth."

I have long learned that Mr. Collins's patroness is no Lady Bountiful in this parish, nor is she in the commission of the peace for the county. Her ways are quite different. Whenever any of the cottagers are disposed to be quarrelsome, discontented or too poor, she sallies forth into the village to settle their differences, silence their complaints, and scold them into harmony and plenty.

Sadly for Hobbs, the tenant of the small and marshy farm on the outskirts of Hunsford, sometimes scolding will not do the office. His poor soil, by way of example, could never be scolded into yielding a decent harvest and, judging by the wet spring we have had, this year will be no exception. According to Lady Catherine, seeing his wife in very poor health and his children close to starving should somehow induce him to apply himself with greater vigour.

I am incensed at Her Ladyship's view on the matter but, as always, I know that open disagreement with her is out of the question. With Mr. Collins, 'tis equally pointless. Charity will have to come stealthily from the parsonage, from carefully-managed household accounts.

My conversation with my husband is promptly concluded. He has my leave to return to Rosings and apologise to Lady Catherine for my *ill-judged actions* in as animated a language as he chooses. For my part, I retire to my private parlour with the ledgers and decide to keep my other tidings to myself for a while longer. Mr. Collins is too concerned about pacifying Lady Catherine, so I imagine he need not know yet that, by the year's end, he will be a father.

My time perusing the ledgers offers some modest satisfaction. Aye, it could be done. Some succour can be given to Hobbs and his large family and, with thrift and care, there might be enough to relieve the Smiths and dear old Mrs. Fenton too.

~

AUGUST 1812

Our plums, blackcurrants, and early-season apples are ripening nicely and, frankly, so am I. Mr. Collins is now aware of my condition. I shared that knowledge around the time when the babe quickened, assuming that by then the visible changes in my size would have served to give the game away. I learned that such concerns were for naught when Mr. Collins gleefully expressed his delight at the intelligence in a less than gentle-manly manner.

"My dear Charlotte!" he exclaimed (one of the few instances when he addressed me without the habitual formality.) "Such wonderful tidings! I had no notion of your happy situation. Indeed, I thought it was your recent fondness for cherry tarts that accounted for the thickening of your waist. How pleased I am to learn that I was wrong! I must inform Lady

Catherine as soon as may be. And my cousin Bennet. I shall write to him on the morrow of our joyful expectation of a young olive-branch."

Much as I knew that Mr. Bennet had no reason to rejoice along with my husband, I made no effort to dissuade Mr. Collins from the scheme. My mother's letter did, on the following morning.

It brought wretched tidings of Lydia Bennet's folly and disgrace. She had eloped, the silly goose, with no thought whatsoever of how her false step would affect her sisters. False step, I say, for it is increasingly obvious to the Meryton neighbourhood that there will be no marriage.

Poor Elizabeth! Her slight chances of securing Mr. Darcy are now completely lost—not that they were too great to begin with. Her good looks and her cheerful disposition must have drawn his interest, but the fact that he had quitted Kent without offering for her plainly showed that her personal charms were not enough to counterbalance the vast difference in their stations.

'Tis a pity that Mr. Darcy seems to be the sort who is ruled by reason rather than sentiment. I have often wondered whether Elizabeth has always suspected that and, consequently, it has pleased her to affect a dislike for the gentleman in the same manner as the fox who tells himself that the grapes he cannot reach must be awfully sour.

She has her pride, my Elizabeth (always had, and always will), which must make her present situation even more pitiable and unbearable. How galling for her, to be shunned and censured for a fault not her own but her younger sister's and her parents'. Lydia should have never been allowed quite so much freedom. This enormity would have never come to pass were it not for Mr. and Mrs. Bennet's downright faulty indulgence.

I am sorry to say that in a heated moment I voiced my thoughts aloud, and Mr. Collins pounced upon the notion like a keen-eyed chicken on an insect.

"Aye, too right, my dear." He nodded with great energy. "My thoughts entirely. I was about to say so myself. Such hoydenish ways in all of them, not just the youngest. Jane has some notions of propriety but, as for the rest, heaven help them. Although what help can they hope for now? Nothing can save them from disgrace."

His countenance brightened, and his smile grew positively smug. "I can only congratulate myself on my most fortunate choice of wife. I shudder to think I might have partaken of their ruin, had I formed a tighter alliance with that unhappy family. As it is, I bask in the knowledge that you bring me nothing but credit. And a babe on the way! My dear Charlotte, what a gem you turned out to be."

I suppose I should have been glad of all this lavish praise and of my husband's overt adulation. Knowing his ways, I doubted it would last long.

Mr. Collins pressed my hand, then excused himself to return to his study.

"If nothing else," he said, "Christian charity compels me to write to my cousin Bennet and condole with him on the grievous affliction he is now suffering under. The death of his youngest would have been a blessing in comparison."

I could only imagine what poor Mr. Bennet would have to say of my husband's notion of Christian charity. I resolved to write to Elizabeth myself and offer my sympathy in a more acceptable manner. However, I imagined it would give no palliation. Under a misfortune such as this, assistance was impossible and condolence insufferable, even when sensitively expressed.

I stayed my hand when I felt the urge to ring for refreshments. Mr. Collins's remark about my girth might have been ever so ungentlemanly, but he had the right of it regarding my growing fondness for cherry tarts. I had better curb it and seek other comforts. It really will not do for me to grow as podgy as my husband.

~

SEPTEMBER 1812

Another letter arrives from Mama about a month later, and it brings exceedingly welcome tidings. Lydia Bennet is married. She is Lydia Wickham now. A patched-up affair at her family's expense, no doubt, but at least she is once more rendered respectable. With any luck, the unseemly beginnings of this entire affair might be forgot in the fullness of time.

Lady Catherine is of a different mind, naturally. As soon as I acquainted him with the contents of Mama's letter, my husband hastened to Rosings to share the intelligence, and I am told that Her Ladyship disdainfully sniffed and declared that no man of honour would connect himself with such a family, regardless of the final result of Lydia's infamous elopement.

Nevertheless, now that my husband's relation is no longer a fallen woman, Lady Catherine has deigned to call upon us at the parsonage again. The timing, however, is most unfortunate. She arrives shortly before the post.

Peggy brings the envelopes upon a salver, mere moments after she came with a tray of tea and buttered scones and teacakes for our guest. The sight of a letter from Hertfordshire excites my husband's interest, and I can only imagine he is eager to reassure his patroness that all is as it should be in that part of the world.

He opens my letter. That is his first mistake.

His second, and a great deal more grievous, is that he reads Mama's letter aloud, without privately assuring himself of its contents.

Lady Catherine has another disdainful sniff for the intelligence that astounds me: Jane Bennet would have her happiness at last. Despite Jane's reserved disposition and her natural inability to encourage a suitor, Mr. Bingley has returned for her, proposed marriage, and they are now engaged. Lady Catherine's sniff is followed by a shrug and a dismissive comment:

"What can one expect? Tradesmen! They have no care for their honour and, for that matter, no honour to care for."

Mr. Collins nods vigorously and resumes reading Mama's letter:

"And that is but half of my tale, dear," Mama had written. *"The second part is even more astounding. It seems that your friend Lizzy will soon follow in Jane's footsteps. There is good reason to suspect she will become engaged as well. A very eligible gentleman was seen beating a path to her door lately. You will never guess who, so I shall tell you: Mr. Darcy, you see, is the man—"* Mr. Collins reads out, then cuts himself off with somewhat of a gurgle.

"Pardon?" Lady Catherine splutters, choking on her scone.

To say that Mr. Collins and I are severely out of favour with Her Ladyship is an understatement. Even before her foray into Hertfordshire, she could do nothing but berate us for the ingratitude and thoughtlessness of asking Elizabeth into Kent last April. Since Lady Catherine's return, Mr. Collins was only allowed to see her once. My husband told me she was livid when she informed him that his cousin Elizabeth is an unfeeling, selfish gal, and an artful upstart to boot.

"I readily agreed with Her Ladyship, of course"—Mr. Collins bitterly resumed his account of that fraught interview—"but that only served to rile her further. *'Then if you knew her to be so, you are as much to blame for throwing her into my nephew's path! That vile vixen has ensnared him now. He is beyond redemption. Nothing I said to him would make him forsake her and do his duty to his lineage. And this abomination would not have come to pass, were it not for you!'* Lady Catherine furiously berated me, and then stormed at me and accused me of the most dreadful schemes. She said"—Mr. Collins gasped for breath—"Her Ladyship said it was all a ploy, to connect myself to an exalted family. A shameful and self-serving scheme, unbefitting a clergyman who should have shown humility and above all, abject gratitude. *'So, this is your way of thanking me for my kindness and attention to you and yours. This is your thanks for the Hunsford preferment. Begone! I cannot bear the sight of you and your repulsive breed.'"*

"Heavens! That is dreadfully unfair," was all I could offer by way of consolation.

"Aye, my dear. You can say that again. Here I am, blameless and honest to a fault, yet other people's disgraceful acts are visited upon me, rather than upon the ones who are rightfully responsible for the crimes. That cousin of mine…! Were I not a man of the cloth, I would go as far as to curse her, for she has been nothing but a curse to me. Verily, the bane of my existence—"

He has not ceased ranting against Eliza ever since, and his diatribes gain renewed fury every time he calls at Rosings and is denied Her Ladyship's presence. I am beginning to fear for his sanity and no less for our future. I have but a limited understanding of the ways of the Church of England and my husband's rights as the holder of the Hunsford living, but I fear that, since it was bestowed at Lady Catherine's pleasure, it might be taken away at her pleasure, too. Or at her displeasure, I should say.

Consequently, Mr. Collins remarks (with more shrewdness than I have ever given him credit for) that since his sufferings could be traced to Mr. Darcy's choices, it is that gentleman who should be his salvation.

"I must acquaint him with my troubles," Mr. Collins states with great energy. "Perchance I could go as far as to transfer my allegiance from his aunt to him. He has a family living to dispose of, too, from what I gathered. Who knows, my dear, where our fortunes lie?"

As to that, I have no notion either. But I dread to think of exposing myself to the humiliation of witnessing Mr. Collins seeking to curry favour with Mr. Darcy in the same ways he has employed to please that gentleman's aunt. Worse still, that my husband might justly expect me to use my connexion to Elizabeth to assist him in his endeavours. It would be an exceedingly uncomfortable situation. Still, this is no bed of roses either—the ill-will verily pouring out from Rosings has become unbearable. I shall make arrangements to travel into Hertfordshire after all. It will be good to see my family—and Elizabeth.

~

NOVEMBER 1812

"Dearly beloved, we are gathered together here in the sight of God, and in the face of this congregation, to join together this Man and this Woman—and *this* Man and *this* Woman—in holy Matrimony; which is an honourable estate, instituted of God in the time of man's innocency…"

Longbourn Church is ever so small. It can barely accommodate the friends and relations who have congregated here to witness Jane and Elizabeth's double wedding. We are all huddled together: myself, my husband, Mama, Papa, Maria and my brothers, the Bennets, naturally, along with Mr. and Mrs. Gardiner, Mrs. Phillips and her husband, and also the Longs, the Gouldings, the Ashworths, and John Purvis and his wife and daughters. There are some predictable additions from outside of Hertfordshire: Miss Bingley, her sister and Mr. Hurst.

It appears that Mr. Darcy's sister and the colonel, his cousin, are the only members of his family who came to stand beside him at his wedding. 'Tis doubtlessly an indication that the others sided with Lady Catherine and took her view on the matter. Still, Mr. Darcy and Elizabeth seem supremely untroubled by this state of affairs. Least of all now, as they stand at the altar along with Jane and Mr. Bingley before Reverend Wickfield, who smiles upon them as benignly as ever and gives voice to the time-honoured words.

The wedding ceremony proceeds in good order. No one speaks up to give just cause why the relevant parties may not be lawfully joined together in matrimony, so the vows are read, the rings exchanged, and their troth duly pledged. Mr. Bingley and Jane, then Mr. Darcy and Elizabeth, are pronounced that they be Man and Wife together, in the name of the Father, and of the Son, and of the Holy Ghost.

Mr. Wickfield smiles just as benignly as he blesses the unions, so that the new husbands and wives might abide in God's love unto their lives' end, then proceeds to instruct them as to their duties to each other and, before long, the ceremony is over and the little church rings with voices raised in a song of gratitude and praise.

'Tis as I watch the newlyweds walking down the aisle together, arm in arm, that I reel in a sudden and most unpleasant shock. There is an ugliness in me, and I discover it now, and I detest it. That ugliness has but one name: envy. Shameful and bitter envy. I know it to be wrong, grievously wrong, and I seek to shun it, yet I cannot be anything but truthful to myself now, in a church.

And the truth is that I envy Elizabeth. Not on account of her new husband's riches, his handsome features or fine stature. 'Tis the look he envelops her in, as they go forth to be man and wife together, that sparks and feeds my bitter envy. 'Tis that warm, blissfully adoring look…

I seek to temper, or at the very least make my peace with, the newly-discovered ugliness within me as best I can, once life in Hertfordshire resumes its course, after the excitement of the double weddings. Mr. and Mrs. Bingley are now installed at Netherfield. Mr. and Mrs. Darcy have long left the country, on their way to Town, and thence to Pemberley.

For the entire time we were thrown together at Longbourn, Netherfield, Lucas Lodge or elsewhere, Mr. Darcy had borne my husband's obsequiousness with admirable civility and calmness, but I cannot say that Mr. Collins had had vast success in advancing his case with that gentleman and acquiring a different living. Doubtlessly Mr. Darcy was too caught in the delights of his engagement and upcoming marriage to give much consideration to mundane matters.

I refuse to ponder on that now. The ugliness in me seeks to fester, but I shall not let it. I tease it out, strand by nasty little strand, and examine it at leisure. Was I feeling smug and superior, silently pitying Elizabeth for thinking she could afford the luxury of refusing Mr. Collins's hand? Was I false last April, when I wished she would make this different and most fortunate alliance? Deep down, did I imagine I could safely play the part of the good friend and wish it for her, knowing it was highly unlikely that it should ever come to pass?

I cannot say, and after a while I grow vexed with myself for even wasting my time on such fruitless speculations. I hope I was neither smug nor false. What else is there to say?

As to my envy, I shall endeavour to subdue it. 'Tis natural but 'tis also fruitless. She made her choices. I made mine. Admittedly, I was not presented with an array of palatable options. I made what I could of what I was given. What purpose is there in wishing I held out for a better fate?

I snort. Stuff and nonsense! What better fate could I have held out for, given my age, my station in life, and my woefully plain appearance? Elizabeth is lucky. Luckier than most. Lucky to be born pretty, to begin with; lucky to grow into a cheerfully engaging woman; and then ever so lucky to meet with such a worthy gentleman and win his heart.

If I were to envy her light and pleasing figure, her comely features and sparkling eyes, would that make *my* dull-grey eyes sparkle? Or make me look any less drab and plain?

The world is misaligned. It has not changed in the two decades that have elapsed since Miss Wollstonecraft penned her courageous writings, and who knows if it ever will? Until it does—*if* it does—the only way women can rise in the world is by marriage, and those of us who cannot boast an independent income or a large dowry have but our charms to recommend us.

What is to be done when one has no charms to speak of? What of those who, like me, enter the marriage mart with no dowry, no gift for witty repartee, a figure resembling a freshly-hewn plank, limp, sandy hair, a poor complexion and features as plain as they come? What should those wretched creatures do but grab the first eligible option that comes their way? And if he should be tedious, selfish, and weak-headed, at least one might take comfort in the fact that he is neither cruel nor vicious, and that he shows himself eminently manageable by a keener wit and a careful hand.

'Tis no concern of mine that Elizabeth's new husband is endowed with very different qualities, and thus her domestic joys will be of a vastly different kind. I *shall* be happy for her. I shall, so help me. And I shall make the most of what I am given. Who can be expected to do any more than that?

~

DECEMBER 1812

I am stunned. I can think of no better word for it. I am too sluggish at the moment to apply myself to finding better words. The intelligence arrived this very morning. I am a widow. How positively odd: I have been a widow since Tuesday, yet I did not know it. Staggering notion, that. Especially to a sluggish mind.

Mr. Collins had been ordered back to Hunsford a se'nnight prior. He had left as early as he could on the Eastbourne coach, to promptly obey Lady Catherine's summons. I was to follow at the month's end, given my condition; Papa had undertaken to convey me in his carriage. Now Papa's main reason for travelling into Kent is to attend Mr Collins's funeral.

From what I gathered, it was my husband's haste to do his duty by his patroness that was his undoing. There was no gig to be had in Bromley for love or money, so he hired himself a horse from the ostler at the Bell. The beast might have been boisterous or not, how should I know? But I do know that Mr. Collins was no horseman. A waggoner found him by the side of the road on the following morning, lifeless, with a broken neck. In view of my delicate state, Mama and Papa insisted I should be spared the details, but I would not have it. Not that there is much else to know anyway.

I am a widow, returned to my father's house. My husband's worldly possessions, such as they are, and whatever I took into Kent upon my marriage, must be collected from the parsonage, to make room for the curate that Lady Catherine had already appointed to do Mr. Collins's office. I cannot imagine there would be much to gather but a few trinkets, clothes and sundry, and some books. As to the rest that Mr. Collins left behind: there is but a few hundred pounds and the babe growing in my belly.

All of a sudden, I burst into laughter, wild, unconquerable laughter. Mama looks at me as if she fears for my sanity. But I do not think of Mama as I continue to chortle uncontrollably. I think of Mrs. Bennet. How pleased must she be if the babe turns out to be a girl. Is this Mrs. Bennet's curse, I wonder, finding myself uprooted and near-destitute? Or is it my just punishment for my thoughts on Elizabeth's wedding day?

I stop laughing and shrug, barely noticing that Mama's arms are tightly wrapped around me. It might be my just punishment. I can believe that. But I do not believe in the power of curses.

Let Mrs. Bennet think what she will. The Longbourn entail aside, to be perfectly honest, I myself almost wish that the babe turns out to be a girl.

Four days after Christmas, in the last week of the old year, I am delivered of a boy. He will be christened William Collins. His father would have liked that. Myself, I choose to think I am naming my babe after my own father.

JUNE 1816

My William is four and a half today. I am touched that Mr. Bennet remembers and, when we call at Longbourn, as we often do, he gives my boy a walking stick which he had carved himself. William is delighted with the gift. He is in no need of a walking stick, praise be. He is as sturdy as any little boy his age and shows nothing of his departed father's tendency towards corpulence. But he has long admired Mr. Bennet's walking stick. Unlike my boy, Elizabeth's father needs such a support when he ambles through the garden. Today, when they go on one of their usual strolls together, my dear William is adorable in his childish delight at being able to mirror his mentor in everything, including the deft handling of a walking stick.

I daresay Papa is not best-pleased to have Mr. Bennet for a rival in my son's affections, but I imagine it cannot be helped. Mr. Bennet is much better company for a young boy, when he gives himself the trouble. And he *has* given himself the trouble, ever since William was old enough to toddle and string ten words together. I cannot imagine why. Perhaps Mr. Bennet has always wished for a son of his own. Perhaps it was because he grievously misses his grandsons, especially Jane's boys, ever since the Bingleys had left Netherfield for their new estate in Staffordshire to be closer to Elizabeth and her ever-growing family.

And before anyone should wonder, nay, I most certainly do not envy Elizabeth that. Of course, I would have liked to have a daughter too. But William is the sweetest child anyone could wish for and is more than able to fill my maternal heart to overflowing.

It must be his adorable ways that have conquered even Mrs. Bennet's reticence about young William Collins who stands to inherit Longbourn. Kitty and Mary were won over ever since he was a bundle of linen in my arms. Mr. Bennet followed suit a few years later, when William had grown from a squealing little thing into a chattering toddler. By the time he was breeched, Mrs. Bennet could no longer resist his cherubic sweetness either.

To begin with, she was heard to grumble that there was *some* benefit in growing closer to the William Collins who stood to cast her from her home. Mrs. Long brought that report to Mama, and one can only imagine how Mama received it. Nevertheless, I managed to persuade her to let it pass and refrain from giving Mrs. Bennet the set-down she deserved. Regardless of that lady's self-serving motives, I too could see the benefit of a closer connexion between Mr. Bennet and his heir apparent. It would do my William no harm to be acquainted with his future property and his responsibilities from as early an age as might be.

Over the years, such considerations have shifted and reshaped themselves into genuine fondness on all sides. These days, there is nothing that my William likes better than his aunt Bennet's sweetmeats and his walks with his uncle Bennet. It was Mrs. Bennet who had suggested the appellations, some years back, and I saw no reason to object, although, strictly speaking, they are cousins. But I leave such trifling details to genealogists, should any of them have an interest in my boy's lineage. All I care about is that he is healthy, happy, and loved.

~

AUGUST 1819

"Let me send for another pot of tea, Charlotte," Elizabeth suggests. "Or would you rather have some orgeat instead?"

"Orgeat, I thank you. 'Tis an exceedingly warm day."

Eliza laughs.

"We had better enjoy the spell of good weather while it lasts. You have lived in the North for long enough to know it shall not be for long."

She is right in that. William and I were asked to come to Pemberley last Christmas, along with Mr. and Mrs. Bennet, as was the case for the last four Yuletide seasons. Only, this time, we did not return to Hertfordshire.

During our planned stay, a month complete, it became increasingly plain that William greatly enjoyed not just the company of Elizabeth's sons but their tutor's instruction. So dear Eliza asked us to extend our stay. Indefinitely, she said. She told me that her boys, Richard and Frederick, were inconsolable each January when they had to part with William. Would I mind so very much if we stayed, and William could further his education?

How could I possibly mind? I miss my family at home, of course, but dear Papa could never afford a private tutor for William. Certainly not one as skilled as Mr. Howard. He seems to have the knack of imparting knowledge in the most engaging manner, so much so that his charges could not object to being excused from the schoolroom for no longer than a se'nnight around Christmas, and then the same again at Easter. And that was largely because his instruction is not restricted to the schoolroom. The boys, and of late Elizabeth's eldest daughter too, learn botany and zoology in the gardens, further their study of the languages in the library, and practise their knowledge of the numbers in every room in the house. Lessons are even held in the housekeeper's pantry, to Mrs. Reynolds' amazement and also vague unease, I should imagine.

Even now, as Eliza and I sit with our refreshments on the south lawn, we catch glimpses of them, as they scamper in the shrubbery (well, the youngsters do) chasing butterflies and I know not what other insects.

Delectable as it is to witness their enjoyment, I am compelled to dart my eyes away once Mr. Howard becomes aware of my scrutiny. It will not do to…

I frown, vexed at myself, and even more so at the hot flush that creeps into my cheeks. Ludicrous flush and ludicrous concerns. *What* will not do, precisely? Mr. Howard is a most sensible man—the least likely to jump to conclusions. He *would* know—would he not?—that I was merely watching William, keen to ascertain the progress of the lesson.

William has the greatest fondness for good-natured Mr. Howard. In the first months of our time in Derbyshire, he missed Mr. Bennet dreadfully. I expect the sentiment was mutual, which was one of the reasons why Elizabeth's father came to stay for several weeks at Easter. For the old gentleman's sake, I am sorry to say that by Eastertide dear Mr. Bennet was largely supplanted in my son's affections by the engaging Mr. Howard, who is more than two decades younger and at least twice as energetic. Mr. Bennet could not keep up with them in their adventures through the grounds and, in the end, he saw it for the losing battle that it was, devoting his time and energy to the youngest Darcys instead. Little Madeleine and her eleven-month older brother, Edmund, had no greater expectations of him than romps in the nursery or, weather permitting, on the lawn.

A maid brings us a jug of orgeat and one of lemonade and on her heels comes Mrs. Reynolds with a plate of some delicious-looking confectionery, which she sets on the table as she casts her mistress a warm smile.

"Should Miss Anne be sad to find these gone on her return, pray tell her that I kept my word and saved her a plateful of her favourites."

"I certainly shall," Elizabeth agrees, smiling. "Have they gone on their ride?"

"I imagine so, ma'am. The master's horse and Miss Anne's were brought at the door just as I was coming 'round with your cakes and sweetmeats."

The housekeeper is wrong, I find. Mr. Darcy and his eldest daughter have not gone on their ride as yet. I know as much, for I can see them emerging through the garden entrance. Anne scampers towards us in a manner that reminds me greatly of Elizabeth at her age and pauses to cast Mrs. Reynolds an engaging smile.

"You do not suppose Papa and I might have some of your raisin bread to keep us going on our ride, do you?"

"Hmm, let me see what I can contrive, miss," Mrs. Reynolds replies with a wink and a motherly grin.

I suppress mine. By the looks of it, Anne can run rings around her parents' housekeeper just as Elizabeth used to do with Mrs. Hill.

"Will you not come with us, Mama?" the girl asks, but Elizabeth shakes her head.

"Not this morning, dearest."

Anne looks crestfallen.

"Are you quite certain? Papa will be so disappointed."

"Your Papa can speak for himself, you know," Mr. Darcy teases his daughter as he comes to stand beside his wife, then crouches at her elbow. "How are you, my love?" he asks ever so softly as he strokes her cheek with the back of his fingers.

"Fine. Just fine," Elizabeth hastens to reassure him, reaching for his hand to keep it in hers.

She lightly brushes his knuckles with her lips, and I look away from the intimate gesture. His oblique enquiry pertains to her morning sickness, as I know full well. Elizabeth has told me a short while ago that she is with child again, some four months gone. Yet that knowledge was not shared with their children yet, apparently, for Elizabeth turns towards her daughter with a blithe remark:

"You know you take after your aunt Georgy in your love of horses, not me. I can only feign it now and then. So, this morning I shall have to leave it to you to keep your papa well-entertained."

Mr. Darcy leans to drop a kiss on her lace cap. I keep my eyes averted. After all these years, I still have not grown accustomed to the fact that the solemn and reserved Mr. Darcy I met in the year eleven at the Meryton assembly could grow to be so openly affectionate.

"I shall have her back in time for her piano lesson," Mr. Darcy promises, making his eldest daughter pout.

"Oh, Papa! Must you?"

"Of course. How else can you hope to become as proficient as your aunt Georgy in your playing, not just your riding?"

Anne makes a pretty little moue, blows her mama a kiss, and the pair of them leave us to our refreshments and our time in the sunshine. I absorb the welcome warmth and the delightful Pemberley tranquillity. For some unfathomable reason, unless it is the very aura of this lovely place, 'tis here that I found that the ugly streak within me is finally ready to be laid to rest. And in my opinion, in cases such as these 'tis best to begin with a confession.

"I envied you, you know," I say, setting my glass of orgeat aside. "Not for your raised consequence or your husband's riches but his love."

I know not what I was expecting, but Elizabeth surprises me with a solemn nod.

"You thought I did not deserve it," she says, and I gasp.

"Goodness, no"—I forcefully protest—"not that, never that. I merely wished I experienced its like for myself. Much as I once claimed I am not romantic"—I conclude, with a self-deprecating little quirk in my mouth.

"It would not have surprised me if you did think me underserving. For quite some time I thought so myself. I certainly did not deserve his love and his hand when he first offered them," Elizabeth declares with energy, and then proceeds to astound me further. "I never told you this, but I was foolish enough to refuse him when he first offered marriage."

I gape. I must make a very silly picture, for Elizabeth laughs softly, then resumes.

"He proposed to me in that little parlour of yours, at Hunsford, and I sent him away with a flea in his ear. Truth be told, with a whole host of them. It does not bear thinking what my life would have been had he taken me at my word. Had he not returned for me. He kept loving me despite my harsh rejection."

I am still speechless. I can do nothing but listen to Elizabeth's extraordinary disclosures.

"I misjudged him so grievously—thought him vain and overbearing. I reproached him for his pride, yet *I* was the one who was unpardonably prejudiced and prideful. I clung to first impressions, false claims, and childish resentments. I thought he wanted a bedfellow and a chattel. It was a very long time until I grasped that what he sought in me was a soulmate and a true companion."

"For love is not to be bought, in any sense of the word," I quote from Miss Wollstonecraft's words of wisdom, in a quiet whisper. *"Its silken wings are instantly shrivelled up when anything beside a return in kind is sought."*

"Just so," Elizabeth says simply, then her fine eyes crinkle at the corners, "I see you have applied yourself to the improvement of your mind by extensive reading."

I shrug and reply just as archly, "I have had a great deal of time on my hands of late."

She gives a rueful little chortle.

"Perhaps he did not know precisely what he sought in me to begin with, and he certainly could have worded his first proposal better, the dear, dear man. But when it comes to ill-judged and intemperate outbursts, I am in no position to cast stones. Hot-headedness is a fault I justly claim for myself as well."

"And so you should," I smilingly reply with the candour of a five-and-twenty-year-old friendship. "But I struggle to imagine your husband as anything but calm and collected."

Elizabeth's arched brow silently indicates she has no such difficulties. I am still smiling as I shake my head.

"Thankfully, since that fateful Eastertide in Kent, I trust we have both learned to communicate our sentiments better."

"A very useful lesson, I grant you," I tease her.

"It can be, with the right teacher," Elizabeth retorts, a twinkle in her eye. "Speaking of which, have you ever considered remarrying?"

The sudden change of topic catches me unawares.

"Remarrying?" I echo her last word like a simpleton, then I force out a chuckle. "At my age?"

"Aye, at the venerable old age of—what? Four-and-thirty? You are still in your prime, Charlotte. If only I could see you as happy."

More like five-and-thirty, I inwardly correct her. In my prime? Hardly. Who would wish to marry plain old Charlotte Collins?

I release another forced laugh.

"Till I have your cheerful disposition and your goodness, I never can have your happiness. Nay, nay, let me shift for myself; and perhaps, if I have very good luck, I may meet with another Mr. Collins."

Elizabeth affectionately rolls her eyes at my quip, then her glance grows rather solemn.

"Hmm. Well, as to that, there is something my husband charged me to mention at a suitable moment, and I can think of no better time than now. You should know that, last night after dinner, Mr. Howard came to see him in his study, and, after much to-ing and fro-ing, asked if he might be allowed to court you."

My hand remains almost comically suspended in the air as I reach for my glass of orgeat. Elizabeth's lips twitch, yet I suspect 'tis not at me but her own sally:

"Now, you always thought me quick to judge, but this time I shall hold myself in check and concede that Mr. Howard might just be very shy, rather than ludicrously right-minded. Perhaps this was his way of indirectly asking *your* permission, rather than merely applying for the consent of the man who pays his wages and owns the largest proportion of his time. So dearest Charlotte, what say you? Shall I ask my husband to put poor Mr. Howard out of his misery?"

I reach for my glass at last and gulp down a long draught, then lower it into my joined hands, crossed palm upwards in my lap. I had hoped for this—oh, *how* I had hoped for this!—from the very first fortnight of our acquaintance. Not because I need to marry—I do not. I am most comfortable at present, and William's inheritance will secure my future. I have no need to rise in the world. Besides, in the eyes of the world, an alliance with a private tutor would scarce raise me.

I could not care less about such paltry considerations, while treasured recollections, gathered over months and months and carefully stored into the deepest recess of my heart, flash through my memory. Engaging conversations. Comfortable silences. His good sense. His unremitting kindness to my child. The very sound of his voice. The look in his eyes when (unobtrusively, he thought) he fixed them upon me.

For six months complete, ever since my arrival at Pemberley last Christmas, we have lived under the same roof. I might as well discount my other visits, for they were far too short. Hardly enough time for conversation or for learning much about him.

The last thought gives me pause. It also gives me the strangest wish to snort. I had not known Mr. Collins a se'nnight before I agreed to join my fate with his. Four days. Four days had made the sum total of our acquaintance on the morning when he had come to Lucas Lodge to ask for my hand. I must be uncommonly apt at making swift decisions. After a four-day acquaintance, I had decided I would become Mr. Collins's wife. A fortnight spent in Mr. Howard's company had been enough make me see he stood every chance to rule my heart. Ludicrous, I know. How is that for one who had never claimed to be romantic? Oh, Elizabeth would laugh if she could read my thoughts.

No, I am being unfair. She would not laugh. Of course not. She has too much good sense for that and would not have the heart to tease me mercilessly, either. I expect she would not have laughed had I taken her into my confidence from the very start of this unparalleled year.

Yet I blush, even as I think of it. What would I have told her? That it was the sound of his voice that had appealed to me in the first place? An even timbre; sensible, some might call it, with a touch of humour when he was talking to the boys. It never rose into pompous and declamatory tones. It never slumped into brusque pettiness or downright incivility towards those who stood beneath him in the household hierarchy. Nor did it ever slither into obsequious deference when he spoke to the master or the mistress of the house.

I should not have made comparisons. I have always known it was wrong, unbefitting a respectful widow. Yet I could not help it. And once I had compared Mr. Howard's tone of voice and his deportment to my late husband's, it was almost as if I could not stop. Nor did I wish to.

One would think I might have compared looks next. I did not trouble myself with that. It served no purpose. A superfluous exercise indeed, for even a passing glance was more than enough to declare Mr. Howard the superior. At least a decade older than my husband would have been, yet leaner, taller, and decidedly handsome. Thinning hair, fading away from the wide brow—nothing like Mr. Collins's dark-brown mane. Not once had I felt the slightest wish to run my fingers through Mr. Collins's hair. As for Robert's, often enough, I would have liked to smooth it with a light caress as I watched him tiring his eyes by sitting in the library late into the night, to read for amusement or prepare his notes for the boys' next lesson.

This was noteworthy too, by the bye, and I duly noted it in passing: he was "Robert" to my mind before I even paused to think about it. Not for a moment in our brief courtship and brief married life did I think of my late husband as anything but Mr. Collins.

Yet I did not trouble myself with such details as days became weeks, and weeks became months. His voice, his looks, his hair, his name—what did they matter? Something else had captured my attention: namely, that I could barely wait for the days to start. I could barely wait for conversations at breakfast; for watching the boys and their tutor at their lessons from a distance. I could barely wait for the nuncheons we shared, for the warmer companionship at dinner, and for the after-dinner hours. It puzzled me, this eagerness. Once I had ascertained its cause, it saddened me. It would not do for plain old Charlotte Collins to make a spectacle of herself.

I tried not to. I tried to feign placidity; keep my distance; keep a matronly air, too, and a still tongue in my head. But how was I to keep an even mien when watching Robert and the children at work and at play?

When watching William hanging to his every word, only to be nurtured with kindness and affection?

How could I not take delight in conversations, when that was what they were: conversations, not sententious monologues? When, time after time, they served to reveal his sterling common sense and honourable nature? How could I refrain from taking part in all those discussions, and eagerly too, even if they should turn into debates, when it was so plain to see that my views mattered? When I could not fail to notice that my sharing them brought a twinkle in a certain pair of dark-grey eyes—a strange twinkle indeed, all the more intriguing because it was hard to discern behind the spectacles? How could I retire early and protect my peace and my heart, when there was joy and excitement below-stairs? When in the whole course of my life I have not had warm, wistful looks settled surreptitiously upon me, nor was I ever listened to with manifest interest—nay, with rapt attention?

It is not an alliance I am seeking but a life companion, in every sense of the word. There is naught amiss with entrusting a man with one's future, with one's very own self, if he can be trusted to respond in kind.

I have long dreamt of openly basking in Robert Howard's affection—and for too long I have dismissed that dream as unattainable and myself as unpardonably missish. The dream is within my reach, it seems. I can scarce believe it.

I feel the sting of tears, but I shall not let them have their way! For goodness sake, I am a grown woman, once married, a mother, not a foolish schoolgirl. Yet, as I glance up at Elizabeth and finally nod in response to her staggering question, I sense that my cheeks are blazing, and my lips are curling up into the widest and most foolish smile.

JOANA STARNES lives in the south of England with her family. Over the years, she has swapped several hats—physician, lecturer, clinical data analyst—but feels most comfortable in a bonnet. She has been living in Georgian England for decades in her imagination and plans to continue in that vein till she lays hands on a time machine. She is the author of eight Austen-inspired novels: *From*

This Day Forward—The Darcys of Pemberley, *The Subsequent Proposal*, *The Second Chance*, *The Falmouth Connection*, *The Unthinkable Triangle*, *Miss Darcy's Companion*, *Mr. Bennet's Dutiful Daughter,* and *The Darcy Legacy*, and one of the contributing authors to *The Darcy Monologues* and *Dangerous to Know: Jane Austen's Rakes & Gentleman Rogues*. You can connect with Joana at facebook.com/joana.a.starnes; joanastarnes.co.uk, facebook.com/AllRoadsLeadToPemberley.JoanaStarnes and twitter.com/Joana_Starnes

KNIGHTLEY DISCOURSES

ANNGELA SCHROEDER

EMMA WOODHOUSE

A witty, intelligent, wealthy woman of a small village in Surrey, Emma has always known she has a charmed life. Her matchmaking tendencies and romantic imaginings make her a questionable rational creature, and yet her kind heart, natural care of others, and steady support from the man she loves has bolstered her good sense as she matures. "**It is very unfair to judge of any body's conduct, without an intimate knowledge of their situation.**" —**Chapter XVIII,** *Emma.*

KNIGHTLEY DISCOURSES

Emma Knightley, still handsome, clever, and rich, had lived nearly thirty-one years in the world before anything of a serious nature set out to vex her. She had resided with her husband and children at her father's estate of Hartfield these last nine years. Until Mr. Woodhouse passed away a year ago, she had balanced the responsibilities of both Hartfield and her duties to her husband's estate, Donwell Abbey. She was of a cheerful disposition and, although occasionally irritated by those in her circle and situations she could not control, was quite content with what life had given her. However, there was one thing Emma had grown to loathe: restlessness.

With her husband off shooting with his brother John, her sister Isabella visiting the tenants of Hartfield (of which *she* was now mistress), and Nanny having just put the children down for a nap, Emma was discontented and knew not how to remedy that state of mind. Looking about the drawing room of Donwell Abbey, she tossed aside the worn copy of the novel she had devoured only the day before and reached for one of her childhood dolls resting on the cushion beside her.

George Knightley, her husband of almost ten years, had brought a trunk down from the attic at Hartfield shortly after her father's death. He had imagined the contents would spur sentimentality and comfort in his melancholy wife. He was right, as he always was. He knew Emma better than she herself did, and the dolls served a balm to her troubled soul.

This one was "Miss Abby," she remembered fondly. She picked it up and straightened its pink silk gown. Mrs. Anne Weston, nee Taylor, her former nanny and now closest friend save her sister, had given it to her upon the death of her mother, an event of which Emma had no memory.

The deep ache with which she missed her father permeated her world, and this moment of solitude only enhanced her need for a diversion.

But what? She worried her bottom lip and contemplated the possibilities.

The children will be asleep for at least another two hours, so a picnic is out of the question. George will be exhausted when he returns from shooting, so an impromptu dinner party will not be appreciated. Mr. and Mrs. Weston are in London, so a visit to Randalls is impossible. She twirled the hair of Miss Abby and continued to think.

She was thus in contemplation when the footman entered the room. "Miss Bates to see you, ma'am."

She did her best to hide the sigh of resignation and reminded herself she needed to offer patience and Christian charity. Her guilt of a misguided statement toward Miss Bates a decade past at the Box Hill picnic yet lingered.

Emma stood, and she allowed a smile to cross her lips at the thought it would most likely not be a visit of minimal duration.

"Miss Bates," Emma said as the aged woman entered the room. "What has caused you to walk all this way to Donwell? Is anything amiss? And please tell me you did not travel by yourself."

The two women sat and Emma called for tea while the elder responded: "Oh, Miss Woodhouse, you are so kind. So kind and thoughtful! Always thinking of your friends and never yourself." Miss Bates tittered away, commenting on the size of the room, the paintings and furnishings, until she stopped mid-sentence. "Oh, forgive me. I have called you Miss Woodhouse again, haven't I?"

She shook her head and tapped her finger on her nose, before chuckling. "I told the young maid, I told Ellen…she is down in the kitchen with your cook. I assured her that would be well with you, as you are such a wonderful hostess. I said, 'Ellen, poor Mrs. Knightley is forced to be patient with my calling her Miss Woodhouse. You see, I have known her for more time than not as Miss Woodhouse and not Mrs. Knightley. Her sister, Miss Isabella, is Mrs. Knightley. Well, truth be told, Misters George and John Knightley's mother was always Mrs. Knightley to me. Especially when we were younger and they would have their strawberry parties and the lot of us would be scampering around–myself, George and John, the Bedford sisters, and others. Mrs. Knightley, God rest her soul, would always ensure we had ample treats—pies, shortcakes, tarts. She was such a regal woman,' and Ellen laughed. Well, she laughs at almost everything I say. She is from Scotland, and I am certain she cannot understand a word I am saying. You see—"

"And have you heard from Mrs. Churchill lately? I have longed to hear how young Master Churchill is faring with his newest pony."

"Oh, yes. Oh, yes. It seems I have been running on with my thoughts." Miss Bates reached for her reticule and began to dig through the bag. "You are so patient with me, Miss Woodhouse—forgive me. Mrs. Knightley. Yes, yes. I have actually received a letter from Jane this very day and knew you would long to hear it, as we have continued that tradition these many years."

She then pulled the missive from her bag and held it up with a triumphant grin. "Ellen understands nothing about our dear Jane's acceptance into the first circles by marrying Mr. Churchill, nor the deep affection he has for her, but you do. You witnessed it first-hand. And I have not even taken the time to read it myself. I was in such a happy state to share it with you, I came directly."

Emma inhaled deeply and pasted a grin on her face, realizing how she would be forced to listen to her dear friend's letter with likely the same news she herself had received in a letter only the day before.

"Dear Aunt," Miss Bates began. What followed, Emma could not recount, for she began to contemplate the fact that the maids needed to reach the corner beams of the room better to remove all the cobwebs (not just those at eye level), that the chair which sat nearest to the fireplace needed to be recovered, and that the chocolate biscuits Cook prepared for tea were the best she had in some time.

She was at the point of determining in her mind where to take the children on holiday, when her thoughts were brought back to the present by a small gasp from Miss Bates. The older woman's cup shook as she picked it up and brought it to her lips.

"Miss Bates, are you well? Was there anything in Jane's letter which troubled you?"

"No, it is only…" She shook her head and set the cup down before beginning to fold up the letter. "It is just that I had no knowledge Jane and Frank were acquainted with the Winthrops."

"Winthrop?"

"Forgive me, Mrs. Knightley. I must call for Ellen and return home before it gets too dark. I do not wish to travel through the woods as the sun is going down."

Emma was shocked at the brevity of Miss Bates's words and realized something had seriously distressed her.

"Miss Bates, please. I will order the carriage for you. You are our friend, and I would not wish to send you home with something troubling you."

She watched as the older woman stood, sat, stood, looked at the folded letter, and sat again. "Miss Woodhouse. I thank you for the kindness and will accept your offer, but I must depart now."

"Very well. Simmons," she called to the footman at the door. "Have the groom prepare the carriage for Miss Bates. Notify me when it is ready to depart. Will you please see that Cook fills a basket with pork and pies as well as a basket of biscuits?"

"Yes, ma'am." The young man nodded and left the room.

"Oh, Miss Woodhouse. You are so good to me."

"It is nothing. I know how you adore sweets."

A long silence hung between the two women before the clock finally chimed three bells, startling Miss Bates.

"Oh, Miss Woodhouse. My true intent of visiting you today was not solely to share Jane's letter. I have recently been remembering my dear mother and, as she has been gone these several years, it made me think of you and our good friend, Mr. Woodhouse. I wanted to offer you my regards for him."

Emma was stunned how Miss Bates's words for her father, whether providential or happenstance, seemed befitting her melancholy disposition of late, and she was at a loss for what to say. But she need not have concerned herself with an answer as Miss Bates continued:

"I was remembering that last dinner at Hartfield when both my mother and your father were still with us. It was Mr. Knightley's birthday, do you recall? And he is so fond of cake and, as it was his birthday, your father agreed a very little might be an acceptable indulgence. Oh, and the cake. The most amazing concoction ever to be sure. And the butter cream! But then, to have mother die only three days later...quite possibly Mr. Woodhouse was correct in his estimation of rich foods?"

Before Emma could answer, the footman returned.

"The carriage is ready, ma'am."

"Thank you, Simmons. Will you please collect Miss Bates's maid from the kitchen?"

"Oh, bless you, Miss Woodhouse...I mean, Mrs. Knightly. Thank you."

Emma took Miss Bates's arm as the carriage was brought around and said, "I only wish you would confide in me if you are in need of solace, as you were a balm to my heart today. Time has not ceased the pain of my father's passing, yet your words today dampened the sting."

"Thank you to no end. You are always kindness itself."

Returning to the drawing room, Emma rested her hand on the window as the small barouche drove down the lane toward Highbury. *Why would a letter from Jane distress Miss Bates? And, most importantly, who is this Winthrop?* Emma Knightley smiled. An occupation had presented itself, and she was no longer restless.

It had been two days since she had visited with Miss Bates. Two days where she had asked everyone *except* her husband the significance of this Winthrop whose mention in a missive seemed to discomfit the elderly spinster. No one had been of any use.

Isabella said she remembered a family with several children by that name who used to reside at Randalls. Unfortunately, the Westons do not return from London for another week, and my letter has only gone out yesterday. And John's reply: "I remember them little but, of course, George would recall them better." She sighed, her frustrated heart pulling at her imagination.

It was then that footsteps could be heard from his dressing room and she leaned over to blow out the candle on her bedside table before the door opened to reveal her husband.

Time had not been unkind to George Knightley—his features were showing little sign of aging with only flecks of silver shot through his dark mass of hair. His frame, silhouetted by the warm glow of the fire in the hearth, was still that of an avid sportsman, and Emma's heart raced as he lifted the counterpane, slipping in next to her.

"Good evening, my dear Emma." His fingertips traced her arms and he softly kissed her shoulder.

"Good evening, Mr. Knightley"—and she leaned to his touch.

"I am sorry I have been monopolized with Donwell business these last two days."

"I thought you were avoiding me," she said with a pout in her voice.

"Avoiding you, my Emma? Whatever for?" He kissed the back of her neck, sending shivers up her spine. "I have actually been thinking much of you lately."

"Hmm..."

"I have. Have you not been thinking of me?" He kissed her again, causing her breath to catch.

"Yes, I have. I have been thinking of this moment for quite some time."

"As have I," he said with a smile which even in the dim light, she could not miss. "And what have you been thinking?"

She turned to face him. Tracing his jaw with her fingers, she slowly arched to kiss him, before pulling away. "I have been thinking about the Winthrops."

"The Winthrops?" He sputtered. "What Winthrops?"

"I was hoping you could tell me."

He sat up and leaned on his elbow, the counterpane falling across his waist. "I had not hoped to have this type of intercourse tonight."

She ran her hand down his back and smiled at the tease in his voice. "I was just curious about the Winthrops."

His laughter indicated his confusion. "The Winthrops? The family that used to live at Randalls years before the Westons?"

"Yes."

"Must we speak of them now? I have discussed business all day and would much rather enjoy my wife." When she did not respond to his entreaties, he asked, "Why are you thinking about them? They were gone long before you would have any recollection of their family."

She shrugged her shoulders and lamented her impulsiveness. "It is only that Miss Bates received a letter from Jane, and she was content reading the letter until she came to the name 'Winthrop'. Then she was so flustered that she excused herself and babbled not another word until I called for our carriage to return her home. Does that not seem an oddity for Miss Bates?"

"Emma?"

"Hmm?"—fidgeting with the covers—"I cannot imagine why you have that tone with me. You cannot have any reason to be exasperated when the uncertainty of my crimes loom before me. I am merely having a conversation with my husband."

"A conversation at *this* precise moment, my dear wife, is your first crime." He reached over and twirled the ends of her blonde curls in his fingers. "Your second is that you interrupted my pursuit solely to appease your curious mind about a missive from Jane to her aunt. That is a crime punishable with transport to Australia." He slid his hand slowly down her arm before raising her hand and kissing the inside of her wrist. "The third: you are obviously on a meddling mission. Maybe some scheme involving Miss Bates. I will warn you now, under no circumstance, are you to allow that clever mind of yours to take up matchmaking again!"

"Matchmaking? I never said anything about a *man* or *matchmaking*!" She squealed, sitting up and clapping her hands. "I knew it! You must tell me, George. I have been riddled with curiosity."

She could see the resignation in his face as he leaned back against the headboard. "Emma…."

"George, darling. I am a married woman of thirty-one. I have four children. Matchmaking was in my youth. I am only concerned for an old friend."

She could feel him studying her and hoped her carefully regulated voice showed no cause for suspicion.

"Very well. I will tell you, Emma. But *no* matchmaking." She nodded soberly until he seemed to believe her, then began. "The Winthrops were a highly esteemed family who owned Randalls before it passed to the previous owner before the Westons."

"Yes, that is what John said yesterday."

"John? You have discussed this with my brother, then? You *are* quite invested—"

"Solely for a friend."

He snorted. "Their brood was a few years older than John and me, save the youngest girl. But our mothers had been at school together, and so we were either at Randalls or they were at Donwell often. I am surprised John did not tell you this."

"Oh, you know your brother. I suppose he could not stir himself to remember." After a moment, she asked, "How would that have affected Miss Bates?"

"Their youngest son was the same age as Miss Bates—"

"Miss Bates is only few years older than you?"

"You knew that, Emma."

"I most certainly did not!"

"Hetty was always amiable. She would make us little boats to sail on the pond when her father, the vicar, would call. She would play hide-and-seek and other childish games with us. Yet when Edmund Winthrop was visiting, we boys did not exist."

"Did she set her cap at him?"

"We were never certain."

Emma paused, absorbing the new information and then— "Forgive me. It is only that you seem so much younger than Miss Bates."

Pulling her close, he laughed into her hair and said, "Because I chose wisely in a bride who would forever keep me young." He tucked a curl behind her ear. "Now, the Winthrops. I must say, I remember a time when John and I were quite disgusted with Edmund and would have challenged him if we could have formulated the idea. We viewed Hetty Bates as quite our own and were quite put out when the Winthrops visited at the same time."

"*You* were smitten with Miss Bates?" she asked in disbelief. "George, I must say, all I thought I knew of the world is now amiss."

A deep chuckle rolled from his lips. "Now you are being nonsensical. I am relating the musings of a young boy of ten who favored Miss Bates solely for her skills at making paper boats and pilfering lemon biscuits from her cook."

"As long as *any* feelings you had for her were of a childish nature..." She kissed him now, reminding him that paper boats were for children and how there were many more advantages to choosing her.

"Emma, darling, you are the most infuriating woman!" He pulled her close and kissed her breathless. "Hetty Bates was a skilled paper boat builder. *You,* Mrs. Knightley, have other arts and allurements."

In the watery light before the sun rose, she reached for him and nuzzled his neck. "Darling... George, are you awake?"

"Hmm?"

"What happened?"

"With us? I hope after ten years and four children, you are aware of the intricacies of marriage."

She swatted him with a pillow. He laughed and turned, drawing her into his embrace, where she rested her head in the crook of his neck. "What happened with Miss Bates and Mr. Winthrop?"

"A lesser man might be affronted how his wife was still deliberating that topic." He kissed her forehead. "He left. His family lost the estate in a bad business venture, and he set out for the colonies. With the war, no one really heard much from him. Miss Bates remained here, her father dying, never marrying, and she and her mother in genteel poverty. Regarding Winthrop, if I understand, he has made a small fortune in trade, but that is all speculation."

George Knightley yawned lazily before snuggling down and allowing his voice to drop, forcing his wife to strain to hear him. "Well, it is all speculation until next week."

"What do you mean?"

"I received a letter yesterday from the man himself. Edmund Winthrop is in London. He has asked if he might trespass on our hospitality at Donwell for a fortnight. I had planned to write that my wife and I would be happy to receive him for the length of his trip into this part of the country."

"George! Why did you not tell me? Why did you make me coax this story from you? How you enjoy vexing me!" Emma sat up and clapped her hands. "This is just as I wished!"

She felt his knowing gaze and steadied her speech. "Now that the house is no longer draped in black, we might host a small party."

"I am sure that has been your concern all along." He pulled the covers up over his shoulders and was soon asleep.

I will invite a few families for a dinner party in honor of Mr. Winthrop and will then be able to observe Miss Bates with her old acquaintance. With any luck, she will benefit from what my husband would deem my officious help and have a future filled with joy of her own.

The gravel crunching under the wheels of a carriage forced Emma to look up from young Lucy Knightley's painting. Recognizing Mrs. Weston's equipage, she handed the baby to Nanny and signaled for the governess to see to the young boys chasing frogs in the garden pond.

As the carriage stopped, she smoothed her gown before extending her hands to her dear friend.

"At last! You have returned."

"My dear, Emma. Yes, two days ago. I am sorry I could not break away from the house until now, but with Mr. Winthrop arriving in the area, my husband wanted little Charles to ride out with him and survey the property. However, I have brought Clarice with me, as she could not miss a chance to play with your dear Lucy."

At that, the sound of squeals and giggles met them, and they turned to see the two young girls embracing.

"Mama, please might I show Clarice my newest doll?"

"Of course, dear. But, you must return to finish your painting for Mr. Winthrop."

"May I also show her your dolls, especially Miss Abby?"

"Of course. But have a care—they are very old. Now run to the house." The two young girls held hands and ran across the lawn, the bonnet ribbons catching on their necks and sending braids flying behind them. "Do you wish to take the air or go into the drawing room?"

"Oh, let us stay out—it is very fine. I have been so confined in London for these last three weeks, I could not wait to return to Highbury. The countryside was calling me."

Emma signaled for a maid to bring them tea, and they sat down on a cushioned bench under a willow by the pond.

"I understand from the letter that you have suspected something regarding our visitor?"

Emma smiled and turned her chin slightly away. "I am afraid, my dear Anne, you will scold me as George will, surely."

"Emma, dear. My days for scolding you are over."

Emma straightened her skirt and waited while the maid set down the tea before sharing her thoughts. "I believe Miss Bates was in love with Mr. Winthrop!"

"Our Miss Bates?"

"Yes!"

"Why would you suspect such a thing?" she asked, setting down her cup and gazing at the woman she once helped to raise.

"She brought a letter she had received from Jane last week and was reading it to me when she gasped and stopped speaking."

"Miss Bates?"

"Yes! I myself was stunned as well and encouraged her to confide in me, but she was too shocked. She mentioned that she did not realize Frank and Jane knew the Winthrops, collected her maid, and left within a trice. There is a story there. I am certain of it."

Anne Weston stirred the sugar in her cup and thoughtfully replied,

"Things are not always as they appear, Emma. We were lately in the company of Mr. Winthrop and his sister at a dinner party while visiting the Churchills. He did mention Miss Bates save a few times but only in reference to her father and the vicarage."

"Oh?"

"Yes. But, he did speak very often *and* fondly of Mrs. Goddard," she said, lifting her cup to her mouth.

"Mrs. Goddard?"

"Mrs. Goddard."

"But, I have not invited Mrs. Goddard to dinner! And now I must find another man to even out my numbers."

"You will need two as Mr. Winthrop is planning to bring his sister."

"His sister? I did not know he would be bringing the sister."

"It appears Mr. Winthrop has taken on many of the American practices. I suppose he was remiss not to mention it to your husband in his most recent letter. Mr. Weston and I said we would convey the message."

"Thank you, my friend." Emma sniffed. "What is Miss Winthrop like? Are her manners as uncouth and American as her brother's?"

Mrs. Weston recognized the peevish attitude and attempted to soothe her younger friend. "I believe they have been out of polite society for so long, they did not understand the faux pas. Remember, even nice people in America have become careless of genteel manners. However, we will not slight them for their mistake."

"Of course not." Emma's eyes brightened— "Mrs. Goddard?"

"Yes, Mrs. Goddard! But, Emma. Do not start plotting any of your matchmaking schemes. Mr. Knightley would not be pleased."

"I am only thinking about bringing two friends back together who have not been in each other's company for a number of years. Oh, I learned my lesson years ago when I almost ruined poor Harriet Martin's chances. Besides, I am certain Mrs. Goddard is not a woman who would take kindly to matters of the heart at her age."

A peal of laughter met this pronouncement, and Emma smiled back at her friend. "What is so entertaining? It was not my intent to say anything amusing."

"And yet, you did. Do you believe because Mrs. Goddard is older that she has no desire for affection? That because she has been a spinster for so long, she has not feelings in that regard?"

"Why would a woman who is so very old wish to change her circumstances? Mrs. Goddard is quite independent running her school, and I am certain she would not wish to adjust to the idea of sharing her life with a man who might muddle things up."

"Is that what men do?" a deep voice behind them asked.

Emma turned quickly, a blush spreading across her cheeks. "George! When did you arrive?"

"In enough time to hear you call poor Alice Goddard too old to want her circumstances to change. I will remind you that she—"

"Is only five years older than you?"

"No, my dear. She is seven years my elder. But, no matter how old she is, or whether you or I believe she would welcome affection at this stage in her life, you are *not* to matchmake. I will say this in front of our old friend and ask her to stand as my witness. I would be very displeased if you went against my wishes. Your schemes cause nothing but trouble."

"Nothing but trouble?" Emma set down her tea cup, squaring her shoulders. "Would you say the joyful union between Anne and Mr. Weston is nothing but trouble? That the marriage of John and Isabella was nothing but trouble?"

"Emma..."

"George, my skills at matchmaking were suspect at times, but I had a very good success rate."

"And did I not just hear you admit to Mrs. Weston how you almost ruined Harriet Smith Martin's chances?"

"How ungallant of you to point out my failings, Mr. Knightley! But you should take comfort knowing I am *not* intending to return to the business of unifying couples. However, if I did, know that it would be efficacious."

"If you did," he said, leaning down and pecking her cheek, "know that I will take up residence back at Hartfield with John and Isabella."

As he walked away, she wrinkled her nose at Anne. "Besides, I have too much to concern myself with. Luckily the house is in order for the Winthrops, but I cannot concentrate on such trivial matters."

"Yes. I am glad you see it that way. Besides, there was one thing I forgot to mention: Mr. Winthrop's sister seemed quite intent on George."

"My George?"

"I am not trying to gossip, but she would not stop recounting the story of how they were once secretly engaged—"

"Engaged?"

"So she would have me believe when the others were occupied. And that the only reason they are not married with grandchildren of their own is because she was forced to leave for America."

"She mentioned grandchildren? How very indelicate!" Emma's ire had risen at the conversation until rational thought took hold of her mind. "I cannot be disturbed by the claim of an unmarried woman past her fortieth year. Of course, she would wish to hold onto any memory which would bring her joy from her youth. And my George is a handsome man, still surpassing the likes of Mr. Elton or, with no disrespect intended, Frank Churchill. I cannot fault her for her misplaced wishes. Do not fret"—she patted Mrs. Weston on the leg— "I will not begrudge her this small fancy."

"And yet... My dear, I have known you these twenty-eight years. I know the look in your eye and the sound in your voice. There is nothing at the forefront of your mind as much as scheming to make a match between Mrs. Goddard and Mr. Winthrop."

"Anne, you heard George...he has—"

"Forbidden you, yes. But, as a wife, I also know it is easier and often times more enjoyable to ask for forgiveness than permission. Might I advise you against that in this instance? I fear your attention should not be diverted. Rosalind Winthrop may be a formidable foe."

"Foe? Do not be ridiculous." Emma stood and brushed off her gown, attempting to hide her annoyance. "George adores me, and I him. I am in no way concerned that his attentions will be directed toward another woman. He is as constant as the sun."

"Yes, my dear. But sometimes there are clouds who feel it is their job to block the glory of the sun for their own amusement and to the detriment of what it knows and loves."

~

She waited until she heard him in the hallway before laying *Evelina* on the bedside table. His knock was swift, and he opened the door without waiting for a reply. She heard him quickly pad across the carpets, before sliding into bed alongside her.

"Ah, my darling Emma."

"Good evening, Mr. Knightley."

Gently kissing her forehead and resting his against hers—"How was your visit today with Mrs. Weston? Did they enjoy London?"

"Very pleasant, and yes they did. Well, as much as one can enjoy London when one is a guest in another's home for any extended time."

"Trouble with Frank?"

She sniffed and nestled into him. "How can they have trouble with a man who is never there? She would never speak ill of him, but I could sense something had occurred."

He waited for her to continue.

Emma shrugged her shoulders, lightly pressing her lips to his neck.

"She told me they had seen him six times. Six times! And he stayed at his club. His club! It seemed left to Jane to attend them, arrange activities around Town, host teas for Anne—leaving Mr. Weston to entertain himself. When Frank was at home, he and his father went riding in Hyde Park or to his club."

Silence enveloped the room, all but the sound of their breathing and crackle of the fire in the hearth.

"And what is it, my dear wife, that you are speculating?"

"George, I know you have never been too keen on Frank Churchill..."

"It is only how he behaved when I first met him. His conduct has... improved since our first acquaintance."

"Do you believe that?"

"In some regards, yes." She waited quietly, unable to voice her concerns, realizing that once it was said, it could not be unspoken but, finding strength in the darkness, she began. "I am afraid, that I believe Frank might have...another woman...."

George did not reply, running his fingers through her hair.

"And you have no response?" She waited for her husband's wise words, finding comfort in his strong arms and the closeness amidst these subtle truths now shaping her world.

He kissed her brow softly. "Emma," he began, "silly men do not want sensible wives. Unfortunately, as often happens, it is too late for some caught up in the excitement of the hunt to realize they have been chasing the wrong prey. It is only then, when they are discontented with their lot, that they concentrate their attention elsewhere, to the dismay of at least one party involved."

"As you say…"

"I am saying nothing. I am merely having a conversation with my wife. Now, let us not discuss Frank Churchill, Prinny, or any other silly man for that matter. This sensible man has chosen the woman who best fits him, and that is all that is important."

She swallowed her questions, thinking of what Mrs. Weston had said about Miss Winthrop, and her ire piqued. *What of this woman who claims to have been secretly engaged to my George? That is not just a statement one bandies about.*

No more was said, and she listened to the steady thud of his heart beat as he held her tightly before she could feel his body relax into sleep.

His words should ease my soul, but they do not. Am I a silly woman married to a sensible man? Shall I become tiresome to him as well?

There were too many truths emerging from this dark unknown. It seemed that the Town life was beginning to impose on the serenity of Highbury, toppling the truths which she had always held dear.

If the conversation from the previous night was supposed to remove her concerns, it did not. All was not right with Emma Knightley's world. Even at her lowest point when her father died, she recognized the depths of people's goodness around her. There was no false pretense. All was as it should be. But now…. She believed that there were things beyond her understanding. A hidden world where men were not as they pretended to be, and not all women were either. What began as an innocent matchmaking scheme all but dissolved, and her thoughts dwelt upon the slow deterioration of a friend's marriage.

What must Jane be feeling? Frank was always a man to ignore propriety, but once they were able to wed, he was quite besotted with her. Or has it always been thus?

She moved around the house, repositioning chairs, straightening paintings, moving vases, plumping pillows in an already perfect scene, awaiting these mysterious guests' arrival.

What is it about a man that would cause him to forsake his wife? The woman who has born his children and is mistress to his home?

Having grown up without a mother but with a father who adored the memory of her, it was a foreign concept that a man would willingly forsake his wedding vows. Especially when it had been a love match.

She had heard of people who married for convenience, who led a separate life away from their home. But she did not move in those circles. The Churchills had, and it seemed Frank had blackened that trust.

George never enjoyed his company as much as he did others. My husband would never associate with people of questionable values.

Emma peered out a long window across the long drive. *Between worrying about Jane and about the propriety of this Winthrop creature, I wonder how I will survive a fortnight.*

She caught a glimpse of a carriage coming into the park. *And yet, can I blame her?* She walked from the room toward her husband's study. *A woman of her age who has no husband, no children, nothing to recommend her, would of course rely upon her memories to bring her joy. The sorry state of poor spinsters can give them little comfort.*

Thinking of Miss Bates and Mrs. Goddard and how time seemed to destroy beauty and common sense, she attempted to soften her annoyance. *George is my husband, but he was likely the only man to show her kindness...that would be like him.* She knocked on the door of his study and did not wait for an answer to enter.

"Our guests arrive."

"Wonderful." Indicating the letter on his desk— "Just finishing a note to my steward."

She studied him in the starkness of daylight. It seemed of late she had beheld him only by candlelight, when their time slowed, allowing them a few private moments. *He is still so striking. Poor Miss Winthrop.*

At that moment, her husband looked up and smiled. "Are you ready, Emma?"

"Yes. Let us go meet our guests."

He held out his arm, and she reached for it, clasping her hands together around the crook at his elbow.

"You must be pleased to reacquaint yourself with your former childhood friends."

"You forget, Emma. All but Miss Winthrop were older than John and I."

"But I am certain you will still have many things to discuss. Mrs. Weston said Miss Winthrop spoke very highly of you. Indeed, she claims to have been once secretly engaged to you."

He blustered and began to fidget with his collar. "Things from childhood can be construed in ways one might wish to remember. Not all are truths."

Her brows raised at this and she attempted to make sense of his words as the great hall door was opened and they moved out to the portico. As the carriage slowed to a stop, she instinctively reached for his hand. *It must be difficult for him to imagine my meeting this woman from his boyhood.*

They walked down the steps to greet their guests. A man with graying hair and a rotund figure, dressed in the latest fashion, exited the carriage. At once, Emma thought that he was certainly a perfect match for Miss Bates based on appearance alone. *Her lot in life is less secure than Mrs. Goddard's, who has her little school. And, some might say her talking is not so inconvenient. Many men appreciate a woman...with something to say.*

A smug look had crossed her face just before an elegantly gloved hand appeared from the carriage and clasped Mr. Winthrop's. Emma swallowed her gasp.

Rosalind Winthrop was no bashful miss, not a mousy spinster a la Miss Bates, nor a practical woman like Mrs. Goddard. Of a sudden, as she straightened to her full height, taking in Emma's measure, the corner of her mouth edged up, and then a smile reached her eyes as she looked on to Knightley. Emma's Mr. Knightley. She was a woman who silently smoldered.

Emma felt herself curtsey to the new arrivals and, by rote, woodenly welcomed them to Donwell. She informed the guests that a light repast would be served in the small dining room at their convenience and that an intimate dinner party in their honor was at six. If they were interested in a tour, she would be available at their leisure.

All this was said, and not once did Emma remember speaking. She was as she had not been in many years—anxious, uncomfortable, and self-conscious—and could not fathom how to remedy the situation.

Dinner had not gone as anticipated. Emma's invitations had been sent out to her friends with the sole purpose of encouraging a match between Mr. Winthrop and either Miss Bates or Mrs. Goddard despite her husband's directive from the previous week regarding matchmaking. But her attention to that task was now at an end. She had items of more significance before her.

Had she perceived the footmen attempting to not gaze upon Miss Winthrop as they walked into the drawing room after dinner? Their sideways glances of her figure, her face, flustered Emma for...well, she would rather not think on it. Having separated from the men, she wanted to observe this woman.

Emma's thoughts were soon interrupted by a measured, cultured voice, more like the purr of a contented feline than a woman past her prime.

"You have worked wonders with Donwell, Mrs. Knightley. I must say, it is far better than I could have done, given the opportunity."

Miss Winthrop had a level of confidence that made Emma's thirty-one years of life seem juvenile. She was more than beautiful. She was mesmerizing.

"Thank you, Miss Winthrop. I have been blessed with an adoring husband who indulges my whims. Only a little modernizing was needed.

His mother did an excellent job caring for the house, as did he, before our marriage."

"Mrs. Knightley was a wonderful woman. I believe you never knew her? No, you would have been much too young to remember when she died. I was a favorite of hers, and she of mine. It is truly a...wonder to be a guest at Donwell when for so long she and I both imagined I would be here in a much different capacity."

She turned to speak to Miss Bates, and Emma bit her bottom lip, while Mrs. Weston clasped Emma's hand with steadying support. Emma quickly collected herself, engaging Mrs. Goddard in conversation. *This will be the longest two weeks of my life.*

⁓

The sound of her husband coming to bed eased some of her insecurities. *George is mine, and regardless of that teasing, flirting Miss Winthrop, my husband is not Frank Churchill.*

"Are you still awake, my dear?"

She rolled over and looked at him in the moonlight. "Yes, but what took you so long to come to bed? Do not tell me John just left for Hartfield. Isabella will not be pleased, as they leave for London in the morning."

"No, he left hours ago. You know he has little tolerance for conversation past eleven."

"I knew you would come eventually." She began to trail soft kisses down his neck. "It is only that I was hoping to–"

"Yes, Winthrop's stories of America were fascinating, but Rosalind's were even better. Do you know she traveled to the West of America? She rode most of the way on horseback and was almost taken by Indians."

Emma froze, her lips halting their movement, as she leaned back. "Miss Winthrop did not retire when I did?"

"She did. However, she returned half an hour later to entertain us with tales of her own adventures."

She sat up quickly.

"She told us she can shoot too. She will be joining us for a day of sport tomorrow."

"Hunting? I have planned for a visit to Randalls. To see her childhood home."

"Oh, that was very thoughtful of you, my love." He yawned and rolled over, his back facing her. "I am certain she would enjoy that the following day. Her heart is set on the hunt tomorrow. Besides, Mr. Weston will be part of the party. I am certain Mrs. Weston will not mind. You and she will enjoy each other's company, as you always do."

Her mouth agape and her brows furrowed in consternation, she became further incensed when her husband began to snore.

She is going hunting, is she? Well, she better not be planning to bag my Mr. Knightley!

"And she is hunting with the men as we speak!"

Mrs. Weston sipped from her tea cup and smiled at her younger friend.

"Emma, what of Miss Bates and Mr. Winthrop?"

"What about them? I can barely spare them a thought," she said, nibbling on a biscuit before dropping it on the saucer. "I am not certain. I believe they spoke to each other well enough last evening."

"And Mrs. Goddard?"

"Once again, I am unsure. I believe they discussed her school and her students..."

Mrs. Weston stirred the liquid in her cup before looking up. "I find it interesting..."

"That?"

"That your attention to this matchmaking scheme between Miss Bates or Mrs. Goddard with Mr. Winthrop has waned in light of Miss Winthrop."

Emma squinted into the sun. "I do not know where to begin." She rubbed her hands on the skirt of her gown and began to roll the edge of the lace. "I believe after our conversation the other day, I was very unsettled." Her dearest friend set her cup on the small table and waited. *How do I tell her? How do I convey my fears without disparaging her husband's son whom she believes is near to perfection?*

"Emma?"

Emma Knightley took a deep breath and began. "It is no secret that when I first met your daughter-in-law, Jane, I did not warm to her."

"You were young, Emma."

"I had lived twenty-one years in selfish conceit, and my dear father was blind to my puffed-up pride that permeated every aspect of my life."

Emma noted Mrs. Weston did not contradict her. "However, now... now I consider Jane to be a dear friend. We exchange letters every few weeks and love sharing the growth of our families."

"I know. I do not understand your disquiet."

With slow, deliberate words, she said, "After our conversation two days ago, I began to think about...Frank...and how he seems to have... allowed his interest in Jane's society to..." She watched for any sign of agitation in her friend but noticing none, continued. "I spoke of it to George, and he...confirmed he had the same concerns...I hope this does not pain you."

Anne Weston shook her head and said, "It is not my pain that I bear but that of my husband. He is a goodly man who can see no fault in his son. It is difficult for me to stand by and allow Frank's treatment to both Jane and my dear husband to occur." Emma nodded. "But Jane holds her head high and shows a level of dignity and honor her husband could only aspire to."

Emma was shocked at the boldness of the statement but grateful her friend was not deceived.

"I still do not understand how this affects Miss Bates and Mrs. Goddard's match with Mr. Winthrop?"

"Frank."

"What do you mean? Frank?"

Emma swallowed and looked across the garden to the children being led on a pony by the groom.

"If Jane—perfectly wonderful, amiable Jane—if her husband would grow tired of her and seek fulfillment from another, could not all husbands?"

"Emma!"

"Well, truly! I could never be concerned about George. Because he is so honorable. And loves me so. And the children. But then Miss Winthrop arrives in all her feathers and velvets, and secret looks, and hunting prowess. Sometimes we do not seek temptation; it presents itself to us willingly! And I confess, I feel as if, like you said, the clouds are trying to block the sun!"

"No, that was unfair of me. Mr. Knightley is not made from the same cloth as Frank—"

"Yes, I know, but is it not possible that this woman could make him forget why he fell in love with me? Could there be something to Miss Winthrop's claim they had been secretly engaged? George says not all is a truth. So not all must be untruth—"

"Emma..."

"But there it is. What am I to believe when he has been acting so strange since she arrived?"

"Emma, has he exhibited behavior which would lend you to believe you are correct in your assertions?"

"No, never. But, it can only be a matter of time."

A deep sigh bellowed from Mrs. Weston. "My dear girl. I am going to give you one more piece of wisdom which will help ensure a happy marriage."

"Yes?" Emma leaned forward.

"Do not imagine your husband less of a man than he is. You will devastate his trust in you and disappoint him. Have faith in the man you know him to be."

Emma and Mrs. Weston both turned to wave as the children called out to them before settling into a quiet lull.

It is not my lack of faith in the man he is. It is my lack of faith in the lady she purports to be!

"Oh, your little girl forgot her doll." Emma looked up to see Miss Winthrop pointing at Miss Abby sitting on the piano.

It was Thursday, only five days into the Winthrops' visit, and the party was listening to young Lucy Knightley perform her newest piece on the pianoforte.

"That is Mrs. Knightley's doll, not young Miss Knightley's," Miss Bates said. "It was given to her by Mrs. Weston when she was just Miss Taylor after Mrs. Woodhouse passed from this earth."

"And you have kept it?" Miss Winthrop asked, turning to Emma with a raised brow.

"I have. I suppose Lucy has forgotten it. It brought me comfort as a child."

"But you are a child no more." She turned her head toward the piano.

Mrs. Weston's eyes met Emma's and an uncomfortable silence lingered.

"And how did you find Randalls?" Miss Bates asked.

"Randalls was lovely. *Almost* as lovely as I remember."

"And what did you find lacking? I am certain Mrs. Weston's hospitality is incomparable." Emma felt the bite in her tone and thought to regulate it after a reproving look from her husband.

She had not intended it to come out quite so harshly, but her patience had been tried these last days. The soup was "delicious but too salty" for her palette, her rooms were "lovely but" she preferred "the view of the gardens more," and the flowers were "well-tended but" she preferred "a less structured style."

The only thing it seems she has not complained about is my husband's company. Although mine has been construed as "charming for one raised in the country." Infuriating! Emma looked at Miss Winthrop and pasted a smile upon her face.

"No, my dear," her guest said, "I was thinking that the only thing lacking at Randalls is the presence of my dear, departed mother."

She felt the eyes of her husband on her and knew she was going to receive a scolding.

"Of course," she replied. "And my sister and brother only lack the presence of my father at Hartfield. Of those sentiments, I can understand." She nodded to the lady and gave her husband a gentle smile, ignoring the brewing storm in his eyes.

"Now, Miss Winthrop. On Saturday, I have planned a picnic to Box Hill. Would that suit?"

"Box Hill. I have not thought of Box Hill in many years. Not since..." She coyly glanced over at George Knightley, who swallowed and turned away, beginning a conversation with Mr. Winthrop about horses.

"Not since...? Pardon me, but if the memories are painful to you, I can change our plans." Emma had intentionally organized the outing at a location which she believed Miss Winthrop had no connection; a place where Emma could prove she had matured since that long-ago picnic when she had insulted poor Miss Bates. Instead, she now felt like a fox about to step into a trap, waiting for the inevitable: a look, an explanation, something that would indicate she had been left out of the joke for whatever reason. It was a hollow feeling and not one she was accustomed to.

"No, no. I would be *thrilled* to relive the happy memories associated with that lovely place."

Emma glanced at George conversing with Mr. Winthrop. *Why do I feel as if I am reading a book and everyone else in the room already knows the ending?*

The clock in the hall chimed, and she heard the door open. He moved across the carpet a bit more sluggishly than usual.

"George? Are you well?"

"Yes," he whispered. "I am well but will have a headache in the morning." Her silence must have unnerved him, because he said, "Do not scold me, Emma. I do not usually imbibe, but Mr. Winthrop brought with him a bottle of whiskey from America which he was gracious enough to share. I had one too many drinks. And if you do not scold me, I will not scold you for your harsh words toward Miss Winthrop this evening. We are even."

"I was not intending my words to be *harsh*. However, as you said, let us forget about it and not scold each other. We are both tired, and I understand your wanting to take a drink or two with your friend."

"I knew you would, my love," he said, kissing her, then rolling over onto his side. "I attempted to excuse myself, especially when Rosalind rejoined the party. But Winthrop entreated me to stay."

"Rosalind? You mean, Miss Winthrop, to be sure. She was drinking with the men in your study?"

"Yes, but…"

Emma sat up. "But what? Do you feel her behavior is proper? Would you approve of that behavior if it was me?"

George looked over his shoulder to her face, his gaze silently questioning. "Of course not. But her brother is her guardian, not I. And you are my wife. You know your proper place."

"My proper place?" She clenched her fists and took a quick breath. "But Miss Winthrop, or as you say *Rosalind's* proper place is wherever she wishes it to be?"

"Once again I agree with your assertions. The only excuse we can make for her is that she is an American—"

"No, she is British, and she is choosing to follow American customs. And why do you call her 'Rosalind,' but her brother is 'Mr. Winthrop?' *That* in itself is improper."

"What are you saying?" he asked, sitting up.

"George, I see how she looks at you."

"What are you implying?"

"It is indecent!"

"I cannot control how a person looks!"

"You admit that she does."

"I have not paid attention to her long enough to determine who or what she looks at. I only know that you are being unreasonable."

"Unreasonable? How am I being unreasonable as I watch a woman make love to my husband without saying a word?"

"Emma!"

"It is true, George, and you know it as well!"

He took a long breath and let it out before replying, his voice steely. "Do you think I have not experienced this situation myself? Have I accused you of delighting in the adoration of every man who glances at the beauty of my wife in a way that would make a maiden blush?"

"You are being ridiculous! That never occurs!"

"Are you so certain?"

He stared at her quietly, as her mind raced. "Whether it happens or not is of little concern. I do not relish the attention!"

"Yet you are implying I do!"

"You do nothing to stop her!"

He stood up and threw the covers off. "Because it is not necessary! I will not encourage her attentions through either acknowledgement or discouragement!"

"Then you are secretly encouraging her!"

"Are you daft, woman?" He stared at her blankly, as her eyes burned with hot tears hidden in the darkness.

After a moment, he cleared his throat. "I will sleep in my room tonight. Discussing this further—now—can accomplish nothing."

"George!"

"Goodnight, Emma."

His steps receded from her room as she lay in bed; her quiet sobs keeping no one in the house awake but herself.

The sun beat down on her through the shade of the trees and a silk parasol over her head. The day had not transpired as she had expected. The entire week had been one she wished to forget. Her husband's frustration had been evident to all in her household as well as their friends and guests.

First, Anne asking after George's odd behavior! Then Miss Winthrop's smug look! Emma could hardly bear it. A foul taste came now with not only the speaking of the woman's name but the thought of it as well.

Emma reached over and picked up a leaf which had fallen on the blanket and spun it in her fingers. She was alone. The other guests—the Westons, Winthrops, Churchills, Mrs. Goddard, Miss Bates, and her own husband—had abandoned her to walk to the summit.

Yes, the Churchills! Their arrival at Randalls one day previous had surprised not only its inhabitants but the neighborhood. True, Jane

Churchill frequented Highbury with her children to visit her in-laws and aunt, but Frank usually remained in Town. It had been two years since he had stepped foot in his ancestral village. His arrival alone was one to cause a stir in the homes of gossip mavens throughout the countryside.

Gossip mavens, yes. But when the Churchills were announced with the Westons at dinner last night, no one stirred.

Emma thought back to how odd Jane's reaction had been when she first laid eyes on Miss Winthrop. *According to Miss Bates, they were acquaintances of the Winthrops. I too could do with a minimal dose of the woman, but to openly snub! However, Miss Winthrop only seemed amused by the slight.*

Emma set down the leaf and took out a fan to cool herself, causing swirls of air to blow wisps of hair about her face. She had not wished to join the others. Her husband was flanked by Miss Winthrop and Frank Churchill, Jane by Miss Bates and the Westons, and Mrs. Goddard by Mr. Winthrop. No, she had much rather sit still and reflect upon that picnic in the same spot all those years ago where she had stepped toward her present state of understanding.

It had been here where Frank had goaded me so; where he had played with my sensibilities. And now, I see him doing the same to his wife. I had hoped that George's anger toward me would not blind him to Frank's actions, but it seems to have done just that. And Mr. Weston, a good man, cannot ever find fault with his son. No, it is best I be alone and collect myself.

Her desires were short lived when a small figure in pale lavender joined her.

The two women quietly gazed over the landscape, enjoying the silence.

"I wanted to thank you for welcoming us upon our unexpected arrival last evening. No one was more surprised than myself of my husband's desire to visit Randalls."

"You are always welcome. Well, I am sure," Emma began with caution, "Mr. Churchill has at last cleared up whatever business has kept him away for so long."

"Yes. I am certain that is it." Jane tugged at her skirt and smoothed it out. After another minute, she began. "I was…surprised to see your other guests. I had understood from my husband that the Winthrops had chosen not to stay in Highbury but instead had continued on to Cornwall and then to Portsmouth to return to the Americas."

"I was not made aware of their plans beyond Donwell. I only know that they will tarry here for another week—"

"Another week?"

"After that, I am uncertain of their schedule."

"Oh."

Emma's nerves were heightened as she looked across at her friend who was once again studying the picturesque.

"Jane?"

"Yes?"

Emma lay her fan in her lap. "I am aware that things...things might not be...easy now..."

An almost indiscernible breath escaped Jane's lips.

"However, I want to extend my friendship and help, if needed."

Emma's declaration was met by silence. An awkwardness pervaded for a few moments, and she was wordlessly berating herself when Jane finally spoke.

"We are not the same girls we were when we last shared a blanket on this spot, are we? You, the mistress of Donwell, and I...I, Mrs. Frank Churchill. How different our circumstances were then—our hopes and dreams."

"Yes, but if you recall," Emma said, laying a hand on Jane's, "we were both here at Box Hill under a false understanding. Now, as married women, we both comprehend our places and can relax in the comfort of our friendship."

A chuckle met Emma's declaration before a quiet resignation pervaded Jane's voice. "The comfort of our friendship, yes, but false understandings still pervade, Emma dear"—staring at the scene before her—"I will be leaving on Monday."

"But you have only arrived."

"Yes, but I feel that it is best to visit my old friends, the Dixons. The children and I will depart and take my aunt with us."

"You are taking Miss Bates to Ireland?"

"She has never had a chance to leave Highbury and, although her chatter can be tiresome, I know of her genuine love for me." She closed her eyes briefly. "She will bring me comfort now."

"And will Mr. Churchill remain at Randalls?"

"Of that I am uncertain. However, I believe as long as there is...diversion...in the area, my husband will remain."

At Emma's curious expression, Jane squeezed her hand. "Never move to London, Emma. Stay in Highbury amongst the people you love and the places you know. Forgive Mr. Knightley for whatever petty squabble you have had. It does not matter who is wrong and who is right. What matters is that your husband comes home to you every night."

The approaching sound of people caused the conversation to cease, and the distinctive voice of Miss Bates could be heard over any others.

"Ireland. Oh, the excitement I feel is beyond any I have ever felt before. To imagine me traveling to a foreign country. But how is Jane to manage so long without Mr. Churchill? I believe he is to remain in London, is he not, Jane? However will we manage the four children, maids, and footmen? I am certain I have no idea how it will be achieved."

"Aunt, if you recall, there was a time I was quite prepared to care for myself."

"Yes, but that was so long ago," she replied, sitting. "Now you have a husband to care for you. You need not burden yourself with such worry. But I know it will be well, and my only concern is the rain. And the Irish."

"The Irish?"

"Yes. I do hope they are not savage. Do you think they will be savage, Miss Woodhouse? Forgive me—Mrs. Knightley?" she asked.

Emma released Jane's hand and smiled, turning to the little party. "I am certain you will encounter no savages, Miss Bates. You will be, after all, guests of the Dixons. And we know they are generosity themselves."

"Well, of course they are! One would never question that. You know, he saved our Jane's life all those years ago. Do you remember, Mrs. Knightley? Mrs. Weston, do you recall the story?"

"I do."

"Oh, I have just realized, I will now be able to thank him properly for the service rendered to our family. What wonderful luck."

"Aunt, I am sure that will not be necessary. It was so long ago."

"Yes, but one does not forget things, or people, just because time has moved on. Look at me. I was so stunned when I received your letter with reference to the Winthrops, I do not believe I spoke for five minutes. You were there, Mrs. Knightley. You recall." She turned a questioning gaze to Emma.

"I do recall, Miss Bates. I was worried for your health."

"I was only worried that Mr. Winthrop would request the repayment of the two pounds he loaned me when we were children. That has haunted me for years, and I had no way to repay it. But he has assured me that the loan has been forgiven, as we are old friends. And now I can travel with a pure conscience and enjoy my journey."

A debt owed? So, it was not love? Emma shook her head. *George was right. I must cease matchmaking.*

"There you are," a male voice interrupted.

The women turned to see Frank Churchill striding toward them with a large grin on his face. "Emma, Jane. What a lovely image! It reminds me of all those years ago. You both sitting just so in that same spot. I feel as if I am in my youth again."

Emma gave a half-hearted grin but felt Jane stiffen beside her.

"Yes. And you have hardly changed a bit, sir. I thought of that only moments ago," Emma replied. She did her best to *not* look away from his eyes, pushing the knowledge that she had of him from her mind.

"But," Mr. Churchill said lazily, sitting down next to the women, "I do hope that you have not left your games at home today, Mrs. Knightley."

"Frank," Jane said, turning her eyes to him.

"Or how about another riddle? No? Well, I have it on good authority that Miss Winthrop desires to know what everyone here is thinking." Miss Winthrop strolled languidly up the path and stopped in front of Jane.

Jane stood and extended her hand to Miss Bates. "Come, Aunt. Let us walk and discuss our trip. I am all aquiver with anticipation. Mrs. Knightley, would you care to join us?"

"Oh, I had hoped to speak to Mrs. Knightley," a purring voice behind them said. "Mrs. Churchill." She nodded, her gaze fixed on Frank.

"If you will excuse me," Jane said, clasping her aunt and Mrs. Weston's hands.

Emma watched the three women, whose company she would much rather join, walk down the path and disappear.

"Mr. Churchill."

"Miss Winthrop," he replied.

"Mrs. Knightley."

Emma inclined her head in acknowledgement. "Please, Miss Winthrop, will you not sit? I am certain the walk has tired you." She attempted to hide the smirk from her voice, as the older woman looked at her with a fierceness in her eyes.

"Little walks do not tire me, Mrs. Knightley. My endurance is much greater than many women younger than myself."

Frank snickered, and Emma realized they were no longer discussing rambles through the woods. She stood to remove herself from the two people with whom she wished to have no more associations.

"Please stay, Mrs. Knightley."

"I thank you, but I must find George."

"He is quite content discussing angling with my brother down by the river. No, I am certain we could spend a few more minutes in discussion before you interrupt their conversation."

Emma Knightley, mistress of one of the most respected estates in England, was being dictated to by a single woman almost twice her age, and she was not having it! "I thank you for the advice but will find my *husband* just the same."

"Frank. I do believe your father was looking for you. You might find him."

"Very well, Rosalind. Emma, stay and rest with Miss Winthrop. I will be back soon with the whole party, and we can then eat luncheon."

Emma stilled, shocked at the familiarity between the two individuals. After Frank Churchill walked away, she turned toward Miss Winthrop. "I was not aware of the intimacy you shared with Mr. Churchill. I believed you to be somewhat recent acquaintances."

Miss Winthrop sat across from Emma on the blanket, and she did likewise.

"Frank and I have been acquaintances, as you say, for a number of years, upon my return from America. He has only recently been introduced to my brother through a business venture, but that is of little interest to you. At any rate, I wished to thank you for your hospitality at Donwell."

"Of course," Emma said, attempting to ignore the feeling of nausea welling up inside.

Miss Winthrop turned from her and looked out over the expansive horizon. "Box Hill holds a special place in my heart, Mrs. Knightley. I understand from Frank that, when you were younger, it was the furthest you had ever traveled from Highbury. For me, the pursuits were not so juvenile. It is here where I could have forsaken the name Winthrop and taken one which has brought you joy and fortune. But alas, it was not meant to be."

Emma stifled a gasp at the brazen declaration and knew not what to say. *Could this woman truly have just spoken of her past with my husband?*

"I know it comes as no surprise, for I am certain Mrs. Weston referred to it, but George and I were secretly engaged and were to marry when he left Cambridge."

Her words took on a hollow quality and, for a moment, Emma could only hear the throbbing within her ears.

"However, I refused to wait and broke our engagement—and his heart. I wonder he waited so long to marry..." She smiled. "He eventually knew he had to marry to secure an heir for Donwell. It appears he chose sensibly on that score. Four children, no less? Three boys and one girl? Very well for a country wife, indeed."

The two women glared at each without pretense, until finally the elder spoke.

"Fear not, Mrs. Knightley, for the virtue of your husband. I am much too content in my independence to want to be shackled to *any* man. Even one as desirable as George. No, my time to attach myself to a husband has passed, and I am quite satisfied with my lot in life: a wealthy, attractive woman who is a threat to all and yet to no one at the same time."

The sound of cackling crows interrupted the woman's declaration and breathed life into Emma's words. "It is not entirely my husband for whom I fear."

A questioning gaze met hers before she continued. "You have stated you have no desire for a husband. Yet you act to lure away others'. You are intent on destroying lives and will take no responsibility for the wreckage left strewn behind you."

The elder woman laughed, licking her lips and shaking her head. "You are not the mindless beauty I took you for. No, Mrs. Knightley. The wreckage I leave is no fault of my own. There is only wreckage when the men themselves heed the song of the siren. I cannot make them listen. They choose to, as you are well aware."

Emma pushed back her shoulders and took in a deep breath. "You prey upon men who are weak, who have no substance to offer you. I do not fear you for my own sake, *Miss* Winthrop. Nor do I fear you any longer for the sake of my marriage. I fear you not at all. Instead, I only feel pity."

With her head raised as a queen, Emma stood and walked toward the footmen to instruct them to begin setting out the luncheon, praying the woman who she had expounded upon with "no fear" would not see her wilt under her own insecurities.

It had been three nights. Three nights since the door from his chamber had opened into hers. She felt her punishment, but she knew it would not, *could* not last for much longer. He had watched her at dinner and when the men had rejoined them after their cigars and port. He had tried to catch her eye, but she felt like a rabbit, skittish at any attention, for fear she would be openly wounded again. She had laughed gaily with Mrs. Weston, had conferred quietly with Mrs. Churchill, and had listened soberly to Miss Bates, all the while avoiding him. Him, and the Winthrops.

Miss Winthrop had not learned her lesson from their discussion at Box Hill. She had simpered and coyly smiled at Frank, even more so than Emma thought possible for a woman of her age. It was actually quite an embarrassment, and it seemed that way for all in attendance. Even Frank had been more subdued, sticking closer to Jane and Miss Bates than Emma could have imagined. She was curious as to why, but the one person she wished to discuss her observations with was not speaking to her.

But there he was. As the clock in the hallway struck two, a light tap could be heard at her chamber door. The soft scrape of wood across the floor and squeak of the hinges supported her claim, but she did not speak. A tear began to form and rolled down her cheek. She lay still, attempting to feign sleep, wondering if he would turn and leave.

As he had done so many nights before, he raised the counterpane and slid into bed beside her. But instead of playing with her hair or kissing her softly, he wrapped his arms around her waist and pulled her to him, cradling her in his arms.

His breath warmed her neck, and she lay motionless, her body rigid. Then he spoke. "Forgive me, my Emma. I was wrong."

At those seven words, she turned to face him and soundly accepted his apology.

Later, when his apology had been exhausted and her forgiveness spent, they lay under the covers, his fingertips tracing her face.

"Emma, you did not deserve my doubt, and I am wholly ashamed I gave it."

She said nothing for a moment, reveling in their intimacy. "I too must apologize. In our marriage, you have done nothing to earn my mistrust. I allowed my insecurity to rule my thoughts." She reached up and pressed her hand over his. "Forgive me?" She leaned into his caress as he kissed her forehead.

"Of course, my love."

After a moment, she continued quietly. "But although we have both spoken our regrets, I admit your actions wounded me." She looked down at the coverlet. "You sided with another woman, George—a woman I have never seen the likes of in all my days, and I am your wife. I know I am younger than you, and Miss Winthrop made sure I felt the ridiculousness—"

"Say no more of her."

She was surprised by the harshness in his tone.

"True, you are younger than I, but your level of understanding does you credit. She is a vindictive woman." Her eyes widened at his pronouncement.

His breathing increased, and she could see his jaw tighten. "No, my sweet girl. It is you who I should have championed. Not another." He pulled her tightly to his chest again and kissed her soundly. "Forgive me?"

She smiled and traced his jaw. "I have forgiven you once, George. I fear I do not have energy enough to forgive you again."

They lay in each other's arms quietly whispering promises of love, until they heard the sounds of servants beyond the doors.

"What happened to make you see things differently?"

He stiffened, then nuzzled into her neck. "Nothing."

"George, tell me. I am your wife."

He kissed her neck and blew out a hot breath. "I had noticed her behavior toward Frank today at Box Hill and then his ignoring her during and after dinner—"

"Yes. I noticed that as well. Do you know why his behavior changed so drastically toward her?"

"He and his father rode ahead of the party on the way home from the picnic. Weston informed him that he was no longer welcome at Randalls."

"What?"

"Emma, what I will tell you now cannot be repeated." She nodded her acquiescence and he continued. "Frank has not been at Randalls for two years…"

"Yes?"

"Two years ago, Mrs. Weston's lady's maid left to take care of her ailing mother and returned several months later."

"Yes. Her mother recovered fully. Anne and I were so pleased."

He was silent and she looked at him, comprehension dawning in her eyes. "She was with child?" He nodded. "And Frank…?" He nodded again.

"It was only discovered yesterday afternoon when Jane's maid overheard Anne's maid telling one of the girls in the kitchen. She was released this morning."

"And Jane?" He nodded, his features reflected in the moonlight. "That is why she is going to Ireland?"

"Not entirely. Miss Winthrop and Frank are...established acquaintances. Jane was told the Winthrops would not be at Randalls, but when Frank discovered they would be here for two weeks, he packed up his family and came."

"Poor Jane."

"Yes, but I am pleased to tell you that Weston has chosen Jane and his grandchildren over his son. Finally Frank will begin to feel there are consequences for his actions."

"And Miss Bates will travel to Ireland."

"Yes, bless Hetty's heart."

They lay there in silence while she burrowed deeper into the crevice of his arms. "Is there anything you have not told me?"

He was quiet for a moment longer.

"As I was retiring to my chambers, Miss Winthrop was discovered in my private study with an improper intent."

Emma sat up and turned to face him. "What?"

"Yes."

"Where is she now?" she began, throwing off the covers and marching toward the door leading to the hall. "I will—"

"Emma, if you're going to leave the room, you should grab a robe, or you will shock the footmen."

"There is no time to joke, George! I will go and have a word with—"

"They are gone."

"What?" she asked, mid-motion.

"They are gone. Her brother had come down to the library to get a book, discovered what could have occurred, and told his valet and her maid to pack them at once. He said he would send his apologies to you upon their arrival back in London."

He pushed himself up and leaned back against the headboard. "I had hoped her attentions to me had changed since we were in our youth. I believed they had, but I was wrong."

Emma walked over to the large chair by the fire and sat down. "What do you mean her attentions to you?"

He took a deep breath and rocked his head back and forth. "Rosalind Winthrop grew up desiring the title of mistress of Donwell. In truth, many young ladies did. Years have passed, and I never thought she would still hold onto those hopes. I felt no threat to you or to myself."

"I do believe you are correct. Being the mistress of Donwell was no longer her greatest hope. Being *your* mistress was. All of the benefits with none of the responsibility."

He was silent and kept his gaze lowered. "My anger with your statements three nights ago was not in the defense of her character but of my own. I could not conceive you would believe such vile thoughts of me."

"I did not wish to believe them, but you did not seem forthcoming. She said you had been secretly engaged."

"Ha!" he barked. "I told you, she *wished* that above all things. When we were younger, our families took a picnic to Box Hill, and she spent the day touting the benefit of a union between us. I was a young man of sixteen with little time for the childish desires of a girl who continued to sneak away from her governess."

"That is not how she explained it to me."

"It would not have been. Rosalind colors her stories as she likes."

"And this is how other people live? This is how other men and women behave?"

He reached his arms out to her, and she walked across the room and melted into them, burying her face like a child, as he stroked her hair.

"No, my love. This is not how other *men* and *women* behave. This is how people who are miserable in their own circumstances attempt to bring others down to their misery. There is a clarity in the darkness, Emma. Ironically, one sometimes becomes strongest living in ignorance of the behaviors of the world. You, my wife, are purity, seeking that light. You are my blessing, and I would not trade you for any woman."

She pulled back and looked him deeply in the eyes. "Truly?"

"Truly. There is only one Emma and I love her for all her imperfections, as she loves me."

As the rooster crowed, she buried herself deeper in his arms, unwilling to abandon the comfort of the last several hours. They had battled demons they did not know they possessed and had been triumphant.

If Emma had still an anxious feeling, a momentary doubt of its being possible for Mr. Knightley to attach himself to another woman, it was not long that she suffered from the recurrence of such uncertainty. It was the occupation of her husband to remind her that, although discourse is valuable in finding solutions to misunderstandings, often it is united silence that brings true joy to a marriage.

And he did.

ANNGELA SCHROEDER has a degree in English with a concentration in British literature and a master's in education. She has taught high school for twenty years and could imagine no job as fulfilling (other than maybe being Oprah). She loves to travel, bake, and watch college football with her husband of eighteen years and three rambunctious sons. Her weaknesses are yellow cake with chocolate frosting, a ripe watermelon, and her father's Arabic food, namely grape leaves and falafel. She lives in California where she dreams of Disney adventures and trips across the pond. Follow her on Twitter: @schros2000, Instagram: Anngela Schroeder-Author, and facebook.com/AnngelaSchroederAuthor/

THE SIMPLE THINGS

J. MARIE CROFT

HETTY BATES

At first glance, Miss Hetty Bates would not be considered a rational creature. Although universally adored by her neighbours, her rambling and nonsensical speeches make her the object of ridicule by Emma, while her often ironic disclosures unwittingly reveal clues to the intrigues in Highbury. Despite living in genteel poverty, she maintains an outward appearance of cheer and contented independence. And yet: *"Seldom, very seldom, does complete truth belong to any human disclosure; seldom can it happen that something is not a little disguised or a little mistaken."*
—**Chapter XLIX,** *Emma.*

THE SIMPLE THINGS

The walls of Quince Cottage shook from the force. Windowpanes rattled. China in the mahogany cabinet jounced. Even the deaf collie scrambled to his feet from a deep sleep, growling at the unknown disturbance sensed in his bones.

Within another body, the shock reached deeper than mere bone. Penetrating skin, passing through sternum and ribs, the jolt—and its resulting irrevocability—lodged in the soft, beating organ sheltered within her five-and-thirty-year-old breast.

An elder lady, knitting abandoned on her lap, fingers clutching the lace-trimmed collar at her throat, looked to the other with sympathetic, watery eyes. Even had the slamming of the door not registered within Mrs. Bates's diminished hearing, her daughter's agonised countenance spoke volumes. Hetty had done the unthinkable.

Mr. Franklin's abrupt, angry departure heralded their own imminent leave-taking. Soon, they would be evicted from the cosy cottage they had shared since the Reverend Mr. Bates met his Maker. Tears welled in the widow's eyes, spilling onto her cheeks.

Smiling bravely as she sat beside her on the settee, Hetty patted her mother's hand. "There, there." Raising her voice, she enunciated carefully. "'Tis as it should be, although I suppose I *should* feel some degree of sorrow or disgrace. Indeed, I should. Me, rejecting an offer. At my age. Imagine! Well, we do not have to *imagine*, do we, Mother? 'Tis all too real." Taking a deep, shuddering breath, she spoke around the lump in her throat. "To be perfectly honest, I feel...lighter now. Less burdened and... and... What is the word? Liberated. Yes, liberated, to be sure! Freed, unfettered...like a bird in flight. Free as a bird!" Hetty's half-suppressed laugh dissolved into a sob. "Emancipated from bonds of slavery. Released from lifelong imprisonment. Unshackled. Ah! That is the exact word, is it not? Unshackled. Yes, unshackled, indeed."

Mrs. Bates gasped. "Hetty! Marriage, as your late sister could have attested, means neither servitude nor captivity. Being a man's wife, his helpmeet, *can* be satisfying if—"

"*If* I respected or, better yet, loved the man. But—heavens!—I can scarcely *tolerate* Mr. Franklin. What woman in her right mind could?" Fingers clamping over lips from which such unprecedented, bitter criticism had escaped, Hetty winced. "Dear me, how unChristian. But, Mother, he called me a silly, spiteful spinster, a tabby. He said I was a feather-headed, old fool. He said I would remain an old maid because no other man would have me. He said... Well, I forget *all* he said. But *he* was the scatterbrain—not scraping his boots before entering our parlour. See? Right there on the floor. Mud! Or worse, for he most likely walked here through his fields."

With a gentle hand on the woman's arm, Hetty restrained her mother. "No, no. Stay where you are. I shall get the mop and... Oh! Do you suppose any of our dishes shattered when he slammed the door? I should check on that pretty plate. You know, the one with the roses and ivy pattern we were given by— Oh, bother!" Hetty tittered. "I have quite forgotten from whence it came. Do you remember? I am sure you must. It was Mrs. Buckley, was it not? Or Mrs. Perry, perhaps."

Returning her daughter's earlier gesture, Mrs. Bates patted Hetty's hand. "You have renounced acceptance of a marriage proposal. 'Twas likely your last chance to wed. You *must* have regrets. Forget broken pottery and mud. Tend, instead, to the painful shards within your heart and the mire in which we are now deeply rooted."

Hetty insisted she had no regrets and, together, they would wriggle out of their current tight spot. Her kind heart suffered only for any disappointed hopes Mr. Franklin might have had for his future.

Teardrops dampening the coarse fabric of her apron, Mrs. Bates wrung her hands. "Your marrying would have had practical advantages. The widower would have taken us into his home, Hetty. Provided for us. All he asked in return was that you tend his needs and those of his children, his house, his kitchen garden, chickens, and dairy. You could have provided *me* with a comfortable old age at Tanglewood. Whatever shall we do now? You threw away our chance at security. A jilted landlord will surely evict us. Once that happens, we will have nowhere to go. No place to live."

"Upon my honour, I will take care of you, Mother. I promise! We shall shift fine on our own. Remember what Father used to say: God helps those who help themselves. So, we shall help ourselves. If ever there were people who, without having great wealth themselves, had every thing they could wish for, I am sure it is us." Gaining her feet, Hetty looked around the modest parlour. "Now, what was I about to do before *he* arrived? Ah! I was going to see if we have any post."

"Of course, we have toast," cried Mrs. Bates, no longer able to see her daughter's lips. "Or we could have, once Patty browns bread over the fire. Tell her I shall have mine with currant jelly. The last of the ham might be nice, too, and a warm cup of caudle."

Hetty reminded her mother their maid had gone to Highbury on an errand. "But I shall be quite happy to toast bread for you. Quite happy."

In the kitchen, she rattled about, talking to herself as she worked. Twice, Mrs. Bates called out, reminding her to bring toast and jelly, ham and caudle. Humming contentedly, Hetty returned to the parlour, making room for the tray on a cluttered table in front of the settee.

"Hetty, my girl," cried her mother upon being handed a plate of seed cake and a cup of weak tea made with twice-used leaves. "Where are the prunes I asked for? Where is my baked apple and gruel?"

"Prunes and—? Oh! How silly of me. I fear Mr. Franklin had the right of it. I *am* a bit absent-minded."

Tut-tutting and taking up her work, Hetty sat, making a dozen neat stitches before jumping to her feet. "Bless me! I have completely forgotten.

Wherever is my stupid head today?" She dashed from the room and was back in a trice, donning spencer, bonnet, and gloves. "Enjoy your tea, Mother, while I fetch the post."

"Wait, Hetty," said Mrs Bates, glancing through the window. "It looks like rain. You know what Mr. Woodhouse would say about being out in the wet."

"'Tis only spitting. A cold, damp day shall not deter me. No, indeed, it shall not. Not if there might be a letter from dear Jane. A letter surely awaits us by now, it being Wednesday. The post office, of all places, shall always have power to draw me out, even in worse mizzle than today. If I do not dally, I will reach home before the rain amounts to much. Should I be caught in a deluge, a letter from my niece will make the soaking worthwhile."

"Are you truly well, my dear? Are you not weighed down by our landlord's anger, our impending situation?"

"Oh, goodness, no. I am well. Stubborn and scatterbrained, perhaps. Resolute and resolved, to be sure. But quite content. One does not need to be married to be happy. No need. Drink your tea now while it is hot. Do not fret over me. A letter from Jane will be the very thing to take my mind off my worries. The doings of a thirteen-year-old girl—the very thing!" After placing a few coins in her reticule and ensuring her mother's comfort, Hetty made to leave.

"Wait. You are not going to Goddard's, are you?"

"No, no. Not there. Mrs. Goddard and I had a nice, long chat the other night at the soirée. I shall, though, while in Highbury, look for apartments to let." Turning away, she sniffled while rifling through her reticule. "Now, where *is* that handkerchief?" Hands on hips, she cast her eyes over the room. "Mister Uff, have you seen the new handkerchief I was working on? I left it somewhere. Did you filch it, naughty dog? Oh, never mind. Come along, old boy. Although it looks like rain, we shall have a nice stroll to the post office."

"Hetty, my girl, wait! The handkerchief you were hemming has been sewn onto your skirt. I will not have you walk about the village with a half-stitched piece of cambric on your muslin. It looks dreadfully like a patch. We still have *some* pride, you know."

~

Along the tree-lined road leading to Highbury, Hetty prattled to the faithful dog trotting at her side. "Pride. We may not have much, but at least we still have *that*. I *do* have pride, Mister Uff. Indeed, I do. What I do *not* have—do not want—is a husband I neither like nor respect, one I might eventually grow to resent or despise. Yet I wonder at the wisdom of loving a person so dearly that when they are no longer with you, it feels as though your heart has been wrenched from your breast." Squeezing eyes shut and sniffing, she spoke in a thicker voice. "I refer to the passing of my sister and father, you understand. No one else. No other. Almost everyone I love, save Jane, is here in Highbury—my mother and...and *you*, of course. I would be sad, indeed, to lose any more of those I love."

Hetty gazed fondly at her black and white dog. He was deaf as a post, but she had loved him at first sight. Old Mr. Martin had scratched his head at her poor choice and suggested another, but she was set on the flawed one, runt of the litter. The collie had been her loyal companion since that day in 1803, four years past. He loved her unconditionally and cared not that Hetty was plain or dull.

"Whatever will I do when the time comes to bid *you* farewell? I have lost too many loved ones, Mister Uff. You must promise to stay with me forever."

Barked at by the collie, a bushy-tailed rodent scurried up an oak, chattering as it went.

"My, my! What a talkative creature. As chattery as a magpie, and— Ah! I remember something else Mr. Franklin said. He said I could talk the hind legs off a donkey. Imagine!" Hetty and her companion took a moment to watch the squirrel settle on a branch and nibble on a seed. "I talk too much. I know I do. I suppose I always have. Being the nervous sort, I cannot help myself. I try *so* hard to please others. 'Tis difficult, though, in certain company, to feign indifference when one feels quite the opposite. Mostly, I am afraid of being off my guard, babbling a secret— someone else's or my own. Added to all *that*, I live with a hard-of-hearing mother and a stone-deaf dog. Well, one must have *some* conversation, after all."

Having slipped down her wet nose, her spectacles were pushed into place. Through them, Hetty peered for a moment into the misty distance, into her past. Recollecting herself, she gestured for the dog to walk on. "Oh, I *know* I say far too much. Yet if people only knew how much more I *want* to say but do not, they would give me *some* credit."

The road to Highbury was a good one, if muddy. The small farms they passed were neat. The hills, woods, and meadows were beautiful. The Surrey countryside, though having nothing wild or bold about it, was exceedingly agreeable. Raindrops splashed into puddles and beat a gentle tattoo on lobed leaves of surrounding oaks. Albeit her day had started dismally and her walking companions were a steady drizzle and a wet, smelly dog, it was almost impossible for Hetty to gaze upon shower-soaked verdure without pleasure.

Above all, she delighted in life's simple pleasures. There was no equal to sharing meals with loved ones, receiving visitors, exchanging letters, hearing a child's giggle, or walking with her dog. Hetty loved all God's creatures—all save gnats, rats, adders, and Mrs. Otway's pugnacious pugs. She could live quite happily without encountering any of those particular creatures ever again.

Also having an unfavourable opinion of her erstwhile suitor, she passed his fields with trepidation, all the while congratulating herself on escaping a martinet's clutches. Briefly, she considered stopping at the fence to chat with one of the man's beasts of burden, but Hetty was too kindhearted to deprive an innocent donkey of its hindmost limbs.

"We are fortunate to not be beasts of burden, Mister Uff. Upon my honour, I would not care to be one of Mr. Franklin's such beasts. No, I would not. To labour for *his* benefit. To tend to *his* needs. Knitting and mending his socks. *Washing* his odious socks. Ugh! Well, I do not know for *certain* his socks are odious, but I imagine they might be. What the man wants is not a wife but an unpaid servant. And his children! How many?" Hetty counted on her fingers. "Bethany, Iris, Oscar, Gerald, Portia... Did I mention Magnus? And— Ah! Oscar. Or did I count him already? Bless me. What an awful mother I would be." A sob escaped, unbidden. "I could not even remember all my children's names." Tears mingled with raindrops as drizzle and heaviness of heart intensified. She gave up blindly rooting through her reticule for a handkerchief, removed her spectacles, and wiped her face on a soggy sleeve.

Taking refuge beneath a leafy oak during a cloudburst, she called Mister Uff to join her. The deaf collie continued down the road until stopping and turning around in search of his wayward mistress. Then, wagging his tail, the dog—wet and mud-covered—trotted back, promptly shaking the mud from his coat onto Hetty's clothing.

Rolling her eyes, she sighed at her predicament while petting the dog's soft, sodden head. "Sufficient unto the day is the evil thereof. *That* is what Father would have said. It means each day has enough burdens of wickedness and suffering, so we should avoid adding to them. Do you understand me, Mister Uff?"

Peeling damp, soiled fabric away from her legs, Hetty fretted over adding to the burdens of their maid-of-all-work. "Patty shall have her hands full now. Oh, fie! I forgot to mop up the mud left by that horrid man's boots."

Hetty held out her palm beyond the tree cover, judging the rain's severity. "Whenever someone was overcome by difficulty, my father would say every bad situation has some good aspect to it. Then he would quote something about sable clouds turning forth silver linings. For the life of me, I *still* cannot comprehend any good to come from either his or my sister's passing. None at all! But, of all the misfortunes suffered during the most harrowing years of that dreadful decade, there *were* a couple good consequences. Jane, after all, was born in ninety-three. But still..."

Shaking off memories and raindrops, Hetty put on a brave face. "Come along. The sun is now breaking through."

As they walked, Hetty prattled on to her dog about the late vicar's love of proverbs. "Do unto others as you would have them do unto you. *That* one I particularly like. I try to always act in accordance with the Golden Rule, but— Oh, look! A full rainbow. How lovely!"

Gaze sweeping over the arch of colour, Hetty, without conscious thought, glanced up the lane leading to Tanglewood Farm and gasped upon descrying Mr. Franklin between the barn and the house, silhouetted against the sun, facing the road, watching her.

Burly and plain as a pikestaff, Ralph Franklin was a landowner but not of gentle birth. Known throughout the neighbourhood as a gruff, clumsy, confrontational sort, he was neither well-educated nor well-spoken. Not an engaging man at the best of times, the widower had not taken Hetty's rejection graciously.

The night prior to her one and only marriage proposal, Hetty and her mother had been invited to a soirée at Donwell Abbey. Perhaps she had envied the few happy couples in attendance. Or it could be she was simply exhausted the next morning from staying out so late. Perhaps she had not been thinking clearly, the result of too much watered-down sherry from the night before. She might have grown tired of everyone asking why she had not yet married. Or, conceivably, it was something else entirely. Whatever the reason, Hetty Bates, the morning after the soirée, in a moment of weakness, had agreed to marry the farmer.

Throughout the rest of that day, she walked around in an anxious, confused state, worried for her future. Tossing and turning during the night, Hetty admitted she had been far too hasty in accepting the man's offer. Her pride revolted at such a union, one in which she would live under a tyrant's complete control.

After Patty had been sent off to the post office the next morning, mother and daughter settled with their work baskets while a pot of thin gruel bubbled, forgotten, over the fire. As Hetty prepared to tell Mrs. Bates about her change of heart regarding Mr. Franklin, the man himself had knocked at the cottage door. Without awaiting an invitation, he strode into the parlour like he owned the place, which, in point of fact, he did.

"Good day, Mrs. Bates," he said, bowing curtly. "Hetty, I would have a word with you." With a jerk of his head, he indicated a corner that would allow them a modicum of privacy, out of the older woman's view.

Hetty followed hesitantly. Without having waited for her to first do so, the farmer had taken a seat. Appalled at his lack of manners, she eased into a chair, trying, in vain, to remember when she had given him leave to use her Christian name.

In no uncertain terms, Mr. Franklin informed Hetty he had been to the vicar, banns would be read starting the following Sunday, and they would be married the morning after the third reading.

Slowly shaking her head, Hetty spoke in the meekest of tones. "No." Unsure if he had heard or not, she met his blank stare. "I thank you, but that is not what I want. Not what I want, at all. I am sorry, so very sorry, Mr. Franklin. Indeed, I am. But I… Well, I have given it much thought. In fact, I hardly slept a wink last night—not a wink, I daresay!—for thinking so much. Think, think, think is all I did. Which is, perhaps, what I *should* have done in the first place…but did not. And, the night before last, I was quite late at Donwell Abbey. So, I have not slept much these past two nights. But, you see, I have decided… That is, I think it best tha—"

"Spit it out, woman! Lawks, you could talk the hind legs off a donkey and still not say nothin'. I ain't got all day!"

Shoulders and back hunched, Hetty whispered, "I think it best the banns *not* be read."

"Not read? Not read! Are you daft? If you think I'm gonna pay fer a license, yer thicker than Tewksbury mustard. The banns *will* be read, as planned." Gaining his feet, he towered over Hetty as she cowered in her chair. "From now on, visits to Donwell and Hartfield are forbidden. We ain't of the same sphere as them families. No wife of *mine* will be putting on such airs."

"Not visit Hartfield? But, but… Mother is Mr. Woodhouse's particular friend! We are blessed to have his—"

"Woman, didn't you hear me? I said no more visits to Hartfield or Donwell!" Slapping his cap atop his head, he snarled, "I'll see you in church the Sunday after next, when the first banns *will* be called."

Surging to her feet, Hetty stood as tall as she could, shoulders squared. "No, sir. They will *not*. I have changed my mind. I am sorry, Mr. Franklin, but I cannot marry you."

"Oh yes, you will! You can't refuse me now. I've already been to the vicar and paid £3. I'll not be humiliated." Grabbing an arm, he shook her until Hetty's teeth rattled. "I won't have it, you hear?"

Hetty struggled to free herself from his painful grasp and a frightening future. "Please, sir! You are hurting me. I am sorry if my refusal has hurt *you*, but…but… Here is a thought! To save face, I give you leave to say *you* rejected *me*."

"I *am* now rejecting you, you feather-headed old fool!" Pushing her aside, he sneered. "Who do you think you are, coquetting and playing the jilt? You're nothin' but a pitiful spinster, so miserable as to be ridiculous and an easy target for taunting remarks of youngsters. Mark my words, Hetty Bates, no other man will have you. Who wants a silly old-maid beyond childbearing years and with tongue enough for two sets of teeth? Not me! You'll always be nothin' but a tabby. An ape leader!"

After bestowing another sneer upon Hetty and a mocking tip of his cap to Mrs. Bates, Ralph Franklin stormed off, slamming the door with such force that the walls shook.

Hetty's decision to walk away from a dismal future had been made almost as easily as she then turned away from Mr. Franklin's glaring at her from the opposite end of the lane. He had not moved from where he stood in his yard. She doubted he had even noticed the beauty of the rainbow before him.

"Well, at least *this* time, the choice to walk away was *mine*. But I *do* feel sorry for Mr. Franklin, Mister Uff. Upon my honour, I do. But I could not agree to live under his thumb. I may live to please others, but total servitude and martyrdom do not, after all, appeal to me. I tried to let the poor man down gently, but he lashed out at me. Quite cruelly, he did. Oh, dear. I pray any resentment will not be taken out on his children. They may be a tag-rag and bobtail lot, unkempt and wild, but they do not deserve misplaced anger."

In vain, Hetty searched her reticule again for a handkerchief. Tears blurred her vision. Raindrops had left her spectacles dotted. "Well, at least Mr. Franklin is an *honest* man…no compunction at all in pointing out *my* faults. But he called me names, accused me of playing the jilt. 'Tis true… I should not have led him on for an entire day. But is it not, after all, a women's prerogative to change her mind?"

Wagging his tail and barking his namesake "Uff, uff," the collie trotted off to greet a bedraggled figure walking towards them.

"Oh! 'Tis our dear Patty. Well, of course, it is. I sent her off earlier to fetch the post."

"Miss Bates! Miss Bates!" In the same splashed condition as Hetty and her dog, the maid ran towards them, panting and waving a handful of letters. "The post come, ma'am. And, as you hoped, one is from Miss Fairfax. There be one from Mrs. Clark, too. I kept them all dry, I did, inside me coat."

Smiling broadly, Hetty accepted the correspondence, hugging the papers to her damp breast. There was nothing in the world so precious as a letter from her late sister's daughter.

"I wish I could break the seal and read Jane's tidings here and now. That would never do, I suppose, to stand in the middle of a muddy road reading one's letters, would it? No, no. I shall wait until I am back at the cottage, warm and dry, although I am as eager to hear Maria's news as Jane's." Stashing the post in her reticule, Hetty turned to her maid. "Now, speaking of news, what have you heard from John Adby at the Crown? He always has the most interesting village gossip."

"Well! Miss Nash told him Goddard's has taken on a new pupil, a Miss Bickerton. And Mr. Weaver-Smythe once again sent Mrs. Goddard enough comfits to share with all the girls, but everyone suspects he's sweet on her and has been ever since that summer the Buckleys come for a visit. Folks say they was all fooled at the time into thinking he fancied *you*."

"Hush, girl! There must be more worthy news than *that* old rumour."

"Miss Bates, you're blushing!"

"I most certainly am *not*! I am merely flushed from…from walking, is all."

"But you was standing still, looking in your retic—"

"Pray, Patty, what *else* did John Adby have to say?"

"All the Perry children have croup, and Mr. Mason's son up and joined the army, he did. The young man won't even be at Highbury's next assembly."

"Stupid wars!" cried Hetty, stamping her foot, sending mud flying. "Why must men be forever fighting wars? Because of war, we have a great scarcity of men. Not that *I* care a fig anymore. But, still, there *are* young ladies hereabouts not past caring about such a shortage."

The maid nodded. "Aye. There's a great scarcity of men in general… and a still *greater* scarcity of any that are good for much."

"Patty! Good gracious." Tittering, Hetty turned towards Highbury.

"But, Miss Bates," called Patty, frowning, "are ye not heading home?"

"Honestly, I do not know where my stupid head is today. Yes, of course. There is no need to go to the post office, is there? You have our letters already. Or *I* do. I put them in my reticule, after all." Hetty looked towards the village. "But... Was there not another reason for my going to Highbury?" Shrugging, she turned, moving into step beside the maid. "Those poor, poor Perry children! Well, their father being the apothecary, I suppose they are in good enough hands. Mr. Perry will treat them with syrups of squill and poppy like he did for the Franklin children. Oh, no!" Hetty's eyes grew wide behind her spectacles. "Patty, please tell me you did not spread news of my engagement. You did not tell John Adby, did you?"

"No, miss. Such an announcement is for you and yer Mr. Franklin to make."

"He is not *my* Mr. Franklin. There will be *no* announcement, and certainly no wedding. Ah! I remember. My other reason for going into Highbury was to inquire about rooms to let. I did it, Patty. I turned down Mr. Franklin. Mother is of the opinion I should have married solely for the sake of being married, no matter the man is an oaf." Hetty gasped, covering her mouth. "Forget I said that. I am still in ill humour, it seems. But, dear Patty, you appear horror-stricken. Come now, why must any woman go from being under her father's influence to being under another man's thumb?" Hetty rubbed at her arm, the one still bearing the imprint of Franklin's cruel grip. "I am as opposed to the idea as a forefinger is to a thumb!"

"Well, you know what they say. What's a queen without a king?"

"What's a queen without a king?" Hetty tittered. "*More powerful*, historically speaking."

"But, ma'am, is not marriage a woman's crowning achievement?"

"I rather think some husbands must be naught but royal nuisances. And if being single was good enough for Good Queen Bess, then it shall be good enough for *me*. I shall remain unwed, reigning over my *own* domain—as tiny and insignificant as it may be. But, dear girl, you are shivering! We must get you warm and dry. Yes, *that* is our first priority, for you are very wet and miserable, indeed. I would not have you catch cold. No, no, that would not do at all. And those boots! Are they not the ones giving you blisters? Tut-tut. We must do something about those, too."

"What about looking for rooms to let, ma'am?"

"Another day, Patty, another day." Trudging onward, Hetty sighed. "Dislodged once more—first from the vicarage, now from Quince Cottage, which I rather liked. Ah, well. Let us hurry home and get you fixed up. Come along, Mister Uff. Mother will want to hear Jane's letter. It will cheer her somewhat, after being so distressed by my decision."

Lips pressed firmly, Hetty warded off another round of tears. "They— Mr. Franklin and Mother, that is—were not entirely wrong, you know. 'Tis certain I shall never again receive a—mind the puddle, dear!—never again receive a marriage proposal. But I have already been years on the shelf. Hah! It *was* Mrs. Buckley. The plate was given to us by Mrs. Buckley, not Mrs. Perry. I remember thanking her and admiring the pattern—roses and ivy, so pretty!—as I placed it on a shelf in the cabinet. We have never used it, though, for it is rather delicate. Well, if a pretty dish may sit on the shelf, then so may plain, old Hetty Bates. Now, as soon as we get home, you must take off those boots, and I will set the kettle to boil."

"Miss Bates, that be *my* job! You are right kind, though. So interested in everyone's welfare. You *notice* things—like uncomfortable boots—and care about people. You'd have made some man a fine wife and been a good mother."

"I may be a middle-aged spinster without beauty or much in the way of intelligence, but I *do* watch and listen"—*and ward off questions of a personal nature with my inconsequential chatter. And, notwithstanding the garrulousness of my talk, I am perfectly capable of rational thought from time to time.* "If a woman cannot marry the gentleman she admires, why should she be obliged to marry one she does not? The sacred institution of matrimony is too often perverted, Patty. Perverted by men and women shackling themselves to a mate for whom they feel no special regard. No attachment. No affection. No ardent admiration. No, that is not the life for me. I will not doom myself to a marriage of apathy, misery, or fear. I would rather live independently, if poor." *And, as blind as I was to another man's faults, I have clearly seen Mr. Franklin's flaws—the scourge! Who needs such men in their life?*

Shoulders squared, chin high, Hetty strode on. "Being single is not such a terrible fate. Indeed, it is not. I have been blessed with an excellent mother, the most wonderful niece, the best of neighbours, and you, such a hard-working maid. Once I find another affordable place for the three of us to live, I shall make our small income suffice. Mother shall want for nothing. Nor shall you. As for me, I have been—and shall forevermore be —content with my life."

In such a state of single blessedness, Hetty wore her muslin mob-cap with pride and devoted her life to the comfort of family, relations, friends, and neighbours. She loved her mother, her niece, her dog; and, while they had lived, she had loved her father and younger sister.

Once upon a time, she also thought she knew how it felt to love and be loved by a man.

Until 1792, the Buckley family had lived a stone's throw from the ill-situated, old vicarage, home of the Reverend Mr. Bates, his wife, and daughters. The two families socialised with the same set of neighbours; and, when they were little girls, Henrietta—or Hetty, as she was known—and her younger sister, Jane, played together with Maria Buckley and endured the teasing of John, their friend's older brother.

Though childhood games had been left behind, Hetty, Jane, and Maria remained inseparable. From their mothers, the girls learned all that was necessary to become fine wives—housekeeping, a smattering of French, the rudiments of music, plus the fine arts of letter writing, dancing, and shopping for ribbons, shoe roses, and other essential fripperies.

Jane sewed a fine stitch without squinting and helped her bespectacled sister do the same. Hetty had not cared for such instruction until, with great patience, Jane succeeded where Mrs. Bates had failed. And, dutifully, Jane practiced her scales. In Hetty's opinion, her sister played their small Broadwood pianoforte with singular skill and sang psalms like an angel in their father's church.

Admired by all for their similar, sweet natures, Jane Bates and Maria

Buckley bloomed from pretty girls into accomplished, handsome young women while the eldest of the three, Hetty, was considered dull and plain.

Upon the return of his womenfolk from a local assembly, Mr. Bates was informed his younger daughter had danced all except one set, while Hetty had been asked to stand up once.

"Yet I had a marvellous time, Father. I tapped my foot and spoke to ever so many of our neighbours. I had a book with me but did not even open the cover. Talk, talk, talk. No time to read. My face ached from smiling so much, and my throat was parched—parched!—from all the chit-chat. An excellent orgeat lemonade slaked my thirst, though. *Three* orgeat lemonades, to be exact. No, no, it was *four*. One while Jane danced with Mr. John Knightley. Another when she stood up with his elder brother. One while she danced with Mr. Larkins, and one last lemonade after my own set with Mr. George Knightley. Orgeat lemonade and a comfortable chair. The very things for one's comfort! I only left my seat to visit the ladies' retiring room, twice, and the one time I danced."

"And you, Jane? Did you have a pleasant evening?"

"I did enjoy the dancing, Father, but I wish dear Hetty had been asked more often."

"Alas, my dear. A good book and a good woman are excellent things for those who know how justly to appreciate their value. There are men, however, who judge of both from the beauty of the covering."

He kissed their cheeks as his daughters bid him a good night then climbed the stairs to their room. On the way, Hetty overheard her mother complaining about muffled voices and the musicians not playing loudly enough.

Mrs. Bates grumbled again about hushed tones when she, accompanied by her daughters, visited the sick and elderly in the parish. But it was on one of those unremarkable calls that the remarkable happened. In a village suffering from a scarcity of eligible young men, Jane Bates met the excellent Lieutenant Fairfax, an infantry regiment officer who had come to Highbury to pay respects to his dying, maternal grandmother.

Seven months later, the same dashing lieutenant returned to the village to woo, then marry, eighteen-year-old Jane. Their wedding had its day of fame and pleasure, hope and interest. Then he whisked her away from the vicarage and from her twenty-year-old sister. It was the same year in which the Buckley family moved to London to ply their trade, saddlery, in a more lucrative market.

Heavy-hearted upon being at once deprived of a most beloved sister and a dear friend, Hetty wrote to Jane weekly and to Maria monthly. Her only comfort came with their replies.

In ninety-three, the post brought joyous tidings of a grandchild for Mr. and Mrs. Bates, a niece for Hetty. Widespread happiness spanned the Channel and lasted three years, ending upon receipt of a letter to Mrs. Fairfax announcing her husband had lost his life in battle on foreign soil. The death that left Jane a widow occurred after the brave lieutenant had saved his superior officer, Colonel Campbell, from a similar fate during a severe camp-fever.

A tear-stained missive from their younger daughter relayed the grim facts to Mr. and Mrs. Bates. A similarly smudged letter to Hetty spelled out Jane's melancholy thoughts. She spoke of sinking in grief and of returning to the bosom of her family once the packing of her meagre belongings was overseen.

Two Janes—one frail, the other an active tot—arrived in Highbury a fortnight later. In hugging her sister, Hetty expressed genuine sorrow. Secretly, she rejoiced in having her small family intact again, and she fell in love with its new addition.

Mrs. Fairfax had returned, in mourning, to her childhood home with not only a fatherless daughter but a troublesome cough in her lungs. Grief, they all thought, had settled heavily upon the young woman. Weight dropped from her frame at an alarming rate. She had neither the strength nor inclination to care for little Jane, but that office was happily taken on by Hetty.

Working with the vicarage's cook, Mrs. Bates tried to plump up Jane's figure, but the once vibrant woman grew ever gaunter. Gladdened when the bloom suddenly appeared again on the widow's cheeks, her family soon discovered the flush was, instead, due to a hectic fever.

At their housekeeper's insistence, Hetty fed her sister Mrs. Wright's concoction of equal parts rum and boiled milk sweetened with loaf sugar. More often than not, she coaxed the mixture between Jane's dry, cracked lips. At the risk of her own health, Hetty settled on a cot at her sister's side, wanting to be there when Jane awoke with night sweats. She read to her, bathed her forehead with lavender water, helped Patty change soaked bed linens and nightclothes, and went without sleep herself. Still, her beloved sister wasted away before her eyes.

When her daughter coughed up blood for the first time, Mrs. Bates sent for the apothecary.

Mr. Perry drew back from examination of the patient, shaking his head. "I am sorry," he told those assembled in the bedchamber, "but I suspect Mrs. Fairfax has the dreaded muslin disease. You must prepare yourselves for the worst. My assistant will bring cobweb pills for her, but there is nothing more—"

"No! No, no, no!" Teardrops slid down Hetty's cheeks as she bolted from the room. Unable to see through the blur, she stumbled outside, falling to her hands and knees, taking great gulps of air, expelling convulsive gasps. *No. Please, God, no. It cannot be. Mr. Perry is mistaken. 'Tis nothing more than a cold. Please, please, not consumption. Not that. Not my beloved Jane. She has a child who needs her. Jane is young and beautiful and may marry again. Take me instead. Please, God, take me instead!*

Mr. Bates found his eldest daughter curled in a ball, sobbing, on the cold ground beyond the back door. Gently, he helped her stand. Cradling Hetty's head against his own heavy heart, he embraced her, then led her into the house where they knelt and prayed together.

Fervent prayers unanswered, the disease claimed another victim. Mrs. Fairfax was interred in the graveyard of the same church in which, two-and-twenty years previously, she had been christened Jane Henrietta Bates.

Little Jane Fairfax became then the property, the charge, the consolation, the foundling of her grandparents and aunt, with every probability of her being permanently fixed there.

Hetty sat in the vicarage, numb, staring into nothingness—an empty space that could not be filled. Life's simple pleasures were meaningless without her sister to share them. *There is no purpose. What is my purpose?* Then she looked down at the girl slumbering on her lap. Lifting and hugging Jane to her breast, awakening her, Hetty wept along with the wailing child. *I am not strong enough for this. I cannot give her what she needs. What sort of life is this for my niece, for any girl? Being taught only what limited means can command? Growing up with no advantages of connexion or improvement? A life of dependence on others?*

Days dragged into weeks, weeks into months. All was grey—the sky, the bare oak trees, her soul, even her hair had sprouted colourless strands, seemingly overnight.

"I cannot imagine from whence the grey came," Hetty complained to her mother. "Do you suppose the essence of rosemary Patty uses when brushing my hair turns it so?"

Mrs. Bates smiled sadly, caressing her daughter's cheek. "No, dear. I am afraid it is rather the essence of *thyme*."

Hetty scowled at her mother's attempt at humour. "Time! If only I could turn back time, I would never let Fairfax steal away my sister. Why did he take her away, only to have her catch that dreaded disease? *He* is to blame. I *hate* him! And where was God when I asked him to save her? I *hate*—"

"Hush! Blasphemy! Your father must *never* hear such irreverence. I am ashamed of you!"

Dashing from the room, dashing away tears, Hetty ran and ran until she found herself on the road leading away from the village to the farms. Slumping onto an unforgiving rock, drawing knees to chest, she tried to have a good cry. But her tears had dried up. Her whole world was dry, cracked open like Jane's lips had been during the consumption.

Away from other eyes and ears, she blamed God, and she blamed Mr. Perry and Lieutenant Fairfax. Mostly, she blamed herself for not being able to save her sister. Hetty even blamed Jane for not fighting harder. *How could you leave us? You bore a daughter, then left her after only three short years. How dare you?* Then she trudged homeward, angry at herself for being angry at Jane.

Quietly, she tiptoed into church, sat in the vicarage-pew, and apologised for every profanity she had uttered. Unreasonable as she knew it to be, Hetty prayed for time to be reversed. She pleaded with God and bargained with him. *If you will make this a nightmare from which I may awaken, I promise to spend my life devoted to the care of others. I promise. Please, God, please.*

~

At the vicarage, the reverend hung up his coat and asked after Hetty. Patting his arm, Mrs. Bates inclined her head towards the back garden. Teeming with late spring greenery, the small space was alive with buzzing insects and birdsong.

"Wait, Henry." His wife passed him a letter. "Read this first."

He found Hetty perched on the bench beside the door. Eyes rimmed in red, she clutched a sodden handkerchief and stared at either the clock in the church steeple or into nothingness while Patty, their young maid, tried to teach Jane how to catch a ball.

"My child, it has been nigh on a half year." Mr. Bates sat heavily beside Hetty on the wooden seat. "'Tis high time to set aside grief, to regain some semblance of cheer. Look how much our dear Jane has grown in so short a time. She has been to us a silver lining set forth by sable clouds. Your niece looks upon you as her mother, you know. She should not witness your sorrow."

"It is *for* little Jane that I weep, Father. What will her future be, do you suppose? Servitude or... I would not have her follow in *my* footsteps. Four-and-twenty. Plain. Dull. Unmarried." Hetty sighed. "If Lieutenant Fairfax had come from a larger family, his relations might have taken her in, given her a proper education. I would *so* love to see Jane become an accomplished lady someday."

"Well, I will do what I can, but, with my modest income, we cannot afford much. School fees were too high for even you and your sister." Mr. Bates handed her the letter. "That might brighten your gloom. 'Tis from Mrs. Buckley. She, her husband, and little John—well, he is not so *little* anymore, I suppose, seeing as he is...what? Five-and-twenty now? Our old friends will come to Highbury this summer for a month-long visit."

"Yes, I know. Maria wrote to me about it. She and Mr. Clark will not accompany the rest of her family. She is with child again."

"Are such tidings not of the gladdest sort?"

Hetty nodded without enthusiasm. Her long-time friend, Maria Clark—three years her junior and the Miss Buckley that was—was already increasing for a second time.

Jane tottered on uneven ground towards her aunt, proudly holding out the ball she had caught. Smiling with unexpected delight, Hetty scooped up her niece, telling her how clever she was, twirling her round, eliciting squeals and giggles. *Is there any sound in the entire world so delightful as a child's laughter?* Kissing the girl's chubby cheek, Hetty rediscovered the joy of abiding love and contentment. It had been a dreadful half year, save for one small, precious girl bringing joy to three saddened hearts. *God willing, I shall often have dear Jane with me to dote on in my declining years. I will be blessed with all the love, all the hope, all the fear of a mother. And, somehow, I shall ensure my niece is educated.*

Life returned to a regular routine at the vicarage, or as regular as could be expected with an active poppet underfoot.

The Reverend Mr. Henry Bates continued to perform the rites of the Church of England: the christening, marrying, and burying—affectionately referred to by him as the hatching, matching, and dispatching—of his churchgoers.

Quiet but amiable, Mrs. Bates spent much of her time visiting her husband's parishioners and her own set of acquaintances, progressively asking people to repeat themselves. Hetty, for one, never complained about having to say things a second or third time.

Having become a favourite of Mr. Woodhouse, Mrs. Bates invited her daughter along on visits to the estate. At times, they—and, occasionally, Mrs. Goddard—were fetched and returned in the Woodhouse carriage, with Hetty talking the ears off James and the hind legs off the horses until he handed her in and the door clicked shut.

At Hartfield, they and Mr. Woodhouse engaged in quadrille and conversation about one another's well-being plus the benefits of drinking tea, staying out of draughts, retiring early, avoiding London air, eating small eggs, thin gruel, and thoroughly boiled pork.

Mr. Woodhouse's attention, when not centred on his own health, often turned to Hetty's with admonishments to eat no rich food, to drink no more than a small half-glass of wine in a tumbler of water, and, most importantly, to remain unmarried. "The less changes in one's life, the better for one's well-being. Spend time with your good parents and niece, Miss Bates. They deserve your affectionate care. And, above all, remain indoors as much as possible. For real comfort, there is nothing like staying inside one's own home."

Hetty smiled, nodding at his advice, but continued to play outside with Jane, to walk in all sorts of weather, and to never refuse a third or fourth glass of watered sherry.

With the arrival of July and warmer temperatures came Mr. and Mrs. Buckley, their son John, and the latter's business partner. Both families were in trade, and the two younger men had set up their own second-hand carriage business in Cheapside, near Mr. Buckley's saddlery shop.

Philip Weaver-Smythe—tall, gentlemanlike, amiable—had a good complexion, eyes the colour of a summer sky, and fair hair so fine it ruffled in the slightest breeze. The night he had been introduced to her at the Highbury assembly room, Hetty thought him nothing short of perfection. He smiled at her, he asked her to stand up with him, and he stood by her side, speaking of his childhood in Haslemere and of his partnership with John Buckley.

"On average, the fair price for a second-hand chaise, if still in fashion, with no more wear than a couple years' worth, newly painted, is £150. Our workers are now refurbishing a number of carriages. Soon we shall have everything from pony carts to landaus available for sale. Should you ever wish to purchase a low phaeton from Ye Olde Carriage Shoppe, Miss Bates, I *promise* it will go off without a hitch." It took a moment, but Hetty eventually tittered, earning from him another special smile.

In such confined society as Highbury, Hetty often found herself in the newcomer's resplendent company. Such was the case during a leisurely morning of battledore and shuttlecock in the small yard of the Buckley's rented house.

When asked by Mr. Hughes if he enjoyed his stay thus far and what he had done, Weaver-Smythe replied, "Well now, let me think. I have been to the Crown Inn, to Ford's, and have walked past your ancient church and vicarage. Have I missed any other points of interest?"

"The Crown Inn is a fine place," said Mr. Weston. "I will not have you mock our little village, sir. Ford's—our principal draper and haberdasher's shop, united—is first in size and fashion."

"Quite right. There may be no historical sites hereabouts, young man," Mr. Hughes huffed with affront, "but we *do* have the friendliest folk. Would you not agree, Miss Bates?"

"Oh, indeed! We are a close-knit, friendly bunch. Blessed with good-will. Surrounded by views sweet to the eye and sweet to the mind. Gentle, rolling chalk hills. So lovely! Upon my honour, I daresay we have the finest downland, woods, and rivers for miles around. Then there is Hart-field, of course. The Woodhouses—lovely, lovely people!—are first in consequence hereabouts. We all look up to them."

"And there *are* two other estates hereabouts," drawled John Buckley. "Randalls, in this parish; and, in the next, about a mile away, is Donwell Abbey, seat of the Knightley family."

"Is that it, then? No noteworthy ruins within an easy distance? I thought it might be splendid to organise an outing. A picnic, perhaps. Is there some celebrated locale *you* should like to visit, Miss Bates?"

Upon being singled out, Hetty gulped, wanting to sip from the glass of lemonade in her hand, but it shook so noticeably that she placed it back on the table with a clunk. "Well, goodness, I…um… Would you consider *seven* miles an easy distance, sir?"

"Indeed, I would. Even *twice* that is nothing in a Ye Olde Carriage conveyance. What do you have in mind, Miss Bates?"

"I have always longed for an excursion to Box Hill. From all I have heard, it would be a marvellous place for a picnic. Simply marvellous!" Hetty swatted at a pestering gnat while ensuring her mother's comfort and keeping a wary eye across the lawn. "Jane, dear," she called, "do stop chasing after Prissy and Piggy with that battledore." Turning back to

Weaver-Smythe, Hetty explained how Mrs. Otway raised pugs and that they all had a mean streak.

"Well, then, madam, we shall not invite *her*, or *them*, on our outing."

"Oh, no, no! Mrs. Otway, herself, is nothing but kindness. I would not exclude her from an outing. But, do you mean it? Are we truly to go?"

"Since you have longed to do so, we must plan on a wondrous day of exploration with nothing but good friends, good food, and good conversation."

Hetty clapped. "Oh, I do love good conversation with friends. Such a harmonious gathering would surely be the highlight of my life. Upon my honour, it would. I *do* long to go to Box Hill."

"Then go there you *shall*. You must. But what is a box hill? Is it square? Rectangular? A hill can hardly be considered gentle and rolling if it has sharp angles. And what does one *do* there for amusement? Fall off its edges?"

"Oh, heavens, no! But… Well, as I said, I have never been." Hetty ran a finger up and down her glass, leaving lines in the condensation. "One would admire the boxes, I suppose. The light of a midsummer sun. Beautiful orchids. Yews, beeches, oaks. Bird song, butterflies, and… Why do you laugh, sir?"

"Admire the boxes? Boxes of what, pray tell?"

"Boxes," scoffed John Buckley, "are evergreen trees." Buffing fingernails on his lapel, he admired the shine. "You, Weaver-Smythe, are either an ignorant *cit* or a simpleton. Both, I suspect. Actually," he said, catching Hetty's eye, "I expect he is having us on. He might have been an accomplished actor, had he a theatrical bent."

"And whilst at yon Box Hill," said Weaver-Smythe, doffing his hat and bowing with an exaggerated, courtly flourish, "I shall climb upon a box and take *another* bough."

As carelessly as she could, Hetty laughed, applauding his performance.

In a letter to Maria Clark, long on praise for her brother's friend, Hetty wrote:

And what a flurry he has thrown me in! Little Jane is shy around him, but he tries hard to win her over. Has there ever been a man of such equal parts handsomeness, cleverness, and amiableness combined? Well, Mr. George Knightley comes to mind. But, as you know, I have never had any hope in that quarter. Regarding Mr. Weaver-Smythe, though, do you suppose...

At the home of Mr. and Mrs. Cole, Weaver-Smythe strode across the room in time to assist Hetty into her chair at the card table. Flipping coat-tails, he took the seat opposite hers. "I enjoyed your father's sermon yesterday about overcoming evil with good. But was there *really* a thief at the vicarage last month? If so, did Mr. Bates *really* hit him over the head with your family Bible?"

Hetty lowered her eyes. "No."

"Nevertheless, your father is quite the entertaining fellow, for a reverend."

"Oh, he can be entertaining, indeed. And, at times, irreverent. Quite irreverent! Father often complains to Old John Adby about our limited income, about being poor. He merely gets teased in return. 'I *know* you are naught but a poor preacher, Bates. I hear you every Sunday!'" Hetty smiled as Weaver-Smythe guffawed. Growing sombre, she shook her head. "Mr. Adby has been my father's clerk for as long as I can remember, but—bless him!—the dear man developed rheumatic gout in his joints. 'Tis sad—so sad!—to witness him, or anyone, in pain."

"You have a compassionate soul, Miss Bates." Weaver-Smythe reached across the table, gently pressing her hand for the briefest of moments.

Hetty blushed at his touch. "Thank you. Unfortunately, Father's wit has put him in trouble with his bishop more than once." At Weaver-Smythe's expectant expression, Hetty told him to prepare for something dreadful. "I was mortified at the time."

"Better and better." Rubbing palms together, he sat forward, smiling in anticipation.

"Have you met farmer Mitchell yet? No? Well, he is a local man nearing his fifth decade. No, wait. Upon my honour, I do believe he recently turned one-and-fifty. Or two-and-fifty. No matter. Last April he took to the altar Miss Ward, the butcher's daughter, who was but fifteen years of age at the time. 'Mr. Mitchell,' cried my father in a voice so loud the entire congregation heard, 'you will find the font at the opposite end of the church.' Poor Mr. Mitchell looked around in confusion. 'Beggin' yer pardon, Mr. Bates, but what do I want with the font?' In his droll manner, Father said, 'Oh, I beg *your* pardon, Mr. Mitchell. I thought you had brought the child to be *christened.*'"

Hetty's face had grown redder while relating the story, but she chuckled along with Weaver-Smythe. "It may be amusing *now*, sir. Yes, quite amusing. The entire congregation laughed, but *I* was mortified. Mortified! Mother hissed at me for slouching down in the pew. I wanted nothing more than the ground to open and swallow me whole. I have never, ever, been so mortified." Palms to cheeks, she closed her eyes. "Now I am embarrassed all over again."

Weaver-Smythe reached across the table, intimately resting, far longer than before, his hand upon one of hers.

That particular hand went unwashed until Hetty arose the next morning.

After a fortnight in each other's company amidst Highbury society, Hetty believed herself in love with Philip Weaver-Smythe. Whether he harboured any special regard for her was less certain. But to have the attention of a remarkably fine young man, with a great deal of intelligence, spirit, and brilliancy was something, indeed.

Save George Knightley, who was always kind, no other eligible man had ever paid Hetty the slightest attention. Weaver-Smythe walked and talked with her. He understood her. He told her she was not at all dull and should not be ashamed of preferring basic comforts and that he, too, delighted in life's simple pleasures.

"Who needs more than modest belongings? Why, a second-hand carriage is as functional as a new one." He smiled the special smile that made Hetty weak at the knees. "Did I ever mention, Miss Bates, that I am a vendor of such conveyances?"

"Innumerable times, sir."

"Are you implying I talk too much?"

"No. *I* talk too much."

"Utter nonsense! If anyone says you talk too much, you must simply talk them out of it. Now, as a special surprise, I have sent for my bespoke curricle. It should arrive within the week, newly refurbished to such an extent that it is even better than new. Wait until you see the improvements I ordered. If you agree, I shall drive you any place you wish to go. Even to Box Hill, if we can get a party together."

Others noticed their peculiar friendship. But Hetty was, after all, nearly a spinster at four-and-twenty. She had no dowry. There could be nothing more than amity between them, no sincere affection, no expectation on either side. Friends and neighbours thought so kindly of Hetty, they simply smiled and turned blind eyes and deaf ears, allowing her a summer of mild flirtation.

"My dear girl," said Mr. Bates, holding her hand, "do not set your cap at him. While he obviously fancies you as a friend, he does not seem the sort to know how justly to appreciate your value. Do you truly suppose he has serious designs on you?"

"Of course not"— *for I am an undistinguished, penniless, bespectacled spinster with grey strands in my hair.*

Hope, however, bloomed within Hetty's heart when Weaver-Smythe invited her and Jane for a drive in his curricle. With the three Buckleys following in their own carriage, they arrived at Bramblehill Park, an abandoned estate in Berkshire. The six of them strolled around the overgrown grounds, inspecting the place, peeking through the manor's grimy, broken windows, and admiring the views. With a great deal of work, the adults all agreed, the place could be an excellent location to settle and raise a family.

Weaver-Smythe had winked, then, at Hetty.

Upon her return to the vicarage, she dashed off another letter filled with all the optimism and exhilaration that day brought forth.

And I pray you are in good health and not terribly cross with me, for it has been well over a fortnight since last I wrote. What a fortnight it has been, Maria! I am almost afraid to tell you how your brother's friend and I have been behaving. Imagine to yourself everything most profligate—nay, shocking!—in the way of standing up and sitting down together, driving and walking unchaperoned, whispering and laughing in corners. Our time together has been heavenly. But— oh!—such breaches of conduct! The first time he kissed my knuckles, I believe my eyes rolled back in my head. Do you remember those contraband novels—the ones I was forbidden to read—the ones you smuggled into the vicarage? Remember how we laughed and laughed at silly, swooning heroines? Such fictions are not as farfetched as we thought. Oh, if only you knew how much more I want to tell you but shall not, you would give me some credit for discretion. Me! And him! Imagine! You must be astounded. Imagine how I feel. I had no idea it could be this way. My cheeks burn as I recall his attentions. I must close now and beseech you, my friend, to burn these pages before someone else sees them. Do answer posthaste, though, for I long to know how you are faring.

Yours &c.,

Hetty Bates

That letter had the misfortune to cross with another by one day.

Above all, I beg you, beware! My husband, upon being asked about our brother's friend, related, to my horror, the most shocking intelligence. Mr. W-S is known to trifle with women's affections, particularly those of wealthy widows and desperate spinsters. Forgive me, dear Hetty, and please believe I do not consider you, in any way, desperate. But marriage, as both you and he must know, is impractical. At any rate, I would not have you bound to a bounder, pressured into a choice that is wrong for you. He plays at courtship, with no serious intent, except where wealthy women are concerned. Even in my limited acquaintance with him, I have observed the scoundrel smiling, flirting, and charming the ladies with gallantry and false flattery. According to Thomas, the rake counteracts ennui by practicing arts and allurements. He makes love to us all, playing his part with more finesse than a renowned stage actor. Please, beware.

Yours &c.,

Maria Clark

By that time, each of the Buckleys, individually, had already taken Hetty aside, hinting at their own suspicions.

Sharp, painful shards of doubt pricked at Hetty's heart, and she emptied her stomach. *Is it possible? Have I been deceived? Am I that desperate? Have his attentions and intentions little to do with genuine preference?*

Weaver-Smythe had taken her several places in his spanking curricle; but not once had he driven her, as promised, on the longed-for excursion to Box Hill. Shards dug deeper. Circles beneath her eyes darkened. Tears sprang forth as she watched him flirt with Mrs. Goddard and with Miss Nash, the head teacher at her school.

One mid-August morn, he was gone—gone to London before the Buckleys, without even calling at the vicarage to take leave of the Bates family.

The day has come and gone, Maria, in which I flirted my last with Mr. W-S. When you receive this, it will all be over. Tears flow as I write. He is gone, you were right, and I was a fool. With him, he has taken my heart and my every hope. I am abandoned, in deepest despair. This anguish cannot be concealed, nor can I endure the pitying looks of whispering parents and neighbours. I scarcely sleep nor eat. I need escape, sanctuary. Might I impose upon you and your husband?

Frantically, Hetty awaited a reply.

Dearest Hetty,

Your request arrived at a most providential time. Yes, please do come to London for an extended stay. A year complete, perhaps. This child I carry is taking its toll, so I would appreciate your assistance in caring for little Tom. I realise this would tear you away from your beloved Jane, but I would not ask if I did not desperately wish you by my side. The sickness which lasted only a few months with my son has diminished not one whit. I am dreadfully fagged. Thomas suggested we hire a nursemaid, but I would rather have my dearest friend with me. Enclosed is fare for the mail coach to Farnham. Thomas and a maid will meet you at the Bush. Your room in our home will be small but comfortable. It shall be your sanctuary, and you shall be my angel. Please, take pity on this wretched creature and come to me in my hour of need.

Yours &c.,

Maria Clark

Hetty showed the missive to her parents. Kind-hearted souls themselves, Mr. and Mrs. Bates agreed she should attend her friend.

Parting with Jane ripped deeply at Hetty's already wounded heart. The brave face she donned while hugging the child and bidding her parents farewell crumpled upon setting off, with Patty, in the cart containing her trunk. Tears slid, unchecked, down her cheeks as Vicarage Lane disappeared from view. By the time she reached the Crown, bid farewell to Patty, and stepped onto the mail coach, her outward composure had been regained.

A month of homesickness and unsettledness gave way to comfort and security in her new situation with the Clarks; but, other than attending church on Sundays, Hetty refused to budge beyond the cosy townhouse. Philip Weaver-Smythe, she learned, resided in the same Cheapside neighbourhood.

"Whatever shall I say, Maria, if anyone asks about him? About my fleeing to London after him? Gossip must be running rife throughout Highbury by now. I wrote to my parents, but they reply without truly answering any of my inquiries."

"You did *not* come here following after any man, Hetty Bates!"

"But he lives nearby! Everyone will think—"

"If anyone has the effrontery to ask, divert your inquisitors by telling the truth. You, my dearest friend, came for the year—at my particular request, expense, and arrangement—to care for my son while I"—Maria caressed her rounded belly—"deliver *this* little one."

Damp handkerchief clasped in her hand, Hetty sniffled, affected by Maria's pitying look. "True, but caring for little Tom was not my *only* reason for escaping here, as you well know."

"You shall have ample opportunity to write your letters. With contacts in the army, my husband can help conduct your investigation. If Lieutenant Fairfax has living relations, we shall find them. If and *when* we do, I pray his people will be in a position to provide a proper upbringing and education for Jane." Maria leaned forward, patting Hetty's arm, smirking. "There now! See how easily I diverted *you*?"

"Yes." Hetty huffed. "Still, I wish *I* had received a proper education. I wish Father could have afforded schooling and that females were entitled to the same levels of enlightenment as the opposite sex." Heaving a quivering sigh, she bowed her head. "Perhaps, if I *had* been better educated, I would not have fallen for him, for his lies. I would not have… Oh, hopeless, stupid creature! Snivelling and feeling sorry for myself. Selfish, stupid!"

"Hetty Bates, listen to yourself, for I shan't! You—devoted friend, daughter, aunt, and neighbour—are filled with universal goodwill. How can such a dear creature be either stupid or selfish? If you had only a shilling in the world, I daresay you would give away sixpence of it. Hetty, you are wonderful with little Tom. He adores you, and I only wish—"

"Stop."

"*I only wish* your spirits were not low, that you were not suffering so."

"All will be well, in time, Maria. *I* shall be well."

"Excellent! Now, let me tell you about the widow next door and the company she keeps…"

Hetty's time with the Clarks passed swiftly, filled with letter writing, compatibility, mutual support, delight in—and exasperation with—a little boy's high-spirited behaviour, plus all the due anticipation and turmoil surrounding a woman's confinement, childbirth, and its aftermath.

Following Maria's churching, a small party—consisting of various Clark and Buckley relations and one Bates—congregated at St. Mary-le-Bow on a cold, January morn. Hetty joined the newlywed Mr. and Mrs. John Buckley at the church's font while little Miss Marie Clark was christened. As one of the child's godmothers, Hetty wept copiously through the entire ceremony, surreptitiously searching for a handkerchief amongst the voluminous folds of her heavy, woollen cape.

In early June, Hetty exchanged teary farewells with Maria and her two children and was handed into the carriage, feeling as though she had left behind a vital part of her life. In company with Mr. Clark and a maid, she was taken to the Bush in Farnham, where she caught the mail coach bound for Highbury.

"Hetty!" At the front door of the ivy-covered vicarage, Mrs. Bates, waving a handkerchief, watched her daughter's approach. "Oh, let me look at you. How we have all missed you, my dear girl."

Dropping her portmanteau on the gravel walkway, Hetty rushed into her mother's arms. Embracing, talking over one another, they took note of the changes ten months had wrought. Mrs. Bates's hearing had deteriorated, her face had aged drastically.

"The Clarks must have taken prodigious care of you, Hetty, and fed you well. You were so languid and wan upon leaving. Now you are returned to us much plumper, your face fuller, skin glowing. Such an improvement but...though your hair seems thicker, it has grown greyer."

Gritting her teeth, Hetty helped Mrs. Bates through the door while Patty fetched the fallen bag. "But you have not changed one bit, Mother. Not one bit! How do you stay so young? How is my father? Is he well? Where is Jane?" Twice, she repeated her questions.

"Your father is poorly, dear. He made me promise not to worry you, but he is failing. Mr. Perry fears he may not be with us much long— Ah! Here is our little poppet. Jane, come greet your auntie."

Four years of age and timid at first, little Miss Fairfax soon revelled in the reunion. Their bond strengthened, and Hetty prayed her letter-writing campaign would produce positive results.

Those fervent prayers would not be answered for four years after the passing in ninety-eight of Mr. Bates. The reverend's death left his grieving widow, daughter, and granddaughter as poor as church mice. Adding to her sorrow, the only home Hetty had ever known was to be vacated before the new vicar arrived.

So they rented Quince Cottage, which sat on a parcel of land owned by Ralph Franklin, a local farmer. The three generations of women lived there contentedly until the year ought-two, when Hetty's copious prayers and letters were answered.

No actual Fairfax relations had ever been located; but, upon return to England, to his own wife and young daughter, Colonel Campbell, superior officer and friend to the late Lieutenant Fairfax, read one of the letters awaiting him—one written by Thomas Clark on Hetty's behalf. With due haste, the colonel replied, was put in contact with Mrs. Bates and Hetty, and was welcomed upon arrival on their doorstep. He had come with an unexpected invitation.

Subsequently, little Miss Fairfax became the Campbells' frequent guest in London, paying them long visits and becoming a favourite with the kindly couple and little Miss Campbell. Before both girls turned nine, the colonel offered to undertake the whole charge of Jane's education. She would belong to his family, live with them entirely, and, one day, become a governess.

The cosy dwelling known as Quince Cottage then became the scene of a tearful parting.

"Do you have your brush and comb set? Have you packed your new hair ribbons? Does Jane not have the loveliest hair you have ever seen, Mrs. Campbell? I daresay she has the prettiest, deep grey eyes, the darkest eyelashes and eyebrows, the fairest, most delicate complexion of anyone I know. Lovely, so lovely! And such a clever, little creature." Crouching in front of her niece, Hetty laid one hand on the girl's shoulder and, with the other, raised her chin so their watery eyes met. "Promise me you will be a good girl for Colonel and Mrs. Campbell."

"I promise, Auntie."

"And promise to send weekly letters."

Jane nodded. "Every Sunday, after church, I will. Mrs. Campbell said she would help with spelling."

"Excellent! I shall expect a letter each Tuesday. You will tell me all your secrets, and I will tell you mi— I will tell you all the most agreeable pieces of news from Highbury. Now, now, Jane, you must not cry. We shall have lovely times whenever you come back to visit. But we will miss you terribly, dear heart. Go give your grandmama a kiss now, but save one for me."

Colonel Campbell handed Jane into the chaise; and everyone waved, smiled, and called out, "Goodbye, goodbye." Hetty merely mouthed the words, too choked up for actual speech. Standing in the lane, she watched until the conveyance drew out of sight. Then she ran to the graveyard, knelt at her sister's headstone, and wept. *I am sorry, Jane! I am sorry I was once angry at you for abandoning a child. 'Tis a very hard thing...being wrenched away from a daughter...or a niece. I am sorry for sending her away. 'Twas for the best. Truly, it was. I pray you know that. She will be looked after and educated— educated!—beyond our means. I made the proper decisions, did I not? Oh, I pray you understand and agree with all my choices.*

To ease her own loneliness and to save one of God's creatures from an uncertain future, Hetty adopted a deaf collie from old Mr. Martin in the year three. In vain, the farmer tried to dissuade his neighbour from such a poor choice, but Hetty was adamant, having instantly fallen in love with the black and white ball of fluff. The little dog trotted beside her half way to Quince Cottage, then was carried, snuggled in her arms, the rest. Mrs.

Bates and her maid-of-all-work, Patty, disapproved of the addition to their small home, but Hetty insisted the collie be permitted inside. Kind to all God's creatures—save, perhaps, gnats, rats, adders, and Mrs. Otway's pugnacious pugs—Hetty more often than not had Mister Uff, as the collie was later named, trotting along at her side, oblivious to her prattle but being told all her secrets.

Patty—a reliable source of information—every few days collected letters for the Bates women from the post office as well as village gossip for them from young John Adby at the Crown. "… and, ere long, little Miss Emma, at only twelve years of age, will become mistress of Hartfield. Her elder sister, you see, is now engaged to Mr. Knightley."

Feeding her collie scraps of ham, Hetty asked, "*Which* Knightley brother?"

"The younger, John."

"What is that you say?" Mrs. Bates looked from Hetty to their maid. "Has that handsome brother of yours been knighted?"

"No, ma'am. Me brother John is still an under-gardener at Donwell Abbey. But there's a rumour in the village about *another* handsome young man. Spotted at Goddard's, he was. Arrived yesterday morning in a fancy chaise with a Ye Olde Carriage Shoppe plaque affixed to its rear quarter. Apparently, he…"

Whenever anyone rattled on about Philip Weaver-Smythe, Hetty, in fine imitation of her mother and Mister Uff, turned a deaf ear. Sorting through letters fetched by Patty, she smiled upon discovering one from Maria.

How delightful it was to see with my own two eyes how well the Campbells are providing for your niece. A proper education, Hetty! Miss Fairfax has certainly fallen into good hands and will be given all the benefits Colonel Campbell can provide, even though he cannot provide her with an inheritance. But, here in London, living with such well-informed people, being attended by first-rate masters, she shall receive every advantage of education and culture…

With little education and even less culture, Hetty and her mother lived a simple but contented life at Quince Cottage. They were called upon there. They returned visits. They wrote and received letters. Though one was nearly deaf, the other garrulous, Mrs. Bates and her daughter were gentle, sociable, kind souls. Besides the housekeeping, they occupied themselves with their work baskets, in helping those even poorer than themselves, and in teaching a few local girls to read, write, and do simple arithmetic. Above all else, they were good neighbours.

Hetty was particularly happy to have the friendship of Mrs. Goddard, proprietress of the local boarding school. The two were often spotted walking together, whispering, gesturing, laughing, sharing confidences, discussing the importance of education for young females.

In the early summer of ought-seven, Maria's parents, Mr. and Mrs. Buckley, arrived in Highbury for a short stay at the Crown.

Upon calling at Quince Cottage, Mrs. Buckley explained that Maria and her husband had planned on accompanying them and thereby surprising Hetty. "They send their apologies, but, you see, young Tom and little Marie have fallen ill with colds, and Thomas has some unexpected business to tend." Sipping from a chipped, delicate cup, Mrs. Buckley winced at the tea's weakness. "Speaking of business, the other half of Ye Olde Carriage Shoppe has been purchased by John. My son is tremendously relieved to part ways with his former partner. By the bye, Mr. Weaver-Smythe recently married the young widow who lives next door to Maria. You know, Hetty... Missus... Missus..."

"Mrs. Mathers?" Wide-eyed, Hetty gawped at their visitor. "Well, what a fine thing, I suppose. The wealthy Widow Mathers and Mr. Weaver-Smythe. Who would have thought? He, such a handsome, ambitious man, and she such a...such a... Well, as they say, there is no accounting for taste. I only met her the once, of course, while staying with Maria. What a coincidence! That your daughter's closest neighbour should be *his* bride."

"Well, you know, Maria never associated much with the likes of *her*. Such a loose woman." Mrs. Buckley sniffed in disdain, then gasped as Hetty choked on a sip of tea. Patting the younger woman's back, she whispered a heartfelt apology.

Hetty dabbed at her mouth with a napkin. "What a surprise, though, about Mr. Weaver-Smythe and Mrs. Mathers. He shall have an artful, pretty creature for his wife, indeed. I daresay she is all *I* am not. Yet, I cannot help but wonder... Well, what is done is done. I am delighted for the happy couple. Yes, delighted! Once they are settled, and I visit with Maria again, I shall take round some doily-napkins for the new Mrs. Weaver-Smythe. Doily-napkins. Yes, a practical yet pretty gift. Mother and I, you see, make the decorative mats to protect our furniture from scratches and spilled tea. The very gift for a bride! But I would not call while *he* is at home. Mr. Weaver-Smythe might feel awkward, you know, having to make a fuss over a few doily-napkins. I am sure he has much better things to do than fuss over lacy table mats or an old...friend."

How unfortunate one's heart cannot be as easily protected from gouges as one's furniture.

Smiling brightly, Hetty reached for the pot. "More tea, Mrs. Buckley?" Turning and raising her voice, she asked her mother the same. Hand shaking, she poured them each another cup, slopping a few drops from the spout onto a decorative table mat. "Oh, fie! Well, as Father often said, 'tis no use crying over spilt milk. He said that to *me* often. 'Sufficient unto the day,' he would say. I suffered enough guilt, enough shame over whatever I had done wrong. My dear father always avoided adding to one's misery."

A sudden thickness in her throat signalled the onset of more tears as Hetty stared out the window in the direction of the churchyard, missing Mr. Bates. *I regret a few things I have done in my life, Father, but how can I regret a trifler like Mr. Weaver-Smythe?*

Over the years, as a consequence of living amidst the close-knit society of a small village plus the occasional trip to London to visit with the Clarks, Hetty often encountered the men who helped shape, for better or worse, the woman she had become.

She visited her father's grave once a month. Addressing his headstone, she told him she loved him. Then, remembering he was not encased within that cold slab of inscribed stone, Hetty raised her eyes heavenward. She praised him for setting an example to male parishioners, for being neither trifler nor tyrant. *Thank you for being a good, caring father to Jane and me, grandfather to little Jane, and husband to my mother.* She apologised for having disappointed him, and she forgave him for leaving behind womenfolk lacking the means to provide for themselves.

In different ways, both Hetty and Mr. Bates were at peace.

Less free from the difficulties of life was the couple who resided in the same Cheapside neighbourhood as Hetty's good friends, the Clarks. Marital status notwithstanding, Mr. Weaver-Smythe sent comfits to Goddard's boarding school once a year, in April, perpetuating rumours of a liaison between him and its proprietress. Such talk neither sat well with his wife nor added to their questionable domestic felicity.

Hetty paid no mind to gossip about an intrigue involving the man she thought she had loved. He had used her ill, and she had learnt a valuable lesson. Lack of interest in his affairs, however, extended only so far. She grinned in unChristian glee upon learning from Maria that, whenever Weaver-Smythe was seen doffing his hat, it was evident his hair—once so fair and incredibly fine—had parted from the top of his head.

Then there was Ralph Franklin of Tanglewood Farm, along the road to Highbury. He and Hetty nodded to one another in passing, he in a dismissive manner, she more civilly. Inwardly, she sighed with relief, knowing she had made the right decision back in ought-seven when she refused him.

Franklin had accused the Bates women of putting on airs by associating with their betters. Had Hetty married the man, he would have forbidden them from further visits to Hartfield. But six years had passed since then, and Hetty and her mother were still welcomed at the estate by Mr. Woodhouse.

Emma Woodhouse had even condescended to visit the small apartment Mrs. Bates rented from a Highbury tradesman after she, Hetty, Patty, and Mister Uff had been evicted from Quince Cottage. Their new lodging, consisting of the drawing-room floor of the house—a mere hop, step, and jump from the Crown—was everything to the women residing within.

And, oh, Maria, little Miss Woodhouse has grown to be as kind-hearted as her dear father. Dotes on him, she does, as I do my mother. Never an inconsiderate remark does she utter, only wit and charity. We have been blessed with their friendship. Now Patty informs me a certain young lady has been invited to Hartfield, befriended by its young mistress.

"'Tis true, Miss Bates. Someone's natural daughter. Accepted by them Woodhouses!" The maid hung up her cloak on a peg and donned an apron. "Rumour has it her father isn't a gentleman at all but a tradesman—rich enough, decent enough to comfortably maintain her. Do you know Miss Smith?"

Glancing up from sewing a chemise, Hetty caught her mother keenly following the conversation. "I do, a little." Taking up her needle again, she carefully stitched a seam. "Although the young woman and I are nothing alike—nothing at all!—coming from such different backgrounds, I cannot help but feel a certain kinship with Harriet Smith. I know what it is, how wonderful it is, to be accepted and befriended by one's betters. Otherwise, she and I have nothing else in common. Nothing at all! Why, according to Mr. Woodhouse, the poor girl seems incapable of completing a full thought or finishing a sentence—and she a former star pupil! I, on the other hand, vex the dear man with how quickly I talk. While I have grown dowdy, Miss Smith—though short and plump—is pretty enough to have gained young Mr. Martin's notice." *A farmer. Perhaps we are not so different, after all.*

"Oh, yes, ma'am. He's smitten, he is," said Patty. "'Tis no wonder, really. She has such fair hair, a pretty complexion, eyes the colour of a summer sky."

Pricking her finger, Hetty yelped. "Speaking of the sky, do you think it will rain today? The clouds look rather ominous. Quite ominous, indeed! Bless me, but I do believe we are in for a cloudburst soon. Come, Mister Uff. We must fetch our letters from the post office before it rains. There have been so many bad colds going around this year, I would not care to be caught in a downpour. No, I would not."

"But, Miss Bates, I come from the post office this past half hour. There be no letters today. 'Tis only Monday, after all. There'll be one from Miss Fairfax or Mrs. Clark tomorrow, no fear."

"Which reminds me, I am a letter in debt to Maria."

And people remark on how well-mannered she is, how sweet-natured. As a parlour boarder at Goddard's, she currently is acquiring the social graces necessary to find a husband. Now she has become Miss Woodhouse's particular friend. Imagine that!

Laying down her pen, Hetty remembered a babe, a fair-haired daughter, delivered in Cheapside by a competent midwife and baptised that same April day by the Clarks' clergyman. Hetty had briefly held the infant in her arms, then handed the angelic creature over to Mrs. Buckley, Maria's mother. The child had been placed first with a country nurse in Haslemere. Then, one early morning in 1806, when she was nine years of age, her father himself conveyed her to Mrs. Goddard's boarding school in Highbury.

Hetty's heart swelled first with pride, then with gratitude to the Woodhouses for offering the girl friendship. *One could not ask for kinder neighbours...but I do wish Mrs. Otway's pugs were not so beastly and that Mr. Franklin was even half as good-hearted as the Woodhouses. Foolish man! Imagine! Forbidding Bates women from associating with their betters. Hah!* Hetty snickered to herself as she picked up the pen.

Truly, Maria, you must not fret over me. I am entirely content in my state of unshackled, single blessedness. My life is devoted to the comfort of family and relations, friends and neighbours. Perhaps I should feel more shame for my indiscretions. Perhaps I should feel ashamed I never married when I had the chance. But a woman must not be obliged to marry a man she does not love. I wrote to my niece recently, upon being asked for advice about a young man she met in Weymouth. I entreated Jane to not commit herself further, to not think of accepting him unless she truly likes him. Anything is to be preferred or endured rather than marrying without affection. I hold a high ideal of the love that should unite man and woman. The worst, most irremediable, of all evils would be a lifelong connexion with an unsuitable partner. I once thought I knew love. What I felt, though, was nothing more than infatuation. Of course, one never forms a just idea of anybody beforehand. One takes up a notion and runs away with it. Ah, well. What man could possibly live up to the shining examples set by my excellent father and men like Mr. Knightley? I believe even you were smitten with the latter at one time, when we were young and foolish. What girl would not have been? Now he has grown to be everything a gentleman ought. Dear

Miss Woodhouse can be such a simpleton at times. She complements him well, in spite of their age difference. I daresay she must be nearly half his age. No, no. Let me think. He is five years my junior. So he would have been a lad of sixteen or so when both Emma and little Jane were born. Goodness, it all seems like yesterday. Well, whomever the gentleman chooses for a wife, she could never be me, alas! He is kind to us, though. His man, William Larkins, sent us apples again yesterday.

Before the end of September, in the year 1814, the Reverend Mr. Elton performed a ceremony uniting in marriage Mr. Robert Martin and a young woman born in London in the spring of ninety-seven. But it was in Highbury, that populous Surrey village, that Harriet Smith met not only her future husband but, unbeknownst to her, her own maternal relations.

Another wedding took place in October; and the Bates womenfolk were all invited to a plentiful breakfast at Hartfield celebrating the marriage of its young mistress, Emma Woodhouse, to George Knightley. The occasion was marked by a veritable feast, complete with soft-boiled eggs, apple tarts, baked apples, custard, and—to Mr. Woodhouse's horror —cake.

There is Mr. Elton—the man who considered himself so superior to Harriet Smith. Well! She is much better off with Mr. Martin than she ever would have been with you. And what a wife you have, sir. You were never worthy of Miss Woodhouse either... I mean Mrs. Knightley. She has always been so kind to me... except for that one incident on Box Hill. The dear girl must have been quite out of sorts that day. But what a fine couple she and Mr. Knightley are. Lovely, how lovely!

Perhaps Hetty envied the happy newlyweds. Perhaps she had not been thinking clearly, the result of too much watered-down sherry. Perhaps she had been irked by someone's voiced opinion that the drabness of certain attendees' attire would not meet the standards of people in a place called Maple Grove. Or, conceivably, it was something else entirely. Whatever the reason, Hetty—in a moment of weakness and having come close to tears of frustration from everyone asking why *she* had never married— answered Mrs. Augusta Elton, the vicar's wife, in an uncommonly sarcastic tone.

"I have always loved life's *simple* things, Mrs. Elton. Upon my honour, I have. But—heavens!—that never meant *I* wanted one for a husband!"

J. MARIE CROFT is a self-proclaimed word nerd and adherent of Jane Austen's quote "Let other pens dwell on guilt and misery." Bearing witness to Joanne's fondness for *Pride and Prejudice*, word-play, and laughter are her light-hearted novel, *Love at First Slight* (a Babblings of a Bookworm Favourite Read of 2014), her playful novella, *A Little Whimsical in His Civilities* (Just Jane 1813's Favourite 2016 JAFF Novella), and her humorous short stories in the anthologies *Sun-kissed: Effusions of Summer, The Darcy Mono-logues,* and *Dangerous to Know: Jane Austen's Rakes & Gentlemen Rogues*. Joanne lives in Nova Scotia, Canada.

IN GOOD HANDS

CAITLIN WILLIAMS

HARRIET SMITH

Sweet-tempered, well-mannered but unsophisticated, Miss Smith is the daughter of nobody knows who. She became the pet of the clever and rich Emma Woodhouse, who believed that, with proper direction and a little matchmaking, she could increase Harriet's chances at a more favourable match than a simple farmer. Impressed by the condescension and suggestable to change, Harriet falls in and out of love no less than three times when, at last, she follows her more rational heart full-circle to the man who has adored her all the while—just the way she is. **"Her character depends on those she is with; but in good hands, she will turn out a valuable woman."** —**Chapter VIII,** *Emma.*

IN GOOD HANDS

The rocking of the carriage augmented the pain in her tooth. It nagged so much as to make Harriet, who was generally possessed of a sweet, even temperament, want to roar or curse like a fishwife and demand they stop at the nearest blacksmith's. There she would order the offending molar yanked out with a great pair of metal tongs—the agonies of such a primitive operation would surely be no worse than the torments she already endured.

Her heart! Oh, her heart was a poor, battered thing. It throbbed and shuddered in unerring sympathy with her tooth.

Mr. Elton, such disappointment!

Mr. Knightly, such humiliation!

And before those two gentlemen, there was Robert Martin. How to describe the swirl of sentiments that man's name produced? She could not fathom them. The only thing she was certain of was her own monumental vanity—to have fancied three men in love with her in the space of a twelve-month!

Who was Harriet Smith, after all? A nobody. Why, she barely existed.

A girl with no name—her father having been either unable or unwilling to grant her his. She lived under a common name which gave all those to whom she was introduced an immediate understanding of her circumstances. It generally prompted pity accompanied by a soft incline of the head.

The stain of illegitimacy, writ large upon her, had previously made her humble, grateful for any notice from her betters. After all, good society might justifiably shun her or refuse her entry to their circles, but people were often kind in response to her tenderness and sweetness. They could not find it within themselves to be ungenerous to a young girl with a pure heart and a pretty face. And they were rewarded for their civility by the warmest feelings of satisfaction—that sort of puffed-up pleasure which invariably follows a charitable deed.

She had been an artless, unassuming girl—just about clever enough to know her place, aware of her limitations—until she had met Miss Emma Woodhouse who, in trying to do well by her, had made Harriet believe in the impossible: that a man such as Mr. Knightley—such a superior man, a gentleman in every sense of the word—might be within her reach. Her ridiculous vanity and ambition had been justly punished by the news that Miss Woodhouse and Mr. Knightley were to be married.

It had been foolish to hope. She saw that now, but its being silly did not lessen the hurt, and her emotions were wild; they had grown teeth with which to gnaw at her soul. The intangible wound was constantly worried at, attacked so relentlessly that it had no chance to heal.

Then a true malady had fallen upon her. Her real teeth had begun to bother her, one in particular.

Upon hearing of Harriet's toothache, Miss Woodhouse had arranged, with a rapidity undoubtedly given extra momentum by her conscience, to deliver Harriet to Mr. and Mrs. John Knightley's house in Town in order that she might receive care from a specialist in such matters. Miss Woodhouse suffered much with guilt, Harriet surmised, but at least she had Mr. George Knightley and the means of sending Harriet away to comfort her.

Lost as she was in these thoughts, it was a surprise to hear the driver's shout telling her they were fast approaching the City. First there was relief but, when the coach began to rattle over the London cobbles, she feared her head might explode with pain. Her discomfort grew, and she had to blink away her tears. When the urge to scream almost overcame her, she was forced to take out her handkerchief, roll it up into a ball, and bite down hard upon it.

Mrs. John Knightley came out to meet the carriage when it came to a juddering stop and brought her excellent mothering skills with her. Upon gaining the pavement, Harriet tried to curtsey, but it was more of a stumble, a feeble attempt she was quickly brought out of. She was gathered instead into the lady's tight embrace. So tenderly was her cheek stroked then that she could hold her tears in no longer. Out they fell, soaking Mrs. Knightley's fine lace collar.

"You poor dear! You must take this," Mrs. Knightley said once they were seated in a comfortable day parlour on the first floor of her smart London townhouse. She held out a tiny brown package folded up tightly and bound by string. "It is nothing but ground peppermint. Rub a little into your gums every few hours. It will not make the pain go away, but it will soothe you."

"You are most kind." Harriet took the package. "And it is so good of you to welcome me here. I hope I shall not be too much trouble."

"No trouble is too great for such a dear friend of Emma's, and I am sure you will not inconvenience us at all. Quite the opposite. We shall get that tooth seen to tomorrow, and then you will feel a good deal better and be excellent company for me."

"Thank you. I already feel quite restored simply from being out of the carriage."

Harriet paused and dreaded having to speak of it, but her many substitute mothers—all those nursemaids and teachers—had taught her well. Felicitations must be given; there was no escaping them. "I ought to give you my congratulations regarding the upcoming...such joyous news... about Miss Woodhouse and Mr. Knightley...that they will be married." She rushed the last of her words out in a long breath. *There, it was done.* She sighed in relief.

Mrs. Knightley's countenance told Harriet that she knew it all, of how Harriet had reached for the stars and fallen flat on her face.

"I have been silly, Mrs. Knightley," Harriet continued. Raising her chin, she tried to look braver than she felt. "But I assure you that, in future, I aim to be the most rational creature in the world. All romance is behind me. I shall never fall in love again."

"None of us can predict the future." The older lady put her teacup gently on the table and gave Harriet a soft smile. "And love, I believe, is something that chooses us, not the other way around. But I suspect a spell away from Highbury will be of great benefit to you. Distance and time will work far better wonders than peppermint."

Harriet tried to smile, but her tooth began to throb anew.

It was extracted a few days later when no other solution could be found, leaving a hole at the back of her mouth large enough for Harriet to dip the end of her tongue into. The surgeon had held the offending tooth aloft for her to see after the operation, with its bloody roots still intact and dangling. The obvious delight he took in his work made her resentful at having to pay him for the tortures he had inflicted upon her.

Yet as the days went by and the hole in her gum became smaller, she became full of praise for his efforts. The pain was gone, and all that remained was a vague feeling of loss, the nagging sense of something being missing. When she examined herself in the pier glass in Mrs. Knightley's hall, she was pleased to discover the gap in her teeth was only noticeable when she smiled very broadly—something she rarely did now anyway.

The Knightley children were her only genuine source of amusement. They were curious, lively, little things, and so affectionate and friendly that Harriet had become rapidly fond of them. In particular, she adored baby Emma. Mrs. Knightley's youngest child, named after her aunt, gurgled so beautifully and had such perfect blonde curls and dimpled cheeks that she charmed all who saw her. Harriet was as susceptible to her smiles as everyone else.

As she was recovering well from her malady and there was still no word of her returning to Highbury, Harriet was beginning to fancy that she might remain in Town for some time. Though it was meant to have been a fleeting visit made necessary by her overfondness for all things sugar, the idea of making herself useful, indispensable even, to the household by way of helping with the children and being a good companion to Mrs. Knightley occurred to her. If they did not mind having her, being surrounded by the love and chaos of the London branch of the Knightley family tree would make Harriet content.

Oh, she would miss Mrs. Goddard and all the friends she had made at that good lady's establishment, but here in Town there was no Mrs. Elton to sniff at her and no Mr. George Knightley to unintentionally remind her of how inferior she was. And if the families met at Christmas or Easter, she could take herself off elsewhere. She was a fortunate girl in some ways to have been always at one school or another. She had collected a great many friends she might visit. To absent herself on that fateful day when Miss Emma Woodhouse became Mrs. George Knightley would be very easy indeed.

And, Robert Martin need never be met with again. She averted her gaze from the glass, could not bear to see her own shame reflected back at her while she remembered how badly she had treated him.

Yet in looking away from herself, she saw him—Mr. Martin was standing in the hall!

Was he an apparition sent to haunt her? She tried to blink him away, but he became more flesh and bone, not less. He moved and, after nodding in her direction, gave her a country half bow. Embarrassed and surprised in equal measure, Harriet could not return the gesture. Heat rushed into her face and she ran away.

The reason for Robert Martin's presence in the Knightley's hall was made clear later when they were taking afternoon tea. Mr. Knightley, who had just arrived home, explained his brother had sent Mr. Martin to Town to deliver some papers. Mr. Martin had called at the house first but, upon being told Mr. Knightley was at his chambers, had gone there instead.

"Robert Martin is a level-headed, clever young man who deserves a great deal more than he has got," Mr. Knightley said. "I think the young girl he sets his cap at will be very fortunate indeed."

"Well, he has gained George's good opinion," Mrs. Knightley added. "He places a good deal of trust in him." She poured her husband's coffee. "Should we ask him to join us for dinner, do you think, before he returns to Highbury?"

"Oh, I am sure there is no need for that!" Harriet exclaimed before she could stop herself. "He would not expect to receive such notice from you."

"No need for it, certainly," Mr. Knightley replied, "but I did enjoy talking to him. Would you not like to see him, Harriet? He might give you news of all your friends in Highbury."

Mr. Knightley's sardonic tone gave Harriet little clue as to whether he was serious or attempting to tease her. Was there a mischievous glint in his eyes, or had they just been caught by the late afternoon sun that streamed in through the windows? Its rays *were* bouncing off the crystal bowl that held the sugar lumps.

Harriet put the biscuit she had been eating back on her plate, fearing she would not be able to swallow it. Her mouth had become dry, her appetite gone.

She was suddenly lost in remembrances of the bright days she had enjoyed at the Martin's farm; long summer days, yet they had flown quickly by, made shorter by wonderful company and a good deal of laughter. She thought of the time when they had spoken of books. Robert Martin had not mocked her for her taste in romantic novels. Instead, he had smiled shyly at her and told her that his land took up much of his time but that he would like to be better read.

"It is not for me to say whether he should come or not. I should not decide it," Harriet said quietly, realising she had left too long a pause, caused a gap in the conversation. "You must do what pleases you, Mr. Knightley."

"But do you object to him, Miss Smith?" Mr. Knightley asked, leaning forward.

"No," she said. "I have not the least objection to Mr. Martin."

The problem was that he might have objections to her! But she did not say that, or that every one of his scruples were well justified.

"Well, we had best ready ourselves for Astley's, if we are to arrive in good time." Mrs. Knightley got to her feet.

Her hosts had kindly arranged some entertainment for Harriet, now that she was recovered. They were to go to the famous amphitheatre on Westminster Bridge Road to see the circus, the two eldest Knightley children accompanying them.

It was the sort of outing that might have given Harriet great cause for excitement a year ago, but all pleasures were dull to her now. Flowers did not smell so sweet, colours were not so bright, music not so uplifting.

Her encounter with Robert Martin that afternoon had further distressed her. She had run away from him, like a child. She ought to have been more civil and tried to express, in some small way, her regrets. Not because she wanted to bring on a renewal of his addresses—she did not deserve his attentions—but because she was truly sorry for any pain she had given him.

Besides, she had resolved to live a life of goodness and simplicity. She would not think of romance.

"Yes, let us go out" said Mr. Knightley, standing up beside his wife, "and consider Robert Martin no more. I shall not feel compelled to have him for dinner if Harriet does not like the idea. We shall send him back to Highbury hungry and never see him again."

But an hour or so later, they did see him again. Mr. Knightley ordered the carriage to stop outside a respectable lodging house on the way to Astley's and, to Harriet's great astonishment, Robert Martin climbed in. The children had to shuffle up closer to their father in order to make room for the farmer's substantial shoulders as he settled himself on the opposite bench. The coach seemed so much narrower with him in it. Harriet was forced to put her knees to one side to avoid them bumping against his.

While Mr. Knightley explained he had asked Mr. Martin to join them for the evening as a thank you for bringing his brother's papers to Town, Harriet could look nowhere but at her shoes. Then, realising she *had* been horribly teased earlier during tea, she managed a reproachful look at Mr. Knightley. He only shrugged and smiled in response.

Her gaze fell back down—to Mr. Martin's boots, which appeared newly polished. His trousers were nowhere near as fine as Mr. Knightley's—they were of a far coarser, thicker wool—but they were impeccably clean, as was his hat, which he threaded through his hands, wringing it one way and then another as he gave his greetings in a deep timbered voice. Though his compliments were given awkwardly, they were so earnest in tone that Harriet, impressed, glanced up again despite her embarrassment, but Mr. Martin immediately looked away and would not meet her eye.

It all made Harriet wish she had the toothache again. That had somehow been less discomforting.

Fortunately, the circus, with its wild colours, thunderous noise, and peculiar, spectacular feats, distracted her from everything, even from herself. The joy and wonder in the children's expressions lifted Harriet's sprits immensely. There was so much to entertain them that she was not forced to converse with Robert Martin, not until the show was over and they were walking out.

Mr. and Mrs. Knightley left the box before them with little John and were soon out of sight, swallowed up by the crowds. It seemed everyone wanted to leave the place at once, and the narrow passages were fit to bursting. There were excited shouts, the audience still caught up in the thrill of all they had witnessed.

They were jostled, yet Mr. Martin was immediately alert to the dangers of pickpockets and of them becoming separated. He had the good sense to keep Henry with him, grabbing hold of the boy firmly by the shoulders.

Harriet, unused to London, panicked by the noise, smell, and heat of the place, could not move for a moment, nor could she speak or even breathe. She grew faint and disorientated until Mr. Martin reached back and took her hand in his. His grasp was strong, unapologetic, and reassuring. He urged her forward by whispering something close to her ear. Though she did not really hear his words, she followed him, and soon they were out. She felt the blessed relief of the cool evening air. The

Knightley's carriage was waiting for them nearby, and the sight of it calmed Harriet's nerves.

As did Robert Martin.

His good, honest face, tanned by the sun, weathered by the wind, was illuminated by the soft golden glow of gas lamps on the bridge, and it suddenly became desperately dear to her. He was still a young man, yet he carried the burdens of his farm with ease while taking care of his mother and shouldering the responsibility for his younger sisters. What a fine man he was, so very fine! No girl had ever regretted a refusal so bitterly as Harriet did then.

"I know I should not say it, Miss Smith, but I wish I did not have to let go of you." Despite his words, he did, however, drop her hand. "Maybe I should not have hoped as I did, but I did not think you were so far above me…"

How he might have continued or how Harriet would have replied, she was never to know. They were called over by Mrs. Knightley and, of course, Mr. Martin still had young Henry with him. If there was a chance of something, a new understanding between them, it had been missed, drowned out.

A war raged within Harriet as she lay in bed that night, sleepless and troubled. In unguarded moments, she gave in to flights of fancy. She imagined notes arriving, posies of flowers, and a young man proclaiming he had never stopped loving her. Then she would scold herself for not paying proper heed to her mistakes.

She needed to be a sensible creature from now on, but the memories of that moment on the bridge when Robert Martin had held her hand, the feelings he had stirred up, were too strong. How might he have finished his sentence had he been free to do so? She relived it in a thousand different ways, but it always ended in a renewal of his addresses.

Then she would shake her head, try to persuade herself it was impossible. "No, he will go home tomorrow," she said quietly to the ceiling, steeling herself for the disappointment that was sure to follow. "And I will probably never see him again."

Turning over in her bed, she gave the pillow a resounding thump, hoping it would help drive her desires deep into the recesses of her mind, bury them forever.

~

Weary, Harriet rose late the next day and was then informed by Mrs. Knightley that Mr. Martin was to dine with them that night! He was not due to go back to Highbury until the next day. Before he had left for his chambers, Mr. Knightley had sent a note to Mr. Martin's lodging house, and the invitation had been immediately accepted by return.

"I am sorry, Harriet," Mrs. Knightley said. "I am afraid my husband has taken it upon himself to make a match for you. I have not mentioned your history with Mr. Martin to him, but when the young man presented himself at Mr. Knightley's chambers, he apparently asked so assiduously and carefully after your welfare that Mr. Knightley believes him to be smitten with you. He ought not to meddle—why, he is as bad as my sister! Worse in some ways, because he labours under the same ridiculous preconception all men do. They assume that a suitor has to do no more than propose for the object of his affection to fall gratefully at his feet. Men have no understanding of the workings of a woman's mind. They cannot imagine that we too might have ambition. Perhaps you hope for more than Mr. Martin can offer, and the life of a farmer's wife is not what you crave. It is no bad thing to want something better."

Harriet got up from the breakfast table, unable to sit still, and paced to the window. "Oh, Mrs. Knightley, you must not think I consider myself above him in any way. I do not! And as for ambition, well, my notion of what is *better* has changed dramatically in recent months. One man can be quite superior to another, in ways that have nothing to do with where his money comes from. What do you suppose?"

Mrs. Knightley nodded and smiled. "I hope Mr. Martin's coming here to dine will not distress you unduly, Harriet."

Though she shook her head in denial and pretended all was well, it did discomfit Harriet. She spent the rest of the day wishing the dinner hour closer. Then in the next moment, she would wish it never to arrive. She wanted him to come; she wanted him away. That Mr. Knightley thought Mr. Martin still admired her made Harriet hope, then she would tell herself not to hope.

Her emotions were as much a circus as the one she had seen at the amphitheatre the previous evening. Her heart was a riot of colour, her soul full of explosions, tricks, and spills. He had accepted the invitation when he need not have; his business completed, he might have returned to Highbury earlier. Did he come to dinner for her sake?

With particular care, she bathed, dressed, and allowed Mrs. Knightley's maid to fuss about her gown and arrange her curls prettily at the back of her head. A few of them swung down to caress her shoulders.

At the appointed hour, not a minute before, she took a deep breath and went down to the drawing room to await Robert Martin's arrival. He was already there!

Deep in conversation with Mr. Knightley, he only briefly turned in her direction. He greeted her, of course, but then went on talking of pigs and chicken, hectares and hedgerows, and rights of way in such an animated fashion and so knowledgably to Mr. Knightley that she feared any interjection she made would make her look foolish.

She retreated to Mrs. Knightley's side and wondered about him from across the room.

There was a pattern to evenings such as these. There would be some conversation before dinner, the meal would last for well over an hour and, at the end of it, the ladies would withdraw while the men remained behind to enjoy brandy and tobacco. When the company came together again, Mrs. Knightley would most likely take to the pianoforte.

Harriet did not play, neither did she sing; it was one of those cases where practice certainly did not make perfect. There were cats that sang better than she. Neither could she draw or even sew particularly well. Her only talent was to be generally agreeable and inoffensive though, to her credit, she was remarkably accomplished at both.

Once the entertainment was finished, Mr. Martin would go. He was not an intimate friend or relation, so he would not linger until supper.

Most likely he would be with them for two, maybe three hours at best. The clock on the mantlepiece ticked off the allotted seconds and minutes of his visit. Harriet adored clocks, had always been fascinated by their movements, had thought of them as the instruments by which happier moments were brought closer. Now the pretty decorated timepiece felt like an enemy, a thief robbing her of the opportunity to say something meaningful to Robert Martin before he went.

The smaller of the hands on the clock made its way relentlessly towards the six. Harriet jumped when the larger hand ticked onto the twelve and sweet chimes began. The butler bowed and cleared his throat but did not need to speak. They all knew dinner was served.

At table, they spoke of the circus. Mrs. Knightley praised the bravery of the trapeze artists who had walked on wires above their heads.

"Are they brave though, Mrs. Knightley, or foolhardy?" Mr. Martin asked.

"Or reckless?" Mr. Knightley added.

"Or perhaps it is all they have ever known," Harriet said. It was the first time she had properly participated in a conversation since they had sat down. "They were likely born into such a life. To them, walking on a wire is probably no different than herding sheep. I think it is the ladies who are the bravest of souls. The way they leap from those great swings with their arms outstretched into the air, trusting the man to catch them. They are not in charge of their own destiny. In that moment, their failure or success depends entirely on someone else."

"They must pick the right partner then, Miss Smith." Mr. Martin's eyes were wide and his forehead furrowed. His look was intent as he leant over his plate a little for a moment, briefly forgetting his manners. "There are some men who would make it their life's work never to let their lady fall, who will always be there to catch them, should they slip or falter."

There followed a long silence while Harriet coloured and knew not what to say. Her heart thudded so loudly against her chest—it reverberated through her just as the noise of the horses' hooves had done when they had slammed against the floor of the circus ring the previous evening. Could anyone else hear it? She smelled the sawdust anew, and her ears rang with the cheers and screams of the crowd. Her hand ached because it was not being held in *his*.

Mrs. Knightley emitted a small cough. "Well, some ladies prefer not to leap. I much prefer to remain on solid ground."

Mr. Knightley laughed. "What of you, Harriet, are you brave?"

"Me, Mr. Knightley? No, I have always been something of a coward, happy to let myself be led hither and thither. I have sat and hoped and wished for things rather than leaped at them. I should like to be braver."

From under her lashes, she gave Mr. Martin a look she had never given any other man. She could not sustain it, however, as she had seen bolder women do.

"But bravado requires opportunity," she added, as she fiddled with her knife and fork, conscious of his gaze upon her. "Here with you, my dear friends, Mr. and Mrs. Knightley, I am happy and content. You have been so very generous that I lack for nothing, and bravery, I think, is also driven by necessity."

Mrs. Knightley, perhaps wishing to break the odd, strained atmosphere that filled the room, found a new subject for them. The one they had been embarking was far too dangerous.

After dinner, the ladies rose to leave the room, but Harriet had no sooner settled herself on a sofa than Mr. Knightley came in. He asked her if she would fetch a tome for him from his small book room along the hall, for Mr. Martin had shown an interest in borrowing it. Harriet blinked, astonished at the request, wondering why he did not retrieve it himself. She rose, as she would never refuse Mr. Knightley a favour, but she trod the highly polished floorboards with trepidation.

As she feared, hoped, dreaded, and wished all at the same time, Mr. Martin was there, having obviously asked for a private audience with her.

She was about to put her head into the lion's mouth. Would she survive the experience?

"Forgive me, Miss Smith, but Mr. and Mrs. Knightley are such good people that no one should ever know of this if you do not wish it." He tugged at his formal collar. Harriet thought she preferred him in the rough tweeds he wore going about his business at the farm. "You see, I was thinking about what you said at dinner about being brave, and so I thought to talk to you."

"Mr. Martin, I must speak to you first."

Harriet wanted him to smile. His face was very grave, as if he expected a refusal from her, but she could not yet relieve his misery.

"You must know that I was born outside of wedlock, was sent away at a young age to live with a family that was paid to keep and raise me. When I was old enough, I went to various schools before finding much happiness at Mrs. Goddard's. Oh, you look sorry for me now, but you must not. I was very fortunate when so many girls in similar circumstances are not. My needs have always been met. I have had gowns aplenty; money would appear in my reticule whenever I required funds.

"When I reached the age whereby a young lady is considered duly educated, and that much more might spoil her, I remained at Mrs. Goddard's. It is a place where I have known acceptance and love, where I have been treated with much affection. I have no other home to go to, so it has become my home. I was raised never to expect much, and I did not, not until Miss Woodhouse took an interest in me.

"She believed me to be the daughter of a fine gentleman, nobility even." Harriet let out a small laugh. "And I, keen to ingratiate myself, flattered by such attention from a grand young lady, let her think just as she pleased. Yet, when I was a small girl, I saw my father."

There was a chair nearby and Harriet sank into it, too full of emotion to stand.

"I was out playing in the fields," she continued, after a deep breath. "I was running and climbing trees when a carriage stopped on the road and a man got out. He was smart and handsome but not a man of nobility. There was no livery. There were only two horses and two servants. He was a man of business, I suspect. As young as I was, I saw the signs of it. He approached me and knew my name. He asked me how I did and pressed a coin into my hand. I ought to have been afraid, I suppose, but there was nothing threatening about him. His countenance was curious, his eyes so terribly sad. He asked after my studies, wished me good tidings. And then returned to his carriage and I never saw the man again."

"Then I am sorry, Miss Smith."

"You are wondering, I think, what all this has to do with you. My point is, Mr. Martin, that I have committed awful sins. Not only did I conceal what I knew about my parentage from Miss Woodhouse, but I also forsook you, and your sisters, and your wonderful mother. You offered me friendship, and I threw it back at you. I was very happy last summer."

"Miss Woodhouse has a lot to answer for…"

"Oh no!" Harriet cut him off. "No, she was blind to what she did and feels so sorry for it now that I cannot blame her. She knew no better, yet I did."

Mr. Martin kneeled before her, bowed his head. "None of that matters to me, Miss Smith. I care not where you come from or what has happened before. I shall probably never read *The Romance of the Forest*, though I told you I would. I am not a learned man. I am a man of the fields and proud of it. I said I should like to read that book because I thought you should prefer it if I did. I wanted you to love me as I do you. We were both deceitful. Harriet, you still have my heart, but do not take it because you feel you can do no better or because I am all that is left for you."

She gasped. "Mr. Martin, you do me the very greatest honour. Indeed, I now feel you are far better than I deserve."

He kissed her hand, then lay his forehead against it. She felt his breath on her fingers like a caress and could think of nothing but what his lips might feel like against hers.

"Could you love me, though?" he asked. His voice was barely above a whisper. It did not matter; so attuned to him was she now, she still heard his every word. "Would you mind being a farmer's wife? Would you live in a place where you are awoken at dawn by a cockerel's crow? Think carefully. You would be mistress of a practical house and, when the rains are bad, you might have to wade through the mud to get to your front door. When the wind blows from the west, the smell of the pigs will invade your parlour. I can offer you little, Miss Smith, but all I have, I will gladly give you. I promise to always catch you if you will leap into my arms."

He remained on his knees before her, his head almost in her lap, as if he were begging. It would not do. She tugged back the hand that he held and used it to grasp his strong jaw, drawing it closer to her. "Mr. Martin, I will take your hand, knowing full well what accompanies it."

He thanked her, and she ducked her head, a moment of shyness overcoming her before she spoke again.

"When I first came to London, I thought that I would be rational, that I should not think of love or romance. Now I see the only sensible path open to me is to accept your offer. A lady can be too careful. To not leap, to not take any risks at all, is to not live properly. You look offended, Mr. Martin."

She kissed him then, bending her face towards his. Their lips met in her very first kiss. She was not disappointed by it. "Yet you must know that when I marry you, I become less of me and all of you. You will own me. I will be controlled by you. That is the way society, the law, everyone sees it. I do not call it a risk because I doubt your love. I have great faith in you, but you must know a woman needs to be in possession of great courage to go down the aisle. It is the bravest walk she will ever make."

He took her hand from his face, turned it over, and kissed the inside of her wrist. She burned; she melted. "I shall make you happy."

"No, Mr. Martin. I shall make myself happy, and we will be happy together."

They spent too long in the small room, finding and understanding each other in sweet, experimental kisses—so long that they had been missed when they returned to the drawing room.

Mrs. Knightley appeared worried, but Mr. Knightley merely smirked. Harriet did not care. She could bear the embarrassment of the moment as Mr. Martin—Robert, her Robert—announced their engagement.

He kept her by his side and they took a seat on a sofa together. Harriet allowed herself to be the centre of attention. She knew she would not often be the main topic of conversation or the cause of excitement. Once she was married, hers would be a simple life mapped out by small milestones. Those small, precious moments: marriages, births, christenings. There would be periods of nothingness when she would feel frustrated, or dull, or put upon, unenthusiastic even, about the life she had chosen. Winters would be hard and unforgiving.

Yet there would be fires and candles, and love. She would be happy in a warm home, surrounded by her family. She looked at her betrothed and saw the strength in his arms, his thighs, his firm jaw. All that he was, was all she required.

It would not always be so. She was rational enough in the ways of the world to understand that there would be times when she would not be so enthralled by him, but he had promised to always catch her, and she silently vowed she would always catch him.

CAITLIN WILLIAMS is an award-winning author of *Ardently, The Coming of Age of Elizabeth Bennet, When We Are Married,* and *The Events at Branxbourne,* that all spin the plot of *Pride and Prejudice* around but keep the characters just the same. Originally from South London, Caitlin spent thirteen years as a detective in the Metropolitan Police but is currently on a break from Scotland Yard so she can spend more time at home with her two children and write. She now lives in Kent, where she spends a lot of time daydreaming about Mr. Darcy, playing with dinosaurs, and trying not to look at the laundry pile.

THE MEANING OF WIFE

BROOKE WEST

FANNY PRICE

Timid, shy, and a poor relation of Sir Thomas Bertram, Fanny prefers to remain quietly unnoticed. At Mansfield Park, amidst lust, sloth, greed, and jealousy, she persisted, ever constant in her morals and sensible in her convictions. *"We have all a better guide in ourselves, if we would attend to it, than any other person can be."* —**Chapter XXXVI, *Mansfield Park*.** In the end, this mild-mannered, quiet, rational creature triumphs. She found her happiness and married the man she always loved—without having to compromise any of her principles.

THE MEANING OF WIFE

That quiet, inconsequential morning would change the course of Fanny Price's future.

Fanny sat placidly at the breakfast table, enjoying what she could see of the grounds through the windows. Hot toast in her hand and a cup of chocolate before her, she was content to halfway listen to the conversation around her and simply *be*.

Tom unfolded a letter beside his plate and harrumphed. "Old Bigby says Lucretia—that's his younger sister, you know—is planning to head off to the Continent at the end of the summer."

"That is lovely." Lady Bertram's soft voice barely carried farther than the rim of the tea cup she lowered from her lips. Though the indolent woman seldom took her breakfast with the family, Tom's return from travels the night before drew her from her bedchamber before eleven o'clock this morning. "Every young woman of consequence ought to have an artistic tour of the continent. Before your father and I said our vows—"

"To study philosophy!" Tom continued, paying no mind to his mother's words.

Fanny felt a brief flash of irritation on Lady Bertram's behalf. She considered at times it was no wonder the woman chose to keep to her bed, when her own family could not countenance allowing her to speak.

"To study, you say?" Sir Thomas Bertram's deep voice shook Fanny to attention.

"His *father* believes it is well to educate young women as far as needed to ensure their intellectual ability to follow the laws of God and our society. Have you ever heard anything so absurd?"

Edmund set his coffee cup onto its saucer; his thoughtful expression that Fanny knew so well brought a gravity to his features. *I may be past pining, but I doubt a day will pass that I will not have reason to reflect on Edmund Bertram's quality.* She watched fondly as his left eye squinted slightly, a clear indication he was about to set someone to rights.

"A woman does not need a formal education to fulfill her role; she need only follow her internal moral compass. Why, take our dear Fanny."

Their dear Fanny, shocked to find herself the subject of this conversation when she had assumed no part in the discourse and sought only to break her fast in peace, froze in the middle of lifting her chocolate to her lips.

"You could not find a less educated but more moral and true woman in all of England." He looked at Fanny, eyes sparkling with admiration, a proud smile on his face. Her face burned, a flush spreading over her cheeks and down her neck. The look he gave her should have made those blushes pleasurable. Instead, the heat under her skin prickled uncomfortably. Something about the way he lauded her lack of education made her wish she had more of one.

"Debate is unseemly in a woman. A clear mind, free from the complexities of academic rigor, ensures her natural sweetness. Her inherent goodness will shine through and light the path for her fortunate husband, illuminating for him the obstacles that he at times will miss, consumed as he is by greater concerns. Only with her unfailing adherence to *rightness* will he excel in his calling." Edmund's gaze lingered on Fanny, his hand resting on the tablecloth between them as if he yearned to reach for hers.

Fanny had long dreamed of seeing such ardor in Edmund's gaze. But his look now, coming as it did on the heels of a celebration of her ignorance, soured the expected delight of receiving his attention. He had not thought debate so unseemly when it came from Mary Crawford, she recalled.

"Too much of that Wollstonecraft, I say!" Sir Thomas said. "Completely turns a woman's head away from her domestic duties. Has her thinking she has a place on the world stage."

Lady Bertram sighed loudly into her teacup, seeming to wilt where she sat.

"It sounds lovely to me," Fanny said weakly, struggling to regain her composure. Edmund had not taken his eyes from her. "Sitting by the Aegean, reading the great philosophers where their works were written."

"I would much rather you not imagine such things at all, Fanny," Edmund said. "The journey alone would be well beyond your capabilities."

Not only am I ignorant, but I am now delicate as well? Too rough for education but too fine for travel? "Perhaps, but assuming the journey were no issue—"

Sir Thomas interrupted, "Even assuming that, the study of philosophy —or any academic endeavor—is a waste of a woman's time."

Edmund must have noticed Fanny's wrinkled brow. "Now, do not take offense! It is simply the natural order of things."

"Natural order of things?"

"Wollstonecraft even recognizes the intellectual superiority of men"— Tom joined in.

"You have the advantage of me. I have not read this Wollstonecraft."

"As always, you prove to be the paragon of feminine morality. Her writings would only pollute a proper female mind so rightly formed as your own. Too much worldliness ruins a good woman." Edmund smiled again in a way that should have made her heart skip a beat but now, feeling attacked by all her male relatives, only made her feel confused and perhaps—though she was reluctant to admit it—indignant.

"Wollstonecraft is a woman?"

"Of course she is!" Tom laughed. "Do you think a man would have written *A Vindication of the Rights of Woman?*" The three men chuckled and turned the conversation to other matters, leaving Fanny to stew in these new feelings of inadequacy and mild outrage.

I had never considered such a writing at all before this morning, but I will have it in my hands before I retire to my chamber this evening.

One week later, Fanny sat on her favorite bench in the garden, nestled among spring blooms yet shaded from the sun by a nearby tree. It had taken her longer than a day to get a copy of *Vindication* in her hands, but once she had, she could scarcely put it down.

> *"Would men but generously snap our chains, and be content with rational fellowship instead of slavish obedience, they would find us more observant daughters, more affectionate sisters, more faithful wives, more reasonable mothers —in a word, better citizens."*

Fanny had long seen the imbalance of power between the sexes but not thought of it in such stark terms. After having read Wollstonecraft's essay through twice, she felt aware, attuned to the inequality of their society. And desirous of setting the balance right.

Footsteps on the gravel drew her notice, and she looked up in time to close the volume and lay it under her hands before Edmund drew too close. He wore the topcoat she liked best on him; the deep blue emphasized his tawny eyes. He smiled at her, amiable as ever, but there was an apprehensive air about him as well.

"Ah, I see I have caught you reading again." His eyes moved to the cover of the book, but Fanny's hands hid the title well. She smiled sweetly and, thankfully, he had the decency not to pry, though he seemed to recognize her intentional furtiveness. "If I may…?" He gestured to the seat beside her.

He looked at her, and she looked back at him, expectant but not hurried. He fidgeted a bit, which was unusual, as he was normally a calm man. The anxious look in his eyes, however, gave Fanny to think that he was going to carry on again about Miss Crawford. It had been weeks since his latest lamentation and, while Fanny hoped Edmund had grown past his sadness, she was wary of another outburst.

"This will come as a great surprise to you, Fanny, for I am certain you have not given a thought to marriage since your disappointment with…."

Edmund looked to the gravel walk and cleared his throat, but his words seem to have become stuck.

"There was no disappointment." Fanny sighed. She had long since tired of having the same conversations about that man. No matter how many times she expressed her feelings on the dissolution of that marriage prospect, no one seemed to take her words to heart. It was almost as though she were not allowed to know her own mind; others must tell her how she felt. While she was gratified by the support and solicitude she had received after the event, discussing it had become all too bothersome.

"Nor surprise, I must say. Mr. Crawford has proved himself to be the very sort of man I considered him to be. I am content to not have to endure his designs on my future any longer. Please, let us not discuss him further."

"As you wish, yes, of course. I only meant ... I mean, we both have suffered at the hands of that family and, try as we might to put them out of our minds, small reminders linger about the Park and the parish house. Fair days they were, before the moral decay rotting through the core of those siblings was made plain to us, their closest friends. And nearly their family! I often wonder, Fanny, whether Miss Craw—" Edmund cut himself off abruptly, a sheepish look stealing across his face.

"It is all right, Edmund."

"Yes. Thank you, Fanny. Your kind nature and understanding of another's troubles are more qualities to recommend you." He hesitated, drawing a breath as though to steady himself.

"To that point, Fanny, I would very much like to propose a ... er, a proposal, I suppose."

He moved closer to her on the bench. His hand raised momentarily from his thigh as if he were going to reach for hers. Like a flash, Fanny recalled that moment over breakfast last week when he looked at her so intensely and seemed to want to reach for her across the expanse of the table. She had felt foolish at the time, reading desire into his expression, but his earnestness and closeness now made her believe her instinct had been correct.

She realized she was staring at his hand, which was resting high on his thigh. Which was covered in a snug buckskin the same color as his eyes.

Her breath caught, embarrassed to think that Edmund saw her forward-
ness. She raised her eyes to his, and her mouth went dry at the open heat
of his gaze.

He fancies me. After all this time. Edmund.

"We suit, do we not?" His voice was raspy, strained, wholly unlike
anything Fanny had heard from him before. He held her gaze and raised
an eyebrow, as if expecting a response, but continued before her lips could
part in reply. "We could be happy together?"

Her heart pounded, barely able to contain the joy of having Edmund
look at her with love instead of simple admiration. But her head ... something inside her head screamed, *He does not know you. How could he love
you?* Fanny was caught between the two impulses. The surge of emotion
flattened with the memory of his earlier words about the "natural order of
things." How those words still nettled her!

"You seek a quiet life of service and devotion, too, do you not?"
Edmund's hand was warm and steady as it held hers. She understood that
he was sure of his decision, his choice. He was choosing *her!*

Fanny's eyes turned to the volume held in her lap, which now filled her
head with new notions of what life could be if she only had the bravery to
seek it. Visions of a life in which she was her own mistress, beholden to
the control of no man by blood or marriage. *Am I so sure a quiet life is what
I seek?*

"I see your modesty, Fanny, and want you to know that, while it
endears me to you, there is no need of it anymore. Not with me. I have
seen the warmth of spirit that burns in you, the fire."

The last word lingered in the air between them. Fanny felt the sting of
heat all over. He had the right of it; she *did* have fire, but, now sparked, her
heat easily had become a blaze of vexation.

Now, Edmund? You wait until now to offer for me? The voice in her head
seemed to be winning.

Memories ran through her mind: Edmund and Mary flirting during
the rehearsals; Edmund encouraging her to accept Henry's affections and
proposal; Edmund pouring the sad contents of his heart to Fanny when he
realized he could not take Mary as a wife; Edmund moping about the
Park for weeks.

He even had the gall to muse on her moments before he offered for me! Fanny could feel her cheeks turning pink as irritation rose within her breast.

"I would be your husband, Fanny! If you would have me." He tipped her chin up to look her in the eye. "Surely the merits are plain to your discerning mind, even without the benefit of forethought—I have always said how you are much keener than others will credit you!"

Fanny flinched at the slight, but he seemed not to notice her reaction nor the insensitivity of his words.

He does not even see you! screamed the voice in her head. *He sees only what he expects from you. That's why he continues to assume you are heartbroken over Mr. Crawford. He simply cannot see you as you truly are.*

He dropped his hand and stood, turning to look across the lawn to the parish house. "But I would be loath to rush you or insist soon upon an answer. I would not hurry you and gladly will wait, should you need time to consider."

Edmund turned back and smiled, appearing at once confident in his proposal and anxious for a response. His expression was all hope and possibility.

Fanny was struck with the sweetness of his smile and could not help but smile in return. For half her life, his smile had guided her through the difficulties and shame of being a poor relative in a great house. Her anger melted away. The voice in her head quieted and she felt like herself again.

She could not, however, shake the disquiet she carried, the suspicion that Edmund did not truly know her at all, choosing only to see the young woman he expected her to be. It struck her as darkly amusing that for years she had longed for Edmund to look upon her with desire but, now that his heart had found his way to her, she could find none of the expected joy.

Fanny reflected upon herself, seeking the thrill, the delight, the divine certainty she anticipated would accompany such a moment. She found none. Her second marriage proposal—two more than she had ever expected to receive—and both met only with disappointment of varying degrees. Henry Crawford's had brought a fierce, visceral repugnance. Edmund's brought a mild sadness.

Whether he knows my heart or not, Edmund would never seek to cause me distress. His words are true. I can rely upon his goodness, and if he offers me time to consider, then time I shall have.

Fanny stood, clutching *A Vindication* in one hand and laying the other on his arm, comforted by his suggestion she not rush a decision. "Edmund, thank you, truly. Yes, I would like to—"

Edmund captured her hand from his arm and pressed it to his lips. "Oh, my dear Fanny! Sweeter and more welcome words never have passed your lips! What a life we shall have together! You have made me the happiest of men this day!"

Fanny felt her face turn hot with mortification. Edmund's lips kept moving but she could hear nothing beyond the sound of rushing blood in her ears and the loud thumping of her heart. Through her anxiety, she could recognize his sincere joy. Fearful as she was, still she was hesitant to correct his error.

But you cannot keep silent and allow your future to be taken out of your hands. Again. The determined and angry voice had returned, more resolute than ever.

Taking a deep breath and forcing her voice steady, she interrupted him. "Edmund, wait. You misunderstood me."

The world around her slowed, and she watched the progression of emotions across his face in painstaking detail. One heartbeat, and he stopped speaking. Two heartbeats more. The lightness of elation and certainty dimmed from his eyes, and then his grin faltered. Five heart-beats. His eyebrows drew together, his confusion growing with each moment of her silence. Ten heartbeats, and his smile was a decided frown.

"I ... misunderstand you?" His voice was small, barely more than a whisper.

"Only a little. I—"

"A little is quite a lot when one has just proposed marriage, it seems."

"Edmund, please. Allow me to finish."

"You do not accept me?"

"No. I mean, perhaps. What I mean is—"

"I know I do not have the wealth of that Crawford man, but I thought what I had to offer you was sufficient to ensure your happiness."

Fanny thought he sounded a lot like his father did when Sir Thomas chastised her for not accepting Henry's hand. It took enormous effort to not explode at the indignation of always having men pass judgment upon her decisions—her most personal and important decisions, at that.

"This has nothing to do with Mr. Crawford, Edmund. If you would please allow me to fin—"

"I had hoped that you would have moved beyond your disappointment, as I have done, and come to the same realization ... the understanding that we suit very well, Fanny."

Incredible! Fanny could not keep the exasperation from her voice as she replied, "I was not *disappointed!* For months you have been overlaying *your* disappointment onto *me!* Do you not hear me at all? Can you not allow me to know my own mind, my own heart?"

Edmund started at her raised voice, eyes wide with shock.

"I do not believe I have ever heard such passion from you."

She felt a little sorry for having shocked him and sought to soothe him. "Is not a marriage proposal the appropriate time to become passionate?"

Her lips quirked into a small smile, and she squeezed his hand. Edmund started again at the pressure, apparently surprised to find their fingers still interlaced. He tried to release his fingers from hers, but she held fast.

"Edmund, I am not sure I ever will marry. I am not sure what I will do with my future. I meant only to accept your offer of *time*. Allow me to consider what life I should like to have. Should I not have an equal say in my own life, mere woman that I am?"

Edmund opened his mouth to speak but thought better of what he intended to say. After a pause and a deep breath, he continued. "Of course. Of course. I apologize. I did not intend to overbear you with my eagerness."

His softened and respectful demeanor soothed the angry voice in her head that had taken over her tongue. He raised her fingers again, barely brushing her knuckles with his soft, warm lips. A thrill of heat shot through her core, unlike anything she had felt before. She wanted to throw herself into his embrace, rushing towards the future of which she had always dreamed.

But, no. *Time. Take your time; find the right state of mind for such a decision.*

Finally, their hands dropped apart.

"The sun has become too hot for me to linger, even in the shade. Shall I escort you inside?"

"No, I should like to remain in the garden for a time. Thank you."

Edmund gave her a slight bow and, with a subdued, somewhat pained smile, turned to go.

Once he was out of sight, Fanny collapsed onto the bench, letting her head fall back. She closed her eyes as she turned her face to the bright sky above, her world only a pleasant light pink color and the chatter of the springtime birds. After a few deep breaths, she felt her emotions calm, her thoughts clearing. The anger receded, allowing her to reflect on all that had just occurred.

It frustrated her that Edmund seemed to have such a difficult time understanding her emotions, her motivations, her desires. They shared common sentiments and values. *There is much to be said for those similarities. To be sure, steady marriages have been built on less. And was not that your chief complaint against Mr. Crawford?* There was no doubt that, between the two men, Edmund was most suited to secure her happiness.

Happiness... What is "happiness"? Happiness is not perpetual, but neither is it a fleeting emotion. Perhaps it is not an emotion at all. No, happiness to me is a contentment with one's life. It is having a fulfilling place in society where one can do those things one feels to be necessary and good.

Fanny pondered what it was that she found to be necessary and good. She imagined herself married to a faceless man, several young, dirty children about her in the kitchen as she prepared the day's bread, her husband lounging with a newspaper by a weak coal fire in the dingy parlor. Her stomach twisted, the image too similar to the life she left behind in Portsmouth.

Putting that grim illusion aside, she envisioned a life touring the Continent and learning about the ancient philosophers, studying mathematics and science. Though the travels seemed exciting, she could find no delight in gathering knowledge simply for its own sake. What good could she do with a head bursting full of knowledge if she never returned home to share it?

Perhaps she could marry a wealthy man and be a lady of a great house with social consequence and exquisite furnishings? This image was met with revulsion. No, she would not elevate herself among others—it felt unnatural and wrong.

Perhaps she should devote her life to the service of others? Work in an orphanage and care for England's abandoned and destitute children? This thought pulled at her heartstrings but did not fill her with contentment.

Edmund thinks I seek a life of service. Once, I would have said the same.

She remembered the tortuous anxiety she felt during those weeks when everyone she loved expected and encouraged her to marry Henry. She had tried to open her heart to him, fighting against all her principles in an effort to appease those around her. She remembered being praised for her selflessness when she agonizingly put her own wishes aside for others—giving up her riding time for Mary, for instance. These attempts at serving the desires of others brought only pain. No comfort. No lightness.

The warm breeze swept across her upturned face. She could hear it rustling the branches of the nearby trees, playing in the petals of the early blooms, a hundred softly whispered words for beauty. She imagined walking in a garden of her own, filled with plants she had chosen. A smile grew on her face. Herbs for the kitchen and for tonics. Vegetables and fruits tended with care to provide sustenance throughout the year. Teaching Susan how to plant a kitchen garden with onions and herbs to keep the rabbits away. Harvesting the garden's bounty and making baskets to share with her neighbors. She would have to plant mint specifically for Mrs. Owens—a strongly brewed peppermint tea helped ease her tender stomach.

She heard Susan's voice from the other side of the house. Her younger sister was probably talking to one of the kittens the stable master recently had brought in.

Fanny's heart swelled with joy thinking of how Susan had grown in her short time at Mansfield Park. Susan was more eloquent and had taken well to all her lessons. Watching Susan develop into a refined young woman was Fanny's greatest delight. She hoped to be able to provide the same constancy and support to all of her siblings, to give them the same chance at a better life than the one they were born to.

She added each younger brother and sister into her imagined garden. The younger girls cutting flowers for the table, the older boys fencing with sticks under the apricot tree. *The apricot tree!* In her mind's eye, she looked up from the garden and took in the familiar surroundings: the small walk behind the parsonage, the distant woods, the imposing silhouette of the manor house. *This! This is where I feel contentment.* She watched her family play in the garden. *This is where I find purpose.*

She was startled to discover that she already was precisely where she wanted to remain. Fanny remembered the misery she felt the prior year when she had been returned to Portsmouth to spend time with her family. Yes, she had longed to return to Mansfield, but that was before she had begun to consider what her adult life would hold.

This new revelation was not borne from a childish fear of change or a selfish desire to not be challenged by life. Fanny *belonged* here, among her family, her friends, her neighbors. She did enjoy a life of service, but in service to those whom she loved and in ways that did not compromise herself.

How then do I maintain this happiness?

Her thoughts turned to Edmund and the offer he made to her not a half hour past. Her heart was on his side, without a doubt. But what about her head? Could she accept being a wife? Would not that be an abdication of her rights as a woman? *Would I not be compromising the integrity of my womanhood by marrying?*

Fanny reached for *A Vindication*, opening to a section she marked earlier in the day:

"It is acknowledged that they spend many of the first years of their lives in acquiring a smattering of accomplishments; meanwhile strength of body and mind are sacrificed to libertine notions of beauty, to the desire of establishing themselves —the only way women can rise in the world—by marriage."

"The only way women can rise in the world—by marriage…" Fanny muttered the words as she closed the volume. "There is some truth to that. And what is so wrong about finding one's way through marriage?"

"I expect I'll marry. Don't you expect to marry?"

"Susan! Where did you come from?"

"Well, I was walking this way—I know you like your afternoon walks in this garden and was hoping to find you—when I heard you and Edmund talking. I sat down in the flowers to wait, but he stayed so long I wearied and went to find the baby kittens Mr. Jones brought from town last week. The gray and white one is my favorite. When I saw Edmund go into the house and you not following, I decided I could still find you here. And here you are! So why are we talking about marriage?"

The lively young girl plopped on the bench beside Fanny, an expectant and humorous gleam in her eye.

Fanny sighed. "Edmund has proposed to me."

"*Today*? Is that what you two were talking about?"

"It was."

"And what did you tell him? Oh, of course you accepted!" When Fanny did not speak or smile or laugh or jump up with delight, Susan's brow furrowed. "Didn't you?"

"Well, no. But I did not refuse him either," Fanny said before Susan could interject her displeasure. Fanny relayed the proposal and her response to her younger sister.

"Surely you will accept him in the end. He is such a good man and a good match for you. He will bring you much happiness!"

Fanny smiled at her sister and took the younger woman's arm in her own, rising from the bench to walk about the garden. "I learned much this past year, dear Susan, and paramount of all the lessons is this: If we women rely upon men for our happiness, we shall be miserable all our lives."

They walked in silence for a few minutes, their boots crunching on the gravel walk.

"Then you will not accept him. If he does not bring you happiness, then why marry him?"

"When you came upon me, I was pondering the meaning of happiness and the purpose of marriage. I do not believe anyone can bring another happiness. *That* we must find on our own. A man can make a happy woman unhappy, but he cannot make an unhappy woman happy."

Again, the sisters lapsed into silence, leaving the gravel walk to stroll through the grass and to the woods beyond.

Susan broke the silence. "Are you happy?"

Fanny smiled, the strings of her bonnet tickling her neck in the breeze. "Yes, Susan, I believe that I am."

"Do you think Edmund would make you unhappy?"

With a jolt, Fanny realized she had been assessing her situation from a skewed perspective. She had been asking her head for a rational reason *why* she should marry Edmund when she should have been asking *why not*.

Her heart was his and had been for nearly half of her life! Her mind was her own, and she had reached a place of contentment with herself. Why, then, should not she take her love as her husband? Surely purpose and peace did not require stagnation to flourish.

Moreover, Edmund was kind and, although he seemed to have some deficiency in his understanding of the female condition, he had always shown himself to be open to discourse. Maybe all she needed was to talk to him about her beliefs. *Imagine having a learned husband as an ally for the rights of women!*

"Perhaps it is through marriage a woman will find her place and elevate the consequence of the female half of our race."

"Fanny?"

"Oh, Susan, I believe I have been most foolish. I must find Edmund!"

I hope he does not throw me over when I tell him I need him to see the woman's perspective. And not just in marriage...

She found Edmund lounging by a warm fire in the library, reading as the sun set through the tall windows.

As she burst into the room, her eyes locked with his. He watched, entranced, as she rushed over and dropped onto the sofa beside him. She had seen the glow of that particular expression on his face before when looking at Mary Crawford, but never quite so intensely as how he wore it now. It was, she realized, a look of wanting, and it brought a smile to her lips. Her gaze never left his even as she placed a book in his lap.

His expression wary, Edmund set his own tome to the side and picked up the book she had given him. His eyes widened as he read the title.

"*This* is what you have been reading this past week?"

She straightened her spine and raised her chin, which quivered almost imperceptibly. Edmund perceived it, however.

"Why do you look so, Fanny? You look … hurt. What has happened?"

"Have you read it?"

"Have I—yes, of course, I have read it."

"And do you find fault in me for having read it? For agreeing with her? Mostly, anyway?"

"Fanny, I—"

"You said worldliness ruins a woman. Well, I believe women *should* receive an education, any education they desire! And men and women should be held to the same moral standards. And that the way women are forced to rely upon men in our society is wrong. God made each of us in His image and we should none of us be subservient to any but Him."

Edmund sat, stunned, staring at her as though he had never seen her before. But it was not displeasure she saw in him. It was an eager sort of curiosity, and, if she were not mistaken, desire.

"I agree with all that you have said." His voice was low, almost rough.

Fanny blinked. "You do? You do not think that I have become polluted and morally corrupt? That I am...I am like Miss Crawford?" Those last words were a whisper.

He seemed to realize in that moment what she needed from him, why she had not accepted him earlier, and why she was here with him now.

"You are the best and most moral person I know, Fanny Price. I do not believe you capable of being polluted. And, I must say, I like this passionate side of you." His hand came up to cup her face, his fingers caressing the curl at her temple.

"As lovely as you have grown to be, all of it pales under the blaze of this new confidence and passion. You are a woman of superior mind, Fanny Price. If an idea takes root in your mind and you find merit in it, then I am persuaded that idea, too, is moral and right. Your endorsement is all I need." He set the book aside and took her hands in his. "*You* are all I need."

All of the fight left her the instant his skin touched hers. She had come prepared to defend herself and her ideas and demand that, if he truly loved her, he would reconsider his views. But none of that was necessary. All she had to do was show him how she felt, and he accepted it. He sided with her.

Fanny thought back to all the times it seemed Edmund's efforts on her behalf ran contrary to what Fanny truly wanted, and she realized that she had never once spoken for herself. *How could he have known? But here, when I tell him, he is right beside me. Unfailingly.*

I ought to have spoken for myself sooner.

"Yes, Edmund."

"Yes? You mean…Is this *the* 'yes'?" His face split in a wide grin, and he clasped her hands tighter.

Her own smile grew to meet his. "Yes. I…thought a lot today about happiness and what it meant to be a wife."

The finger that caressed her curl teased the curve of her brow. She felt a shiver of pleasure at this small, heartfelt gesture. "And what did you discover?"

"That I am happiest surrounded by my family and able to aid those who are dear to me. And that, while equality of the sexes is vital, marriage does not, as has been suggested, further entrench the current inequities but can be an excellent tool for bringing about needed changes."

He leaned forward, tantalizingly close. His forehead came to rest against hers, a symbol of their united future.

"I am impressed by your thoughtfulness on the matter, and I look forward to long evenings with you. Discussing the equality of the sexes."

Fanny blushed at the intensity of his gaze, his closeness, and the way he emphasized certain words. He sat back suddenly and peered at her.

"But are you certain? A parson's wife?"

"A clergyman's wife is precisely the role I would have chosen for myself. How else would I be so well positioned to assist and bring comfort to the neighborhood?"

Edmund bit his lip. "A lady of a great house, surely, can do more than a mere clergyman's wife."

"She would be tied to her great house most of the time, to be available to callers. And when she does visit among the needy in the parish, they will open their doors to her but never their hearts or minds. No one ever wants to bother a great lady, but a parson's wife is meant to be bothered."

With a brisk laugh, he pulled her into his arms. Her hand on his chest, she could feel his heart beating. The soothing heat of his arms around her body and the sound of his laugh in her ears filled her with a contentment she had never known—the satisfaction of both her rational mind and her emotional heart.

BROOKE WEST always loved the strong women of literature and thinks the best leading women have complex inner lives. When she's not spinning tales of rakish men and daring women, Brooke spends her time in the kitchen baking or at the gym working off all that baking. She lives in South Carolina with her husband and son and their three mischievous cats. Brooke co-authored the IPPY award winning novel *The Many Lives of Fitzwilliam Darcy* and the short story "Holiday Mix Tape" in *Then Comes Winter*. She also authored the short story "Last Letter to Mansfield," which you can find in *Dangerous to Know: Jane Austen's Rakes & Gentlemen Rogues*. Find Brooke on Twitter @WordyWest.

WHAT STRANGE CREATURES

JENETTA JAMES

MARY CRAWFORD

Charming, witty, and handsome, this orphaned heiress has all the makings of a heroine, and yet her rational sensibilities, survival instincts, and questionable values might be found wanting by polite society. *"There, I will stake my last like a woman of spirit. No cold prudence for me. I was not born to sit still and do nothing. If I lose the game, it shall not be from not striving for it."* —**Chapter XXV,** *Mansfield Park.*

WHAT STRANGE CREATURES

When Hoskins announced that she had a gentleman caller, Mary Craw-ford looked at the clock in disbelief. A morning call in the morning? What manner of gaucheness was this? To be awake and abroad when polite society, as one, was still abed. Whoever could this creature be? Mary put aside her book, for it did not do to be caught in the act of reading (unless the audience specifically admired such a pastime). Then, she slipped her dainty feet from the silk-covered chaise, straightening her gown. "Show him in, please, Hoskins." Possibilities rattled through her mind, and she was suddenly interested in the day.

In a moment, Mary was idling by the tall window, gazing nonchalantly onto the bustle of Hill Street with her best side to the room. The door swept across the surface of the carpet, but she did not turn. She had learned long ago never to be caught in the act of inspecting others. It did not do to appear too eager. Rather to her surprise, Hoskins' familiar voice was joined by another, more brusque.

"Am I addressing Miss Mary Crawford?"

At this, Mary surely did turn. In the corner of her vision, Hoskins stood, open mouthed, eyes darting. The outward display of shock was a habit Mary expected in others but forbade in herself. She therefore wore her practised, blank expression and looked the newcomer square in the face. Being in no hurry to answer insolence, she paused before speaking.

"You do." She lingered over the words, taking his measure. All men and many women towered over Mary. But this man was taller than most. Well-dressed but not impeccably so. Not at all dandyish. Mud-splattered Hessian boots, well-cut frock coat. A knowing face but not an old one. Accent not quite out of the top drawer but, Mary surmised, a creditable effort. Undeniably, discomfortingly handsome. "Sir." Tilting her head, she gave him a reserved glance before continuing with the obvious question. "And who are you, please?"

"I am Mr. James Hunter." He said this as though it were explanation enough and handed Mary a card. She ran her finger over the rough surface. Black copperplate on cream. "Magistrate."

"Good heavens. You must wish to speak to my uncle, the admiral. Hoskins, please fe—"

"No, miss. I am not mistaken. It is you I wish to speak to. Admiral Crawford cannot help me."

Mary blinked. She comprehended it likely that her uncle knew she was to be interrogated in this manner but had thought neither to introduce her decorously nor accompany her. She felt, not for the first time, the pangs of lost love, lost confidence, lost protection, the gaping chasm where true affection once lived. For a moment, it stung, but it was of no consequence.

"Thank you, Hoskins. That will be all."

Thus, Mary and he were alone in the drawing room. His eyes were grey shot through with green and he had a face that repaid inspection. In other circumstances, it might be admired. The impropriety of the situation did strike her. However, for some time now, her life had lacked so much that was appropriate. Proper affection, proper care, proper direction. Mary had searched for those things on her own account. And she had grown used to the feeling of having been cut free from the usual run of things. A moment alone with a strange man could not trouble her. She turned his card over in her hand and regarded him.

"I declare that you cannot be from Bow Street, for you do not have the waistcoat."

She said this playfully, jauntily. It was Mary's experience that most people responded to humour. Sweetness, even if it need be counterfeited, was the thing. She would wager this man was no different. A whisper of amusement crossed his face.

"I am a magistrate, miss. Not a runner."

Hmm. A lack of jollity and a sense of self-importance. She resolved to discover his business and send him on his way.

"My apologies. Perhaps you shall do me the favour of explaining why you are here?"

Her arch tone, usually so effective, appeared to have no impact on him. He simply commenced pacing the room, quite as though it were his own.

"I am here, Miss Crawford, to speak to you about your friend, Miss Verity Stanhope."

"Verity? What about her?"

"I regret to say that she has disappeared."

"Disappeared." She repeated the word to disguise her own surprise. Mary was not accustomed to ignorance, to being taken unawares. She sat on the sofa and clasped her hands until they whitened. "I see." Silly Verity. What a waste of good prospects.

"I believe that you attended Lady Attenborough's ball with Miss Stanhope on Tuesday last?"

"Yes. Yes, I did. We had a marvellous time."

They had. A smile, involuntary and without artifice, came to her face. The memory in her head was warm, vivid.

Looking up, she noted the man's brown buttons, matching breeches. No signet ring. No cane. A man without a trace of decoration. She could see immediately that he was not quite of the same class as she. And yet, he did not appear uncomfortable.

"Do you like to dance and be seen in society, Mr. Hunter? I do not believe I have ever observed you."

He wore a rueful expression, not unfriendly. Mary imagined him sitting beside a humble fire somewhere, smoking a pipe.

"I shall tell you what I know already. It had been a usual manner of day for Miss Stanhope. She rose late, lunched with her parents, received her cousin Miss Franks as a caller afterwards. Later she visited the modiste, a

Madam Villechamp in Chancery Lane, before returning home, readying for the ball, which you know she attended. She is reported to have departed Lady Attenborough's in her own carriage at two o'clock on Wednesday morning with her brother, who had escorted her. Her father's servants recall their arrival home. Her maid helped her to bed at about three o'clock. She has not been seen since."

Mary's mind flitted back in time. She had left later, danced longer. Her brother, Henry, who had obligingly escorted her, had departed much earlier than they had agreed he would. A memory came, of clambering into her carriage in the dark, flushed, fatigued, alone. Her dance card had been full and dozens of eligible gentlemen had solicited her conversation in between reels, even during them.

She could not now recall Verity's departure, and nobody had thought to tell her that her friend was missing. That was a knock to her. How unthinking and fickle the world could be. Mary drew up her fine shawl against a slight shiver.

"I did not know. Would you like some tea?"

She rang the bell without waiting for an answer. "Sir Horace must have asked that it be kept hush. Possibly a mistake. It is the deserted father's conundrum, is it not? To tell the world that one's daughter is gone and thus enlist help in finding her. Or to keep it close and pray one does not need the assistance of others. He must have thought he could manage alone."

The magistrate nodded.

"Yes, I believe he did. It appears to me that his anxiety for his daughter has now overtaken his fear of scandal. He and Lady Margaret are beside themselves."

Mary felt a flutter of sympathy. The loss of a person one loves, however so occasioned, can draw a line through happiness as surely as any of life's misfortunes.

"So they have called in Bow Street?"

He confirmed the same, his hands behind his back as though they were tied there. Mary wondered that Verity's parents would be so unthinking. She felt for them, she really did. But paid mercenaries from the lowest portion of society were the last people to be in a position to find their daughter.

"And how may I help you, sir?"

"I would like to hear your recollections, please, Miss Crawford. What do you remember about the night of the ball? Did Miss Stanhope seem to be as you would normally expect her? Did anything appear to you to be amiss or out of keeping with the usual? Did she say anything to you which now appears suggestive?"

Hoskins appeared, and Mary asked for tea and cakes. This strange visitor surely required some sugar.

"Of course. It may be easier for me to recount events if you were to sit down, Mr. Hunter." Mary arched her brows, and he complied. From his pocket, he produced a small brown book. They sat opposite one another with the sun streaming through the windows as she began.

"I fear you shall throw me over for a hopeless witness. Verity and I spoke but little, as we were both engaged in dancing all night. It was a lovely ball. Teaming with the best gowns and the smartest names." Mary edged forward on the chaise, her mind going back in time. "Sweetmeats piled upon foreign fruits. Spiced punch and Madeira. Candlelight trembling on silk. Lovers on balconies. Do I shock you?"

"No, miss." He did not hesitate in his reply. He simply said it and Mary wondered what he had seen, where he had been. Far beyond the drawing room and the gaming table, she should think.

"In any case, it was a rather hectic affair. I spoke to Verity at the beginning, if I recall. She and I are great friends. But no single young lady of marriageable age ever uses such an occasion to commune with her friends. Nor should she. Verity sought a good marriage, as do we all. Please do not tell her parents, but she once had rather a fancy for my brother."

Mary paused and edged closer, watching his face. She had great faith in the power of candour in one's dealings with other people. No person alive does not have a hidden truth of which they wish to speak.

"It came to nothing. Henry is like a fish that no net can catch."

In fact, Verity was one of three of Mary's friends who had been so disappointed. Who knew how many others there were?

"Yes, I know of that connexion. I have already spoken to Mr. Henry Crawford. He has an unassailable alibi for the night in question, and my agents can find no suggestion that he is harbouring Miss Stanhope in any way."

At this, Mary let go of her composure and flushed. It was not the flush of a young girl in the company of a handsome stranger. She was furious. She did not know whether to be more furious at this Hunter creature for the suggestion or at Henry for not having warned her of the coming interrogation.

"I see that you are shocked, miss. I am afraid that, in a case of this sort, there can be no room for the sensibilities of grand families."

"Our family is hardly grand, Mr. Hunter. Rich, yes. But not so grand as most of its members would like."

"Well, it is of no importance. The point is that a young girl is missing. She may be in great danger."

"I am sorry, but I cannot help you. Verity was engaged all night. So was I. We are, neither of us, girls to be left sitting at the side during a ball. I wish that I had paid more attention to her, but I did not."

He nodded in a commonplace way, but his eyes were studying her.

"I appreciate, although I have no direct experience, that these balls are busy affairs. I can imagine. But if I may say, miss, you seem remarkably unperturbed at your friend's disappearance. Are you not concerned?"

Had she possessed less restraint, Mary should have raised her eyes to heaven.

"Of course, I am concerned. But I am a rational creature, Mr. Hunter. Verity has had admirers and those whom she admired. She has a fortune, one that she will come into in a few short months. If she has disappeared, I will wager that she has eloped. As many have done before her. It is a scandal, of course, and will be for some time to come. Because people like to gossip. Particularly if it makes them feel more moral, better placed, better judged. It is one of the less attractive aspects of human nature. But it is hardly cause for bringing in the magistrates."

"You make a great assumption, Miss Crawford. Did Verity mention a beau to you?"

A dull feeling of regret, uncertainty, clouded with worry started in

Mary's mind. It was like a marble rolling around. First here, then there, next where?

"No, she did not."

"Would you have expected her to?"

The marble rolled some more. "Yes," said Mary, quietly. "Yes, I would, rather." But one cannot count on always getting that which one expects. A pause lasted for longer than she planned or was comfortable with. "But, of course, that does not mean she did not have one. Verity may have intended to tell me but been unable to do so. I am her friend, sir. Not her keeper."

"You are awfully ready to dismiss her disappearance as though it were an event in the gossip pages."

"What else could it be?"

Mr. Hunter leaned on the arm of the chaise and paused before speaking. Mary had the impression she was being appraised.

"Have you heard of a Miss Elizabeth Archer? No? She is a young lady of good breeding. Not quite as exalted as Miss Stanhope, but she is far from being lowly. She also disappeared from her home—and has not been sighted since only last month. Last year, the Honourable Veronica Keythorpe went missing. She was first thought to have eloped—"

"Yes. I recall."

Mary shuddered. She read the news sheets when the admiral was finished with them, although she preferred to keep it quiet.

"Then thought to be missing. Then found dead."

The word hit the floor. Mary's fingers, which had been playing about the ribbon on her shawl, stilled.

"No person has ever been apprehended for causing her death. So I hope you see, miss. I am obliged to treat this as a matter most serious. It may be as you say. But it may also be much worse. Miss Stanhope may be presently wresting with a danger from which she can be rescued."

Mary observed a softness in his eyes that had not been there before.

"Yes. Yes, of course I understand. I am rather ashamed to have been so flippant, Mr. Hunter. I wonder if you can forgive me?"

She turned her finely featured face to his, but there was some brightness missing. She could feel it. Mary knew when she looked her best, when she shone her brightest. At this moment, her appearance was marred by her mood. She could not account for it.

"I am willing to trade my forgiveness."

"And what is your bargain, sir?" Mary perked up, for she liked a bargain as much as frank speaking.

"That you remember this conversation. If you hear anything or recall anything. If you learn any new matter. Please come to me in the first instance. I gave you my card. Keep it. Write to me, and I will call on you. Or visit yourself, whatever is most convenient. I can be found at Bow Street. If you cannot locate me, ask any of the fellows with the waistcoats. At any time."

"Any time? Do you have no wife, Mr. Hunter?"

A flicker of a smile, a hint.

"Sadly, no, Miss Crawford. Too many criminals to round up. Not enough society."

～

"What a bloody rogue."

Admiral Crawford croaked from beyond the news sheet. The remark called for no response from Mary, and she did not offer any. He was always better behaved when her brother, Henry, who was his favourite, was present. In Henry's absence, and without her dearest aunt alive, the admiral had been increasingly objectionable. Irritable and absent, by turns. Cursing freely, reddening, raging, growing in every dimension except good grace.

Mary continued buttering her toast. Sunshine broke through the morning room, a cascade of yellow light. A footman moved noiselessly behind her. Carriages clipped along in the street outside like well-trained dogs. Under the table, she slipped off her silk slippers and allowed her stockinged feet the luxury of the Persian carpet.

The admiral shook the news sheet and let out an indistinct, animalistic noise. Fearing another tirade on the Whigs, Mary spoke. "I have heard from Henry, Uncle. He shall join us next month, in time for the Haverfords' ball. Is that not good news?"

For a moment, he gave no appearance of having heard her. But shortly, and by degrees, the news sheet was lowered, and the white head and ruddy nose of a man long at sea appeared.

He grunted.

"Oh, I nearly forgot. We have been invited to Mrs. Fortescue's for supper and cards. She has been so kind since—"

"When?" The word came out as a bark.

"Next Wednesday."

"I am out. So, no."

Mary searched his features, but she knew better than to ask where he was going. She had heard whispers in corners, observed pointed looks across other people's tables. Mary turned away from it. Her uncle's life was his own, as he never neglected to inform her.

"Do you object to me going alone, Uncle?"

He looked up, a sneer playing about his countenance.

"'Course not! Why ever should I? Go. You have your own carriage."

Mary returned to her plate. She had her own of everything, save a home. Marriage would be remedy to that malady, but she was anxious to make the right choice. There was no merit in it unless one could do it properly. The admiral let out a sawing laugh as he continued to read and Mary ate in silent horror. Her poor aunt.

Mary did not solicit further conversation for her own felicity but felt compelled to do so.

"Uncle, have you heard anything of this Stanhope business?"

"Why should I?" he asked, laughter tinged with disdain. "She was your friend."

"She still is my friend, Uncle. But I do not know where she is. Would that I did." Mary poured herself another cup of tea. "I thought perhaps someone at your club may have said how the search proceeds. Some of those gentlemen are terribly thick with Sir Horace Stanhope, are they not?"

He exhaled and took an ungainly mouthful of his breakfast. Soft yolk oozed from the corners of his whiskery mouth. Mary looked away.

"It has been mentioned"—he spoke through his food, the words half desiccated—"but no one appears to know where the little chit is or whom she is with. Lucky escape for your brother, that's what I say."

Mary looked up, alarmed, reacting despite herself.

"How so, sir? Surely a baronet's daughter with a fortune of thirty thousand pounds would have made a perfectly proper wife for Henry, if only he would agree? If I recall, you yourself encouraged the match."

His voice, when it came, was almost a snarl.

"Nothing wrong with the colour of her money. But a girl who runs off at the drop of a hat, with god knows bloody who, is a bad bet, Mary. No judgement. Not to be trusted. Even your aunt had more sense than that."

Mary flinched. Inside her, anger rode on the back of love and regret. She was used to his unkindness, of course. And she was resolute that she would never show him any of the hurt he caused her.

"Mark my words, Henry will not now regret his choice." Admiral Crawford then returned to his news sheet, and uncle and niece spoke no more.

Mary did not regret the silence, but in her mind there was darkness. How could there be no news of Verity when all society was looking for her? How could a well-known girl of the *ton* suddenly disappear without a trace? It was one thing to run off. But the offending parties could usually be relied upon to reappear married or be found in compromising circumstances.

A worm of misgiving had been laid in Mary's mind. Thus, she wrote to Lady Margaret, offering her sympathies and friendship. She had paid morning calls to Verity's other particular friends, asking questions, openly pondering, in the hope that somebody may know. They did not. Worry had begun to mount around her. Fear climbed on the back of ignorance until she could no longer see. At night, she had taken to lying on her back, awake and contemplating the canopy of her bed growing into shadow. A great, sightless black above her. She closed her eyes and replayed the night Verity disappeared, but nothing new came.

She carried about the card of the man from Bow Street in her reticule, occasionally reaching in and checking it was still there. She thought of him often too, his staid clothes and determined expression. A strange conviction took root in her mind that he could find the truth and, although she knew nothing of him, she put her faith in that.

One hundred memories of Verity flitted through her mind, like butterflies breaking loose. Their arms locked on walks in the park, their laughter careening about ballrooms as they danced, the joyful and confiding conspiracy that great girlfriends invariably have with one another. Mary's heart ached with it.

The effort involved in disguising disquiet turned out to be considerable. Mary discovered that her first weapon was activity. Therefore, she resolved one day, in addition to her morning calls, to go shopping. She left Hill Street with every expectation of keeping herself extremely busy. Thus, having purchased some gloves for her half-sister, Mrs. Grant, and some sheet music for herself, she proceeded to a bookshop she knew well.

It was a dark, cavernous place, full of treasures, lacking fashion. Mary luxuriated in it for a while. The rows of leather spines reminded her of Mr. Hunter and his little book. Unmolested by the man at the counter, she stayed longer than was seemly and, having done so, selected a couple of books to purchase.

It was as she made her way into the bustle of the street that her temporary contentment deserted her. Her mind dwelled on the missing Verity and other intractable losses. She thought of her social engagements. So many frock-coated gentlemen on silk covered chaises, so many calls for her to play her harp whilst all society watched.

Suddenly, she was less willing than she had been before. For how could she sit about in drawing rooms when Verity remained undiscovered?

At Madam Villechamp's, she stopped and gazed at the window display as though in a dream. Sunlight glinted on glass. Subtle movement beyond the curtain spoke of fashion, of womanhood, of preening for the battle that passed for life during the season. Mary recalled her aunt tugging at her arm as they passed and the note of disapproval in her voice. "No, Mary. Madam Villechamp's is not for you." She had inherited that censure and was inclined to criticise by default. Aunt had meant, of course, that

Mary did not have need of the arts of Madam Villechamp, but now she wondered.

Suddenly, the sun was too bright, the crowd too great, the street too encroaching. Wishing to be home but knowing that her carriage was awaiting her some distance away, she quickened her pace. Her kid half boots clicked on the sand dusted ground. Clutching her parcels, she rushed through a mass of souls: sisters shopping for ribbons, young boys lugging boxes of goods.

Despite her haste, she became aware of a small, plain carriage that seemed to clip steadily at the edge of her vision. Try as she might to look properly without turning her head, she could not. Wishing to throw off the irritation, the nagging sense that she was imagining it, she paused suddenly at the next shop window. It was a bonnet shop, and Mary cast her eye over the array of colours and shapes, ribbon cascading about inside the glass. But when she turned back to continue her walk, the carriage had stopped. It was stood in the road with a traffic of persons swelling past it on each side.

Alarm gripped her and she held her parcels tighter. Later, she realised that she must have betrayed her discomfort, for the door swung open with a click and out stepped Mr. Hunter.

"Miss Crawford."

He bowed. She had not imagined his handsome face. It was his entirely.

"Mr. Hunter. I thought you were following me."

"I was. But when I saw that you had spied me, miss, I had to reveal myself. It was not my design to make you afraid."

"Then what is your design, sir? What is the meaning of this?"

"Would you do me the favour of walking with me a while, miss?"

Mary, who had been too long alone with her thoughts, consented.

"Yes, I would be happy to. My carriage awaits me on The Strand. Shall we go that way?"

He answered with his feet and, in unison, they advanced.

"Do you have any news of Verity?"

"I wish I did. It is not for want of seeking her, Miss Crawford."

"I have been asking amongst our acquaintances. But, I am sorry to say that nobody appears to have the least idea where she might be. It makes one feel quite hopeless."

That, Mary reflected, was the heart of it. They ambled on in silent companionship.

"So, sir. Shall you explain what you mean by following a respectable lady about her shopping?"

The skin around his eyes crinkled as he smiled. He was tanned by the sun, more weathered than most men she encountered.

"If I speak to you in confidence, may I depend on you, Miss Crawford? My instinct tells me that I may. But I should like to hear it from your own lips."

"Yes, of course. It shall be a perfect secret."

"I saw you looking in the window of Madam Villechamp's. I know not whether you frequent her. But the establishment has come to my attention as part of the search for Miss Stanhope. You see, Madam Villechamp was Verity's dressmaker. It was that shop that she visited on the day she disappeared."

"There is nothing unusual in that, surely?"

"No, not in itself. But Veronica Keythorpe was also a customer, and she also visited there on the day that she went missing. Even more remarkably, Miss Archer, the girl I spoke to you of when I met you— she had been there too. She visited with a cousin some weeks before her disappearance. It may be wrong, but I cannot turn my mind from the suspicion that there is a connexion. I would be obliged…I mean, I would prefer it if you could see your way clear to not go there for the time being."

Mary rolled it about in her mind. Whatever would Aunt Crawford say? Her suggestion to Mary had always been that the establishment lacked respectability, nothing more. Too much flesh, not enough fabric. Mary regarded her companion doubtfully. His concern warmed her, but she could not quite credit it. This world of disappearing girls and Bow Street heroes was radical, fanciful.

"How clever of you to notice that. You must not worry about my safety though. For I never use that modiste. My late aunt was much against it. I know not whether it was the fashions or Madame Villechamp herself. She is known for louche styling. It is said that she has a husband and children who sit deserted in France. Maybe you know that already. You may have it in your little book. My aunt, I believe, feared for my morals. To her, marriage was utterly sacrosanct; whatever happened, she believed in faithfulness. As to that, I cannot say. But she brought me up to avoid the place, so I shall."

Her voice was touched with reverence, with fondness. She left the question of her own morality open.

"You miss your aunt?"

"Yes. Greatly. My parents died some years ago. But my aunt cared for me as though I were her own child. You may say that she was mother, father, sister, friend."

"And the admiral?"

Mary looked him straight in the eye and smiled. They did not break step.

"I see."

For some time, they simply walked. The streets peeled past, polished black doors and iron railings vanishing behind them. Mary thought it likely that she would be observed by somebody she knew, but she could not find it in her to mind. They were, after all, in the open and she had a perfect excuse to be conversing with him. He, Mr. Hunter, was a permitted escape from fashionable society, and an agreeable one. Too soon, her blue bodied carriage appeared in sight. Roberts, who had been kicking his heels on the road, looked up, and Mary knew that her time with Mr. Hunter was short.

"One thing."

"Yes?" He slowed and looked to her.

"If you are right about this business. If the modiste has some hand in it…."

"Hmm?"

"How shall you ever discover the truth of it? You can hardly go there for a fitting."

His broad chest convulsed gently as he laughed.

"There are many things I cannot do, Miss Crawford. Whether by reason of social convention or otherwise. But there is always good old-fashioned questioning. I have my methods. Please do not trouble over it."

Mary arched her brows and continued walking. She was by no means persuaded. The modistes of fashionable London were closed boxes, known only to the wealthy ladies who patronised them and the scanty and largely unfortunate staff within. Poor Mr. Hunter could no more be expected to penetrate that than he could gain admittance to high society. What he needed was an assistant. A friend.

"And where do you learn your methods, sir? Is there a school for magistrates? A college where industrious young men might learn to battle villainy?"

Mary looked up at him. The sun warmed her skin and she knew that it glowed, the beginnings of a bronze. It was not fashionable, but fashion was not everything. If circumstances had been different, she should have liked to take his arm.

"There is not. But perhaps there should be. No, I am afraid that I rely on slightly more practical experience."

"Meaning?"

He exhaled and slowed. His expression spoke of discretion. He was not likely to tell her.

Mary arched her brow, returning to old certainties, tried methods, and said, "I still believe that Verity will appear with a feckless husband. But I applaud your efforts. And I shall do anything at all to help you. Thank you for walking me to my carriage."

"You are welcome, Miss Crawford."

And with that, Roberts opened the door for her. Mary climbed in, keeping Mr. Hunter in sight as the door was closed between them.

Mary sat beside her brother in the carriage as it rolled through the streets. This was the pitch dark of the early morning, the moment before the dawn. He had appeared, as Henry was wont to do, the day previously. With no notice and in a noisy hail of good wishes. Mary was happy to see him, the admiral thrilled. He was in Town for two nights only, a short ration, before departing for a house party in Wiltshire. The siblings had left Gussie Faraday's house in gales of laughter, and now Mary leaned back, pushing her body into the thin leather seat, stretching out her legs, her arms. Henry, who never showed fatigue in public, yawned. Then, he turned to her with his brow creased.

"Oh Mary. I should not have played that last hand."

"How much did you lose?"

"It is probably best that I do not say. Better for you not to know, dear."

He leaned over and kissed her hairline, his breath sour with Madeira but his smile like that of a puppy on a long walk.

"Just don't tell old Nelson."

"I shall not tell him, if you stop calling him that. It does not suit him. Too heroic."

"Now, now." He took her hand and squeezed it. "Do not dwell on that. Life, darling sister, is all about seizing opportunities where they lie. And making them where they do not."

"Says the gentleman who has just lost his allowance at the faro table."

"Yes, well. One cannot expect to be always in the pink." He grinned, winningly. If all else was lost, Henry would always have that: a way with people, a spark of merriment, a sense of levity. And one day, all else may well be lost.

"I noticed that you had a lot of attention, sister dear. Old Peter Armitage and that cousin of Maxwell's. Remind me of his name?"

"William. He looks better than he talks."

Henry stretched his legs out, too. He let out a quiet bubble of laughter.

"Fortune?"

"Sadly not. I believe he may be interested in mine. And I cannot consent to be a man's banker."

"You might, Mary. If you were getting value in return. A title, an estate. And if you want to get away from Ne— our uncle, then that is the surest way, is it not? Marry one of these young bloods that linger about you."

Mary sighed. These young men were rather like dogs, padding about, hoping for preferment. They were entertaining in their way, but they had their limits.

"The problem, which you yourself know full well, is finding the right person. Many are agreeable in company, possessed of standing, handsome, even. Some are wealthy, some are clever. But uniting with another for life is no small business. I am anxious not to throw myself away on the wrong bet. For *I* should never escape."

She eyed him; she could have said more but held back.

"Do you suggest that I should do so? I do not deny, Mary, that I have had my share of romances. But I have never had a wife to desert or neglect. I hope that I never shall. You mean, I suppose, to suggest that wives have the poorer bargain."

"Of course they have the poorer bargain! In *their* lives, wives cannot make free as husbands do. If a husband is displeased with his wife, well, there are solutions, possibilities…. For a wife, she can find neither escape nor compensation."

He flung his head back. "Indeed. You want too much. You cannot see into the future, dear. Seize the day; seize your own advantages. Otherwise, what is the point in all of these evenings gadding about, all this fashion?"

He gestured to her evening gown, blush pink and terribly becoming, if she said so herself.

"Interminable hours playing the harp, singing."

Mary turned her hands over and regarded her fingers, quite sore from the strings. She had played long that evening but, in truth, she loved it. The soft melodious hum, the comfortable shape of the frame against her body. Singing she could well manage without. Being asked to entertain with her own voice always gave her alarm. It seemed excessively giving, leaving her throat dry and her chest constrained. There was always the fear of missing the note, going flat, and looking a fool.

"Verity is a lovely singer. I miss her voice, Henry."

"Oh, Mary. Not again."

"Are you sure you have heard nothing? Did Gussie say anything to you? How can she just be gone, like a puff of smoke?"

"I do not know, darling. But please stop asking me about it. If I knew, I would tell you. It has nothing to do with me. Now stop talking about the wretched business. It is too solemn for a night such as this one."

Mary looked out of the window, a marble of enquiry rolling about her mind. The sky had begun to lighten, the night crack up, disintegrate.

"Actually, it is morning. And, we are home."

They juddered to a halt in Hill Street and abandoned the carriage for the house. Her uncle's hat was not on the hall table. For a moment, Mary felt troubled. She squinted and wondered.

"Thank you, Hoskins," she said as the butler took her cloak, somewhat sleepily. "Has our uncle returned?"

"Not yet, miss."

Madam Villechamp had a certain reputation, and Aunt Crawford had not been the only respectable lady to turn away from it. It was the sort of establishment to which a lady turned when she wished to make matters obvious. Purveyors of ensembles that make men look and women talk. Mary could name a dozen girls who, desiring to shock or to startle a man into forming an attachment, had procured their gowns from there. Memories appeared to her, of plump creamy bosoms and cut away shoulders, of wispy fabric, like gossamer threads wrapped about curved forms. Audible gasps. Indecent, indecorous, people said.

People were right, she thought primly. Madam Villechamp was, Mary reflected as she entered the shop for the first time, successful for all that.

The shop was rather a step from Hill Street, nestled between a milliner and a haberdasher on Chancery Lane. This part of the city felt different; dirtier, hotter, lacking in elegance. Mary knew a pang of misgiving, a twinge in her belly.

Walking in, she forced that feeling away. The interior of the establishment smelled of lavender and oranges. Mary's nose twitched, and she opted to stand in the receiving room. A young woman with a squint spared her a greeting and said that "Madame" would not be long. Mary settled her body with an effort and returned a serene expression. After all, she did need a new day gown and there was nothing wrong at all in a well-known lady of means visiting an established modiste, was there?

The days since she had met with Mr. Hunter had slouched by, still with no news of Verity. Henry had high-tailed off to his weekend house party and left a considerable paucity of fun in his wake. The admiral was much the same as ever, save that he was absent more and more. In the day,

Mary shopped, paid calls, and played her harp. At night, she lay awake, contemplating the darkness.

It was in such circumstances that she had resolved to call at Madam Villechamp's. Enough of hopelessness. Enough of ignorance. She, Mary, would go forth and assist Mr. Hunter by doing that which he could not do. Who knew what she may find?

Mary paced, considering how best to execute such an ambition. Curiously, she was being kept waiting. Mr. Hunter's words came into her mind, and she began to feel a prickle of nerves. The girl with the squint reappeared with a pile of material before smiling sheepishly and removing herself. A peel of laughter sounded in the middle distance.

Like many such shops, the interior was draped with curtains, and a wall of fabric trembled around Mary. She did, too, but forced herself to be still. Beyond the curtain, Mary could just make out an outline of a desk, a chair—no person attending either.

Verity had been in this room on the day she disappeared. What secret might be concealed within? It would be the work of a few minutes, she thought to herself. Almost of a moment. If she delayed, she would reason herself out of it.

And so, grasping the moment, she stole across the room, through the curtain. It flapped behind her, upsetting the air. Beyond, Mary found herself in close quarters. A low table and a rickety chair stood in the middle of the room. A chaise was littered with fabrics, pieces of lace. The desk was festooned in paper, news sheets, drawings in charcoal, spilled ink, letters with the seals broken. Mary's heart thudded in her chest, and her hands grew clammy. She steadied herself and forced her eyes to look.

Quickly, she began to search. Quick moving fingers leafing through papers, lifting, sorting, skin dry with dust and guilt. And fear of being caught. Mary's eyes danced over many words in many hands, but the word she searched for was "Verity"; might some clue be written here, waiting to be discovered?

So determined was her mind that she almost missed it. At first, the folded letter with its broken seal was glimpsed at in passing and placed back down. It took Mary a moment to understand the gravity of her position. And then she read it again.

My love,

You know I do not ordinarily write, but I must. That was a poor parting, Lucille, and you cannot expect me to put up with it. Not now, not ever. When my wife died, I did not miss her for a moment. But without you, I am quite vanquished. Our love has been of many years' duration, and you cannot end it now on such a sour note. Come back to me and I will give you anything it is in my power to give. Carriages, gold. They are yours. If you were free, I would marry you in an instant. Unless you can obtain a divorce, which you tell me is impossible.

So, I offer you the next best thing. Come to Hill Street and live with me. People will talk, but bloody well let them. I do not care for society, in any case. You shall have the satisfaction of a comfortable home in one of London's better streets, the warmth of my bed every night, and everyone shall know that you, Lucille, are the choice I make. Make haste.

Your lover,

Edward

Mary's hand quivered, and the words, which were so clear, seemed to swim on the page. The writer had not signed his surname, but Mary did not need to see it. She knew the hand well enough; the man's name was her own. For this was a letter written by her own uncle.

Her head ached, a pang of stinging pain fit to burst it. Matters, long pushed away, came to mind. His frequent absences from home, her aunt's disapproval of Madam Villechamp. Old matrons whispering behind fans at assemblies, girls giggling as the admiral passed them. The reality of it came at Mary like a carriage in the fog. How long had it been there? And how close had she been to being hit directly, killed in an instant?

Reality returned. A sour, bitter taste rose in Mary's throat that she was in this place, standing upon this woman's carpet, breathing in her wretched scent. She, Mary, was a voyeur and a traitor.

Somewhere in the distance, a woman laughed and a door opened. Her heart raced and roared in her ears. As quick as a whip, she put the letter back and swept through the dividing curtain. Then she picked up her skirts and ran.

The air in the street was unseasonably cold, but it relieved her to feel it against her skin as she bolted towards her carriage. She boarded with utmost speed and, breathless, leaned back on the leather seat.

"Roberts."

"Yes, miss?"

"Bow Street, please. As fast as you can."

Mr. Hunter looked up sharply as Mary entered the room. He jumped to his feet like a scalded cat.

"Miss Crawford!"

Mary, who had regained some of her composure, bobbed a curtsey in answer to his courtly bow. The room was dingy, spartan, almost bare. There was one chair beside Mr. Hunter's own. In the corner stood a dusty cabinet. The gentleman gestured for her to sit and then did so himself.

"I have just returned from Hill Street. I spoke to your uncle, briefly. And, although he assured me that he would pass on a message to you, I have just taken the liberty of writing this note. I had intended to send it this afternoon. But since you are here, let me place it in your hands, Miss Crawford."

He passed the small note, neatly sealed, and Mary took it. As she did so, their hands almost touched. Almost, but not quite. Mary, who was still short of breath, broke the seal. Her eyes scanned the page, but he spoke before she read.

"Allow me to save your heartache and say that Miss Stanhope has been found. She is safe and well. Although, as you correctly predicted at the beginning of our acquaintance, she is no longer Miss Stanhope. She was married in Scotland, to a Mr. Wise."

A breath escaped Mary's mouth.

"Never heard of him."

"No indeed. Neither had her father. He is, or was until recently, a tutor of the pianoforte."

Mary blanched and then laughed. She could hear the gasping from here to Mayfair.

"So, you were right. I must apologise for having made you afraid that something more sinister was afoot. It is not my business to go about frightening young ladies."

Mary flashed him a fiery eye.

"You did not frighten me, Mr. Hunter. I do not scare easily. And it would seem that, but for a little scandal and the regret that Verity may one day come to feel, there is nothing more to be said. Scandals are two a penny. And as for regrets… Thank you, sir, for thinking enough of my friend to search so tirelessly for her. I am indebted to you, as is she. Now, I believe that I should take my leave."

Mary began to stand, her body heavy, her mind spinning, flailing.

"Wait—"

He said it sharply, swiftly and Mary stopped. Time slowed, creaked.

"Why were you visiting me?"

"Oh, it was nothing."

Nothing, thought Mary. Nothing, save the final proof that her current way of living was insupportable, unsustainable, could not continue. Mr. Hunter had a face one could trust and a shoulder one could lean on. Had she been a weaker girl, she would have cried. But as it was, her face hardened, she drew her body up poker straight, making to leave.

"I do not believe it was, Miss Crawford. I do not believe that a lady of your standing would visit Bow Street in person unless you had a reason to do so."

Accurate, of course. Mary paused. Very little escaped him, and that deserved acknowledgement.

"I could almost believe you on the verge of saying 'out with it', sir."

He simply raised his eyebrows.

"I came here to tell you that I had visited Madam Villechamp's."

"Yes?" He blinked, face blank as a sheet.

"Not as a customer. Well—I did pretend to be a customer. But my real motive was to search for evidence relating to Verity. While I was waiting to be seen, I slipped into the office and searched through papers on a desk. There was nothing there, Mr. Hunter. Measurements, invoices, letters, little nothings. But I thought you should know I had done it."

"Did anyone see you?" His voice faltered and she looked away.

"I do not believe so. But I left without attending my appointment and without saying goodbye."

"Is that not simply bolting by another name?"

"Do not attack me with your semantics, sir." Mary blinked. The ribbon containing her way of life had fallen loose, slipped away. "It shall no doubt be remarked upon. They shall have me down for a peculiarity, maybe worse. Let us hope that they suspect me of ill health. The sort of lady who is taken by fainting fits and ill humours at a moment's notice."

"Do you care what they think?"

"Foolish fellow. I should sooner be taken for a spy than a wilting Jenny."

"Nobody could take you for a wilting Jenny, Miss Crawford." His gaze held her for a moment, pinned, every line drawn.

Then he stood and, without seeking her leave, poured a glass of brandy. Wordlessly, he handed it to her. The thin light from the window played upon the amber fluid and glowed. Why ever not? Mary reached for the glass and took a sip.

"Now, why did you not take your leave properly? Why did you bolt?"

Mary considered saying nothing. She considered thanking him and departing the room with her secrets. It is what most ladies would have done. To tell a man, a perfect stranger, such truths was folly. It was indiscretion bordering on madness. It was not, by any measure, *proper*.

"Because I found information that…touched me."

"But you said that you were not a customer."

"I am not, was not. It was a letter to Madam Villechamp. From my uncle. It was not"—she paused, choosing her words—"the sort of letter one writes to an indifferent acquaintance. I suppose it puts things somewhat beyond doubt. It is proof, were proof needed, that men are strange creatures indeed."

Mr. Hunter sighed in acknowledgement. His eyes were full of sympathy and kindness, and something else as well. Mary had not one regret for having told him. "Strange. And worse. For he asks her to Hill Street. To live."

"Will you stay?"

"I cannot. It would be impossible. Even if my pride could stand it, my heart could not. In any case, I cannot hope to make a proper marriage living at Hill Street in such circumstances."

"So where shall you go?"

"I know not. I have many friends, Mr. Hunter, but few true allies. My parents are dead, as is my aunt. My brother has an estate. But—well, he cannot settle to read a novel. I have a half-sister who would take me in. But she is older than I. Her husband is a country rector, a distance from Town. Their life is a far cry from mine."

"I hope you do not take this ill, Miss Crawford. But I cannot imagine you in the country."

"Neither can I. Do you suppose that I shall cease to exist?" She laughed, inwardly unravelling, unfolding.

"I hope not."

"As do I. Thank you, Mr. Hunter. I cannot explain quite why, but I feel better for having spoken with you. Even before today, I have enjoyed our talks. Now, I must be away. I have a new life to arrange."

"Miss Crawford." He bowed. "You can always find me here, miss. If you need an ally."

Mary left without speaking further. But an odd sense of settled calm had stolen over her. Was it better to live in ignorance and be comfortable, or to know the truth and be moved by it into uncharted landscapes? She did not know but was willing to try. Her boots echoed on the wooden steps inside the building on Bow Street as she made her way into the sunshine.

JENETTA JAMES is a lawyer, writer, mother, and taker-on of too much. She grew up in Cambridge and read history at Oxford where she was a scholar and president of the Oxford History Society. After graduating, she took to the law and now practices full time as a barrister. Over the years, she has lived in France, Hungary, and Trinidad, as well as her native England. Jenetta currently lives in London with her husband and children where she enjoys reading, laughing, and playing with Lego. She is the author of *Suddenly Mrs. Darcy*, *The Elizabeth Papers*, and *Lover's Knot*.

AN UNNATURAL BEGINNING

ELIZABETH ADAMS

ANNE ELLIOT

Persuaded at nineteen to break off her engagement to a promising yet insignificant young naval officer, this daughter of a baronet remains lonely, overlooked, and undervalued by her family. As she grows older and closer to inevitable spinsterhood, the weight of regret causes this rational creature to vow that if ever applied to by a younger person in similar circumstances, she would offer no such guidance. *She had been forced into prudence in her youth, she had learned romance as she grew older: the natural sequel of an unnatural beginning.*
–**Chapter IV**, *Persuasion.*

AN UNNATURAL BEGINNING

KELLYNCH HALL, LATE SUMMER 1809

Anne walked along the garden path, her hand tucked neatly into the crook of Mr. Musgrove's arm. He was telling her about a hunt he planned to participate in at a neighboring estate.

She looked past him at her mother's roses. Lady Elliot had spent hours designing the walled garden and supervising its installation. She had known every flower, every variety, and watched over it as if it were one of her children. Anne loved to walk in it, to sit on the stone bench beneath the trellis covered by yellow blossoms, or to trail her fingers through the fountain at the center. It reminded her of her mother, of the days they had spent together sheltered by the stone walls and high hedges. Lady Elliot had been the only member of Anne's family whom she could see herself in, the only one who understood her quiet second daughter, the only one with whom Anne felt truly herself with no need for amendments or excuses.

Anne sighed and looked about the garden. The pale pink ones were her favorites. The smell was not strong from a distance but, if one leaned in close, the sweet fragrance was intoxicating. She had been compared to these roses once, years ago.

They were nearing the center now, and her mind was awash in memories both real and imagined. How she would have preferred walking with her mother! How she wished her mother had been with them three years ago when Anne had needed her wise counsel and steady affection. She could imagine them sitting on the bench by the fountain, the fragrant blossoms perfuming the air.

Anne would have told her all about *him*, how he made her feel, how he reminded her, just a little, of her dear mother. Lady Elliot would have listened and asked to meet him. She would have laughed at Anne's thinking two such disparate characters were in any way similar. Anne would have shaken her head with a smile, knowing that what she saw in both her mother's eyes and his was not a similarity of character, but of preference. They would have sat together in the garden as he told them stories, and her mother would have been as beguiled as Anne had been.

Would she have acted differently if her mother had been there three years ago? Would she have been so easily persuaded? She could not know. But she hoped...

Her companion asked her a question, and she returned her attention to the man walking with her. It was sad, really, how little she wanted to talk to Charles Musgrove. He was a perfectly decent man. Kind, respectable, well-mannered. But alas, he possessed one fatal flaw that not even the best of manners could redeem.

He was not Frederick Wentworth.

He had gone silent for a moment. She looked at him from the corner of her eye and saw he had paused in his speech but did not look particularly expectant of an answer. She made a noncommittal noise, he was satisfied, and they continued their dull amble through the garden.

No, he was most certainly not Frederick Wentworth. And she was no Anne Wentworth, to her everlasting shame.

~

SUMMER 1806

"Have you met Commander Wentworth, Miss Anne? He is visiting his brother in Monkford."

"No, I have not." She turned her gaze to the gentleman standing next to the hostess and tilted her head back until she reached his eyes. Her own widened in response, and she quickly nodded her head and dipped into a brief curtsey.

He bowed, longer than she had, and smiled in such a way that she thought he had a great secret he would never tell.

Or perhaps he was seeing her secrets.

The hostess left them with a knowing smile, and they began a conversation about spring, the weather, and the general countryside. The topics were inane and the words benign, but something passed between them and, before the night was through, a tiny piece of her heart had taken up residence next to Commander Wentworth's.

The second time Anne saw the commander was at a picnic hosted by a neighboring vicar. Her sister Elizabeth did not wish to attend and, indeed, had not been invited herself, though Anne had offered to include her. Sir Walter Elliot was not enthused by his second daughter's friendship with such lowly people but, as Lady Russell was also a friend of the vicar, and Anne was so little a nuisance, and he was so little bothered by her absence, he did not forbid it or even question her about the particulars when she applied to him for permission to attend.

The vicar, Mr. Browning, was a young man with an even younger wife. She was a pretty, fair-haired creature with a tinkling laugh and a kind heart. She immediately took Anne by the arm when she arrived and led her to a blanket spread out beneath a sprawling oak tree. Two gentlemen were sitting near a handful of ladies reclining on cushions, and they stood when the ladies approached.

"I believe you know Mr. Ewing." Mrs. Browning gestured to the man on her right. "And this is Commander Wentworth. He is visiting his brother nearby."

Anne dropped her eyes to the ground as she curtsied, feeling the blood rush to her face. She chanced a glance back up at Commander Wentworth and saw him smiling at her, his countenance open. Mrs. Browning flitted off to continue her duties as hostess, and Commander Wentworth stepped forward to lead Anne to a cushion, then lowered himself to sit beside her. She could not help thinking he moved like a cat, so graceful was he.

"Are you enjoying your visit, Commander?" she asked politely.

"Very much, Miss Elliot." He proceeded to tell her of the sights he had seen with his brother, and how yet another brother and his wife and son had come to visit. He had taught his nephew to fish, and the little scamp had repaid him by spilling ink all over his new waistcoat.

"So as you see," he said charmingly as he held his arms out and gestured to his attire, "I am forced to wear a clashing waistcoat with my new blue coat. I hope your eyes are not overly offended."

She could not but smile at his good humor. "My eyes are not too badly injured, though I do wish I could have seen the other waistcoat. It must have been terrible to see it ruined before you ever wore it."

"Oh, it was a sight to behold, Miss Elliot," he said in exaggerated tones. "Fine blue silk, shot through with gold threads. My tailor chose the material particularly to match my eyes."

She could not help looking at his eyes then. They were a bright shade of blue, like forget-me-nots, and filled with merriment.

"It must have been splendid, indeed."

His cheeks pinked, and she felt a rush of feminine pride at having caused it.

The third time she saw him, she was returning from visiting a tenant. He was riding in a neighboring field and changed his course to join her. He tied his horse to a tree and relieved her of the empty basket she had been carrying.

"Do you have many tenants at Kellynch?"

"Not too many, only nine farms."

"And do you tend to them often?"

"Of course. It is my duty."

"Your sisters do not accompany you?"

"Mary is too young and she is currently away at school. Elizabeth finds she does not have the time for such things. She prefers to leave it to me."

He raised a brow at that, and they walked on in silence for a time.

She eventually asked him about life in the navy, and he regaled her with stories of ship-board mishaps and the horrors of living on salted ham and stale biscuits for months on end. His ship had once been attacked by marauders when he was a lad, and she listened in astonishment as he told her of being tied up and thrown into the sea.

"However did you survive?"

"Not as heroically as you'd expect in a grand tale," he said with a mischievous smile. "Several other men had been thrown in but not all were tied. Some had been wounded but were able to swim. I kept my head above water until a lieutenant fished me out and cut my bindings. We were able to board the ship and rejoin the fighting. I'm afraid the only assistance I offered was tripping a sailor as he ran past me."

She was caught between returning his smile and gaping at him wide-mouthed. Pirates! She had never thought to meet someone with such vast experience or such great adventures. It was so far removed from her quiet life in Somerset.

"Please, tell me more, Commander."

He smiled and continued talking until they reached the boundary of Kellynch's park. She could not remember when she had spent a more enjoyable afternoon.

⁓

KELLYNCH HALL, 1809

"Mr. Musgrove to see Miss Anne," the butler said in somber tones.

Anne could not help thinking their butler resembled an undertaker in that moment and how apt a comparison it was, for was she not dead already? Her sister Elizabeth spared their caller a quick glance and went back to her cards. Sir Walter Elliot seemed mildly happy to see Mr. Musgrove but not enough to do more than greet him, inquire of his parents, and sit back down again with his eldest daughter.

Anne tried to compensate for her family's lack of manners but realized belatedly that he would take her enthusiasm for encouragement, and she thought to temper her behavior. Yet how he could think her lukewarm responses and lack of interest as encouragement, she did not know. She was horribly dull and, what was worse, she knew it.

She had been engaging once. She had never been gregarious and she never held the entire room's attention, but she had been pretty and occasionally witty and often gay.

Now, her bloom was fading. She could feel it like an autumn wind come to rob the trees of their leaves. Regret was stealing away with her youth, and half a woman was left in its place.

"Would you agree?" asked Mr. Musgrove.

She returned her attention to the man at her side and chided herself for letting her thoughts wander yet again. "I beg your pardon. Could you repeat the question?"

He did not seem to mind her inattention and rambled on about hunting rifles. She nodded and smiled, occasionally adding a word or two. His calls were becoming more frequent, and she was beginning to think he was preparing to make his proposals. She had thought her lack of encouragement would deter him, but perhaps a more direct refusal would be necessary.

Charles Musgrove proved surprisingly persistent. He called twice per week and sat next to her at dinners and in drawing rooms. He offered his arm any time it was plausible and even when it was not. She had been escorted to the pianoforte, across the room for tea, and to the punch table at a ball more times than she could count. He often asked her father if they might walk in the gardens, and Sir Walter always agreed before Anne could think of an excuse to avoid the exercise or find someone to accompany them.

It was on one such walk, in the Italian garden so in fashion that season, that Mr. Musgrove turned to her, his face earnest and his eyes excited, and said, "Miss Anne, I do so enjoy your company. There is hardly a better way to spend an afternoon than in your society."

"Thank you, Mr. Musgrove. It is kind of you to say."

"I wonder, would you want to spend more afternoons like this?"

She looked at him in confusion.

"That is to say, would you accept my hand? In marriage?"

She hardly knew where to look. "I, Mr. Musgrove, I..." She stumbled and tripped over her words, but finally said, "I thank you for the offer. I am honored you would choose me. But I cannot accept it."

He stared blankly at her. "You cannot?"

"I cannot. I am sorry to be the cause of any pain or discomfort, and I do hope we may remain friends."

"Friends?" He looked at her as if he were trying to solve complicated mathematical equations. "You are refusing?"

"Yes, I am refusing. But I thank you for the offer, and I would like to remain friends."

"I see. Well, yes, very well." He continued to look flummoxed, but he made no effort to leave the garden or even to walk apart from her.

He showed neither anger nor any wounded feelings, so unlike her other experience. She could only surmise from this that, while Mr. Musgrove might value her as a friend and neighbor, and even *like* her a good deal, he did not have a strong attachment to her. Anne could not but be relieved. She did not wish to be the cause of a broken heart. Again.

SOMERSETSHIRE, 1806

Anne might have been alarmed at how quickly she gave over her heart to Frederick Wentworth, but she was so very young and he so very good at inspiring her trust that she could not wonder at it. He was all that was delightful. She could not but marvel at how well they complemented each other. Where she was steady, he was vivacious. Where she was quiet, he was outgoing. Where she was cautious, he was daring.

It was their fourth meeting when she realized she was developing tender feelings for Commander Wentworth. It was their fifth when she began to think those feelings might be reciprocated.

They had been together on many occasions, and he always found a moment to speak with her and often sat near her. Mrs. Browning was a helpful accomplice. That good lady often hosted the kinds of events designed to further acquaintances and promote lasting friendships rather than merely to entertain.

Anne and Commander Wentworth always had thoughtful discussions, the occasional friendly debate, and plenty of time to converse on a variety of topics. He told her of the places he had sailed to with the navy and of his months at sea. She told him of life on an estate that had been held by her family for more than a hundred years. He questioned her about her care of the tenants and her work with the vicar at his school for local children. She told him about life at a girls' school and being the daughter of a baronet. He told her of his large family of brothers and his eldest sister, of whom he was very fond.

"Sophia is sometimes my only link to home when I am away," he confided on their eighth meeting. "That is likely because she is married to a sailor herself."

"Your brothers do not write to you?"

"They are poor correspondents, though Edward is better than the others."

She smiled at his reference to the young curate he was visiting.

By their tenth meeting, she was sure she was in a fair way to being in love with him and, on their eleventh, he looked at her with such warmth in his eyes she felt her breath catch.

In early autumn, Anne was invited to spend a fortnight with a friend whose father's estate was a few miles distant from Kellynch. Mayfield was a beautiful property, and Anne accepted readily, glad to spend time with her friend and even gladder to be within an easy distance of Monkford, where Commander Wentworth was staying with his brother.

The Wentworth brothers were a regular fixture at Mayfield. They came for tea and cards, were frequently invited for dinner, and joined the party for excursions and musical evenings. Anne saw Commander Wentworth nearly every day and in such intimate circumstances that she wondered how she would do without him when she returned to Kellynch. Her feelings were such that she struggled to conceal them. Her heart was no longer her own, and her entire future happiness depended on the dashing commander.

Two days before she was set to return to Kellynch, he asked her to walk in the gardens after dinner. The sun was dipping toward the horizon, and the landscape was bathed in a warm glow. The air was pleasantly cool, and he draped her shawl about her shoulders with deliberate care.

She was filled with anticipation when his bare hands touched her shoulder, and then the skin above her elbow, and she told him that she knew the perfect place for an evening stroll.

Anne led him to the east garden, on the opposite side of the house from the drawing room where the party was gathered. He smiled as they rounded the corner into the high hedges and narrow paths, and she wondered if her choice of location, clearly a bid to have his company to herself, had been too bold.

He took her hand and threaded it through his arm, then pulled her as close to him as he could, making their steps a bit awkward.

Not too bold, she thought.

They walked quietly for a time, Anne too full of happiness to say anything. Frederick broke the silence.

"This garden is lovely."

"Yes."

"I must applaud you for choosing it for our walk," he said with a smile.

She flushed and looked down, then met his gaze. "You do not find my behavior bold?"

"No, I do not. I find your behavior perfect. But if you wish to be bolder with me, I will not deter you."

She was certain she had never flushed as red as she did in that moment. He looked at her with kind eyes and tipped her chin up gently, then stroked her flaming cheek with the barest touch of his fingertips.

"Do you find my behavior bold?" he asked, his voice hushed.

"No. I find your behavior perfect."

His eyes softened, and he suddenly looked younger to her, innocent and whole, unvarnished by the troubles of life or the claims of time. He leaned forward and rested his forehead against hers, his warm breath washing across her face.

"Anne, dearest Anne. Do you know what you do to me?"

She shuddered and swallowed thickly, her breath ragged. "No. Is it like what you do to me?"

He released a startled laugh, and she looked up at him, unsure. He pulled her to him. "Darling, you are delightful. Never did I think I would be so fortunate as to find you."

She sighed in relief and rested her head on his chest. His arms tightened about her, and she felt him kiss her hair. What bliss was this!

"Please say you will marry me," he whispered into her hair. "I love you quite desperately."

She gasped, astonished and pleased and thrilled beyond her wildest imaginings.

"Yes, I will marry you, Commander."

He pressed her tighter, and she returned the embrace, wishing they could remain thus forever. He pulled back and looked in her eyes, a tender expression on his face, and tucked a lock of hair behind her ear. "Will you call me Frederick, my love?"

"Yes, Frederick. Will you call me Anne?"

"You have been Anne in my mind for some time now." Then he bent his head to hers, slowly but without hesitation, and kissed her lips.

She was nervous and did not respond as she wished to, her inexperienced lips pursed firmly and her head tilted at an awkward angle. She should have equaled his fervor, but she could do nothing but listen to her staggered breathing—or was it his?—and force her unsteady legs to remain standing.

"Too bold?" he asked as he withdrew.

"Not at all. Will you find me too bold if I ask you to repeat it?"

"I will find you perfect."

She smiled brilliantly at him, and he looked at her for a moment, wonder in his eyes, and kissed her again. This time, she was better prepared and kissed him back, her lips soft and her head tilted just so, her passion urging her to wrap her arms around his neck. He seemed to find this encouraging and pulled her close until her feet were off the ground.

Somehow, deep in her heart, she knew she would never be as happy as she was in this moment.

Would that she had been wrong.

∾

KELLYNCH HALL 1809

"Young Musgrove has not been here this week. Is he from home?" asked Sir Walter one evening after dinner.

"Yes, your suitor has been remiss of late," added Elizabeth.

"He is not my suitor," said Anne quietly to her sister.

Elizabeth merely smiled back at her with a disbelieving expression.

"I do not believe he is away from Uppercross, Father," said Anne.

The subject was dropped, and she thought she had escaped unscathed. However, as they were going up the stairs and separating to their own apartments, Sir Walter said to Anne, "I had thought he would make you an offer."

Anne could not prevaricate and quickly stepped into a small parlor near her father's room to avoid Elizabeth's too inquisitive gaze. Sir Walter followed her and studied himself in the mirror over the mantle, running his hand along the hair over his left ear to assure himself of its thickness, and then turned to face his second daughter. He looked at her impatiently.

Anne gathered her courage. "He did make me an offer, Father." She took a deep breath and looked him in the eye. "I refused him."

"You refused him?"

"Yes."

He paced to the end of the room, then turned quickly on his heel. "You will not accept him?"

"I cannot feel for him what a wife should feel for her husband," she replied evenly.

"And you will not reconsider?"

"I cannot, Father."

"He is not the handsomest man, but Mrs. Musgrove has kept her looks remarkably well."

"Be that as it may, my answer is no."

Sir Walter sighed. "Very well. Perhaps he will do for Mary."

~

ANNE'S PRIVATE CHAMBER AT KELLYNCH, OCTOBER 1806

"You have done what?" asked Lady Russell. Her shock and dismay were evident on every feature.

Anne stared at her mother's dearest friend. "You disapprove?"

"You do not?"

"I think we will be very happy together. His temperament is ideally suited to my own and he cares very much for me, as I do him."

Lady Russell sighed and sat forward in her chair. "Dearest Anne, you are but nineteen. I know you believe yourself in love with Commander Wentworth. Indeed, he is a worthy man and very handsome, but love alone is not enough to sustain a marriage. Where will you live? What will you live on?"

"Frederick believes he will make his fortune with the navy, and we might be very comfortable," said Anne uneasily. She did not mention her own dowry—if in fact there was to be one.

"When will that be? Years in the future! You are in your bloom! You could attract a husband from a fine family with a healthy income."

"The Wentworth family is nothing to be ashamed of," said Anne with quiet vehemence.

"Of course not," said Lady Russell in soothing tones. "I merely mean that you are just now coming to the notice of men who could give you so much more."

"Let Elizabeth make a fine match with a wealthy gentleman. I only wish for Frederick!" She felt tears welling up in her eyes and looked away.

"My dear, dear Anne!" cried Lady Russell. She hastened to sit beside her goddaughter on the sofa and rubbed a familiar pattern on her back, moving from her neck down her spine and back again in a rhythmic motion. Anne found it comforting, to her annoyance.

Lady Russell carried on with her campaign. "Commander Wentworth cannot support a wife at this time, can he?"

Anne shook her head. "But in a year or two, when he is made a captain, and we could write…"

Lady Russell made a tsking sound. "Who knows how your feelings will have changed in that time? You may find yourself bound to a man you no longer wish to live with. We have all seen the consequences of a hasty match."

"When have I ever been hasty?" asked Anne, insulted.

"You have not known him long, only four months. And you know little of his family, of his life away from Somerset."

The older woman shifted in her seat. The room was quiet but for the sound of her hand gliding over Anne's silk gown and the ticking of the clock on the mantle. She spoke tentatively, "In the absence of your excellent mother, it is incumbent on me to advise you as a mother would."

Another pause, then Lady Russell's quiet voice: "As much as I hate to say it, my dear, you must consider the possibility of him not returning home, or worse."

Anne snapped her head up and looked at her godmother more harshly than she ever had.

Lady Russell met her gaze. "He is in the navy, and we are at war. It must be considered."

Anne could not argue with Lady Russell's points and thus remained silent. After she had gathered her thoughts and could be certain of the steadiness of her voice, she said, "I may not have known him long, but I know him well—better than some I have known my entire life." She raised her chin. "And I have faith in the commander. He has already seen some success and believes he will see more. I have no reason to doubt him."

Lady Russell made a sympathetic face and tilted her head. "Think on what I have said, my dear, and bear in mind that you are nineteen. Nothing need be decided today."

Anne nodded and Lady Russell left her with a cup of strong tea and a kiss to her forehead, like she had done when Anne was a child. Anne leaned back on the chaise near the fireplace and stared, unseeing, at the empty hearth.

She wished desperately for her mother. Lady Elliot would know exactly what to do. She would calm Lady Russell and know best how to break the news to Sir Walter. The baronet was difficult to please at times, but Anne was of so little importance to him that she could not think he would truly object. She knew he would dislike the lack of connections and rank, but Frederick was handsome and that was in his favor, as was her father's apathy for all things relating to his younger daughters. Oh, that her mother were here!

Alas, Anne was on her own and must manage this situation without her mother's counsel. She thought of the future and the Royal Navy and the war with France. She thought of her courtship with Frederick and his family she had yet to meet. She thought of her sisters and her father and Kellynch. She thought so long and so hard, she feared she would go mad.

Hours later, as she was lying in bed trying to sleep and failing horribly, she heard a tapping sound. She tilted her head to the window and heard it again. Something was hitting against the glass. She climbed out of bed, wrapped a dressing gown around her, and approached the dark window. Another object plinked against the pane, and she realized it was a tiny stone.

Knowing who must have thrown it, she threw open the window and leaned out, a wide smile on her face.

"Anne!"

"Frederick! What are you doing? If someone catches you—"

"Come down! I want to see you," he called as quietly as he could.

"In the middle of the night?"

He held out his arms with a grin. "As you see."

She bit her lip and nodded, then ducked back inside and pulled her curtains tight. She hurried into a simple gown and tugged on her boots. She twisted her braid up and pinned it above the nape of her neck, her breath coming faster with every moment.

She crept down the corridor and out through a side door, then slipped away from the house, feeling more daring than she ever had in her life.

Just as Anne reached the edge of the garden and out of sight of the house, she felt strong arms reach about her waist and pull her close. She squeaked, and it was met with a laugh and a hand gently pressed over her mouth.

"Shh, my love," Frederick murmured in her ear.

The feel of his arms around her was so thrilling she closed her eyes to savor it and leaned back into him. He bent his head down to her ear and nuzzled the soft skin beneath it. She gasped and tilted her head to better accommodate him. She could feel his smile against her skin as he breathed deeply the scent of her neck.

"Anne," he whispered, low and filled with longing. He kissed her throat gently, and she surprised herself when a whimper escaped her.

"Come." He grabbed her hand and led her deep into the gardens, farther from the house.

~

THE WALLED GARDEN, KELLYNCH, 1809

Anne sat in her mother's garden, staring blankly at the flowerbeds before her. She had sat on this bench before, long ago. She remembered the whispered words and the shy smiles. If she held very still, she could feel the heat of his leg pressed against hers when he sat too near. Her neck tingled with the remembrance of his touch and the way his breath ghosted across her skin, his lips on her ear, her hair, her upturned face.

He had compared her to the flowers in this very garden. One particular variety had been his favorite. It reminded him of her, he had said. It was not bright, or especially large, or ostentatious in any way. It was a pale pink blossom, early to bloom and late to wither. It always turned to the sun, glowing in the bright rays.

He had been more accurate than he knew. If she was a flower, he had been her sun, turning to bask in his warmth and glean some of his radiance for herself. She had never thought she would be one of those ladies whose life began and ended with a gentleman. But how was she to go on with only half a heart? How was she to find happiness with a tormented soul, her memories tainted by her own betrayal? How was she to look on another man with favor when they all paled in comparison to Frederick?

Here she was, two-and-twenty, unattached, and without a single prospect. Having spurned the man she loved and turned down a most eligible offer, she could not expect to receive another. Not after what she had done. She had been tested and tried, and she had failed, most spectacularly. Fate would not smile on her again. Of that she was certain.

~

KELLYNCH, NOVEMBER 1806

"You are breaking your promise?" he said icily. It was not a question but a statement of disbelief.

She looked down and shuffled her feet in the gravel. "It is for the best."

"The best for whom?"

She swallowed, still unable to look at him. She was a good girl, and rebellion did not come naturally. Not against her duty or against those she loved. "You do not have a ship. A wife will only hold you back. And we are so different," she trailed off, her conviction wavering.

He placed his hands on her upper arms and pulled her to him with more force than she had ever felt from him. "You need a fine house full of servants, is that it?" he asked bitterly.

"No!" she cried, looking up at him. "You know that has nothing to do with it. You are at the beginning of your career. You must focus all your energies on the navy. A wife and children will be a distraction." Lady Russell had given her a frightful account of navy wives raising cottages full of children without assistance nine months of the year. It was not a pretty picture and she could admit to herself, though never to him, that the image quite alarmed her.

"Children?"

She flushed. "My mother was fecund, and so were her sisters. I have reason to believe children would not be long in coming."

He almost smiled, and it was her undoing. Tears began their ceaseless track down her face, one behind the other, without mercy. She would never see those children. Those tiny souls would never exist. No son with his father's eyes and easy smile. No daughter with her mother's hair and her father's charm.

His eyes filled with anguish, mouth twisted in pain, he choked: "Anne, you are the only woman for me."

She grasped his wrists so firmly her knuckles turned white. "Frederick, I could not bear it if something happened to you. If you were thinking about me or in a rush to return and you made a dangerous choice…" Lady Russell's arguments against his headstrong character and utter fearlessness, his courting of danger, played in her mind. Unsure of her reasoning, she was certain of one thing: her heart would not survive news of his demise.

"Do not say it is for my benefit! I will look after myself."

"The navy should have the greater part of your attention. You will need to campaign for a ship and must go wherever they send you. We likely would not see each other for months, perhaps years." She knew she was only repeating another's arguments, but she was quickly losing sight of her own reasons for disappointing him. Had she even had any? "After you have seen more success and been without me for some time, you may change your mind."

"Never!"

"You might regret me and wish you hadn't married so hastily. I do not wish to be a youthful mistake!"

He stepped back, disbelief written on his features. She saw the moment when he decided to stop fighting for her. His sky-blue eyes turned cold, and icy fingers tripped down her spine. She could not know if it was because he saw the merits in her arguments or if he was so disgusted with her for breaking her word that he wished nothing more to do with her. The hardness in his expression, the stubborn set to his jaw, told her he would never believe it was the right choice.

His voice was like shards of ice—hard, but ready to shatter from the slightest blow. "So this is your decision? Your father is unhappy and Lady Russell prefers a more illustrious suitor, so you will do their bidding, like a good little girl."

She flushed as if he had struck her. Her voice was trapped in a throat that could not swallow, her lips too numb to form words.

"Very well, Miss Elliot. Goodbye." He bowed correctly and turned to leave the garden. His steps were long and exact, his motion stiff compared to his usual careless grace.

She could not watch him go, not like this. This would not be her last memory of him. She ran to catch him, the gravel crunching beneath her feet and flying up against her skirts. She threw herself against his back, wrapping her arms about his waist and burying her face in the wool of his coat. She felt him take in a great breath as her own body shuddered and sobbed against his, and then his hands grasped hers and gently pried them apart, lowering both their arms to his sides. Her eyes remained riveted to the back of his coat, willing him to turn around and look at her, to let her see his face one last time.

They stood there for a moment, perfectly still, barely breathing. He squeezed her fingers once, long and steady, and then released her before walking to the gate. She thought he would hesitate before he stepped through, but he did not turn back or look over his shoulder. It was over. He was gone.

She would never see him again.

~

KELLYNCH, AUTUMN 1809

The broadsheet was on the table, as it always was. She glanced through the headlines, looking for anything to do with the Royal Navy. There, in the center of the page, was a description of an attack in the West Indies. The Laconia, led by Captain Wentworth, had successfully captured an enemy ship, and the captain had come away from the action a wealthier man for the prize money.

She set down the paper with shaking hands. She knew he had been successful, but to see his name in print, leading a siege on the seas, affected her more than she thought it would. Her fingers trembled as she traced them down the length of the article, absorbing all the information she could, desperate for word of him.

Had she not broken their engagement, this would have allowed them to marry. He could now comfortably support a wife, and she was as much in love with him as she had ever been—more so, if such a thing were possible without seeing the object of her affection for nearly three years. They could have been writing to each other all this time. She would have heard an account of the action in his own hand; the words would have leapt off the page as he described the most exciting parts to her, telling the story as only he could, and she would hear his voice in her mind as she read them.

She would eagerly await his arrival in Somerset, or perhaps she would travel to Portsmouth to meet his ship. They would fall into each other's arms, giddy with relief and expectation, and they would marry as soon as possible. He would insist on it. She would not argue. They would rent a cottage near the coast until he had to return to duty, and she would stay with his family while he was at sea, or perhaps return to Kellynch, though that idea was less appealing than it had once been.

But they were not engaged. He had not written to her, and she had not spoken a word of him since that fateful day when she had dashed all his hopes and broken her own heart. Her feelings had stood the test of time, with no encouragement. Had his?

She could only hope that in his heart, beneath his anger and pain, he still loved her. She had to believe that such precious feelings as theirs, such hopes as they had had, could not be so easily done away with. One argument could not lay waste to all that had been between them. Harsh words could not erase the tenderness of his arms wound about her, her cheek pressed against his chest. They had shared too much to lose it so simply.

Her sister's voice in the corridor sent her hand flying to her face, where she was surprised to feel the evidence of tears streaming down her cheeks. Not wanting to be seen, she quickly made her way out a side door and walked straight to her mother's garden.

Once she had gained the privacy of its walls, she ran all the way to the back, not stopping until she was panting and her hair was disheveled. She collapsed on the bench and drew ragged breaths, one behind the other, stemming the tide of emotions that threatened to overwhelm her.

When she was master of herself, she looked around at her mother's rose bushes, dormant in the chill of autumn, and thought how very like them she was. Their bloom gone, but the potential for so much life waiting beneath the surface and the bare stems. She felt it sometimes, her own possibility, when she stood in this garden, surrounded by memories of those who had loved her. She spared a moment to mourn the innocent girl she had been, so ready to love and be loved, so naïve in the ways of the world.

She sighed when she thought of those who had ostensibly protected her, professing their devotion as they ripped her apart. Her father, Lady Russell, even her beloved Frederick. No one had thought of the position they were putting her in—asking her to choose between the family to whom she owed loyalty and the man who held her heart. They lobbied for their own desires, uncaring of how she was tossed about between them. Did they even realize how untenable the situation was for her? The impossible choice she was forced to make? For a girl such as she was then, unused to open defiance and not born for revolution, it had been intolerable.

She knew Lady Russell had meant to act in her best interests, but Anne was no longer a girl, and the woman she had become could clearly see that even those one loves, dear as they are, can be blinded by their own prejudices and wishes. She more easily acquitted Frederick; his heart had been broken, his honor insulted, his trust betrayed.

She burned with shame when she thought of her own spineless reactions. He was right. She had behaved as an obedient child, not a rational creature able to make her own choices. Lady Russell had said that nothing need be decided soon; Anne had been nineteen, after all. There was time. But Anne had decided, and regret was her constant companion.

She thought very differently now than she had been persuaded to think three years ago. Faced with the same decision again, she would choose her own happiness and his.

She would not be persuaded again.

She would wait. Frederick would come for her. He must. And when he did, she would be ready. She knew her own mind now. He need never doubt her again.

ELIZABETH ADAMS is a book-loving, tango-dancing, Austen enthusiast. She loves old houses and thinks birthdays should be celebrated with trips—as should most occasions. She can often be found by a sunny window with a cup of hot tea and a book in her hand. She writes romantic comedy and comedic drama in both historical and modern settings. She is the author of *The Houseguest, Unwilling, On Equal Ground, The 26th of November,* and *Meryton Vignettes: Tales of Pride and Prejudice,* and the modern comedy *Green Card.* You can find more information, short stories, and outtakes at elizabethadamswrites.wordpress.com

WHERE THE SKY TOUCHES THE SEA

KARALYNNE MACKRORY

SOPHIA CROFT

Rational and wise, sister to Captain Frederick Wentworth, Mrs. Croft is half of one of the few examples of a happy marriage that Jane Austen ever wrote. As a well-travelled and confident woman, she sets the standard of a good navy wife and helpmeet. *"...as long as we were together nothing ever ailed me, and I never met with the smallest inconvenience."* —**Chapter VIII,** *Persuasion.*

WHERE THE SKY TOUCHES THE SEA

1817, SOMERSETSHIRE

"Oh George, mind the rut, dear, or we shall—"

I spoke too late, for we are now mired in the thick sludge built up along the side of the lane, pulling our gig quickly to a halt. Taking hold of the seat beneath me, my legs shoot forward to support myself against the front of the equipage, preventing me from going with the carriage into the muck.

It would not have been my first time finding myself in such trouble. I am no stranger to going overboard on the gig—nor finding myself in a bit of dirty water. Just the other day, my husband and I had such a mishap; the very remembrance pulls the edges of my mouth up! Lost in conversation, we had not been minding the ribbons. I very well could have fallen portside were it not for his quick hand pulling me back into the gig.

When all was determined to be well, my side pinched in laughter, reminding me of the way the waves crash into the rocks along the Isle of Wight, so constant and unrelenting was my hilarity. "Ah, Soph, I have done it again it seems. Blast if these wheeled contraptions are not harder than navigating the helm of a barque," he had blurted, and my heart had swelled with affection. Together, we had coaxed the horses to pull the equipage back onto dry land and we carried on our adventuring through the sleepy hills of Somersetshire.

This is our way—the only way we have learned to thrive together. Whatever storms we encounter, we batten down the hatches and sail through together.

Now my lips twitch with a smile despite my near miss, as we are not about an easy jaunt but on our way to dine with our neighbors, Mr. and Mrs. Musgrove. Again, the gig tilts evermore slightly as the wheel wedges itself quite securely deeper into the mud each time that George or I unsuccessfully try our luck with the reins. I give way to laughter when my husband coos words of encouragement to the matched pair. His eyes twinkle at me and, before long, we both give up and lean into each other with amusement.

With a good-natured sigh, I look at my husband of fifteen years, rear-admiral of the white, and survey our predicament.

"Well now we have gone and done it, haven't we, Soph?"

"Indeed we have, dear," I report, leaning starboard to better survey the extent of our trouble. "What might our hosts at the Great House think of us now? We were meant to dine there in twenty minutes. The carriage, George, we should have taken the carriage. And we might have persuaded Fred to come with us."

"Your brother expressed the desire to ride from Kellynch to Upper-cross and I thought, with such a clear evening, a bit of breeze in the gig would be more to our pleasure. Ah, Soph, you know how I like the feel of the wind in my face."

I pull my husband to me as I rest my head against the broad strength of his shoulder to let him know I assign him no blame. My cheek presses against the superfine of his jacket, the warmth of him seeping through to me. He is no man in his youth, all wiry muscles and ensnared energy. And yet, he is still my sturdy anchor.

I ponder about Fred's wish to ride, remembering my brother's agitation before we all set off for dinner at Uppercross. Freddy, usually so even-tempered, seemed to bear an unusual amount of restlessness this evening.

I turn my attention to my husband, gray about the temples and cheeks ruddy from the wind and a lifetime at sea. He is still quite a handsome man, in my opinion. When he looks at me with his blue eyes surrounded by smile lines, I know right away the next words from his mouth: "Well, Sophie, I am sorry to have to say it, but I fear we will probably be more than late to dine at Uppercross." With a look down at the ground, he heaves a dramatic sigh. "We may even expire here."

I fall into laughter but manage to acquit myself reasonably with a solemn expression. "Admiral Croft, it has been a pleasure to be married to you. And were we to indeed find our mortal end along this rural stretch of lane, it shall be a comfort to know that it was at your hands."

"Ha! You wound me, woman!" (First we laugh, then we teasingly predict the worst, then we get to work. That is always our way.) My husband hands me the reins and climbs out of the gig, reminding me of the many times I have seen him climb the rigging on his ship. As he nears the muddied band of the wheel, he steps backwards, lands on the soft turf beyond the mud, and winces. My heart lurches. I suspect he may have a bit of the gout.

"Soph, guide the horses to your right as I try to push this wheel out."

His words snap me out of my worried musings and I work the horses to help my husband free our wheel. Together we make a good pair. He never places me in a glass case to be admired as his wife. He values my opinion, is willing to see my ideas through, and comes to me when he wishes for sound counsel. I likely even surprised Sir Walter's lawyer, Mr. Shepherd, by asking the majority of the questions about Kellynch Hall, and the terms and the taxes, as the admiral is less conversant with business.

With no little effort, the gig attains more solid ground and my husband climbs back in. The seat bounces when his weight settles next to mine. He turns to me with the look of triumph I have seen many times after overcoming some difficulty. My heart swells with a tide of contentment only a long-tested love can produce. It is love, and well do I know my luck to have it. I love this man with greater feeling than the youthful passionate offerings my heart once made some fifteen years ago when we first wed.

I lace my arm through his and nestle into his shoulder only briefly. We can afford no more time, and so I pick up the reins where they rest on my lap and resume our course.

"We've cheated death once again, Admiral Croft."

I glance from the lane up to my husband's face, anticipating his humorous retort. My laughter forestalls any witty remark of his, for tiny flecks of mud speckle his face and he looks as if he might have contracted some spotted disease.

Warm hands encapsulate mine, gently taking the reins again lest I be the one to drive us off the road, for tears obscure my vision. He brings our gig to a careful halt. His lips tremble, telling me he finds my amusement contagious even if he does not understand its source. I attempt to speak numerous times but can barely manage to point to his face.

George removes his soiled gloves, lifts his hand to his nose and wipes at a spot, smearing it. My laughter is breathless and silent. My insides squeeze taut and it is all I can do to regulate myself. He laughs too upon seeing the smudge of mud on his finger.

"Well, we are a pair, are we not, Mrs. Croft?"

"I beg your pardon, sir." I gasp for breath, humor painting my tone while observing my own pristine gloves. "But how do you think to match me to your state?"

"You are perfectly correct, Sophie dear"—reaching into his pocket for his handkerchief—"You are far more handsome than I ever might have claimed to be." With a soft smile about his lips, he gently wipes a smudge on my cheek.

My smile warms and my heart contracts. I reach for the cloth in his hand and begin to clean the smudges on his face. When I finish, I sit higher and place a kiss on his cheek.

"How do we get ourselves in these scrapes, Admiral?"

"It doesn't much matter to me, dear, as long as all my scrapes are with you."

With that, he lifts up the reins and orders the horses to walk on. Within minutes, we are pulling through the gate and winding around the wide gravel circle to the front of the house of Mr. and Mrs. Musgrove.

Our eventful journey plays at the back of my mind while I look on at the antiqued stone of Uppercross, anticipating a pleasant evening of food and conversation. On previous visits, I have found the host and hostess to be charming, unaffected people, and their daughters, if a little high-spirited, to be blessed with everything youth desires. I also expect to meet Miss Anne Elliot again, in whom I found a steadiness much to my liking.

As I reach across my husband to tug the left rein a little to the right to encourage the pair to center the gravel lane again, I believe I could not have felt more happiness in the evening than I have already found stuck in the mud on a nameless country lane.

"I tell you, George, I was really quite surprised by Fred this evening. All that talk of women and their delicate needs. As if we were all fragile flowers, beautiful and useless at the same time!"

My husband gently pats my shoulder as he crosses our room towards the decanter of sherry. While he pours us each a small glass, he chuckles. His good humor is from an evening with engaging, energetic-minded people speaking of his favorite topic—the navy! While I enjoyed the company at Uppercross and sharing a quiet conversation with Miss Elliot, I find myself enveloped in melancholy.

"Your brother may have found his fortune as a captain in the navy, but he is poor in understanding. He will soon learn, like all men must do at some time or another, that when a woman speaks, his answer is and must always be, 'You are quite right, dear.'" To this he lifts his glass in a salute to me.

"Oh you!" I tut as I turn back to my looking glass. I avert my eyes, not wishing to see my countenance reflected back and resume removing the pins from my hair. With a "hmmph," I say under my breath, "We *are* rational creatures who do *not* expect to be in smooth waters..."

My fingers slow from the sure, efficient pace I have employed all my life when letting down my hair in preparation for bed. Soon they are heedless and lost in my tresses as my mind drifts—lost in remembrance. Smooth waters... No, I have not been in smooth waters all my days. The memories this evening are a series of clear, scattered parts in a dark haze. Still, those lucid fragments—I could swear, time has not passed at all...

~

The nip of the winter wind coming up from the coast was as fierce as any beastly bite. My reflection of its howl still sends a shiver down my spine and holds more significance than much of the other aspects of that dour, wet garrison town of Deal. The wind was like a demon tormenting the residents, including half-pay sea captains awaiting their next command—or wives of navy men, with hope in their eyes, watching where the sky touches the sea and praying their heart's wishes could prove power enough to wade their loved ones into port.

The reminiscence of that winter wind strikes me with such clarity and stands prominently, curiously, in my mind, considering what had happened to me there. The weather—I heave a humorless snort—was not the worst of it, although the permeating cold is perhaps a fitting symbol of that darkest winter of my life.

Besides the wind, my mind only recalls fragments of that winter I spent there without George, then Captain Croft. Like paintings of certain moments, the rest blur into grays and blues of indistinct recollection. I mused years ago that every biting breath I drew in that town was scored in my brain, but the years have a way of softening the etchings, smoothing with the healing touch of subsequent years, as other remembrances are dulled for self-preservation. Even the clear portions are difficult to think upon. How does one describe the feeling inside when a heart breaks in two?

Deal is such a small town for how essential it is to the navy. The Downs provide a sheltered anchorage for small vessels transporting necessary goods to the larger ships. The Naval Yard provides materials for repair and supplies. From shore, one can see hundreds of ships anchored beyond: every one provides the means of happiness or continued isolation to those waiting on land.

How similar that seemed to my experience there; sheltered at times, and despite having such a view of my future, still hopelessly desolate. Furthermore, my time there was both small in the span of my life yet significant.

Captain Croft at the time was stationed in the North Seas. I remember mentioning my travels to Mrs. Musgrove at her dinner table. I have never been a woman often overcome with emotion. I am practical and useful. I find ways to solve my predicaments and dislike the idle occupations of most of my sex. But this is not to say I am not a soul of deep feeling. My heart aches like others when I am filled with that powerful dark angel, Loneliness. However much my heart may feel, I do not like to lose command of my emotions, and never have, even with my dear George. Though it is with him that I feel safe enough to do so. And it was there, in Deal, where I nearly broke from his mooring.

I had acquaintances enough in that small Kent town. It is not as if that winter was one of complete desolation. Dear friends, wives, mothers, and families of other sailors created a safe netting for me. I was young then in the year three and, while never prone to rash decisions, was still plagued with the impetuousness of youth. George and I had only been wed a short six weeks when we were stationed there before his departure. In fewer weeks than we had enjoyed matrimonial life, he was captained on a ship headed to the North Seas for a twelvemonth. Were it not for those ladies, rational creatures themselves, it does not bear thinking whether I might have survived that winter.

Slowly my eyes focus again to the present and, through the looking glass, I behold my husband. I am not a small woman, neither fat nor tall, but there is strength in my frame that came about by necessity on our travels. It was not always so for me. Upon our marriage, I was perhaps more like the delicate silhouette of Miss Anne. My husband too once had the vigor of youth with wiry muscles and a trim waist. Now his shoulders have broadened with years of work on the ships—assisting his midshipmen in their duties when waters or war became rough. The sinewy muscles of his youth were replaced with the seasoned bulk of manhood. As he advanced in his profession, he began to grow soft about his middle and the slight effects of a long sea life began to pick at his health. To me, he is still a most handsome man, made more so by the laugh lines, graying temples, and knowing looks.

Perhaps this evening's topic at dinner with Fredrick and the Musgroves has placed me in a reflective mood. When my brother related the history of his time in the navy, I recalled the admiral's early years. And very rarely can I think on those years without my mind traveling down this melancholy path.

I recall how worried I was day in and day out for George. The worry was tangible at times. A gripping plague of emotions—made all the more disconcerting for a practical woman like me. Word of him could not come more dearly. Some news might come from returned officers, but most precious—the arrival of a letter! In my hands, I would then hold a piece of George. It was as if the sun parted the ever-present clouds and shone warmth on me for a few moments. The letter provided reassurance of his having been well and safe as of such-and-such a date. Still, as the weeks passed, little nets of anxious thoughts would draw those clouds closed again and every new ship was wished to be his. Every small vessel rowed into town for supplies was hoped to carry him to me.

I lived in perpetual fright all the time. This overwhelming anxiousness caused me to suffer in body and mind, the only time in my life I ever fancied myself unwell. Most mornings, for many weeks after he left, I was so troubled that I found myself ill. My already slim figure became gaunt and my very vitality seemed to drain away.

A very kind, wise woman of twice my age and experience lived in the apartment beside me, and upon some intuition, came to pay me a visit one afternoon. This memory rushes through me, causing my back to arch as if the recollection is a cold hand running up my spine. I feel at once all the emotions of that perverse yet beautiful day. I know not in what state she found me, for my mind recalls only a hush of whispers, a doctor called, and some warm broth pressed to my lips. I marvel how it is possible for one to have a recollection of shame and yet not feel it. I remember having become neglectful of my toilette and at the same time feeling that I had somehow failed George, allowing my worry to consume me thus.

With the ready care of my dear neighbor, I was very soon brought some relief. My anxiety, it seemed, was not the sole cause of my bodily discomfort. When I was again sensible to my surroundings, I learned that the doctor had examined and declared me to be with child. For the next hours, I faced every range of emotion, mostly elation and joy. I also experienced thoughts and sensations I shudder to recall even now.

My heart beat thunderously with a strange mixture of excitement and fear. It was exactly what would save me. I could be a mother to George's child! The distraction might ward away the waves of worry for him.

But alone. Most of the time, I would be on my own. Though I could and would draw upon the experiences of the other kind women of Deal, it was still a task I would have to strive on my own. The thought of being with child sent phantasmal icy ribbons all over my body. A mother. It was a powerful, terrific prospect.

Can any mother adequately describe the wonder that accompanies such a discovery? It has been nearly fifteen years and still words lodge in my throat, feelings constrict my heart, and expressions escape my mind, unable to describe the all-encompassing sense of magic that came with life growing within.

I longed to speak with George, to share this terrifying joy with him. I knew in my heart he would be a most devoted father and that he too would wish to be by my side. A little calculation and it was determined that the babe would most certainly arrive before he returned. The future instantly petrified me and made me wish even more fervently for my husband's return. But I was not the only woman to endure this process alone. I did not claim to deserve any sort of extra compassion for myself. Although there were times, I am ashamed to say, when I raged against that fate that attached me to a naval officer, I knew this was the life that I would have and I would never want anyone different.

Those next several weeks are a blur of mismatched memories. The weather was as perpetual as the tides: cold, rainy, and windy. Correspondence was sparse, as the ships in the North Seas were likely experiencing fiercer weather than we were at the South of England. At times, I held my secret treasured-soul growing inside me as a personal luxury. The babe bound me to George and was to be a joyful surprise for him when he was once again ashore.

Years have seasoned my decisions and built up my sensible mind, for as a woman now of many more years than the woman I was then, I am aghast that, despite yearning to share the news with my husband, I never once put the words to paper. I wonder now if it was this secret I kept— and my reluctance to disclose it—that clouded my mind so that I did not see the shifting of tides that were to come.

~

"What has you so quiet this evening, Soph?" My husband breaks through my musings, placing my glass of sherry on the dressing table in front of me.

Shaking my head to clear my thoughts, I stand, reaching up on my toes to kiss him. "I am only thinking of Deal."

A look sweeps across his features, almost too quick for me to be certain of it. But George and I do not keep our thoughts from each other. Fifteen years of marriage to your dearest companion provides you with the security necessary to never keep your own counsel. Besides, I have since learned there is no benefit in that.

I believe he intends to say something but instead simply embraces me. It is enough to express his understanding. It was not always like this for us, this easy knowledge of each other's needs and feelings. I suppose that also comes with our years together.

Nobody tells a young miss how different her husband will be. The male sex is a different sort of creature. I had brothers, and I was still not prepared for the nature of a man's feelings. It has been my understanding from my years with George that men do not feel *less* than a woman; instead, they *feel differently*. My proof was the overwhelming joy in my George's eyes when at last he did step off that transfer vessel onto the shore and saw me waiting for him. In addition, I witnessed the expressions on the faces of numerous returning men starved for months of seeing their loved ones when they again beheld those dear ones safe and hale. It cannot be denied then that a man feels as ardently as a woman. But they certainly express it differently.

Like the bow of a boat made glossy by the constant caress of the water as it rushes over it, the years have eroded the worst of my recollections. But it pleases me that the engraving in my mind of my husband's countenance when he returned to me that day remains as fresh as if it were yesterday. Time cannot wear down some things. And though I may not be as effusive as others of my sex, there is very little I can do to keep the tears from welling in my eyes as I reminisce on the brightness in those of my husband then.

Together we walk to our bed in the master suite at Kellynch, our hands entangled, and after extinguishing the candles, we climb atop it. When together, it has always been thus for us, sleeping in the same bed. I am thankful on a ship there are not such vast accommodations as to make me adhere to society's standards of sleeping separately from my husband. As long as I am with him, I have nothing to fear.

"Do you blame me for not writing to you when it happened, George?"

He knows of what I speak. Warm hands reach across the bed, roughened from work but exactly the touch I long for. He pulls me gently to him, and I readily take my place, long made comfortable from habit, at his side.

"I understand now why you did not."

"I told myself at first that I was not in the right state to give such communication. That I should not do it justice as I ought. Then I reasoned that it might not get to you before you arrived home again anyway. In the end, I believe it was that I was simply not brave enough."

He is quiet and I listen to his breathing. I know that it is not that he has nothing to say but that men need time to manage their emotions. I listen quietly to his heartbeat in my ear and content myself that my husband always shares with me his thoughts and that I need only wait.

In time, the deep rumble of his voice breaks the silence in the room.

"Sophie, you were all I longed for. A babe would have been an extension of you, a part that added to your allure. But I fear that you will think me a brute when I say that if all I ever receive in this life is the portion of heaven that is you, and no more, then I am content."

I admit my eyes flood again and I smile. It is a sentiment he has expressed in different ways over the years when we have spoken of the events of that late January. They are not made trite for the repetition of them, rather rendered more sincere. My arms pull me tighter to him, and I try to hold all my concentration to the sound of his heart in my ear but once again the veil of time slides past my mind's eye and I am swiftly back in Deal.

〜

I did not give George a child before his return.

For those short weeks I knew motherhood, I alone carried my secret. Again I marvel with the vision of maturity, making hindsight full of clarity. I ought to have told him. I admit I did not feel equal to sharing my condition through a letter. And in the end, it did not matter much if I had.

I have always supposed that I owed the doctor an apology for my actions that evening. When my condition became grave enough, the symptoms evident that I had lost the babe, I became quite insensible to anything but the grief. Like a dam that had given way, I was carried down in the current. I suppose I could blame some of it on the fever that gripped me in the days before the babe was lost. I was fevered, in spirit, not just in body. This was not what I had chosen when I married a naval man. Living alone, waiting for him…I knew would be my lot—but having this dearest prize so recently won snatched from me and to have no husband to cleave to? No husband to bear my painful cries as I came face to face with my grief? I was in a prison walled by emotions. I could not see past them nor did it seem fair. The whole of it took on the quality of a horrific dream.

"I am sorry, madam," he said, wiping his hands upon a cloth after examining me. All I could look at was that towel, twisting and being pulled through his fingers. Being soiled with…

I did not look at him when he told me that there was some irregularity with the shape of my womb. *Damaged. Wrong. Failure.* That is how my ears interpreted the words from his lips. By then my erratic burst of insensibility had grown numb. I did not express any feeling when he, with muffled, useless apologies, declared that it would be unlikely for me to ever conceive and carry a babe. He said my fever would likely prevent future conception anyway, regardless of my condition. I remember he said the word miracle. And I scoffed. He called my conception a miracle and, in the same breath, told me my womb had failed. I suppose now I can see how he would call it that. The term does not now hold the bitterness it did then. It *was* a miracle that I experienced that brief touch of motherhood.

To this day, I shudder at the animal-like cry that ripped from my lips then. As the doctor turned to depart, it tore from deep inside me like a feral cat, and I lobbed the nearest item to me at his back. My hurt was such that every subsequent pain must always be compared to it. The doctor did not turn; he simply lowered his head and slipped out the door, taking with him any claim to heaven I had dared to believe was mine. I found my tormented outburst had resulted only in the impotent throw of that soiled cloth.

Anyone who has ever experienced grief will tell you what a cloying thing it is. It ebbs and flows, not unlike the tides that I know and love so well. It comes and sneaks in like a rogue wave, pushing you off balance and at once adrift for a moment. At other times it lurks, hazy like the shadowed fog on the horizon, tempting you with the fear that it foretells rough waters ahead. Sometimes those rough waters come. To me, the worst is when they do not. When I can see Grief on that horizon as if to say, "I am here. I am always here."

When George returned, he found the *me* that grief had created. I cannot describe that person, for I lived inside her. With his homecoming, he brought with him all the impassioned longing and love with which he had left, only to find a hollowed-out woman with little to laugh about and far less heart to give.

I do not blame George for the way he acted. He could not have known what had happened to me. For a time, we grew distant. At times, I felt resentment toward him. He had been out in the world, completely spared from the torment of the loss of our child. I was at home and my feelings preyed upon me.

"Why do you think on such times?" There is emotion in George's voice, though one who did not know him as I do would not recognize it.

I settle closer to him, using his warmth to chase away the chill of nostalgia. I try to empty my mind enough to answer his question. As his fingers begin comforting paths of lazy swirls on my back, my muscles melt, and with them, the pangs of that time. Once again, I reflect on the events of the past with the eyes of the present, with all their enlightened, love-healed, wizened lenses.

I cannot recall the event, look, or word that helped to anchor me again in that dark sea. But I do believe I finally recognized that same heartbreak in George. When George could neither bear living with, nor could he understand this pitiful creature that he called his wife, he too came to know a bit of grief. I wish I could say that my feelings upon seeing it were noble. Instead, for a time I allowed bitterness to enslave my heart and I relished in his pain, for now I was not the only one. We were both ships at sea without sails.

He received his next assignment on a sloop headed south, eventually to the East Indies. Faced with the possibility of a longer estrangement from him, a cord snapped inside me and, immediately, I felt more than grief. I bore a need for George so fiercely it swallowed my whole being like a tidal wave.

I cried to George then; I begged him not to leave me again and any cords of grief around his heart snapped as well. He was angry at me. I had never, before or since, experienced his anger directed so severely at me.

His eyes darkened with passion as he coldly declared, "And what am I to you, ma'am?"

Stunned, I stared at him. Did he not know he was my everything? That for him I had endured torturous months of waiting, worry, and toil? Of a sudden, I understood that he did not know these things. I had not fostered the love I felt for him above my grief for the loss of motherhood and my—our—child.

"I do not choose when these reflections will fill my mind, George. But I am at peace now when they do. For they remind me how very close I was to losing you as well and how we learned to navigate our way back together."

"I do not like the sadness it brings to you."

My lips lift in a soft smile against the heat of his chest. I suppose that when difficult memories assail us, we do have a tendency, as humans, to have our emotions painted a different hue. But as I reflect on the entirety of this momentous time of my life, of our life together, I see these remembrances as times that changed me from the girl of my youth, full of passion but without substance, hopes and dreams without contentment, and love without a sure foundation. It was Deal where I learned how to begin to build the type of love that fills my heart now as I embrace my husband. It was in Deal where I began to see that hopes and dreams held all the power to crush you—or become your reality—depending on whom you shared them with.

That evening years ago, I realized that George ought to have been more to me than my husband and lover. I ought to have remembered he was my closest companion and friend. With him, I could share my sorrow, unburden my shattered plans, and I could burn away that nagging fog of grief like the sun as it blazed up over the horizon. As I poured out to George the events of the months of his absence, it would have been ideal to say that he understood immediately, and we were in communion again. But he was young and full of the ensnared energy that I saw in Freddy lately. His temper had flared and, briefly, I understood how betrayed he had felt that I had not shared with him all that I had been forced to endure. I misinterpreted his feelings at first, for I was as impetuously youthful as he was. I saw his anger and felt it directed at my failure to tell him, to trust him, to provide him with a child.

As the long hours passed, I learned his anger was directed at himself too. He was tortured by the thought of what I had endured and how little he could have done for me if he had known. He was away on a ship, hundreds of miles to the north, while his wife grieved at death's door, alone. I learned that and many other lessons regarding the way a man might feel. I grasped that I ought to have trusted him with my pain. We cried for the loss of our child, the loss of any future children, and then, after hours of the searing expulsion of diseased spirits, we could see in the eyes of the other a little of the person we had loved before.

As a naval officer's wife, I have learned that, when rough waters come, you cannot sit upon the decking and rage against the storm. You cannot scream at the wind and lash out at the rain on your face. Doing so will do nothing but allow the storm to beat upon you with greater vengeance and perhaps steal from you your life. No, when the waters are not calm, you must secure the boat, rigging and sails. Brace yourself and, with your crew beside you, face the storm.

～

"It's hard for me to think of what you went through, Soph. What I would do to have been ashore then and at your side."

"You were soon there beside me."

"But not without quite a squall first!"

I laugh, as he expected. George always pulls me from any solemn thoughts with humor. I am glad to know that we can now speak lightly about such a deep cut in our marriage. It is proof that we have healed.

"I suppose we ought to have had one good row in our marriage, else we would have been doomed, I am sure."

The rumble of his laugh makes my smile widen. How I love the feel of it against my ears. The sound vibrates, tickling my ear.

"You are a good man to me, George."

He makes a low noise in his throat and I smile to myself. When he speaks, his voice is rougher than usual and my heart beats against my chest in an attempt to be closer to his.

"Enough of that, Soph. Let us sleep now. I want to take the gig out on these country lanes again. I have a mind to take you down that path we discovered yesterday. Charles Musgrove tells me it takes one very near to Winthrop, which I am told is the estate his cousin is to inherit."

I readily agree, for I love nothing more than to spend time with my husband. After Deal, we traveled everywhere together and I was never away from him. It is true what I told Mrs. Musgrove: as long as I had the admiral at my side, I never did fear and was always quite comfortable on the ships. When George left for his next assignment, he took me with him. Through the passage of time and the years on the sea, my memories of that winter were smoothed and weathered away; some remained and contributed to my eventual healing and the foundation of love that I now benefit from with George.

My thoughts shift like a quiet breeze back to our earlier journey to Uppercross and getting stuck in the mud. I might laugh again at our scrapes if I were not reminded that what I feel for George is a *seasoned love*. The unexpected timbre of George's voice catches me off guard, for I had thought he had begun to slumber while I muse my good fortune.

"Do you ever regret coming aboard with me, Sophie? We could have likely found children to adopt and raise if you had stayed ashore."

I sit up abruptly to be assured of his eyes on mine when I speak. "Admiral Croft, you have been more than enough for me. I followed you to the East Indies and I would follow you to all the ends of the earth. Besides, many a young midshipman have I raised."

"As long as you do not have any regrets, my dear."

"I do not."

"As for me, Mrs. Croft, I am grateful you are not one of those fine ladies. I am grateful that you are a *rational creature*."

I lie back down against my husband and embrace him tightly, my mind shifting entirely away from the past. Once again, finding amused irritation at the absurdity of my brother mixed with the desire to either shake him or laugh at his lack of understanding, I say, "Really! What could Fred have been thinking?"

George chuckles again, and my ear tingles at the sound. "One day he will find himself with such a woman as you, Sophie. Impossible to live with—"

I jab him in the side, and my ear feels his laugh again.

"Impossible to live with*out*, my dear. And then he will find his opinion of ladies aboard ships to be quite different." George punctuates his words with a kiss to my temple.

"Indeed."

It seems my husband has changed his mind about sleep, for George then begins to debate which of the Misses Musgrove would suit my brother best, but I cannot form an opinion myself. Privately I do not feel either would suit Fred. Neither of them has the strength of character required to be a naval officer's wife. Shrugging, I realize, neither did I at their age. Life bore me many instances after my time in Deal when waters were not smooth. And yet, from then on, George and I have always determined to be happy and to be together. With those two resolutions, nothing ever ails me, and I never meet with the smallest inconvenience.

KARALYNNE MACKRORY is no newbie to the writing world. She made her debut as an author at the tender age of thirteen when she wrote her first collection of bad poetry. As a young adult, she steered clear of bad prose and achieved a degree in social work. Years later, she has published four Austen-inspired novels so full of romantic sensibilities as to give you a swoon and hopefully a few laughs: *Falling for Mr. Darcy, Bluebells in the Mourning,* the IPPY award-winning *Haunting Mr. Darcy,* and *Yours Forevermore, Darcy.* Her books turned out much better than her poetry.

THE ART OF PLEASING

LONA MANNING

PENELOPE CLAY

When chance throws Penelope Clay, a poor widow with two small children, into the company of Sir Walter Elliot, a widowed baronet, her only rational notion is to charm and wheedle her way into becoming the next Lady Elliot. She befriends Sir Walter's oldest daughter, and though others stand in the way of her schemes, Mrs. Clay is *"a clever young woman, who understood the art of pleasing..."* —**Chapter II, *Persuasion.***

THE ART OF PLEASING

"Why did you tell them I am a widow?" I demanded as soon as we drove out of earshot of the footman who had helped me climb up into my father's pony cart.

"I did not say anything of the kind," my father answered. "I told Sir Walter your marriage had not prospered and that you had returned to live with us. That is no less than the truth, only less than the *whole*. Would you rather I had told them that the father of your children is a fugitive from the law? That he abandoned you? That he was—is—a fraud and a criminal?"

"But I heard Miss Anne Elliot ask Miss Elliot who I was, and Miss Elliot said I was a widow. She mistook you."

My father glanced at me, at my worn black boots and my old grey gown and my cheap straw bonnet. "Your dress and veil must have added to the misapprehension that you are in mourning."

The veil, we both knew, was to keep my freckles at bay.

"What if we are in company together and they introduce me as a widow? What should I say?"

"They will no doubt introduce you as 'Mrs. Clay.' Fortunately, it is a common enough name."

"'Common as mud,' Mr. Clay used to say."

"Nobody in Kellynch will think it worth their while to wonder if you happen to be associated with some minor scandal in Plymouth, some brief paragraph about a Mr. Clay, that appeared in the newspaper several months ago. With sufficient caution, we may conceal these disgraceful family matters."

We proceeded in silence for a time, while I pondered on the difference between my father's way of speaking when he was in the presence of Sir Walter—"I must take leave to observe, Sir Walter" and "I venture to hint, Sir Walter"—and his asperity with me. No doubt the irritation and impatience he suppresses whilst in attendance at Kellynch Hall must find its vent somewhere. And so, rather than whip our horse, he must lash at me with his tongue.

Finally, I said, "Miss Elliot was quite civil, don't you think? I believe I made a good impression."

He nodded but added, "Do not do anything to jeopardise this promising beginning, Penelope. You are just genteel enough to be an acceptable companion for Miss Elliot, if you guard your tongue carefully. Follow my lead when you are at Kellynch. Sir Walter and Miss Elliot must be guided, as one would guide a flock of sheep, with their debts nipping at their heels. We must show them the promise of green and open pastures ahead."

"Well, that is apt, is it not, for our name is Shepherd," I said.

"Do not attempt anything like wit or repartee when you are at Kellynch, Penelope."

It might be supposed that a woman who finds herself without a farthing at the age of two-and-thirty must be ignorant about money matters. On the contrary. I kept the books (both sets) for Clay & Company. When I had to return in disgrace to my father's house, I quickly realised that disaster threatened him as well. My father is a solicitor and Sir Walter Elliot is his most illustrious client. But Sir Walter Elliot does not pay his bills while my father, on the other hand, must pay his clerks. And now he has three more mouths to feed at home. He was no more pleased to receive us than I was to be there, but I had no alternative.

At least this state of affairs provided a means whereby I could make myself useful—to be a sort of spy at Kellynch Hall, Sir Walter's grand country estate.

"Nothing was of so much use for my poor daughter's health as a drive to Kellynch," my father would say when he brought me with him and, indeed, compared to the utter monotony of home life, I preferred to sit in the second-best parlour with Miss Elliot, drinking tea and eating little cakes.

I was to befriend Miss Elliot and report on our conversations. Did the Elliots truly understand that they faced a crisis? Were they serious about retrenching? To be fair, only Sir Walter and Miss Elliot had been profligate. There was another daughter at home, Miss Anne, who was all for making strict reforms, but, as I soon learned, her voice had no weight with her father and older sister.

Miss Anne was very reserved. She would come into the parlour just long enough to greet me. "And how are your children, Mrs. Clay?" she would always say in her polite, quiet way, but I am certain she really meant, *"Why aren't you at home with your children—where you belong?"* Then she would excuse herself, and we would hear her tinkling away on her pianoforte in some distant room while I did my best to charm my way into the good graces of Sir Walter and Miss Elliot.

At first, I felt like a graceless heifer in Miss Elliot's company. After all, I had spent almost half my life working in a warehouse on a dockside in Plymouth—not exactly a centre of refinement! I studied her manner and her movements: how she poured milk into her teacup last, not first; how she said "drawing-room" and not "parlour"; and how she sat and stood and moved.

I was not a little gratified at how quickly I became a welcome visitor at Kellynch—received with smiles, invited to stay, given my own bedchamber! A favourite companion of both Miss Elliot and her father!

Sir Walter would sometimes comment on what a pleasing contrast we presented. I think Miss Elliot chose me as one might choose a bonnet. I set off her best features. She is tall and slender, whereas I am short and inclined to plumpness; she is dark, and I am fair; she is elegant, even down to her smallest gestures, where I am clumsy; and…I am altogether well-looking, I am told, even handsome, but she is a beauty.

She is prone to changeable moods. I put it down to the fact that she has no interests to occupy her during the day, no one interesting to occupy her at night, and she must be nearly thirty.

Sir Walter is easier to manage. Although he is almost as old as my father, he is not unpleasant to look at and he fancies himself a wit. I laugh at his sallies (demurely of course, using my hand to cover my crooked front tooth) and hang on his every word. I would not say that I flirt with him, not quite, but I do frequently remark to his daughter what a well-looking man he is, and no doubt the compliment is passed along.

Patiently, all through the month of June and into July, my father and I made our visits back and forth in our little pony-cart. My poor father laid the memorandums he had drawn up before Sir Walter, showing him how strained his finances were, how paying the interest alone on his debts was swallowing him up alive, and how he could not possibly go on any longer as he was. There was some talk of retrenching, less travel, dismissing some servants (who had not been paid for two quarters), but the baronet refused to consider it. It would be too humiliating.

Then, to our great surprise and relief, Sir Walter suddenly resolved that he would rather quit Kellynch Hall than remain there under reduced circumstances. This was the best solution to his debt problems, for he could rent his great estate for a handsome sum.

Thanks to me, we swiftly and discreetly found a tenant. Of course, my father, as Sir Walter's indispensable agent, must have all the credit. I am not complaining. This is often the easiest way to get something accomplished—let the man think he did it. In fact, my own great disaster came about when I gave way to my husband, against my better judgment. We were doing well, buying stale-dated navy salted beef and biscuit at auction and re-selling it to the merchant ships. But my husband was too greedy. He was confident that no one would catch on to his little schemes and fiddles. He was wrong.

At Kellynch, I had said of myself, "I returned to my parents' home after I lost poor Mr. Clay," which was true enough, in the sense that I no longer had Mr. Clay with me, though I did know where he was. After I helped him escape from the constables (he hid inside one of his own barrels and was trucked out of our warehouse in a handbarrow), he went to London, from whence he would occasionally write by styling himself "Aunt Grace" just in case our letters fell into the wrong hands. "My dear Penelope, can you spare some money for your poor old aunt? I need more medicine." That sort of thing.

It was he who let me know Admiral Croft was looking to settle in Somersetshire and that he was gone to Taunton, where my father made his acquaintance.

I knew Admiral Croft would be an excellent tenant for Kellynch. I had never met him, but I knew of his reputation in Plymouth. Once, my husband hinted to Admiral Croft's purser that it would be a simple matter to substitute the ship's stores of fresh cheese for some older stuff, and then they could sell the good cheese and split the profits. The purser practically kicked him down the gangway and told him, "Admiral Croft runs a clean ship with no gutter rats aboard."

By means of testing the wind, my father mentioned the desirability of having a navy man as a tenant. "If a rich admiral were to come in our way, Sir Walter..."

I added some flattering remarks about how only landed gentlemen (like Sir Walter) could preserve their good looks, compared to sailors who must toil in all weathers, but father scolded me on the ride home and said I had talked too much. I was there to listen, not to hold forth, he said.

"'*Men but what lose something of their personableness*'? Is that even English? And why did you say that you knew a great deal about sailors? Do you *wish* to invite questions about your past?"

"You are overcautious, Father. Miss Elliot did once ask me what my husband did, and I said he had been a chandler, and even before I finished explaining what a chandler was, she lost interest and began talking about her new gown."

"Nevertheless, do not volunteer unnecessary information about yourself at any time. Be as useful as possible while Miss Elliot packs up her things and settles her affairs. Having rounded up the sheep, so to speak, we must now guide them to safer pastures. Sir Walter cannot get himself into a scrape in Bath as he could easily do in London. There is some hope that he might contrive to live within his means in Bath."

I stayed away from Kellynch when Admiral Croft and his wife came to visit. I do not know if the admiral's purser told him about my husband—if the name "Clay" had any associations for him—but I was taking no chances. My father told me the meeting went off well, and it was settled that the Crofts should take possession at Michaelmas.

My new task was to steer Miss Elliot towards Bath—always Bath. How mild the winter season! So kind to the complexion! What a figure she would make there! And Sir Walter could still be Sir Walter, with no loss of pleasure or consequence and with a larger audience. As for all the toils and vexations of sorting and packing and removing themselves from Kellynch Hall, naturally, I was at their entire disposal. In fact, I began to spend more time at Kellynch than at home. Miss Elliot began to call me "Penelope," but I, of course, continued to address her as "Miss Elliot" and not "Elizabeth" to her face.

As September approached, two extraordinarily fortunate things occurred: *I* was to go to Bath and Miss Anne was not! Miss Elliot—Elizabeth!—invited me to come and help set up her new household, while Miss Anne was to visit all the autumn with their youngest sister, a married lady who lived nearby.

My father was pleased with me, for once.

"You must write me regularly. Ensure they keep their expenditures within bounds," he lectured as he took me and my travelling trunk to Kellynch Hall. I would go in state in the Elliot carriage with Sir Walter and Miss Elliot. It was to be the last journey for the carriage, for it would be sold at auction, and the horses as well.

"Yes, Father. The four subjects at my boarding school were sewing, sums, grammar, and 'telling baronets what to do.'"

He gave me a sideways look and met my spirit of raillery.

"Well, let's hope that you learned more than you ever did at your dancing lessons."

Cutting but true. I was a most ungainly dancer. I could never remember the steps, and the dancing master was forever crying, "Mam'selle Shepherd! One, two, three, four—*un, deux, trois, quatre! Non! Non! à droite! à droite!*"

However, despite my protests to my father, I was well prepared to manage a town home, thanks to my experience managing my husband's business. Elizabeth needed no housekeeper so long as she had me. I could drive a sharp bargain with all of the Bath tradesmen. I could direct the housemaids in their duties, while she need only exert herself for the more genteel tasks like approving the menus. We had only eight servants at Camden Place, and yet we managed to present a creditable face to the world.

As an example of how I reined them in, Elizabeth wanted fresh flowers several times a week for all the principal rooms, and I persuaded her to purchase some potted palms and other tender plants instead. "For here, just off the parlour—drawing room, I mean—is a lovely little bow window that would make an admirable greenhouse. Why pay for cut flowers, which will only die, when you can have flourishing live plants every day? And, unless gentlemen have changed in their ways, Miss Elliot, may I venture to predict that armloads of flowers will soon be arriving at your door."

When I first met her, I had wondered, since she did not play, paint, or read, how Elizabeth passed her days. Somehow, she kept me and her lady's maid on the hop all day.

"Where is that latest letter from Anne?" she asked one morning. "I suppose I should answer it and get it over with before we go for our morning calls. I have been meaning to do so for a fortnight."

"I shall fetch it for you, dear Miss Elliot," I said, placing her writing slant for her on the breakfast table. "Why, this one must be a new letter. It's not opened."

"No, I have not read it yet," came the answer. "You can read it to me, a little at a time, Penelope, and I shall answer as you go along."

"I should be happy to, if you and Miss Anne have no objection to my seeing your private family correspondence."

"She can have nothing to say which would be of interest to anybody."

I did not contradict Elizabeth, but I found the letter to be very pleasant to read, even though it described ordinary activities in the country, visiting back and forth, and long walks in the fields. Miss Anne wrote well. Her handwriting was beautiful and clear, and so was her English.

"Mrs. Croft's brother, whom you knew as Commander Wentworth, has come to stay at Kellynch for some indefinite time," I read. "He is now

Captain Wentworth and has been visiting frequently here in Uppercross—"

"What? Wentworth back!" exclaimed Elizabeth.

I paused. "Were you acquainted with this Captain Wentworth then, Miss Elliot?"

"Slightly, and only briefly. He was an impudent, beggarly sort of man who had the presumption to make an offer for Anne. Father and I managed to chase him off. He had no fortune, no rank, no family connections."

"Well, then, you did right by your sister. So very careful of her happiness! I honour you, ma'am!" I said. There were many times over the past fifteen years when I wished someone had performed the same kind office for me.

"We had to consider the Elliot name and our rank and dignity. But we do not speak of it. Go on with the letter. Does she say anything more of him?"

"He is described as dancing and walking out with the Misses Musgrove very often."

"He must still be single, then."

But I learned nothing more, as the housemaid interrupted us with a request that I come inspect the laundry delivery.

Despite Elizabeth's moods, she was clearly pleased to be out of the isolation of the countryside, and I was beginning to think that my husband's disgrace was the best thing that had ever happened to me. Not a year ago, I was arguing over the price of lumber and tar and rancid butter with some rascally quartermaster. Now I spent my days making social calls with Elizabeth, receiving guests in the drawing room and eating and drinking better food than ever the Clays could afford! And whenever I could not endure her waspish remarks, I volunteered to do some errands for her and walked down the hill into town.

As for Sir Walter, even back at Kellynch, it had idly crossed my mind that I might attempt to attach him. At first, I thought of it only for my own amusement.

But time, and my patient application of the arts of pleasing had done a great deal for me. I was very much a part of the household, consulted in many daily matters: "What shall we do about the squeaking pantry door?" "What do you think of the lining to this waistcoat, my dear?" Chiefly, Sir Walter valued me because I would listen to him. Every day he told me all about his outings, what he did, who he saw, how wretched they looked. I listened and nodded and smiled and laughed: "Oh, Sir Walter!"

I sensed that Sir Walter's growing reliance on me was triumphing over his prejudices against my lowly rank. His attentions and compliments increased perceptibly. He said my complexion (by which he meant my freckles) had improved, and that I was a truly discerning woman (because I said so many flattering things about him).

What did Elizabeth think of all this? I am certain *she* never thought of me in such a light. I think I would have been out on the street, bag and baggage, if she'd had any fear of gaining me as a stepmother. Elizabeth kept me with her, however, and I never detected the least uneasiness.

By December, I dared to imagine myself—freckles, crooked tooth, and all—as the future wife of Sir Walter Elliot. His daughters would have to call me "mother." Or maybe "dearest mother." I would be the mistress of Camden Place and one day, of Kellynch Hall. And to crown it all, I would give Sir Walter a son and heir who would grow up to become a baronet.

I did not share my ambitions with my father, not with anyone.

In this fashion, the old year ended, and we began the new.

When you are in trade, you quickly learn to recognise a salesman. They are different from customers. Customers enter the shop and grow impatient if they are not served on the instant. Salesmen come in when you are busy. They wait with a good-natured smile on their faces, content to indulge in their own pleasant reflections until they can beg a few moments of your time.

Mr. William Elliot reminded me of the salesmen who wanted us to buy their candles and rope and jackknives. There was nothing hurried about him. He was all ease, all good nature. From the first time he called upon us, he was selling *himself*.

I knew of Mr. Elliot's existence because Elizabeth and Sir Walter had spoken of him occasionally—but not kindly. He was the heir presumptive to the baronetcy, some kind of cousin, but I gather they threw him off years ago when he married a wealthy merchant's daughter. Fortunately, the unworthy Mrs. Elliot did not live to pollute their bloodlines with her offspring. She died last May.

Mr. Elliot is about three-and-thirty. Rich, thanks to his late wife. He is also exceedingly charming, as I mentioned, and although the Elliots gave him a cool reception at first (and they are very good at being cool), his conversation was so engaging that they quite forgot themselves, and we sat together for some time.

In answer to a question from Elizabeth, Mr. Elliot explained that he had recently made a tour of the coast as far south as Falmouth, then back through Sidmouth and Lyme Regis.

"A curious time of year for such a journey, I should think," observed Sir Walter. "Unless you are fond of sea-bathing in winter?" He looked about expectantly, so I laughed softly.

"I confess to be a romantic, Sir Walter, and there is something very stirring about contemplating the vastness of the ocean at this time of year," came the answer. Mr. Elliot hinted that he was trying to lose himself in contemplation of the glories of nature but found, when he gazed over the bounding waves, he longed for someone to share its beauties with him.

I enjoyed watching the effects of his eloquence upon Sir Walter—and especially on Elizabeth.

"Lyme, I think, had the greatest charms. I should like to visit there again—but not as a *solitary* traveller," said Mr. Elliot

"Lyme? Did not your sister say that she had also been to Lyme, in her letters?" I asked Elizabeth.

She shrugged. "I do not recollect."

"Miss Elliot, have *you* ever been to the southern coast?" Mr. Elliot asked, leaning forward in a most ingratiating fashion. "I do think it affords the finest scenery of that sort, excepting Scotland, of course."

"Not I," answered Elizabeth. "Mrs. Clay, until recently, resided somewhere in that vicinity. Did you not, Penelope?"

"I have lived in Dawlish, Mr. Elliot, and Plymouth. I should very much like to see the coast of Scotland. I have never been to Scotland."

"Is your husband a naval officer then, Mrs. Clay?" he asked, turning to me.

"My late husband was a chandler."

Well, Mr. Clay was never "on time" for anything.

"I am sorry to know of your loss, madam."

"Likewise, I am sure, Mr. Elliot," said I.

But he turned his head so that Elizabeth could not see his countenance, and he gave me a significant smile as though to say he was *not* sorry to hear there was no husband in the case! Do not think that I was mistaken in that look, for I have seen that smile and that gleam in the eye many a time before, ever since I turned fifteen and my figure bloomed. I may have freckles and I may have a crooked tooth, but the gentlemen have always taken an interest in me.

Well, that first visit was followed by another one, and another, and within a week he became the favourite guest at Camden Place. It did not displease Sir Walter that Mr. Elliot was not quite so well-looking as himself. That was when I learnt what "underhung" meant, for I was quite startled when Sir Walter first used the term. It referred to Mr. Elliot's jaw, which was quite long. But Mr. Elliot's conversation was so good, and he was so thoughtful and generous!

For example, he was taking tea with us and Elizabeth was trying to decide if she should hold a supper party. "But fresh fruit is so…" We all knew she was about to say "expensive at this time of year" but she caught herself in time and said, "…so insipid when it is out of season."

And the very next day, a man delivered a large hamper of fresh fruit, including a pineapple, with the compliments of Mr. Elliot and a note saying he had found a good fruiterer and we must not deny him "the pleasure of sharing the bounty with the ladies of Camden Place."

Likewise, I had let him know that Elizabeth was fond of flowers. From then on, handsome bouquets arrived regularly. He was soon on a most intimate footing with us, coming and going at all hours, every day, and attending us to other social gatherings or taking Elizabeth and me for an airing in his carriage.

His attentions to her were all entirely proper—as became a man still wearing mourning for his wife. Of course, Elizabeth believed that Mr. Elliot admired her, and perhaps she was correct. But when she invited Mr. Elliot to dinner and he was seated between us, his hand found its way to my knee under cover of the tablecloth. I pushed it off but was more curious than affronted and told no one. *What are you about, Mr. Elliot?*

Had we been sitting far apart at a long, large, formal dining table, Mr. Elliot could not have reached me. But we had no such table in Bath. When Elizabeth was thinking of converting one of the two drawing rooms and buying a dining table and a dozen chairs, I told her, "My dear Miss Elliot, I must confess, I so enjoy sitting with you and your father at the little breakfast table. It is much more snug and comfortable! You can seat six persons with ease, and your guests will think it a greater distinction if they are the only guests at your table! And you have only the footboy to help the butler serve, after all."

This last point decided her, and she gave no large dinner parties.

About a fortnight after Mr. Elliot came into our lives, Miss Anne concluded her visit with the Musgroves and came to Bath. She greeted me in her usual way, asking after my health and my father's health, and then: "And how are your two fine boys, Mrs. Clay?"

"Very well indeed, Miss Anne. The country air agrees with them, and my mother dotes upon them."

"You must miss them a great deal."

I gave a little smile and a nod.

Miss Anne was quiet and thoughtful, even more than usual. I do not know if she was tired from her travels, or unhappy that I was still there, or disliked Bath, or was no fonder of her nearest relations than they were of her—or perhaps all of those things together. She was on the point of retiring for the night when Mr. Elliot called, and we discovered that he and Miss Anne had already met in Lyme!

"Surely there is an element of predestination in all of this, Cousin Anne?" cried Mr. Elliot gallantly. "We were all meant to meet and be friends, even though, in the awkwardness of my youth, I was afraid I had displeased you"—he nodded gracefully at Elizabeth—"and was too diffident to intrude myself upon you. The loss was mine. At last, I have the pleasure and honour of calling myself your friend as well as your relation! What arrogant fools young men are when a mistaken sort of pride or delicacy prevents them from making an overture to someone who, if they only knew, would welcome the renewed acquaintance!"

A strange expression passed over Miss Anne's face at that moment which I could not understand.

"If you can credit it, Mr. Elliot," said Sir Walter, "a similar, unfortunate estrangement arose in our family once before..."

Miss Anne looked at him, surprised.

"It was between myself and a noble branch of our family in Ireland."

And then she relaxed.

"I would also find it exceedingly awkward to make the overture after the passage of so many years."

Miss Anne changed the topic. Did Mr. Elliot enjoy music? Then the two of them spoke of Haydn and Rosetti, and she began to grow cheerful and more animated. In fact, she looked prettier altogether than I had recalled of her at Kellynch.

Mr. Elliot did seem taken with Miss Anne, so I was both curious and apprehensive to know if Elizabeth perceived it as well. Perhaps she found it inconceivable that he could. Her sister and I were merely planets orbiting her sun. He was gallant to us all, but she was the centre of her own universe.

However, I was uneasy—and for more than one reason. I believed Miss Anne had a determined dislike of me (though she was never less than polite). What if she prejudiced Mr. Elliot against me? *He* would have some influence with Elizabeth where Miss Anne did not.

I lay awake late that night, pondering. I vowed I was not going to be chased out of Bath by Miss Anne. She and I would have to come to some kind of understanding if I was to continue at Camden Place. Staying in the city afforded me the best opportunity to make a new start, perhaps find a new business partner. The idea of returning to live out my days with my parents in their dismal village in the middle of nowhere was intolerable.

I had no money, no position, and no power—only my wits to help me survive. That would have to be enough.

The next morning when I heard Miss Anne coming down the stairs, I said to Elizabeth, "I have been delighted to have been of some use to you, my dear Miss Elliot, but I shall now prepare to return to my father's house. Now that your sister has returned, I cannot suppose myself at all wanted."

"That must not be any reason, indeed," Elizabeth answered in an undertone, glancing towards the door of the breakfast room. "I assure you, I feel it none. She is nothing to me, compared with you."

And as Miss Anne came in and joined us at the table, my triumph was complete for her father added, "My dear madam, this must not be. As yet, you have seen nothing of Bath. You have been here only to be useful. You must not run away from us now"—and more besides!

Miss Anne must have heard the warmth in Sir Walter's voice, his ingratiating air.

I modestly smiled my gratitude to Sir Walter and asked Miss Anne if she had slept well to show I bore her no ill will. I even brought her a cup of coffee.

I fancied I should not hear any more enquiries about my two fine boys from Miss Anne after such a proof as that!

Still, she was by no means reconciled to my presence. That evening, we sat at an elegantly late dinner. Mr. Elliot was with us again, and I was clumsily attempting to cut my quail. When I pushed my knife into the breast, the bird flew off my plate and landed in my lap! I was mortified, and I saw Miss Anne, across the table, give the tiniest ladylike shudder.

Mr. Elliot, who was seated at my side, immediately said, "Oh! How unpardonably careless of me, Mrs. Clay. I nudged your elbow. My most sincere apologies. Pray, allow me to carve my bird and share it with you."

The butler took the quail away and brought me a fresh napkin. I sat with my cheeks burning, seething at Miss Anne but feeling that the next time Mr. Elliot put his hand on my knee, I would not push it away!

~

Sir Walter and Elizabeth thought so well of themselves that I was astonished to see how they were thrown into a fret when they heard that Lady

Dalrymple and her daughter were staying in Bath. These were the noble Irish relations that Sir Walter feared he had offended.

Sir Walter wrote an apologetic letter, which was graciously received, and he and Miss Elizabeth were in ecstasies. We were all invited to Laura Place, the finest address in Bath, guests of Lady Dalrymple and Miss Carteret. Of course, I only spoke to them when spoken to, which was not often, but they were not at all frightening. They were not more elegant than Elizabeth, nor were they more well-informed than Miss Anne—and no one was as charming as Mr. Elliot!

We all vastly enjoyed his company. He seemed to have come to Bath for no other reason than to attend on us at Camden Place. He was with us again one evening when we were all sitting about in the drawing room, and Elizabeth and I were talking over the details of another party she was planning. Miss Anne was in conversation with Mr. Elliot. I heard him say: "My cousin Anne shakes her head. She is not satisfied. She is fastidious."

Yes, that is just the word. Fastidious. She cannot help it. He learned towards her, and although I could not hear the rest, his tone and expression were all that was tender and sincere. *I should not like to see what Elizabeth is like when she is jealous.* Almost without knowing what I did, I asked Elizabeth if we ought to sample the pastries the cook had prepared for the party, and we left the room.

What are you about, Mr. Elliot? I pondered for the hundredth time, and I resolved to ask him directly. Before he left that night, I took care that he heard me say I would go out to purchase some fresh decks of cards the next morning, and which shop I would attend, and at what time, etc.

And it worked! To my great gratification, there he was, waiting for me. He had already bought the cards for me. I let him take my arm and guide me to a quieter side street. He was a well-made man, and he stood close, looking down at me most intently. I felt extremely conscious of him, conscious of the fact that I had not been with a man for over half a year since I *lost* my husband.

"Mr. Elliot. This is a pleasant surprise indeed."

"A surprise? Did not your bewitching eyes invite me to meet you this morning? I think they did."

"You may save your flattery for the Miss Elliots, sir. Rather, I want you to tell me honestly, what mischief are you brewing? What do you want?"

"What do I want?" he said, his eyes roaming past my face and down to my rather (if I say so myself) fine bosom. "I should be delighted to make your better acquaintance, Mrs. Clay."

"But what would Miss Elliot say to that?"

"You may rely upon my discretion, my dear Mrs. Clay, of course."

"And you likewise wish me to be discreet? You wish me to smile and look on as you make love to Miss Elizabeth and Miss Anne together? I think I am no better than any other woman in that regard. I doubt I could conceal my jealousy in such a case."

"Just as I must conceal *my* jealousy when I observe how much Sir Walter admires *you!*"

"Nay, Mr. Elliot, what are you suggesting?" I turned away, feeling more muddled than before. *He knows that I am angling for Sir Walter and, if I succeed, then he will be displaced as the heir, should I have a son. He has every reason to wish that Sir Walter remains as he is.*

"If only I could trust you, Mr. Elliot!"

"Trust me, Penelope"—he leaned closer and whispered in my ear—"let us be friends."

I felt a deep flush spread across my cheeks. I thought I was too old to blush—but evidently not! I had meant to confront Mr. Elliot, but he had taken complete control of the conversation.

"You are afraid of placing your reputation in my hands. Do you not see that I am also placing *my* reputation in yours? One word from you to the Miss Elliots about our conversation today and I would be banished from Camden Place forever." His lips gently brushed my ear and I shivered.

"The next time Miss Elliot sends you on an errand, please make sure it is in a distant part of town and that it will occupy half-a-day at least. I will engage a room in some unfashionable place."

Ah, such weakness on my part! I gave him no answer but toiled back up the hill to Camden Place. I tried to look composed with nothing upon my mind but card parties, but within, I was plotting and planning, consumed with the desire to feel that man's hands on my bare flesh, to feel his lips, to feel…. *Oh! What expressions must be crossing my face!*

There was a letter from my father waiting for me upon my return. I had been keeping him informed of events (well, most events, at any rate) and he replied:

I must commend you, Penelope. You really have curbed their habits of extravagance. I am finally able to collect some small portion of the fees owing to my firm, and this September, if all goes well, we shall be able to send Henry and John to a good school. For now, they are doing well under your mother's care and are much improved in their manners and habits. I request, therefore, that you remain at Camden Place for so long as the Elliots make you welcome.

You say that Mr. Elliot is making himself agreeable to both daughters. If possible, encourage his suit of the eldest. It would be highly advantageous to have Miss Elliot married and off her father's hands. It was her expenditures, not her sister's, which contributed to the near-bankruptcy of Sir Walter.

Please destroy this letter after you have read it.

Mr. Elliot joined us again that evening. We managed to exchange a few words in secret. He told me that he would take a room at Westgate Buildings and asked me to make some excuse to come away a few days hence. I could not say "no," nor did I say "yes," but my eyes told him that I had yielded.

"You are looking particularly well tonight, Mrs. Clay," Sir Walter observed genially. "Your colour is so high! One might think you were a rosy-faced maiden of one-and-twenty."

The next day, Sir Walter, Miss Elliot and I paid a morning call to Laura Place. Lady Dalrymple had a head cold and was even stupider than usual, and I was rejoicing when Miss Elliot finally rose to depart. Our hostess invited us to return that evening and, of course, her offer was eagerly accepted.

Once we were home again, Miss Anne was informed, and she instantly declined, saying she had promised to visit an old schoolfellow. Her father and sister could hardly believe their ears. They demanded the particulars, and we learned that she was a lady suffering greatly from rheumatism who had come to town for the hot baths. I listened, wearing the usual look of polite interest on my face until Miss Anne told them where this lady lived.

Sir Walter exclaimed, "Mrs. Smith, lodging in Westgate Buildings! A poor widow, barely able to live, between thirty and forty! A mere Mrs. Smith—an every-day Mrs. Smith, of all people and all names in the world —to be the chosen friend of Miss Anne Elliot and to be preferred by her to her own family connections among the nobility of England and Ireland! Mrs. Smith! Such a name!"

I murmured an excuse and left the room, for I could not hide my anxiety at the thought that Mr. Elliot might be, even then, settling upon a room for "Mr. and Mrs. Goodworthy" or the like in the same building that Miss Anne Elliot, against all probability, was also frequenting. How I berated myself for my folly and weakness! It was such a mad scheme.

I wanted to send Mr. Elliot a note by the footboy, but that was, of course, far too risky on several counts. We would see him that evening at Laura Place. I had to contain my agitation and impatience.

To my great surprise, as I was dressing for the evening, Miss Anne came to my room and asked me if I was feeling well. Then she added, with every sign of true concern, "You left the room so abruptly. I was a little worried that my father's remarks might have...wounded your feelings. His wit can sometimes have a tinge of cruelty, I fear."

Well, to tell the truth, I had not even thought of the connection between the poor widow Smith and myself, the supposed widow Clay. I had to turn away quickly to hide a bark of laughter and succeeded in converting it into a cough. But I will give Miss Anne credit. I believe she was truly worried that my feelings had been deeply hurt. Miss Anne may be fastidious, but she was never unkind, and one could certainly *not* say that of her sister or father.

How fortunate that I was feeling well-disposed towards her, for at Laura Place that evening, I sat near the formidable Lady Russell and had to listen politely, nod my head and say "indeed" and "very true" while she and Mr. Elliot engaged in a long conversation about Miss Anne's many virtues.

I had not been in company with Lady Russell above once or twice. She was a neighbour and a longtime friend of the family back in Kellynch. I suppose she was a motherlike figure to the three daughters of the house since Lady Elliot died many years ago, but I found her to be quite intimidating. She was also something of a bluestocking, preening herself on her understanding and her information and, of course, she had no time for me at all!

Mr. Elliot was visibly moved to hear that Miss Anne had forsworn the delights of an evening at Laura Place to visit an old schoolfellow fallen on hard times. Lady Russell did not mention the name "Mrs. Smith"—of that I am certain—but I took care to repeat "Westgate Buildings" several times, and I had to give Mr. Elliot credit. He did not react at all, unlike me, who had almost lost my composure earlier. He only continued to praise Miss Anne: her calm temper, her excellent manners, her well-informed mind.

Ah, Lady Russell would like a match between Miss Anne and Mr. Elliot, I realised. *And my father wants me to steer him to Elizabeth. As for me, it would be best if Mr. Elliot were gone, so that I can work on Sir Walter. Good heavens, how complicated!*

Mr. Elliot brought me a cup of punch, and he leaned in and whispered, "I have not been able to think of anything but having you in my arms. I must see you alone, and soon."

A lady would have said, "Sir! What do you take me for?"

I whispered, "Yes."

The ideal time came courtesy of Admiral Croft, for he and his wife were come to Bath on the first of February, delivering their calling cards at Camden Place and a letter for Miss Anne from her sister Mary. How cheerful that letter made her! She said she was relieved that their young friend Miss Musgrove was mending so well after having fallen on her head at Lyme. Heartened! Yes, I should say so! I watched her practically float up the stairs, clutching the letter to her bosom.

But at any rate, I asked Elizabeth if I could go to the hot baths when she and her father went to return the visit to the Crofts. She had no objection (she never went herself), so I took a chair to the baths and walked around the corner to the Colonnade where Mr. Elliot was waiting for me.

Many would condemn me, of course. The moralists would call me a sinner and the worldly folk would say I was being reckless. But I had always been a woman with a hearty appetite and I had gone without carnal pleasure for a long time.

Once he had me in a cosy, little bedchamber with an adjoining parlour, he said, "Now at last I may call you Penelope, may I not?"

Well... He already had my gown half off. I suppose there was no need to stand on ceremony.

He stripped me down to my stockings, unbound my long hair, and bid me stand where the sunlight was streaming in through a high window so he could admire me.

"Now, I behold Aphrodite. Elizabeth is Hera and Anne is Athena, of course. But even without viewing them as I now see you, I render my judgment—I will award the golden apple to you."

I had no idea what he was talking about. "Golden apple? What am I to do with a golden apple? I should much rather have a new gown."

He laughed, "And so you shall, my dear. But first..."

How curious to be performing this most intimate act with a stranger! To feel so close to him and yet conceal so much from him! I had no notion of his past, he had little of mine, and I assumed (I told myself) that the affection he showed for me must be just a contrivance, a lie, a trick to use me in some fashion. It had all to do with the Elliots and nothing to do with me. And yet, our union was an awakening I shall never forget.

He knew how to draw me to heights of absolute abandon such as I had never experienced. There are ladies, I am told, who sometimes express more passion than they feel. Such was not necessary in this case.

And I have never heard of a man dissembling during the act, as some ladies will do. I was in no doubt that he was entirely gratified.

Thoroughly sated, we lay entwined, and he played with my hair, holding it up so the sunlight made it glow, all golden-red.

"This...schoolfellow that Anne goes to see at Westgate Buildings...Would you happen to know her name, perchance, my dear?"

Now, *there* was an unexpected topic! Where had his mind wandered, and why was he thinking of Miss Anne and her friend Mrs. Smith as he lay with me? He sounded careless, very "oh, by-the-bye," but he had posed his question at the moment when I might be supposed to be most complaisant, most unwary.

I pondered. Clearly, I had information that he wanted. I had every reason to believe he and I were working at cross-purposes so far as the Elliots were concerned. I decided to let him grope in the dark.

"Why, yes," I said. "Miss *Cooper* is the name. Yes, Cooper. They were in school together. Poor girl. So afflicted with the rheumatism, and so young! I believe she is a little younger than Miss Anne."

I felt him relax. *Why? What if I had truthfully said, "Her friend is Mrs. Smith?" Was this the name he was expecting? Who is Mrs. Smith to him?*

"But"—laying my fingers lightly on his lips—"you must never, never mention her name in Camden Place, for Elizabeth and Sir Walter are most seriously displeased that Miss Anne should have a friend in such lowly circumstances."

He took my hand and kissed my palm. "I can promise you that, Penelope. Her name shall not cross my lips."

I sighed and stretched. "I had better be going."

I have never had a man pour water into the basin and wash me himself. And he used a bottle of mineral water from the Pump Room!

"I will send you home to them smelling of sulphur," he said, and he sprinkled some water all over my hair as I was pinning it up. Then he dressed me, kissing and caressing me as he did so. We were hungering for each other as powerfully when we left the room as when we had entered an hour before.

No one suspected us. Life continued in its usual pattern. We had social engagements almost every evening, and Mr. Elliot was often with us. I felt certain he would be paying his addresses to Miss Anne once his year of mourning was over, and I was equally certain that Elizabeth confidently expected he would go down on one knee to her! How could one man be so audacious as to court two ladies who lived under the same roof as his mistress? Ladies and gentlemen, I give you Mr. William Walter Elliot, Esquire.

At any moment, I could speak and destroy his hopes. And at any moment, he could speak and destroy mine.

"There is a letter for you, Penelope, from your aunt Grace," said Elizabeth one morning in mid-February. "What an unusual hand she has for a woman! So bold, almost mannish."

"Thank you, Miss Elliot," I said, and I took the letter to my room to read. *Aunt Grace* told me that he wanted passage money to go to the West Indies. He thought he might set up in business again.

I know you are in a good situation, my old girl, and you would rather the boys stay in England. I am sure you will do well, whatever befalls. Can you not lend me some money, for old times' sake?

I had only one possession of some value—my great-grandmother's pearl choker. I kept it always with me, but it was a trifle too small to fit around my neck, or my neck was a trifle too fat to fit inside the choker. And the clasp was broken. Even though it was a family heirloom, I resolved to get it repaired and then sell it in the hopes that it would rid me of Mr. Clay.

Elizabeth, Miss Anne, and I had planned a shopping excursion for later that week. On that day, I brought the choker along in its little box, but before I could get to the jewellers on Union Street, it began to rain. We took shelter in Molland's, and Mr. Elliot (for he was attending on us) spied Lady Dalrymple's barouche not far away and went off to ask her to take us home. She agreed but had only room for two.

Of course, I assumed that the Misses Elliot would take the seats in the barouche. After all, I was only Mrs. Clay. But Elizabeth was determined to show how low she rated her own sister. She said, "Penelope has a little cold" and "Penelope's boots are not so thick as yours, Anne," while I protested, "It barely rains!" and "My boots are very stout, I assure you," and Miss Anne said, "I would rather walk, indeed." And so, it was finally referred to Mr. Elliot to render his judgement, and he chose Miss Anne to stay with him over me!

I handed him my little box with the pearl choker. "Then would you please be so good as to take this to the jewellers, Mr. Elliot, on my behalf."

"I can do it now," he said, "while you are waiting." Maybe he did not want to stay there and feel my resentful eyes boring a hole through his back while we waited for the carriage.

"Good," I said. "Perhaps they have some golden apples, as well."

I looked about Molland's while Elizabeth tapped her foot and Miss Anne looked out the window. I was arguing with myself that it was foolish to feel slighted and even more foolish to let him know. The bell above the door tinkled and a small party of gentlemen and ladies entered, and the tallest of the gentlemen appeared to know Anne and she him. They spoke for several minutes. I had not a good view of the gentleman, for he had his back to me, but my impression was that he was quite handsome.

The servant came to the door to fetch us to Lady Dalrymple's barouche. Elizabeth pretended she did not hear so that the footman might repeat, more loudly, "Lady Dalrymple for Miss Elliot!" Finally, she proudly passed through the store, ignoring Miss Anne and ignoring the man she was talking with. I scurried along behind her, consumed with curiosity. But Elizabeth said nothing of the matter on the way home.

The following day, I was again lying next to William in our little room, listening to the rain.

"Sir Walter says my freckles have faded because I am using Gowland's Lotion. I think it is because I never see the sun here in Bath. He hates freckles, you know."

"The old fool! My dear Penelope, I will not rest until I have kissed every freckle on your body, from your head to your toes."

"Did your first wife have freckles? What was her name?"

He was silent for a while. "No, she did not. Her name was Jenny."

Another pause.

"Well?" he said. "Are you not going to ask me if she was more beautiful than you? Or did I care for her more than... Did I care for her at all?"

"Well, was she? Did you?"

"She was beautiful, but she was a giddy, stupid little creature. I do not mean 'ignorant'; I mean 'stupid.' Her conversation was worse than tedious. We simply rubbed along till the end."

He looked at me, waiting for the next question. But I did not need to ask it.

"She miscarried, and she died. I was miles away in Tunbridge Wells."

"Oh."

"And the last thing I will say about her, is that if I had to do it over again, I would have tried to be more patient with her. Her money made me independent, after all. But resolutions like that are easier to make after the fact."

"You couldn't have known she was going to die suddenly."

"No."

I yawned and stretched. "I wish we could sleep together all afternoon and I could wake up in your arms, and then we could order up some roast chicken and a bottle of wine, and then I would tease you and play with you until you begged me for mercy…"

But, of course, we could not. We rose and got ready to return to our lives. I was to call upon Laura Place and obtain a receipt for a cream cake that Elizabeth had particularly enjoyed during her last visit. William offered to go with me, at least as far as the entrance to Laura Place.

We had reached Pulteney Street and we were walking comfortably together, our arms linked under Mr. Elliot's big umbrella.

"It rains very heavily. I am sure you will get your feet wet, Penelope."

"Nay, I am enjoying this," I said, thinking of his earlier walk in the rain with Miss Anne. "A little rain won't hurt me! I am not made of sugar, William."

"I should say not!"

A small party of gentlemen, walking in the opposite direction and engaged in some animated conversation, passed us by. Among them was that tall, handsome man who had spoken to Miss Anne in Molland's. By his bearing and posture, he was undoubtedly a military man, army or navy. And by his air, he had to be an officer. His expression was alert and intelligent as he conversed with his friends.

"Twenty minutes ago, you were in my arms, Penelope, and now you are looking after strange men in the street," William teased.

Just then, though, a carriage passed by, and I looked up to see Lady Russell peering at us out of her window. She craned her neck and watched us as her carriage went by.

"Oh, this is most unfortunate! That was Lady Russell!"

"What of it? You were on an errand and were detained by the rain but, fortunately, I happened along and offered to escort you."

I sank back on his arm, relieved and happy. "Of course, of course."

"Evil to him who evil thinks, Penelope."

When we finally got back to Camden Place (I was always careful to say "Camden Place" not "home," and "the drawing room" not "our drawing room," and so forth), Elizabeth told me my new gown had been delivered.

Oh, joy! I explained it away as a gift from my father as Mr. Elliot stood there smiling.

"I shall be able to wear it on Thursday at Lady Dalrymple's concert!" I exclaimed.

Racing up the stairs to try it on, I overheard Mr. Elliot say to Elizabeth, "You cannot expect me to depart, now that I have this rare opportunity to converse with you alone, my dear Miss Elliot..."

I could not help but be impressed! The man was tireless!

My new gown fit me well and was in a flattering shade of green with black trimmings to suit my widowed state. On the night of the concert, I was happily conscious of looking to good advantage as we waited in the Octagon Room for Lady Dalrymple.

Others began to arrive. Suddenly, I saw that same tall, handsome man. He spied Miss Anne and made a little bow, then made as though to resume walking. She stepped forward and he paused. They both seemed to hesitate, to waver, but then she smiled.

I saw his face. I saw hers.

I knew instantly that William plotted and planned in vain. Anne Elliot loved and was loved in return.

And as I watched them talk, utterly engrossed with one another, I felt a powerful longing. It was not mere jealousy. I just longed for someone to look at *me* the way that the tall, handsome man looked at Miss Anne.

"Miss Elliot, pray, who is that man addressing your sister?" I whispered.

Elizabeth looked, frowned, then murmured to her father. "It is—I think I am not mistaken—that is the curate's brother. Do you recall, Father?"

"Oh, yes. Hmmph. He looks to have risen in the world, I think."

Just then Captain Wentworth looked our way. Sir Walter and Elizabeth acknowledged him, very slightly, very formally, and he did the same. Soon after, Lady Dalrymple and her daughter appeared with Mr. Elliot and his friend Colonel Wallis, and we were all swept up in the rush to greet them.

During the first part of the concert, I tried to concentrate on the music, but it was much more interesting to watch William whispering to Miss Anne and hearing her laugh. "For shame! For shame! This is too much flattery!"

She was glowing, as though she were lit up from within, and poor William thought it was for him.

During the interval, Sir Walter stood and moved about, I suppose the better to see and be seen, and there was Lady Russell further down on the bench. Lady Russell ignored me in general, but she was too well-bred not to respond when I asked if she was enjoying the concert.

"Indeed. The violinist is quite superior, and the counter-tenor has good expression, although his ornamentations were a little too showy for my taste."

"Oh... Indeed yes. I really have very seldom had the chance, and no doubt you have seen many such concerts. It is no wonder that you spend part of your time in Bath, ma'am, where you can enjoy such"—I waved my arm vaguely—"such...*things*, rather than always be immured in the country. I dote on music, ma'am, but seldom have I had the opportunity to attend such festive gatherings as this."

She was being genial enough, for she looked at me and said, "Penelope, is it? Your good father must have enjoyed his classical studies when he was at school to have given you such a name. Did he not see to it that you received a good education?"

"Oh yes, ma'am, I was sent to a very respectable girls' school in Dawlish."

And I climbed out of the bedroom window in the middle of the night when I was seventeen and ran away with Henry Clay! I didn't learn anything about ornamentations (whatever they are), but I certainly learned a lot about life!

"Ma'am, you are so very well read, I know. I wonder, do you know about the Golden Apple?"

"The Golden Apple of Paris?"

"Nay, Lady Russell, I think you will find it is a Greek myth of some kind, not a French story."

"Paris," Lady Russell said, "is the name of a man. A man who had to choose which of three goddesses should receive a golden apple upon which was engraved, 'For the Fairest'."

"Indeed!" I said with a knowing air.

"The apple," Lady Russell said, "represents discord. It is allegorical, of course."

"Oh yes, of course."

"The rivalry of three women as a figurative representation of impending disaster."

"Very interesting," I said.

"I think that you and Mr. Elliot are quite friendly," she suddenly said. "I saw you on Pulteney Street the other day. I did not inform Miss Anne, who was in the carriage with me. I told her I was looking for some particular window curtains."

"Yes, I recall it, ma'am. I was doing some errands for Miss Elliot but was caught in the rain. Mr. Elliot happened by and offered to escort me. He is a perfect gentleman and I have never had a moment's unease when alone with him. He is friendly, that is so, but he is never improper. Do you not agree with me, Lady Russell, that he greatly admires Miss Anne?"

She smiled, obviously relieved. "We do see eye to eye on this matter then. They are so extraordinarily well suited as to rank, taste, feeling, education, and background. I must say, Mrs. Clay, for your sake, that if you ever choose to marry again, I trust you also will make a *suitable* match, amongst your own set."

I understood her perfectly this time, of course, the meddling old woman! "Thank you, Lady Russell. I am most obliged. Oh, but I see the violinist has started playing again."

"He is merely tuning his instrument, Mrs. Clay. We shall have the second half shortly."

Before the concert started again, Mr. Elliot was invited by Elizabeth and Miss Carteret, in a manner not to be refused, to sit between them. Perhaps she had noticed how marked his attentions were becoming to Miss Anne.

Yes, you had better change your quarry from Anne to Elizabeth, for Anne has escaped your grasp and you don't even know it.

Sir Walter returned and resumed his seat. Beside me.

"How did you enjoy the first half, my dear Mrs. Clay?"

"Oh! Extremely. Very much. The counter-tenor was a little too showy for my taste, though."

He patted my thigh affectionately and then gave it a little squeeze, while looking straight ahead.

I wanted to bask in my triumph. I was dressed as a lady in a beautiful new gown. Lady Russell, the intellectual Lady Russell, was utterly hoodwinked. I would win, and William Elliot had lost. This was what I had worked for. Security, respectability, a good future for my sons.

But all I could think was: *Tonight, I saw a man in love and a woman who loved him back. And I do not love Sir Walter that way. Or any way at all.*

The next morning, Miss Anne went out directly after breakfast. William had a little difficulty hiding his surprise and wounded pride when he called on us to "beg that you had not caught cold" after staying out late at the concert. He fancied that she was panting for him, that she was as good as his.

William and I never took any chances at Camden Place—no stolen kisses or little notes slipped from one hand to another—but on this occasion, he said as he was leaving, "Oh! Mrs. Clay, your necklace has been repaired. I took the liberty of redeeming it myself from the jewellers. Here it is."

THE ART OF PLEASING

And he looked at me intently and glanced up the stairs, which I understood to mean: *Do not open this in front of anyone. Open it in your
bedchamber.*

Inside, I found my little pearl choker with a new clasp as well as a long
strand of pearls. I held them against my skin. They were exquisite and
must have cost a great deal. It truly distressed me that I would have to sell
them immediately to send the funds to Mr. Clay—for, whatever occurred,
I wanted a new life without him.

Miss Anne returned a few hours later. I concluded that she had not
seen her handsome captain, for she was quiet and thoughtful.

"Mr. Elliot asked us to tell you he was sorry to have missed you, Miss
Anne," I said, "and he is going away for a few days, early tomorrow."

"But," Elizabeth said, "he returns to Camden Place this evening."

This was my signal. "He finds it so difficult to stay away, does he not?"

"I had not the smallest intention of asking him," said Elizabeth, "but he
gave so many hints, so Mrs. Clay says, at least."

"Indeed, I do say it," said I, playing my part. "I never saw anybody in
my life spell harder for an invitation. Poor man! I was really in pain for
him, for your hard-hearted sister, Miss Anne, seems bent on cruelty."

"Oh!" cried Elizabeth, "I have been rather too much used to the game to
be soon overcome by a gentleman's hints. However, when I found how
excessively he was regretting that he should miss my father this morning,
I gave way immediately, for I would never really prevent an opportunity
of bringing him and Father together. They appear to so much advantage
in company with each other, each behaving so pleasantly, Mr. Elliot
looking up with so much respect."

"Quite delightful!" I cried, but I did not dare look at Miss Anne for fear
I should burst out laughing. "Exactly like father and son! Dear Miss Elliot,
may I not say father and son?"

"Oh! I lay no embargo on anybody's words. If you will have such ideas!
But, upon my word, I am scarcely sensible of his attentions being beyond
those of other men."

"My dear Miss Elliot!" I said, lifting my hands and eyes, as though I was
too amazed at her modesty to say anything more.

As that evening was far from the first occasion for me to observe how

 339

capably William courted two women at once, it did not arouse so much wonder in me as it had in the beginning. Elizabeth was still the dupe of his pretended regard, but I thought that Miss Anne was more guarded in her manner.

The only thing worth mentioning about that evening is that William managed to whisper to me, "Tomorrow morning. Meet me at our usual place."

~

I reached the Colonnade and there was quite a throng of people there that morning, as it was a popular gathering spot. William had chosen it for that reason; if we were seen there, we could always claim to have met by chance. I looked about me but could not see him.

"Mrs. Clay!"

I turned, and there, to my great dismay, was Captain Brand.

I knew him from Plymouth. A shabby, dishonest, lazy, conniving fellow, a confederate of Mr. Clay in his little schemes. Pay the jollyboat men six shillings to transport the barrels and claim you paid them eight. Loosen the bindings on the barrel and drain out the rum. Get the captain to sign the claim form for the "damaged" barrels and the lost spirits and then split the proceeds.

Next to Mr. Clay himself, this was the last person I wanted to see in Bath.

"Ah, Penelope!" he exclaimed. "The famous legend of Penelope. The wife of Odysseus. Faithful wife. Sitting patiently at home for years. Waiting on her husband. Rejecting all the other suitors. Penelope, the chaste."

"You would do well to mind your own business, Captain Brand, and I will tend to mine."

"Your business? Your business? What was that, exactly? 'Clay & Company, Chandlers,' as I recall. Whatever happened to your business, Mrs. Clay?"

"Sir, you were just as deep in the mischief as Mr. Clay was, if not more!"

"Yes. Strange thing. Some have tried to bring a complaint against me. My brother, the admiral, always persuades them they were quite mistaken."

He put a firm hand on my shoulder and leered in my face.

"I made a new friend t'other day. Name of Elliot. Nice fellow. Told him I was from Plymouth. Asked me if I knew a Mrs. Penelope Clay. 'I have that honour,' says I. Tells me you have quite enchanted Sir Walter Elliot. Bid fair to be Lady Elliot. Heartwarming story. Like a fairy tale."

"Captain Brand, I have nothing more to say to you."

"But, *I* have. A lot more to say. Not to you but to a magistrate."

I looked around anxiously for William. I saw no friendly face, but Captain Brand hailed an older man who was walking to the King's Baths: "Justice Pettigrew, sir, well met! Happy day!"

"Captain, how are you, sir? And your excellent brother?"

"Tolerably well, sir."

The man he called Justice Pettigrew looked from the captain to me, expecting an introduction of course, but Captain Brand only said, "Justice Pettigrew, sir, a quick question. Begging your indulgence. What is the penalty for bigamy? Asking for a friend."

"Well, sir, I have tried a few cases in Taunton. The men I send to Australia. Despicable bounders."

"And the women?"

"Women of such depraved character are sent where they belong. To prison."

"Much obliged, much obliged. Good day to you, sir. Enjoy the baths."

Captain Brand kept smiling as he spoke low to me, "What a pleasure to see you, ma'am. Brings back memories. Such good times, your husband and me. How is he? He was in excellent health, when I last saw him."

I fixed a look of pure hatred on him. His smile only broadened.

"I could develop a poor memory. Perhaps. For a generous consideration. Give you time to think on it, shall I? So good to see an old friend. Surely, we'll meet again soon. Perhaps I'll call on Sir Walter. Good day, madam."

He went into the baths, laughing.

I knew it would be futile to beg for mercy. He would not go away after one bribe; he would be back, again and again, to threaten me with expo-sure. He would never be satisfied; I would always be at his mercy. I had already, in my heart, rejected the idea of marrying Sir Walter, but I was utterly furious to be threatened and thwarted by that disgusting orangutan.

"You look downcast, my dear Penelope."

There was William at my elbow.

"I think I saw you speaking with my new friend, Captain Brand. He was quite surprised when I told him you were a widow. I might have blundered when I mentioned you would be passing by the Colonnade this morning. Can you ever forgive me?"

"You have won, William." I sighed. "I will not be marrying Sir Walter, nor providing him with an heir to steal Kellynch Hall away from you. In fact, I had better make my exit from Bath soon."

He was a gentleman, even in victory.

"You have lost the game, Penelope. But may I say, I have never enjoyed a contest more nor had a more admirable rival. You must admit that I have not been an ungenerous adversary."

"Indeed not, William. Thank you for the beautiful pearls. And the gown."

"May I express my hope that our friendship may continue? After I marry the lovely Anne and have deposited her in some remote, old pile in the country, you and I perhaps…?"

I still know something you don't know about Miss Anne. And I could tell you that I don't want to marry Sir Walter anyway, but you probably wouldn't believe me.

"I have, at best, three hours before I will be missed in Camden Place, and I've errands to run. Let us not waste time in talking, shall we, William?"

We went to his rented rooms and, if possible, our coming together, though brief and hurried, was even more satisfying than our previous encounters. I let myself go and surrendered to the moment. What must the other tenants have thought of my unabashed cries of pleasure! I did not care. And as for William, how different was the man in bed with me from the Mr. Elliot the world knew. Mr. Elliot! So discreet, so polished, so restrained when in company!

Only I could reach the inner core of him, the blazing need, the hidden passion. When he gasped one final time and convulsed in my arms, I felt my power over him.

We had to resume our false selves as we put on our clothes. He escorted me back to Bath Street. "Here, Penelope, you had better take a chair and get home quickly before you are missed. Let's step across to the White Hart." He pointed across the street where a great many porters and chairmen were touting for customers in front of the inn.

"Nay, William. I still have to go to the printers for Elizabeth to pick up more calling cards. I shall take a chair from Milsom Street."

I suddenly had a most fearful thought.

"You will not expose me at Camden Place, will you, William? You would not glory in your triumph over me?"

"Of course not. Remember, I placed my reputation in your hands when I succumbed to your charms. And I am grateful that you do not resent me for succeeding where you have failed. You understand we all have a duty to do the best for ourselves. Only one of us could win. *Carthego delenda est*, you know."

Well no, of course, I did not know what that meant, but what did it matter? And I knew that *he* had not won, either. He had lost Miss Anne. But he still had a chance at Elizabeth—if he wanted her.

We parted. He went his way, and I went mine.

The feeling that my carefully built, comfortable life in Bath was crashing around my ears only grew worse that evening. Elizabeth was going over every detail of tomorrow's card party with me (the most elaborate entertainment we had yet arranged) when Miss Anne, who had been sitting and looking at a book without turning the pages for an hour altogether, suddenly sat up and said, "We were surprised to see you, Mrs. Clay, opposite the White Hart this morning with Mr. Elliot when he had told us he was going to Thornberry."

"Oh dear," I replied as though I had just recollected it. "Very true. Only think, Miss Elliot! To my great surprise, I met with Mr. Elliot in Bath Street. I was never more astonished. He turned back and walked with me to the Pump Yard. He had been prevented setting off for Thornberry, but I really forget by what, for I was in a hurry and could not much attend…" And I babbled on for what felt like an eternity. Elizabeth was satisfied; I was not certain of Miss Anne.

My lie sounded clumsy and stupid, even to me. Perhaps I was getting tired of lies, of always having to play a part.

My life with Mr. Clay had been filled with duplicity as well, but half the chandlers in Plymouth did the same or worse. We sold inedible victuals to unsuspecting captains; he stole empty casks from one brewery yard and sold them to the next. "The brewers stole the barrels from the navy yard to begin with, old girl," he reasoned, "so they have no cause to complain if someone steals them again."

The first falsehood, of course, was that we were legally married. I was only seventeen when I ran away with Mr. Clay. He promised we would go to Gretna Green, but we never did. I have never been to Scotland, alas. He bought me a second-hand ring, and we lived as man and wife, and everyone in Plymouth accepted that I was Mrs. Clay, the chandler's wife.

Of course, that would not mend matters with Sir Walter when Captain Brand exposed me. "Pray do not be alarmed, Sir Walter. I am not a bigamist. I am merely a fallen woman."

Even if I *could* have become Lady Elliot—even the satisfaction of revenging myself upon everyone who thought me lowly, clumsy, and ignorant (oh! only imagine the rage of Elizabeth, the reserve of Miss Anne, the indignation of Lady Russell), it would not be a sufficient reward for marrying that vain, ridiculous old man. I did not want to wake up to him every morning, god forbid!

I wanted to wake up with someone who liked me for who I was, and who would not mind if I ate roast chicken in bed and who would make love to me until the world fell away…

The next morning, I returned the pearls William had given me to the jewellers (oh lord, they were even more expensive than I realised!) and took the money to the bank. Then I posted a letter to "Aunt Grace" to tell him he could withdraw the funds for his voyage to the West Indies. *Farewell and God speed, Henry Clay!*

I hurried back to Camden Place and was still untying my bonnet when Miss Anne came in, as well. I was surprised I did not notice her on the walk home—she must have taken a most roundabout route today.

She did not look happy. This did not bode well! She did not look sad, either. She walked past me, saying nothing, and went up to her room.

What was going on between Miss Anne and her captain? I had heard he was to attend the card party tonight; I hoped my curiosity would be satisfied. I should like to know how it all ended before I left. Would William court Elizabeth instead of Miss Anne once the truth burst upon him? Would Miss Anne be happy? I found myself wishing that she would be. *At least one of us deserves to be happy, and I suppose it is she who deserves it the most. She had never done anything so imprudent in her youth as I had done. And I was still reaping the consequences of it.*

On the other hand, why did Miss Anne give the captain up so many years ago, and why did it take so long to get him back if she still loved him? If I were to guess, she was too well-bred to admit it. All those years, all of that longing and heartache, and the only thing keeping her silent was some rule of society, some so-called law of conduct for gentlewomen.

Perhaps I am not cut out to be a gentlewoman.

She did not join us for dinner, and I grew increasingly worried. Should I have gone to her and asked if she was indisposed? I knew she would think it presumptuous. Finally, as the footboy and I were lighting all the candles in the drawing rooms, she appeared, dressed for the evening. She looked calm and radiant.

"You are in good looks tonight, Anne!" Even her father noticed, and then he went to hail Mr. Elliot who, with the privilege of a close relation, was the first guest to arrive. Miss Anne retreated to the little greenhouse area when she saw him come in, but, of course, he followed her. And I followed them both.

"Good evening, Cousin Anne," I heard him say as I approached. "I need not enquire if you are well, for anyone can see that you are more than well. Can you really be looking forward to this evening so much that it brings the glow to your cheek and that enchanting light to your eye? Is it the prospect of cards and idle conversation that thrills you? Or, may I flatter myself, is there some other cause?"

"I am quite well, I thank you, Mr. Elliot," was all she said, and she was spared further conversation, for everyone else seemed to arrive at once. Here, at last, I saw Admiral Croft and his wife. They looked to be very pleasant people. Here were half-a-dozen other people of fashion. Here were the Musgroves.

I stayed close to Mr. Elliot, for I wanted to see his face when Captain Wentworth arrived. And he in turn was shadowing Miss Anne, though she was determinedly trying to avoid him.

I caught him saying to her, "I know you do not care for card parties, dear cousin. Cards are indeed the resort of people with no conversation, a description that hardly fits you."

I noted with amusement that Miss Anne was barely listening to him, and her eyes were fixed on the entrance to the front hall.

"I know you do not occupy your time with trivialities, and that is but one of the many reasons I have come to feel such...such a deep respect and ardent—"

"You are too kind, Cousin. There is no need for so many compliments. Pray, take your ease and enjoy the evening. I think I shall take a turn about the room."

"Ask her about Miss Cooper," I whispered to him. "She went to see her today, I think."

"Stay, my dear cousin. I was just going to enquire after your friend Miss Cooper."

She turned, perplexed.

"Miss Cooper?"

"Why, yes, Miss Cooper. Your old schoolfellow who lives at Westgate Buildings and who you so kindly visit. I trust she is feeling better. No doubt she is, because of your goodness to her."

Miss Anne gave him an odd look. Something like pity. She shook her head and said, "Mr. Elliot, you have been misinformed; I cannot think how. My old school fellow is not 'Miss Cooper.' But since you enquire, her name is Smith. Mrs. Charles Smith. I think you will recall the name, as Mr. Smith was your dearest, most generous friend, was he not? And although you refused to help her after he died, believe me, I shall see to it that she receives the help she needs."

She walked away, and this time he did not follow.

I had the satisfaction of seeing Mr. Elliot—the calm, the elegant, the reserved Mr. Elliot—briefly lose his composure. His mouth opened, once, twice. He made to say something. He looked at me and shook his head.

"So that's why you wondered who Miss Anne's old schoolfellow was," I said. "You happened to know someone who went to school with her. And this Mrs. Smith gave your true character to Miss Anne."

Just then, Captain Wentworth was announced. Miss Anne went up to greet the man she loved. His countenance hid nothing; neither did hers.

I sighed theatrically. "Ah. In the end, you know, I am a sentimental woman. How I love a happy ending. I wish them joy—do you not, Mr. Elliot?"

"You lied to me, you little minx. You let me waste my time in a futile effort to win Anne's affections."

"Truly, you have my sympathies. We all must do the best we can for ourselves, Mr. Elliot. Cart-horse *delenda est,* you know."

"That's Carthage, not cart-horse, Penelope."

"You were wrong when you said, 'Only one of us can win.' In fact, both of us have lost—at this game, at any rate."

He gently steered me behind the greenhouse plants, where we lingered, and pretended to admire them.

"So, what will you do now?" I asked. "I suppose that William Walter Elliot, Esquire can choose any sort of wife he wants. You could court Elizabeth or some other woman of rank."

"After spending so much time with Elizabeth and Miss Carteret and the other ladies hereabouts, that notion has lost its appeal. Anne is the only one I might have tolerated."

"You could marry a rich merchant's daughter."

"I have done that and, while I've no objection to marrying money, I no longer need to marry *for* money."

"Or you could marry a"—I searched for the words—"a true partner. Someone who understands you."

"You make a persuasive case, Penelope." He took my hand and raised it to his lips. "Someone who understands me and, what's more, someone who is a wild, abandoned hoyden in the bedchamber. That would suit me very well. We are birds of a feather, you and I. What a pity it is that you are already married. If only you were free, I should indeed be tempted, I vow."

He smiled that utterly sincere William Walter Elliot, Esquire smile that I knew so well.

I smiled back.

"Well then, I have very good news for you indeed, William…"

[Mr. Elliot] soon quitted Bath; and on Mrs. Clay's quitting it soon afterwards and being next heard of as established under his protection in London, it was evident how double a game he had been playing, and how determined he was to save himself from being cut out by one artful woman, at least. Mrs. Clay's affections had overpowered her interest, and she had sacrificed, for the young man's sake, the possibility of scheming longer for Sir Walter. She has abilities, however, as well as affections; and it is now a doubtful point whether his cunning, or hers, may finally carry the day; whether, after preventing her from being the wife of Sir Walter, he may not be wheedled and caressed at last into making her the wife of Sir William.
—Persuasion, Chapter XXIV.

LONA MANNING is the author of the *Mansfield Park*-inspired novels *A Contrary Wind* and *A Marriage of Attachment*, along with numerous true crime articles, available at crimemagazine.com. She has worked as a non-profit administrator, a vocational instructor, a market researcher, and a speechwriter for politicians. She currently teaches English as a second language and with her husband divides her time between China and Canada. You can follow Lona at lona-manning.ca where she blogs about China and Jane Austen.

LOUISA BY THE SEA

BEAU NORTH

LOUISA MUSGROVE

Lively and fashionable, Louisa Musgrove is an accomplished daughter of a country squire. After she and her sister return from a school at Exeter, she imagines herself in love with Captain Wentworth, Anne Elliot's former betrothed who has recently returned from sea. *"Would I be turned back from doing a thing that I had determined to do, and that I knew to be right, by the airs and interference of such a person, or of any person, I may say? No, I have no idea of being so easily persuaded. When I have made up my mind, I have made it."* — **Chapter X, *Persuasion*.** Though full of verve, her foolish whims lead her to calamitous consequences, throwing her at the affectionate heart of another.

LOUISA BY THE SEA

THREE HOURS

At first, there is only pain, brighter and more blinding than the sun skimming across still water. Touch, taste, movement, sound—all are lost to me. I cannot tell if I am screaming, though it *feels* as though I am. I do not know how long this feeling lasts before the darkness eclipses my awareness, leaving me in absolute quiet. It is more like a state of *un*being than being. I am aware of nothing, not even my own name. I cannot say I mind so very much. I would stay in this state forever if it would but spare me the agony of feeling that pain once more.

Alas, it cannot be. I find my consciousness rising, breaking through the surface of my immovable unbeing. When my eyes first crack open, the pain of the candlelight slices through me. I am in an unfamiliar place, which I do not find unusual, as I am a stranger even unto myself at present. People speak in low voices, but I cannot separate one voice from another. Someone props me up and another person tips liquid, cool and cloyingly sweet, into my mouth. I drink, glad I remember how this function is performed, as I have the impression that coughing would be excruciating. Hands, gentle but firm, touch my wrist and my throat, before beginning a careful exploration of my head. I want to protest, but I find myself unable to speak. It is just as well. As the examination continues, I find myself pulled back into the dark. A voice chases me down as I go.

"*Sleep, Louisa. Be well.*" A man's voice. Salt-roughened, but soft and lovely all at once. I do not recognize his voice, but for the first time I feel safety and comfort, and I allow myself to drift.

~

THREE DAYS

"Sleep the sleep that knows not breaking, Morn of toil nor night of waking…"

"How did Miss Henrietta and Miss Anne fare on the journey back to Uppercross?" Voices again. The low murmurs of men talking nearby.

"What could she have been thinking…"

"The fault is mine, I should have stopped her. What have I done?"

"Dear God, please let her live."

"Oh Louisa, Louisa! Charles, I think I may faint."

The pain was still there, digging into my head with cold fingers. There had been another voice that was speaking softly, but it is silent now, listening. I do not know how I know, but I am certain I know him somehow, my now-silent guardian. The other men are also known to me, though I know not how.

Their words conjure images, context in my quiet mind: *sister* and *friend* and *home.* And then I see them! Cheerful Henrietta, cheeks flushed in merriment. Lovely Anne, clear-eyed and tranquil. And then there was Uppercross. *Home!* I could not see it, but I had the feeling of it, as if I could smell the fragrant gardens, feel the sun-warmed stone of the house under my palm. Solid, constant Uppercross, which would remain tall and proud long after the likes of Louisa Musgrove turned to dust.

Louisa Musgrove! I am Louisa Musgrove!

Memories, awareness floods me in a tide so powerful my eyes fly open for the first time in…I do not know how long. They are met by dark, steady eyes. Extraordinary eyes, truly. So deep brown they are nearly black.

I open my mouth to speak, and the eyes widen.

"Louisa?" *I know that voice!* How do I know that voice?

My throat works. "I am," I manage to say. The effort saps me, and this time I rush to meet the rising dark.

~

ONE WEEK

"My loveless eye unmoved may gaze on thee, and safely view thy ripening beauties shine…"

The gentle murmur rouses me from my slumber. My awakening brings a tide of familiar feelings, the strangeness of my surroundings, the soft cadence of the words—lines of poetry, I believe—the ever-present pain in my head. Today there is a new sensation, that of hunger. The smell of fresh scones are a torment to me. It causes me to sigh, perhaps more loudly than I intended, and the voice beside me quietens.

I open my eyes and look over at him, both hoping and dreading to see Captain Wentworth. Disappointment and relief flood me in equal measure. This man is not Captain Wentworth, who is a study in shades of gold and bronze. The person looking at me is quite his opposite, with dark hair and shadowed eyes. His face is slight, his features fine. He holds my gaze a moment before standing and leaving the small room without a word. *Benwick.* I recall his name as I watch him leave. *Captain James Benwick.*

"Louisa! Oh, my darling!"

I turn my head, slowly and painfully, and see a familiar sight sitting to my left. Dear Mama! I raise a hand weakly in her direction and feel tears sting my eyes as she takes it in her own.

I am able to speak but find that I am so overwhelmed I can only say "mama."

"Oh, my dear girl! How do you feel, Louisa?"

"Very hungry," I say, making her giddy with delight.

"A good sign, I should think," my brother Charles says as he enters the room, a cautious smile on his face.

I try to smile; my lips feel as heavy as if they were tied by anchors. A strange sort of melancholy passes through me like sudden storm clouds rolling against the sky. *My life.* I am too much aware of how abruptly it nearly ended. All for one moment of unbridled happiness, a solitary second experiencing what it must be like to fly. *But I did not fly. I fell.*

Mama sees that some emotion has overwhelmed me and flutters about to give me comfort. I turn my face away, strangely ashamed. And, I am astonished to admit, I am angry as well. Why did Captain Wentworth fail to catch me? How could he have let such a thing happen? I ponder this as I allow Mama and Charles to assist me in sipping beef tea and a bitter brew left by the surgeon that makes me feel languid, and I feel myself once more pulled down into the cool depths of sleep.

~

THREE WEEKS

"It is a fine thing, to see you moving about once more."

Captain Benwick offers his arm to assist me to the table in the corner of my room, where Mrs. Harville has brought me a fine supper of cold ham, warm bread, and tart cheese, a small pudding, and a glass of Captain Harville's wonderful beer, an almost sweet and nutty concoction that I have come to love. It amuses my hosts that I enjoy it so much, fine young lady that I am, but I believe it pleases them as well.

"I think you will be very happy to have your room back when I am gone, Captain."

There—in the depths of his dark eyes—a shift. Have I said something wrong? He only responds with a quiet "not at all" and holds my chair out for me.

In the weeks since my injury, it has become a necessity to teach myself certain things anew. I find some tasks quite beyond my abilities, such as needlework, a task I cannot apply myself to for more than a quarter hour without inciting a most violent headache. That is no great loss to me; I have never been particularly fond of the employment.

I have learned—through some trial and error—that loud noises have an alarming effect on my person. In the earlier days of my recovery, the sudden slamming of a door by one of the Harville children caused me to shake uncontrollably and I was unable to leave my bed that whole day.

Since then, I always dine privately, sometimes with Mama or Charles for company, though I could tell they always wished to be dining with the Harvilles, who did nothing without a great deal of laughter and good cheer.

Unlike the jolly Harvilles, Captain Benwick is a quiet presence. It should have put me at ease, but I often find myself feeling strange, unsettled in his company. I cannot account for it; he is nothing if not a perfect gentleman toward me at all times, though there are moments when I catch him looking at me with a singular gaze, as if he were trying to assemble puzzle pieces. The carefree girl I was before would not merit such a close study. Now I could not be so certain. The broken girl who leapt from the Cobb. It mortifies me to think he might see me as such.

Even as I ask him if he would not join me for dinner, I am overcome with a giddy sort of self-consciousness and cannot be easy. I believe he senses this, for he sits down opposite me but does not touch the food he has brought, only stares into the amber-colored beer in his glass without drinking. I apply myself to my dinner. He would speak or not, though it will always be my preference that he *do* speak. He has a lovely voice and a way with poetry. When he reads to me, the sound seems to cover me like a second skin, making me feel untouched by injury, whole, and longing for more.

"Harry has had a letter today," he says in an oddly flat tone, so unlike his custom. "From Frederick."

I still for a moment, then concentrate my efforts on spreading cheese on a slice of bread. "Oh?" is my only reply.

"He will return to Lyme by Sunday next."

"I see." I shove the bread and cheese into my mouth in a most unlady-like manner. Anything to avoid this topic. I do not wish to think of Captain Wentworth, let alone speak of him with Captain Benwick. "I am sure he will be greatly relieved to see you so improved."

I hold back a snort of laughter. Yes, I am certain he *would* be glad to not have the stain of my life's blood on his hands. Still, he has stayed away so long, I cannot but wonder at his purpose in coming here now.

"Will you not eat, Captain?" I ask when I am able once more. Benwick looks up at me; a gleam in his eyes makes him, in that moment, uncommonly handsome.

"I thank you, I am not hungry. Please, do not let me keep you from enjoying your repast."

He begins to push away from the table and, before he can rise, I place a hand on his arm, lightly, afraid suddenly of being alone with my thoughts.

"Please, Captain. Will you not stay?"

I have never seen war, or battle, or even a fight between men but, in that moment, I see a great struggle in Benwick's eyes before he nods his dark head and quietly says, "If you wish it." I do not know what has just happened, but I do know that I am soothed and find that I can manage a smile.

~

ONE MONTH

There is no joy like mine, for Captain Wentworth has brought, not only himself, but dear Henrietta as well. My sister and I embrace in a shocking display of laughter and tears for everyone to witness. I cannot care for propriety when my other half, the dearest person in the world, is with me again.

As for the captain himself, Wentworth strides into the room, golden hair still blown back from his clear brow, his eyes bright with challenge. He takes my hand and bows over it, his lips not quite meeting my fingers. Does he feel that hand tremble in his own? My curtsey is more a *suggestion* of a curtsey than a curtsey proper but, if this offends him, he does not say. He smiles at me, brightly, but I see regret in his looks as well.

"It does my heart good to see you so recovered, Miss Musgrove."

My eyes flick to the man who lingers in the corner of the room, attempting to disappear into a shadow. Benwick holds my gaze a moment, then looks away. The loss of it stings. I look back at Captain Wentworth. Somehow larger than life, he seems to fill the entire room with his presence. I find it is too much for me and ask Henrietta if she will take a turn with me out of doors.

"Oh yes, for I have so much to acquaint you with!" Henrietta smiles and blushes in such a way that I know what her news will be, that our cousin, Henry Hayter, has at last asked for her hand.

Fear rises in me. I am not ready to lose her now, not so close on the heels of the folly that nearly ended my life. But as Henrietta tells me of her joy, she blossoms, her pretty features made quite lovely in the glow of her happiness. I gather all my courage and affect a tranquility that does nothing to belie the tumult raging within. Am I to lose my only companion so soon? And, even if I were to have another year in her company, could I ever explain to my sister the stark loneliness I have felt during my recovery? I have been alone with the specter of my own death for these weeks, the ending that almost was; I feel the shadow of it clinging to me at all times. It has changed me in some elusive way I cannot grasp.

And, though I would never admit it to anyone but myself, I am in some small way envious of Henrietta. I would never begrudge her cousin Henry, of course, but she is now taking a step that is expected of all genteel young ladies. It marks me out further as different, as *other,* that I am not likely to have such an offer now, now that I am so damaged. Since the accident, I do not know that I could manage a fine large house like Uppercross, but I would like to have companionship, someone to share my life with. Someone to light up my nights and banish the shadow that hangs over me now.

I glance behind me to see the tall, handsome figure of Captain Wentworth following as he talks with Captain Harville, his gestures animated, though I cannot hear his speech. And there, some paces behind them, stands Captain Benwick; his attention is not on his friends or on me, but his eyes, his figure, all of him seems turned toward the sea. His expression is of such longing that I quickly turn away, feeling that I have invaded his privacy.

I increase my pace, pulling a chattering Henrietta along with me. It does me good to walk, to climb the gently sloping hills, feeling my legs, little used in weeks, burning with the effort. The hills are not steep, but the effort costs me. A pulsing sensation in my head warns me to stop, to rest, but I cannot stop until I have put a great deal more distance between myself and the men.

I wish to outrun that expression on James Benwick's face. It plagues me. He is mourning for the sainted Fanny Harville, no doubt. How could any single woman have possessed so many accomplishments, such good taste, such a sweet temper and gentle disposition as Harry Harville's late sister, Benwick's departed love? Had death erased all her flaws, or had she always been a superior woman, to be matched by none among the living?

I stop in my tracks, dizzy with sudden understanding. Henrietta clings to my arm. "Oh, dear Louisa, you are so pale! We must turn back at once!"

I fear I am unequal to the task. I have only realized how deep my envy is for the late Fanny Harville. Because I must be forced to live with the shame of my folly, always dining alone and in fear of loud noises, while *she* was rendered more perfect in death than she likely had been in life. *Surely, I will find myself in hell for such uncharitable thoughts.* I sway, clinging to my sister, who cries out for help.

"Etta, I am afraid," I say quietly, using my nursery-room name for my sister. "Pray for my soul."

Strong arms lift me, carry me easily. I know without looking that it is not Captain Wentworth who carries me but Captain Benwick. There is a familiarity to his scent...rosemary, for remembrance, and the ever-present smell of the sea that seems to live in his skin. I glance over his shoulder to see Harville and Wentworth looking on in surprise, Henrietta clinging to Captain Wentworth's arm. Captain Benwick shifts my weight and grunts.

"You do too much too soon."

How had he come to my aid so quickly, when he was well behind his friends? I can only assume he ran when he saw me falter. I picture the hundreds of tiny gestures since my accident. A steadying hand on the elbow, a strong arm for me to cling to. He has been propping me up since I began to walk again.

"I do not wish to be an invalid any longer."

"You could sooner carry water in your hand than you could wish yourself cured, you silly girl. Do not play about with your health. Do you never think of your family and what they would suffer if you perished out of foolishness?"

I bristle at his tone but say nothing until he says, "And what of Frederick? What on earth must *he* think?"

Why would *that* matter? Captain Wentworth was not the man I thought he was. And perhaps I am not the girl I thought I was.

"By my heel, I care not."

He startles, then grunts once more. I think it might be a laugh. "Perhaps you should," he says in a more serious tone.

I look up at him and am certain then that my envy of Fanny Harville had little to do with her seeming perfection. I envied her because of *him*, because she possessed the heart that I wished to claim as my own. Somewhere amid his lines of poetry, I have fallen helplessly in love with James Benwick. His dark eyes bore deep into my own for a moment before he looks away first.

"Do not look at me like that."

I rest my head on his shoulder. The Harvilles' tidy, little house is in sight. "Like what?"

"Like I am some sort of hero coming to your aid."

"But you *did* come to my aid."

"I am no hero."

I sigh. "I am quite able to stand now. If you will but lend me your arm, I will return to bed and not stir my foolish head all day."

He looks at me once more but, instead of putting me down, he pulls me closer toward him.

"I am sorry I said that. I've known many foolish creatures in my day, but Louisa Musgrove is not one of them. You are young, and full of vitality, and not wishing to be confined. I understand you very well."

Mama and Mrs. Harville have not returned from their sojourn into Lyme to visit the sweet shop. The house is, for the first time since my coming there, completely quiet and still. I am carried back to my room and placed with care on the bed. The hushed air of the house, the awareness that we are alone, makes the action one of great intimacy. He does not pull away from me at once, but hovers over me and, in a gesture of great tenderness, he brushes my hair away from my face, as some of my pins have come loose while he carried me. Voices echo through the house, the sounds of the others having finally caught up to us. Still, he does not move. I observe the smallest of tremors in his lower lip. The sight of it affects me powerfully. If I were not already lying down, I would certainly need to.

I ache to touch his face, to trace the surprisingly delicate lines of his brow, to feel the softness of his full lips under my fingertips, but I remain motionless, still wondering at this new knowledge that I have found love, and the hopelessness of him ever returning my feelings. How could I compete with a ghost?

"Frederick is a fine man," he says. It vexes me. Why would he bring Captain Wentworth here, putting him between us where only a moment ago there was nothing but layers of muslin and wool to separate us? I turn my face away.

"Thank you for your assistance. I would only wish to be with my sister or Mama. Please do not let me keep you from the business of your day."

A moment later he is gone, leaving me alone with my troubled thoughts. I turn my face into the pillow and scream.

∾

ONE MONTH, THREE DAYS

"And thus the heart will break, yet brokenly live on."

"I thought I might find you here," Charles says as he takes a seat beside me. I look up from the book I have borrowed from Captain Benwick for my daily attempt to read a few lines before the inevitable pain sets in behind my eyes. It helps that I have found a lovely vantage point, near the Harville home but not too close to the Cobb, which I do not think I shall ever visit again. I sit here often, watching the sea churn against the rocks or lap gently at the shore.

I like the rages more than the placidity. It reminds me of dear old Mrs. Croft, who I once heard admonishing her brother: "None of us want to be in calm waters all our lives." I knew that, no matter what followed, I had these weeks in Lyme to thank for teaching me this truth of myself. I was not cheerful or content, but I felt a sense of freedom I imagine few women my age ever attain.

"Good day, Charles," I greet my brother.

"I've heard from Wentworth. He's going to stay on with his brother in Shropshire for some time and does not know when he is to return."

I smile. This is becoming a bit of a game to me. How many people expected that I was pining for Captain Wentworth? I imagined that I fancied him once. He is a brilliant, charming man with happy manners and a great fortune. My family encouraged me, society expected it of me.

But I cannot love the man who let me fall. I can only love the person who caught me. It is a secret I carry with no expectation or hope of such feelings ever being returned. I shall never burden *him* with my love but have determined that I will live my life, unmarried and free, and love him from afar. *"And thus, the heart will break, yet brokenly live on."* Indeed.

"I think I shall bear the deprivation very well."

"I must say, Louisa dear, you surprise me. One would almost think you never had any designs on Wentworth."

"Perhaps the old Louisa did. But life is short, and I will not settle for less than I deserve. The worst sort of life I can imagine is one lived out of obligation."

A pained expression passes over my brother's face, and I know he is thinking of his own marriage to Anne's sister Mary, his own disappointed hopes. I put my hand in his. Charles, poor Charles, knows something of unrequited love. He had been so very fond of Anne, after all. She would not give up her freedom for a man she did not love. It is unfortunate that she is beholden to a family as unpleasant as the Elliots, but she has not compromised her essential self to escape them.

"Is that all you've come to tell me?"

He smiles and is his usual self again. "Not at all! I have far more pleasant news. The surgeon has informed me that you may be well enough to return to Uppercross within this fortnight."

My expression does not change. When I speak, my voice sounds very small to my ears. "So soon?"

"You've made remarkable progress, and think how happy it will make Mama and Henrietta to have you home and helping to prepare for the wedding."

I wish to rail and roar and stamp my feet, but instead I smile and say, "Yes, Charles. That will be lovely."

~

ONE MONTH, ONE WEEK

Despite the rumble of thunder outside, the air in the dining room is one of celebration, albeit a quiet one, as the Harvilles toast my recovering and my impending return to my own county. Charles has already returned to the inn for the night, wishing to write some letters home to his wife Mary, and one to Anne. I feel strangely close to Anne now, even as she is so far away in Bath.

In the corner of my eye hovers the beloved shadow of Benwick, who does not celebrate but stares sullenly into his wine in a way that has become familiar and dear to me. I find I cannot let him sit there so unengaged and decide to tease him out of his melancholy.

"In a week's time, Captain Benwick need not suffer my company when he wishes to dine in his own room."

Benwick looks up at me and scowls; I smile sweetly at him. "I have never begrudged you the use of my room."

My smile falters. "No, indeed not."

"Come, James. Miss Musgrove was only teasing you," Captain Harville chides gently. He turns to me and says, "Miss Musgrove, I would make him sleep with the pigs, if we had any, if it would bring you any comfort."

The thunder crashes outside, rattling the windows. A strange sensation, like a high-pitched buzzing between my ears makes me sway. The room spins.

"Miss Musgrove?" Benwick is grave, looking at me so intently that I cannot hold his gaze.

"Too much wine, I think. It all went to my head." I put my glass down with trembling fingers.

Mrs. Harville leaps from her seat. "I'll make you some tea, dear. That'll set you right."

I manage a smile and thank her warmly. I shall miss the Harvilles when I return, almost as much as the person whose eyes I now avoid.

"A moment, if you please, Mrs. Harville."

I stand and lift my glass once more. I look at my hosts. "Words cannot express the gratitude I feel for the hospitality you have shown me. You have taken me in, a spoiled girl and a stranger, and cared for me as if I were one of your own. Family, I am learning, is not only who we share blood with. *You* are my family too. Thank you, Captain Harville, Mrs. Harville, all your dear children, and Captain Benwick, of course." I say this last without looking directly at him but feel him startle at the mention of his name.

"Thank you for your tenderness and care. For being there to catch me when I fell."

This last I direct at *him*. Mrs. Harville rushes over to embrace me, and Captain Harville's eyes are bright with emotion.

"Oh, you dear girl!" his good wife says. Captain Harville stands and makes his way painfully over to me. I know his injured leg brings him additional misery in damp weather, so the gesture is not lost on me. He takes my hand and bows over it.

"You are always welcome in our home, Miss Musgrove. I hope you will think of me as another brother."

"I would be honored to call you such."

And then, *he* was there, his darkly handsome face as solemn as I had ever seen it. He touches my hand.

"Lou—er, Miss Musgrove, I..."

Please do not say you think of me as your sister! I could never bear it!

A boom of thunder, closer than the last, crashes around us. The buzzing in my head grows louder, more intense, and I experience the horror of my body moving uncontrollably as I tumble backwards, thrashing and flopping like a fish thrown ashore. Pain explodes in my head, brighter and more brilliant than the sun in high summer. On my lips, I taste blood.

"Louisa!" Benwick's shocked cry echoes through my mind. I want to speak, to comfort him, but I cannot. Something is placed in my mouth, a leather strap the surgeon left in the event this happened again, and I feel the darkness rise once more to greet me.

~

ONE MONTH, ONE WEEK, ONE DAY

"And on that cheek, and o'er that brow, So soft, so calm, yet eloquent..."

"But how will this affect her recovery?"

"She is not the same as she once was, Mr. Musgrove. Your sister may expect such fits in the future, though they may lessen in severity with time."

"When may she be returned to her family?"

"Oh, I would not let her any farther than this room for a se'nnight. I shall be back tomorrow to check her progress."

The voices die down to a low bubble as the heavy wood door is pulled nearly closed. I know that *he* is with me and that we are alone. I smell salt spray and rosemary and the uniquely spicy aroma of books. I do not want to look at him, now that my mortification is complete.

"I know that you are awake, Louisa." I keep my eyes closed, my form still. I realize something, there in my self-imposed dark. He has always called me "Louisa" when we are alone. I am only "Miss Musgrove" when in company. It strikes me as intimate, as though he sees me—me as I am, not the proper, docile version of myself that society tells people to see. He sees that I am stubborn and quarrelsome, that I laugh whenever possible and that I love poetry...but only when read by him.

"I can always tell when you are listening. Come now. Tell me what I should read next. Have I made you weary of Scott and Byron? Should we have some Wordsworth?"

"Mary Wollstonecraft," I say without opening his eyes. *"A Vindication of the Rights of Women."*

A low chuckle from Benwick. I believe it is the first time I have ever heard him really laugh.

"I see. You care not for these romantics, then?"

How can I tell him that every word he had spoken was burned into my very soul? That I treasure every syllable that had ever passed his lips in this room?

I open my eyes and look at him, seeing a tenderness I had never witnessed in him before.

"Do not look at me like that." I repeat the words he said to me the day he carried me back from my walk. He remains where he sits, perfect and still as a statue, eyes gleaming in the dim firelight. His lips curve up into a smile. I bask in it, vowing to hold the sight in my heart until my dying day.

"How do I look at you?"

"Like I am a broken thing, an object of pity."

He laughs again, and *this* time I feel warmth spread through me, touching every intimate part of my person. Good heavens, if his *laugh* could do that what would it be like to kiss him?

"Louisa, I have never seen a creature so strong as yourself. How could I pity you? You have danced with Death and lived! You, a broken thing? You, who bends like the reeds, unbreaking, no matter how violent the storm?"

Tears fill my eyes, making the room waver.

"Please, no more. I cannot bear it."

He pauses. "I do not wish to cause you pain."

"And yet..."

"And yet?"

I shake my head. I feel my death clinging to me once more, that grey shadow I had slowly peeled off in my weeks of recovery. I am afraid of dying and being tethered to this place. What if I had died without telling him my heart? Would I be condemned to haunt him, watch him grow older, or marry another? If I were going to meet my maker, I would do it with no secrets, no burdens.

"I love you, James," I say, my eyes never leaving his. "I love you horribly. I did not want to tell you, but there are moments when I am so full of love for you that it fills me to the point of pain. I know you could never love me, that your heart is buried with Fanny. But I have loved, and do love, only you."

Moments go by, marked only with the steady beat of my heart, the most obstinate part of me. Each beat, each breath felt an age. Empires rise and fall as I lie there, waiting for him to speak.

"But...Frederick..."

"Captain Wentworth is a good and fine man, but I could never love him the way I love you. How could you even think it? Have you not seen it in all of my looks?"

He stands, turning his back to me.

"I…I should go. You need rest. We shall talk more, soon."

I do not reach for him or ask him to stay. He would do as he wished. I would not have him by my side out of any misplaced sense of duty.

"Yes," I say as he walks through the door, "you should go."

ONE MONTH, ONE WEEK, THREE DAYS

"And I am telling you, Harry, it is not like her. I fear this last episode has affected her spirits greatly."

I overhear Mrs. Harville and her husband discussing my condition. I must do better to smile and act cheerful, but I fear she is correct.

"If only James had not left yesterday." Mrs. Harville sighs. "He seems to have a way with her."

"It is right he should visit Fanny's grave, for we can't leave the children to go ourselves," Captain Harville says. I get up and pace my room, my hands smoothing the sprigged yellow muslin gown. Once, it had been quite becoming on me. Now I fear it only emphasizes how thin and sallow I have become. I take a deep breath and emerge from the room. The Harvilles look up at me in surprise.

"Louisa, my dear, are you well?"

I smile, feeling foolish as I do. "Very well, Mrs. Harville. I was wondering if Charles might be fetched from the inn and the surgeon called round. I…I feel it is time to return home."

ONE MONTH, THREE WEEKS

"I shall be very happy to see Uppercross again," I say to Charles as the carriage rolls toward home.

He looks up at me with a raised brow. "Will you?"

"Of course! Whyever not?"

My eldest brother—only brother now that poor Dick is dead these last six years—shakes his head. "It has been some time since I have seen you happy, duckling. Since…before."

"Before I threw myself from the Cobb like a damn fool?"

Charles laughs and shakes his head. "Do not let Mary hear you speaking so! She will say you've picked up bad habits from living with sailors."

I find (and this discovery is a liberating one) that I am looking forward to saying a great deal of things for the sole purpose of deviling my sister Mary. Perhaps, in some respects, I am much improved.

"It is a shame," Charles says, watching me closely, "that we did not get a chance to take our leave of Captain Benwick."

"Indeed." I avoid my brother's eye by looking at the passing scenery.

"It seems as though you two became good friends during your time there."

"Yes, I suppose."

Charles sighs and falls quiet a moment. After several moments of silence, he speaks again.

"Do not live with regrets, as I have, Louisa. Should you be so lucky as to find love, do not let it escape your grasp. Fight like hell to keep it."

I look over at my brother and smile. "I will, Charles. I thank you."

"And please"—he takes my hand and gives me a brotherly smile—"never a word of this talk to Mary."

ONE MONTH, THREE WEEKS, THREE DAYS

I will not say I am satisfied with the watercolor, but I am happy to have found an occupation that does not bring me pain. My harp I have already gifted to Henrietta as an early wedding present; the harpsicord sits closed and abandoned in the corner of the room. Perhaps one day I might have a small cottage of my own and Mama can take up her old spinet once more, but for now the house moves about its business in hushed tones.

I do not know what has made me want to take up my watercolors. It was not a practice I found great enjoyment with at school. Perhaps I paint because I miss the views at Lyme. I miss the shining sea and the sight of the sun dancing on water. I have replicated my favorite view from memory as faithfully as I can, but still it does not fill my heart the same way. I cannot feel the ocean mist on my brow nor taste its salt on my lips. For all the pretty splendor of my home county, I find that I miss Lyme.

A maid enters and tells me I have a visitor.

"Tell Mary I am lying down," I tell her, deciding to add a touch more orange to my paper sunset.

"If you please, miss, it is a gentleman who has called."

Strange. *Perhaps it is Captain Wentworth on his way to Bath.* He had not come 'round to Lyme to wish me farewell, though my mind was too occupied with another captain to remark upon his absence at the time. I put my brushes away and discard my smock, not stopping to check my reflection in the mirror. I have little use for vanity of late.

That other, more dear captain was the vanguard of my every thought. I thought of nothing without wondering first *"What would James think of that?"* or *"If only I could relay that to James, I do believe it would make him laugh."* He had, at some point, replaced the phantom of Death that had clung to me since my fall. His words became my shield against the darker turns of my thoughts, the memory of his rare smiles an indulgence I allowed myself only in the quiet gloom of my bower when sleep could not find me.

I take a deep breath to calm my nerves before I enter the drawing room and, to my great surprise, it is not Captain Wentworth's dashing figure I see standing at the window. This man is more slender, his dark locks shorter than I had ever seen them. I freeze, drinking in the sight of that much-loved profile, the high cheekbones, the small, almost pretty nose, the full mouth, but it is not *him* until he turns, the weight of those warm, brown eyes on my person, smiles and says, "Louisa."

He opens his arms and I forget myself. Forget to curtsey, forget to greet him, forget that we may not be alone in the room. I rush at the invitation to fill that unoccupied space, feeling lighter than air when his arms close around me. My thoughts are addled, for when his lips meet mine, all I can think is *I am flying. At last, I am flying.*

He loves me. It is certain, and it is true, however strangely it has occurred. A natural sequel to an unnatural beginning but, as he kisses my cheek, my temple, my brow, he says my name over and over like lines of poetry.

"Louisa, Louisa, my dearest heart."

"How is this possible?" I manage to ask through tears. I cannot stop my joyous exploration of his person, the softness of his hair, the scrape of shorn whiskers, the heart that thunders under my palm. "Could you really love me?"

He smiles and kisses the tip of my nose. "I have loved you for some time now. I thought it quite impossible that someone so young and bright could ever care for such a moody fellow as myself."

"But you did not stay to say goodbye!"

"No. I shall never say goodbye to you, my heart. I had other farewells to make. To beg Fanny's understanding. Not forgiveness, for I do not think she would ever have begrudged me this happiness."

"She will always have a place in your heart, and that is as it should be," I say, surprised to realize I meant it. For Fanny Harville had, in her way, made him the man I came to love.

"We must let the past remain where it ought and look to the future. Could you marry an old sailor, Louisa Musgrove?"

"Only if that sailor is you, James Benwick. I choose a life with you over any other future this world has to offer."

He takes my face in his hands, his thumbs caress my cheeks. "Are you certain? I made enough on the *Laconia* that we could have a very comfortable life together."

I put my hands over his. He feels warm and vital and so beautifully *alive* to me. I have cast off Death and embraced Life with every particle of my being. I smile up at him.

"Am I certain? No, my dear captain, it is far worse. I am *determined*."

And then we find other, less vocal ways to express our joy. But that is ours alone and does not bear repeating.

∿

TWO MONTHS

"Are you sorry to not be joining your family in Bath?"

A laugh bubbles up from inside of me. I feel I am more myself now, as if the carefree fool and the broken girl have merged to become one happy, somewhat sensible, young woman. I link my arm with James's and answer him in all sincerity: "There is nowhere else I would rather be."

We are walking through the garden at Uppercross, and it is a perfectly lovely day. How could I want to be in Bath, where it is cold and rainy and far too noisy?

"I have had a letter from Frederick," James says, and for the first time since our engagement looks rather pensive.

"And how is Captain Wentworth?" I ask without much interest.

"He is engaged. To Miss Anne Elliot."

I could not have been more astonished if he had told me Captain Wentworth was to become the next monarch of the empire.

"Captain Wentworth? To *Anne?*"

"Surely you have heard the gossip that he was once engaged to a lady in the county?"

I affirm that I had heard as much from Mama, who heard it from Mrs. Croft herself. That it should have been Anne astonished me indeed.

"I suppose this does explain why she would not have poor Charles."

"Does this news affect you?" James asks nervously. I consider the question, thinking of all that had transpired between myself and Captain Wentworth in full view of Anne Elliot and find that I cannot be easy. How it must have plagued her! I remember something else, from our first days at Lyme.

"Does the news affect *you,* Captain? We all believed you rather fancied Anne."

He chuckled and patted my hand. "I am fond of Miss Anne but had no thoughts beyond those of friendship."

I am not certain this is entirely true but find that I do not care. We are an unlikely match, one made of mutual understanding rather than circumstance of birth. If I am secure in anything, it is in my feelings for him, and the return of his regard.

"Frederick tells me they discussed our impending union," James says, smiling at me. The warm sun does marvelous things to his eyes.

"Oh, have they indeed?"

"Yes, Miss Anne hopes that, through your influence, I might gain high spirits and liveliness, and Frederick thinks you will now have a relish for morbid poetry."

I laugh again. "I relish any words you say."

"Then perk up your ears, my heart. For there was never such joy for me than sailing through life with my Louisa by the sea."

I shiver and lean into his arm. I believe that, without him to anchor me, I will take off in flight, up, up into the perfect blue sky, content to soar.

BEAU NORTH is the author of three books and contributor to multiple anthologies. Beau hails from the kudzu-strangled wilderness of South Carolina but now hangs her hat in Portland, Oregon. In her spare time, Beau is the co-host of the podcast *Excessively Diverted: Modern Classics On-Screen.*

THE STRENGTH OF THEIR ATTACHMENT

SOPHIA ROSE

CATHERINE MORLAND

Young, naïve, and in possession of no remarkable skill or gift, a more unlikely heroine there never was. Yet, she has survived a harrowing adventure on the road from Northanger Abbey, found love with a handsome and sensible gentleman, and emerged a rational creature, developing grace and forming her own ideas and judgments. *"Her heart was affectionate, her disposition cheerful and open, without conceit or affection of any kind..."* —**Chapter II**, *Northanger Abbey*.

THE STRENGTH OF THEIR
ATTACHMENT

JUNE 1800, FULLERTON, WILTSHIRE

From my customary place at my father's right hand, I observed that his reading of a letter from my aunt Tate did not bring welcome news. The clamor created by a large family of children at the breakfast table went unremarked by him. The lack of receiving my own letter these last three weeks suppressed my own natural high spirits, making me a mute witness to my father's quiet tapping of forefinger to cloth, throat clearing, sipping from his dish of tea, and now a slight frown forming on a face used to more convivial expressions.

"What is it, my dear?" Mama asked, dabbing at little George's spilt milk and leveling a stern eye at Willie before he could push his uneaten and unwanted portion onto Betsy's plate.

Until I began attending to the way Mama ran her household in anticipation of my own future status as helpmeet, I had not given Mama her due for her ability to attend to more than one matter at a time. And, for her part, Mama was full of wonder to discover her oldest daughter was moderately able when it came to the domestic arts, though success was tempered with some failure. Repairing holes in the stocking heels so that knots did not form to make the wearer uncomfortable was my downfall, it seemed. The nods of satisfaction and the pride in Mama's voice when she told Mrs. Allen of her oldest daughter's new interest had prevented me from admitting that my betrothed, Henry Tilney, was the instigator for this practical course of study—a practice to help while away the time as we waited on his father to give our nuptials his blessing.

Papa looked up from the letter over his spectacles. "My sister's spirits remain low since the loss of Mr. Tate this past March. She claims she is much alone, but Minerva cannot fault those friends who choose to stay away. Her tears and grief would only make them uncomfortable."

Mama returned, "And yet, their duty is clear if they call themselves her friends. What else does Minerva say?"

"She writes me a tale of a fowl's fate. Her favorite hen died and her cook was displeased that Henrietta's corpse must be given over to the workhouse for their comestible pleasure because"—Papa paused and fluttered his hand with the table linen like a lady's handkerchief as he dramatically concluded—"my sister could not possibly eat her."

This drew guffaws around the table. Papa smiled as he adjusted his spectacles. I was well aware of whom I could thank for my own vivid imagination.

Not to be distracted by the woeful tale of the fowl's fate, Mama ventured a second inquiry: "Was there anything else?"

This time Papa was grave. "No, she is sorry to report that she has had no more success than we."

Mama excused the younger children from table. Only Sarah and I witnessed our parents growing concern for our brother James's uncharacteristic neglect of his correspondence home following his return to university. As a resident of Oxford, Aunt Minerva Tate was well placed and gladly took Papa's commission to call upon her nephew. Joining in the family's general unease, she admitted in her last letter that James had not called upon her save once when he first arrived back in Oxford. It was as unlikely for him to neglect regular family visits with his aunt as penning his letters back home.

After his sad disappointment in the spring involving the adventuress Isabella Thorpe, James had spent time in the bosom of our family before returning to Oxford for the next term. We had thought that we had sent him off a little sad and embittered, as most would be who suffered a jilting, but well along the path toward equanimity. However, four letters from home remained unanswered, and now this lack of reply when Aunt Tate's own man hand-delivered her note, to the very door of the college, in case all the letters had somehow gone *astray* in the post.

Mama pursed her lips as she straightened the table covering that young George's departure had disarranged.

"Mr. Morland, I think it is time to write the dean and make deeper inquiries."

"James would not appreciate our interference. He wished us to allow him to find his own way through this disappointment, if you recall."

Mama nodded.

Seeing my parents troubled, my own vivid imagination threatened to overset me with lurid images of James's injury or demise, but I stamped these out. Albeit, an imagination was not entirely useless, as I set it to the issue at hand. Regulation and moderation were the keys. Therefore, unlike most days when James's broken betrothal was mentioned, I was not about the business of vilifying Isabella Thorpe in my thoughts. I learnt something after my recent adventures in Bath from the pair of Thorpe siblings, who practiced no economy in their words nor much forethought in their schemes, causing great harm as a result. Hence, I did not immediately launch into speech but weighed the idea carefully.

Finally, I spoke: "Mama, Papa, what if, instead of a letter to James's headmaster, which might indeed make him cross when this gentleman sought him out on behalf of his family... What if a personal visit was attempted?"

My plan was not immediately rejected.

Emboldened by their thoughtful expressions, I pressed on. "Might I go on your behalf? I could stay with Aunt Minerva. I would make James aware I was in Oxford so he might wait upon me at my aunt's, and I could satisfy us all that James is in good health."

Not one to envy or even want to attend school, I had not demurred when Sally (or rather, Sarah, as she desired us all to call her now) was sent to Mrs. Hutchins's school in Bristol with the small legacy Grandmama Nicholson bestowed in her will for one of her granddaughters to be trained up as a proper lady. Since her return home, Sarah had regaled us all with the benefit of Mrs. Hutchins's knowledge of ladies' deportment, and she did not hesitate to do this now.

Sarah artfully splayed hand to her heart and gasped, "It would not be proper, Catherine. How could you think of such a thing? A lady never goes beyond her own hedgerow unaccompanied, Mrs. Hutchins says."

After a time, when no one challenged this pearl of wisdom, Papa shook his head and patted my hand. "Thank you, Catherine, but we have no one to accompany you into Oxfordshire, though I am sure your aunt would welcome your visit."

At Sarah's self-satisfied sound as she looked at me over her cup of tea, likely meeting Mrs. Hutchins's exacting standard for genteel cup holding, Papa said, "Your sister displays proper feeling for a brother, and we appreciate her offering to go to him on our behalf, Sally."

Papa's use of "Sally" made her wince and, though it did me little credit, I secretly crowed over my sister. He squeezed my hand, folded the letter, and kissed his lady's hand that reached for him on his way past as he adjourned to his study.

Sarah huffed. "I would hope I display proper feeling for James. I was merely pointing out that it would not be appropriate for Catherine to travel alone." She glanced at us both to make certain we understood. I knew that Sarah did not intend to sound overly prim or unfeeling. She was simply exhibiting her training.

Privately, I was relieved that it had not fallen to me to learn to sit, stand, walk, dress, eat, sew, draw, and play an instrument to such strict guidelines. As oldest granddaughter, Mama had spoken to me of the possibility of this gift and I happily deferred to the next in line, who would take more pleasure from the experience. Sarah had quoted aphorisms about a lady's role in the home and society that made me cringe for her. Mama had explained that this was a confusing time for Sarah and we must be patient. Sarah was not like me or the other children and had her eyes set on Town rather than country.

Mama mirrored Papa's actions and patted Sarah's hand.

Sarah nodded to us, dabbed her lips, and excused herself to practice scales on the pianoforte.

I had no strong hopes that my suggestion would be accepted, but I was as concerned for James as my parents. I felt his pain keenly, having observed Isabella flirt with Captain Tilney, my own Henry's older brother, her duplicity on several occasions, and her disgust for James after she learned the exact details of the settlement Papa offered.

Mama stood and removed the doorstop, and the door fell shut. She returned to settle in with her tea while contemplating me as if she were measuring me up and concluded the fit would be right.

"Yes, Mama?"

"Your aunt Tate keeps a carriage and she is fond of her nieces and nephews. Would you accept her invitation to stay with her, if it came?"

I took Mama's meaning perfectly. My growing smile was my reply, even as I tipped my head at Papa's empty place.

My surprising fellow conspirator seemed to have matters well in hand. "I will speak to your papa. He does not oppose your visit, provided it is accomplished with you properly attended. We must prepare your things. How are you coming on the rent in your second-best gown? You cannot go to Minerva in tatters. What will she think of us?"

I laughed, knowing my mother was teasing. "I think even my aunt would approve the state of my gowns these days, thanks to your guidance and that of Mrs. Allen. I will be ready to take leave as soon as arrangements are made, Mama."

Fear welled up in my Morland family as James's silence stretched. Further, I had not told my parents of the stranger who had been inquiring for James in the village. Mr. Harry Stuckey ran the local inn and shared all the goings on with his brother over a pint. Mr. John Stuckey, who owned the village shop, in turn shared this curious bit of gossip with me when I was collecting Father's paper order. The stranger had left without calling round to the vicarage once it was known that James was not at home. Something in the furtive way he comported himself left me unsettled, but why worry my parents more when I had only my qualms and hearsay that the stranger was significant. Even Papa would view this as my imagination at work.

Had Henry been there—and, oh how I felt his absence keenly—I would have consulted him about what the stranger's inquiries might mean in light of James's silence and then received his impartial perspective on the matter. Yes, I would write. Perhaps I would find the courage to also inquire into his present feelings about our understanding, as each day without word from him diminished my hope that I would ever stand with him before the altar.

~

OXFORD, OXFORDSHIRE

A se'nnight later, I was established in my late uncle's townhouse. It was well situated on a quiet, respectable street just off High, a short distance from Merton and Magdalen Colleges. In truth, everything in Oxford was *near* to a young lady used to walking many a country mile and not necessarily over a convenient footpath or road.

Uncle Tate's attorney chambers on the ground floor were now rented and occupied by his former law clerk, Mr. Withers, new attorney-at-law. The handsomely appointed rooms on the two floors and attics above were occupied by Mr. Tate's widow. Aunt Tate kept a fine establishment with housekeeper, cook, footman, maids, boy, lady's maid, and a coachman who, with the rest of the male staff, lived over the mews behind the building.

My aunt's writing desk was placed to take advantage of the light, and the window further presented me with a view of the center of Oxford beyond the facing building. I saw spires and heard bells ringing throughout the day. I had no doubt that I would know the names of each tower and spire before long.

In a letter to inform my family that I arrived safely, I wrote how my aunt and I approached the porter at James's college the day after my arrival, wherein we learned that James had not retrieved Aunt Tate's earlier note.

This was all easy to put down on paper, but I could not bring myself to pen the rest. I had assured my aunt that I would inform the family at Fullerton of all that we learned. Instead, I was pouring it out in a letter to Henry since I was unfit to write such dreadful details to our loving and proud parents:

Mr. Roberts, the porter at James's college, shared news that disturbs us greatly. He told Aunt Minerva and me that he had not observed James coming or going, but his mail has been retrieved. As you know, from your time here pursuing your own education, the porter at the gate knows all. Mr. Roberts visited James's new room that he has occupied since Easter term when he vacated the one just across the landing from Mr. Thorpe. He discovered that James had collected some of his things and is gone.

Mr. Roberts did not wish to admit us into further confidences. However, my aunt persuaded him, and we learned there are rumors of ungentlemanlike conduct and that James had been sent down. To his knowledge, which can be relied upon, the latter is not true and, as to the former, Mr. Roberts does not credit it. He repeated assurances to my aunt that 'no one who has the privilege of knowing young Mr. Morland would believe such faradiddles.'

What were the rumors? Untrue, one and all, I say! It is rumored that James owes debts at shops around Oxford as well as gentlemanly wagers on curricle races, horse races, cock fights, and boxing matches. He has made no assurances that he will discharge these debts, particularly the debts of honor. Mr. Roberts mentioned a particular gaming house run by a Lady Clarissa where the wagers were made. How is it that she can make claim to be a lady, I wonder? My aunt was overset at the discovery that a female would play host to these deep wagers in her own house. Perhaps a loo party would be acceptable, but to devote her public rooms to all forms of gaming including an E-O table! I must ask if you are familiar with Even Odd and could enlighten me. Mr. Roberts indicated that a man spinning the wheel was akin to flinging his coin into the sea.

Henry's continued silence was deafening. Perhaps he was unable to send a letter through his sister. Perhaps Eleanor had been busy planning her wedding to the viscount. At least this was what I hoped was the explanation. I feared that these rumors about James might reach the general's ear and he would be set against me becoming wife to his son for good. And what of Henry? He was already estranged from his father after the villainous way the general treated me when he was imposed upon by John Thorpe's lies and cast me from his home to make my own way home. Henry saw little of his beloved sister when he denied himself visits to the abbey. Would he now find himself connected to a family who was thought to produce a cad who avoided his debts? Should I be unable to locate James and squelch the rumors, would I be placed in a position of releasing Henry from our engagement due to scandal? Better that it not come to that, I told myself firmly as I dipped my pen to continue the letter.

My heart tells me that there is some mistake. James does not play at cards, and he has never shown an interest in wagers. He is not one to spend beyond his means. Yet, according to Mr. Roberts, the debts are genuine and James's name is attached to them. How can this be?

Mr. Roberts promised he would attempt to locate the source of the rumors and be on watch for James. James's tutors and the headmaster are under the impression that there was a dire family situation that drew Mr. Morland home to Wiltshire. This fabrication seemed to amuse the porter. I suspect that James must have some friends who are attempting to protect him by perpetrating this misrepresentation, which I refuse to call a lie.

Now give one of your smirks and lecture me at your leisure, dear Henry. Notice I did not dare refer to Mr. Roberts as a nice man, though he is prodigiously so, because I quaver at the thought of your opinions on the overuse of the word 'nice'.

My aunt is brought low. She cannot sleep well, and her head aches beyond what a body can endure, she says. She eschews such sorry tales about her beloved godson, but it pains her nonetheless. She charges me that my need for action is unbecoming and that we must approach the dean, as he is better situated to give James assistance. I can only privately eschew this advice. This is no time to be trimming a hat or painting screens. I cannot remain still. Every feeling demands that James is alone and needs support.

I persuaded her away from approaching the dean, as my parents do not wish to take this course of action. Yet. I—

There was a knock at the door of the morning room, and Aunt Minerva's handsome footman Donnie was there.

"Miss Morland, is it still your intention to walk out this afternoon? Mrs. Tate is resting, so Jennings is free to accompany you now."

My walk! I had forgotten that I planned it.

"Yes, thank you, Donnie. Please tell Jennings that I will retrieve my bonnet."

Donnie was an affable sort, and he did not hide a small smile before retreating as I capped the ink and slid my writing under the blotter to finish later.

Once achieving the street, my motive was to watch the busier thoroughfares for the familiar face of my brother. Not the population of London or Bath, Oxford was still a substantial city to a young lady accustomed to a country village.

Jennings had been lady's maid to Aunt Minerva since before her wedding. She walked at a sedate pace, pointing out fashionable ladies or acquaintances of the Tates. The footman Donnie had come fresh from the estate of Mr. Tate's older brother not two years earlier and followed behind us. Both servants knew my reason for going out. Jennings did not approve but saw no harm in walking about town as any gentle lady might do in fine weather. Donnie, however, seemed to enjoy the afternoon stroll and my purpose.

I noted a bookseller for a future visit, though I would make no purchases and content myself with my aunt's subscription to the circulating library. Everywhere I looked was evidence this was an erudite center, and I studied each youthful face for familiar features. I reminded myself to look beyond the scholarly robes to other men along the way. James did not own a mount or even a light equipage, but I did not neglect any of those either. Along our way, Donnie drew my attention to several young gentlemen that fit James's description.

For two more days, I continued my afternoon walks, lost a day to rain, and, on the following day, fortune rather than intention befell me when my expectations had grown low. I gave up on discovering James by chance. It had been a foolhardy notion but relieved my need for action, any action. Today was devoted to seeing one of the local sights.

Henry had attended Christ Church, where he received his degree, and I was eager to see the lovely old buildings, particularly the cathedral. I thought of Henry when Great Tom, Christ Church's old bell, rang out, and I could see Tom Tower from St. Aldate's Street. Donnie navigated us safely across the busy High Street and eventually onto the cathedral grounds when I noticed Jennings' limp. I took pity on the lady's maid, who had explained it was but a blister on her heel. (Perhaps she had been the lamentable victim of a poorly repaired stocking heel.)

Jennings would have continued hobbling along if I had not persuaded her that her heel would fare better after a period of rest. Jennings only yielded when Donnie solicitously escorted her to a comfortable bench in the shade.

"This will do fine, miss. Take Donnie and walk about. Remember, do not stray far."

"I will not leave the cathedral grounds. I promise."

I was compassionate for the suffering Jennings but longed to look over such an edifice steeped in history. Oh, the stories this place could tell! I could imagine Henry grinning at my awestruck expression before carefully explaining all that was before me.

The cathedral had once been St. Frideswide's Priory. I admit, I was imagining ghostly nuns and priests walking these grounds, perhaps surrounded by mists in the dead of night when I heard a familiar voice behind a nearby border hedge.

"Damn, but they almost caught me last night."

John Thorpe! He sounded breathless, like he was still fleeing someone. I had been set to slink rapidly away from the odious man until—"Lady Clarissa's Mohawks came at me for a right good beating, but I evaded them. Not to boast, but I have something of a reputation for being quick of mind and fleet of foot."

Lady Clarissa! That was the name Mr. Robert's gave us for the woman owning a gaming establishment.

"I thought you said they would follow James Morland," an unfamiliar tenor stuttered. "You gave them Morland's name when you made your wagers to Lady Clarissa."

At this, I gasped and my indignation rose. It was only Donnie's gentle hand on my shoulder, shake of the head, and finger to his lips that halted my charge around the bush.

"And, so I did!" John Thorpe snarled. "I heard they got past Roberts and went to his room and then his favorite public house, but he was not in either place. Someone warned him. He has too many friends who help misdirect Lady Clarissa's brutes, so they lurk about hoping to catch *me*. They know me by sight as *Morland*. But James Morland looks nothing like me. Unremarkable fellow, really."

"What about the rumors we scattered around, discrediting Morland? Forcing his hand?"

"Some damage. It ran him off. I could barely keep my countenance to hear old Greeley going on about the sin of gaming and staring at Morland's empty seat in our lecture room. That bloody Baddage, though!"

"Who is Baddage and what has he done?"

"Edward Trevor, Viscount Baddage, has taken up the cudgels on Morland's behalf. I think he suspects me. I saw him once on the street near Lady Clarissa's."

My heart raced and I no longer felt the urge to immediately castigate him. However, before much time passed, John Thorpe would feel the lash of my tongue for his perfidy! Poor James! Where was my brother? Was he hiding away in a rat-infested cellar?

"Would not have expected it of Baddage. He likes the distinction of class, and Morland does not have the Town bronze or blunt to impress the likes of Baddage and his set. Style themselves as Corinthians and expect the rest of us to step aside with hat in hand, but I made him take note of me when I scotched his chances with a certain lady. People are credulous when I tell them things. The Right Honorable Miss Fairborne now believes Viscount Baddage has lost a fortune to gaming and the dissolute pursuit of lightskirts." Thorpe laughed at this admission. "He is having a devil of a time persuading the young lady she is mistaken. M'sister says it's odious how I can sway people to believe what I want. She is jealous of all the times Mama favored me."

"You assured me that Mr. Morland would learn of the debt and, to save his reputation, attempt to pay it with funds he inherited from his godfather. You said when he pays the debt, this would free up funds you would use to pay me back. You said this would sink him with Miss Thorpe for good and she would accept my suit. If this is all a hum—"

"It will work. Morland cannot hide forever. He has no funds."

"You just said he has got fu—"

"His father keeps it for him. He will go home to Wiltshire, and I shall know it if he does. I have been collecting his post. His family knows nothing of his whereabouts, so he has not attempted to gain their support. I already hinted to Lady Clarissa that I, in the guise of Morland, might have to go home and get my father to raise the two thousand. Do not go into the vapors. It will work."

The voices drifted away with the sound of retreating steps. Donnie and I were left alone on our side of the hedge.

All at once, the full import of what I heard descended on me. I was trembling and might have collapsed if the footman had not given me his arm. Within moments, Jennings stared with concern when I collapsed to the bench and sat imitating a statue.

Donnie paced nearby as I collected myself.

"Miss, you seem disturbed. Did something occur?" Jennings asked.

I looked back to where I overheard John Thorpe. My voice was surprisingly steady when I replied to the lady's maid. "Thank you. I am well, Miss Jennings. I encountered the brother to the young lady who was once pledged to James. That is, I avoided the encounter."

"I see. My foot does not pain me after the rest, and I am prepared to walk back to the house. We shall return a different way so as not to encounter him again."

After a sleepless night, I had determined on a course of action that would likely end in a scold from my aunt or being sent home in disgrace. If only Henry or Papa or one of my other brothers were here…but they were not and sending for them would take time that James did not have. Even now, Lady Clarissa's brutish enforcers (or Mohawks, as John Thorpe called them) might discover him.

I waited until my aunt was conducting her weekly meeting with her housekeeper, stole into her desk for one of her cards and slipped downstairs. I had the door open when I was discovered.

"Mrs. Tate would be right put out if she were aware of you stealing away like this." Donnie loomed over me.

I drew up and attempted to look commanding. Unmoved, he merely lifted a brow and tilted his head toward the back of the house.

I lowered my chin. "I must help James. I believe I know how to find him. Please do not interfere."

"I will not, but you're not going alone, miss."

I had images of being hauled back by my collar in disgrace, then being locked in my room and forced to subsist on bread and water. Not that my aunt would be so cruel! But I would not be deterred.

"You have my word."

Reluctantly, the footman trailed behind me.

Truth be told, when I stood at the porter's entrance at James's college watching several young scholars finish up with Mr. Roberts, I was glad of the footman's presence. I dreaded encountering the dean unescorted.

I wore my best walking dress and bonnet, new gloves and half boots, and carried the pretty reticule Sarah made me. While knowing myself not to be a great beauty, I thought I looked well today. Any boost to my confidence would be welcome for this endeavor. A young gentleman listening to a fellow scholar caught my eye as he passed me and winked. I promptly looked at my shoes, feeling my face burn.

What Henry would think when he learned of my actions did not bear thinking, or my courage might fail. I had sent my letter telling him of my search for James and the conversation I overheard at the cathedral. How to tell him of this latest escapade...? I would have to think on that later.

Mr. Roberts came directly and bowed. "Miss Morland, is it not?"

"Mr. Roberts. Yes. I offer my compliments and a desire for a few minutes of Lord Baddage's time. Here is my card. You may tell him I only wish a few minutes and it is in regard to Mr. James Morland. Please."

My hand shook when I held out my aunt's card with my name penned below. I was rewarded for my boldness when the porter did not deny knowledge of Lord Baddage; I assumed correctly that he attended this college with James.

Mr. Roberts hesitated as I experienced a sinking feeling, knowing that gently bred ladies did not make calls on single gentlemen, but his eyes filled with pity as he took the card, leading me away from the inquisitive eyes of the young men strolling past.

"Do wait inside my parlor, miss, and I shall see if His Lordship is in."

Mr. Roberts escorted me to a chair and glanced at Donnie before leaving us. Since leaving the house, the footman had remained silent and moved like my shadow.

I nervously glanced around this bachelor domicile—the very gate of a great institution of learning, instructing young men for centuries. I felt the weight of my actions for storming this all-male citadel. Many believed and even wrote in their published works that a woman's educational focus must be toward marriage and the home, that women's minds were not capable of learning the subjects taught within this college and other institutions of higher learning. I was intimidated, but then recalled that a dunderhead like John Thorpe was allowed to matriculate from such a school, and I straightened my shoulders.

At the distant sound of voices and movement in the quad where the residents of the college moved between buildings, Donnie paced to the small window and glanced out. Did he envy these gentlemen's sons? He was quick and bright. I rather thought he would have done well here had he been born into the right class.

A boot scraped in the passage beyond. I rose as the door opened and a gentleman dressed in buckskins entered with Mr. Roberts.

"Miss Morland, this is Lord Baddage, and he would be *delighted* to give you a quarter hour of his time. My lord, Miss Morland."

The porter hesitated but, at a nod from Lord Baddage, closed the door.

I swallowed the lump in my throat. Other than on my journey from Northanger Abbey in the public coach, I had never been this close to a strange male, alone, and had never met a viscount, but at least I remembered to curtsey.

"Thank you for seeing me."

"What can I do for you, Miss Morland?"

A narrow face, long nose, high cheekbones, thin lips crooked up in amusement matched watchful gray eyes. I hazarded a guess that this was someone not easily overset.

He swept the tails of his blue coat aside to settle on the only other chair after setting down his hat and driving gloves. I realized he must have been on his way out when Mr. Roberts found him. He shook flaxen hair from his eyes and waited.

In for a penny; in for a pound, I thought.

"I am looking for my brother, my lord. His family is worried that he has not returned our letters, and Mr. Roberts tells me he has decamped."

"And you believe I might assist you?"

He was not much older than me. Twenty, perhaps, but his composure belied his youth. I caught myself from nervously picking at my glove button as he sat back, showing little interest in my troubles.

"Yes, I think you can. I am told that you have helped to protect his reputation with the dean and his tutors by vouchsafing a fictitious journey into Wiltshire. You must count yourself one of his friends to do so. I am aware there are ugly rumors about him." I pierced him with a most ardent expression after stating as fact what was pure conjecture on my part about Lord Baddage's involvement. "It's all a fudge!" He raised his brows at my outburst and my face grew hot. "My brother is neither one to frequent a gaming house nor refuse to honor his debts if he has them."

Still silent, he no longer seemed disinterested, but neither did he display an air of helpfulness.

"I know who spread these falsehoods, and I know who ran up debts with Lady Clarissa. He has acted spitefully. He has interfered with my family and caused my good-hearted parents to worry for their son. John Thorpe is a loathsome toad. If I were a man… But no; he is beneath calling out. He is no gentleman."

Lord Baddage glanced away and took up his hat like he had never examined it closely before.

I worried all was lost and he would refuse me, but then he turned back with a mischievous grin. "I see you are fly to the time of day."

There was an elegance to his movements, even as the viscount crossed his legs, setting the hat across his knee. His face turned grim. "Morland is safely away. You need not fear for his safety."

"While I am happy to receive these assurances, I wish to speak with my brother, my lord."

"Not possible at present."

This was not to be borne! "Where is James? I need to see him. We must scotch the rumors and further mischief."

I suspected the viscount found me a tiresome female; nevertheless, I persisted. His countenance was patient, manners perfect, and leaning forward, he said, "There is no need."

I rather thought there was and opened my mouth to say as much, but Lord Baddage stood, indicating this was the end of our interview.

I could think of nothing that would induce him to tell me what I wished to know. Instead, I said, "You will tell James that I wish to see him or my next call will be upon Mr. Thorpe. Good day, my lord." I curtseyed and swept out as I imagined a grand dame might.

I was on the walking path when Lord Baddage called out. "Miss Morland, stay a moment!" Passersby turned to his calling my name. "Come aside, please."

He guided me by the elbow away from the foot traffic and a handsome steed waiting for him with a groom. Donnie followed along into the shade of the nearby trees.

Lord Baddage's voice was low. "Miss Morland, please. Refrain from such a precipitous action, I beg of you. We have a plan in motion. It depends on Morland staying out of sight and giving time for those who hold Thorpe's vowels to detain him. Thorpe's at low tide but continues to toss the die in hopes of his luck changing. He grows further in debt and, if his bad luck continues, he will be following Brummel to the continent."

I felt a slow smile form on my lips.

"You wish to assist James, possibly, but I believe you have your own grievances against John Thorpe in regard to *Miss Fairborne*. Perchance, is she your reason for involving yourself in James's business?"

At this, he stiffened and stepped back. I understood he would not be sharing confidences about his choice to actively align himself against Thorpe.

"Your brother is not my pawn, if that is what you fear, Miss Morland."

"I do not know what to think, my lord. I am hopeful you are acting honorably."

"Oh, I am." He smiled, this time with warmth, his eyes roaming my face. "He is fortunate in his family. Please, do not approach Thorpe, as it would hinder our efforts."

"James's reputation—"

"Is not in doubt by those who matter. We know what we are about, Miss Morland. You may trust I act as James's friend."

"Very well"—and inclined my head.

He bowed. "Thank you. Now allow me to escort you to your lodgings."

I thought of Aunt Minerva and said, "Oh, no! That is…there is no need. I know my way about. I have Donnie here …and I have upset your plans already"—nodding toward his horse and groom.

"Not at all."

I smiled and retreated swiftly. I felt his eyes on me until I rounded the corner but did not look back.

"Well"—glancing up at Donnie when we were back on the High Street—"Mrs. Tate will be wondering at our absence by now."

He smiled. "Did we not look in at one of the shops on the High this morning?"

"Yes, I believe we did." And I could not help but smile back.

Four days later, I was absolutely convinced that patience was not one of my virtues. Neither was a good temper, apparently. I was out of countenance with everyone. I had heard nothing from my betrothed, though surely my letter would have reached him! However, what had my bowstring strung tightest was no word from James or Lord Baddage.

Aunt Minerva had lectured me about not communicating my plans to go out. She repeated this more than once, even after receiving my apology and promise I would not leave the house without telling her again.

I stopped pacing before the cold fireplace. I had not even realized that I had left my seat. My body was rigid, and I felt my face pulled into a frown. I attempted to lighten my expression and unclench my hands and shoulders.

"Catherine. The day is fine, and I recollect there is a cricket match that caught your notice. You mentioned it over yesterday's breakfast. Take yourself off and do not return until you have rid yourself of this dismal mood."

"I am sorry, Aunt. I did not mean for you to regret my company with my display of such poor manners."

Aunt Minerva waved this off. "I worry about him, too, child. Away with you."

"Thank you." Like my father, Aunt Minerva was not easily overset and had a good heart. "Take Jennings and Donnie."

We walked east toward Magdalen Bridge and the River Cherwell. I hoped to see boaters on the warm July day. Henry had spoken of going on such excursions.

Near the river, the city fell back, and I could breathe clean country air and look out over green meadows. Laughter, birdsong, and the nearby cricket match made my gloom dissipate. I did not walk all the way to the bridge but meandered toward the playing field where distant figures all in white showed the match to be in progress. I listened as Donnie attempted to explain cricket to Jennings.

They drew ahead of me, and it was then that I felt a strong hand wrap around my arm and tug me behind a tree.

"No screechin' if yer know wot's good for yer," a big man growled in my face.

"Where's Morland?" an even larger man demanded. "We know yer his sister. Heard that fancy viscount call out your name on the street, didn't we?"

Terrified, I felt the tightness of my stays. My breath sawed through me as my heart raced.

"Where is he?" barked the bigger man.

"I do not know," I blurted. "Are you Lady Clarissa's Mohawks?"

Their eyes narrowed.

"How d'ya know that name if you know nuffin' about it?"

"I have been searching for my brother. My brother is not the man you seek."

"No, 'course not." They laughed.

"I tell you the truth. John Thorpe used my brother's name when he went to Lady Clarissa's. I overheard Mr. Thorpe confessing his perfidy to a gentleman to whom he is indebted. He laughed at how he tricked you. He said he laid a false trail into Wiltshire and thought it was vastly amusing that you went there to track down my brother while he stayed here and continued with his affairs without reprisal."

It was plain they did not like the idea of someone duping them.

"The legitimate James Morland shares my features. He has light brown hair and hazel eyes like me. He is average in height and figure. Like me. If I could find him, I would prove to you that you are on the trail of the wrong man."

I could see that they were doubtful.

"Listen!"

I winced as the shorter one gripped my arm tighter, and he hissed, "If yer lyin'—"

"I am not lying!" I gasped with fright.

"Miss Morland!"

At this, the men released me and scurried off toward a stand of trees near the river. The shorter one looked back with a menacing expression.

The footman found me behind the tree. "Miss Morland! What happened?"

I pointed toward the river as I found my voice. "The ruffians! Lady Clarissa's men wanted me to tell them where James is."

"Well, they are gone now. You are safe. I am sorry, miss. I thought you were right behind us but, when I turned around, I could not find you. I saw two rough characters and then I spied your blue coat."

"I think they have been following us since the other day, hoping I would lead them to James. They heard my name on the street when Lord Baddage called out to me. They would have found a way, no matter what. It is not your fault, Donnie. You scared them off."

"Miss Jennings is walking this way. We will see you home."

"I do not want her, or my aunt, to know. They will fuss and draw more attention to James's plight. We must keep things quiet."

"Right."

He fixed a smile on his face and strode out from behind the tree. "She is right here, Miss Jennings. Saw a pretty butterfly she wished to draw."

I startled. Butterfly? Draw?

The falsehood served its purpose, and I wondered if I should be concerned with the footman's easy ability; he had exercised it more than once during our short acquaintance.

Jennings began to chide me and so I said, "Look, Jennings! A lemon ice stand. I am surprised there is ice left this late into the year. Let us have some and cheer on Merton." I pointed to a stall with several standing about enjoying the refreshing treat.

"That would be lovely, miss." Jennings was agreeable and forgot her lecture. The footman smiled as I took out the coins to pay for three. Donnie had certainly earned his.

~

Not a half hour had passed when I heard: "Miss Morland? Damn! It is you."

I considered ignoring Thorpe and walking away as fast as my boots might carry me. Unfortunately, he was before me in a trice, doffing his hat.

I hesitated over giving him the cut direct, but rudeness would not drive him away.

"How do you do, Miss Morland? I was unaware you were in Oxford. Have you friends here? Does Morland join your party?" His eyes shifted, looking for James, no doubt. "Surely he would not leave his favorite sister to her own devices. Perhaps he is off making a friendly wager on the outcome of the match?"

"No, James does not join me, but my aunt is awaiting my return. Good day, Mr. Thorpe."

An arm snaked around my own, right over the place that was still aching from the previous rough handling, "No need to hurry off, Miss

Morland. Your aunt can spare you a few minutes to an old friend, surely. I've got a pony on Baliol, but it is early so I won't miss the crucial portion of the match."

I tried to pull away but his other hand clamped down more securely.

"Mr. Thorpe—"

"Miss Morland, it is such a great pleasure to encounter you here. Fortuitous, in point of fact. Let us walk along the river path so you may tell me all your news without our being interrupted. I am certain you have tales of your time going out on the Town with Morland here to squire you about."

I caught the footman's eye, alert and concerned. I hoped my voice sounded steadier than I felt. "Miss Jennings, Donnie, let us continue along the water." There was cheering as someone was bowled out. The Merton bowler had been quite exceptional at dismissing Baliol batsmen. I would give a pony to swap John Thorpe's company for the cricket match!

"Mr. Thorpe—"

"Fate was kind to brighten my day with your presence. I have heard nothing of you since Bath."

He held up his hand as if I had protested and laid it back down, keeping me locked at his side. "But do not think I rebuke you on that score. Sly minx, to insinuate yourself in with the likes of the Tilneys!"

At that, I did protest. "I did no such thing. Miss Tilney and General Tilney were kind enough to extend an invitation, which I did not seek out. I had not the slightest notion the family was leaving Bath until not long before I was invited to journey with them into Gloucestershire. Now, really, Mr. Thorpe—"

"Ah, that might be so." He continued to boast how he had used his influence with General Tilney to look upon me with a kind eye and it was his doing that brought me the invitation, and thus, I should feel indebted. Insufferable man!

I caught the welcome sight of Lord Baddage and two unwelcome yet familiar figures converging on us from two different directions. Lord Baddage signaled me to continue along, allowing the encounter with the unwelcome party.

Thorpe spotted Lord Baddage and drew up. He opened his mouth, but Lord Baddage bowed to me—and only me.

"Miss Morland, you are a difficult lady to track. I have a message. Thankfully, your aunt directed me here, and your footman alerted my attention to your party."

John Thorpe sputtered. His arm released me as he went to address Lord Baddage. Then the two brutes approached from the opposite direction and laid hands on John Thorpe. The larger man winked at me.

"Didna ken to his whereabouts, you say?" he laughed.

"This is not my brother!" I said sharply, wholly done with Mohawks and Thorpes. "This is John Thorpe. Tell them!" I looked at Lord Baddage.

Thorpe clamped his lips together while his eyes darted about, looking for escape. Lord Baddage said, "She speaks the truth, gents."

"Unhand me." Thorpe protested and struggled like a fish caught on a hook. He was hit in the stomach and doubled over.

"Let's jes take a little walk together so we can help call to mind yer obligations to a certain lady, shall we?" The shorter one's grin flashed displaying a missing tooth.

"Come, Miss Morland, we must away," said Lord Baddage, urging me from the violent scene. Donnie offered Jennings his arm, who looked ready to faint.

I had thought about someone planting John Thorpe a facer but had not realized until then that perhaps I was not so keen on violence as I had previously thought.

"What of Mr. Thorpe? You guided me to let them intercept us. They might kill him."

"One could hope, but not likely," His Lordship murmured. Then he smiled. "They will rough him up a bit, but nothing of a permanent nature, my dear Miss Morland. Lady Clarissa wishes to be paid, after all."

"He made up lies about James because he does not have the funds, so there will be no payment forthcoming."

"He can raise it." Lord Baddage was lacking in sympathy. We walked up the slope to the path along High Street near the bridge.

"I do not understand."

"He can sell off his hunter, his equipage, a diamond cravat pin he is fond of displaying. He can sell out of the Funds. His debts are of his own making in an attempt to live beyond his means, and his troubles have come back on him."

I heard all this with astonishment and realized that John Thorpe could have paid his debts all along. He had not needed to drag James into this. He had acted, not from desperation and fear as I supposed, but malice. Any sympathy I might have had vanished.

"Is James safe now, do you think, my lord?"

"It is more than likely. Thorpe will be forced to confess the truth, and word will get around."

He was smiling and I had little doubt that he would make certain of this. I recalled he had his own reason for word to travel as to John Thorpe's true character and deceit. I hoped Miss Fairborne, who had been duped by Thorpe's false testimony about Lord Baddage, would reconsider for the viscount's sake.

Lord Baddage drew my attention to a pair of matching chestnuts pulling a curricle. "Fine cattle those."

I was more interested in their driver. "Henry! How do you come to be here?" I rushed forward, only to be stopped by his frown.

Henry raised an eyebrow, taking in Lord Baddage.

The viscount stepped up and, belatedly, I remembered to introduce them. "My lord, allow me to introduce Mr. Tilney of Woodston, Gloucestershire? Mr. Tilney, Lord Baddage. He is James's friend who has been helping with his difficulty."

Lord Baddage and Henry touched gloves to hats. Then, with an enigmatic smile, the viscount hastily took his leave. "Forgive me for not seeing you back to your aunt's home, Miss Morland. I wish to discover how matters are progressing. Mr. Tilney, if you might see to Miss Morland, she has had a fright just now."

The young lord bowed and walked away. I observed him go, but he could not keep my attention now that Henry was here!

"You there," Henry called to my aunt's footman. "Take their heads."

Donnie went to hold the horses' bridles while Henry descended and rushed to me. He took my hand in his and drew me close.

"Does he speak truth? Have you had a fright?"

I trembled and the tears came. I had been holding myself in check but the sight of Henry's beloved face wreathed in concern allowed me to let go. I clutched at the hand he raised toward the bruise forming on my arm.

He did not wait for me to speak but handed me up into his curricle and turned, with hand out, to a trembling Jennings. Fortunately, Jennings was of a slender build like myself. When Henry joined us, I saw the immediate benefit of a snug fit as I nestled against him and felt his movements as he quietly handled his team, wearing that same taciturn expression he bore when I first walked up on Lord Baddage's arm.

Henry gripped the reins, and Donnie took the valet's customary place. I felt Henry's leg muscle strain and his arm brush my own as he gave the horses their office. If I felt pleasure to be this close after so long apart, I doubt any lady in close proximity to this handsome specimen of a man would blame me.

Henry returned me back to my aunt's house, negotiating the High's traffic easily. John Thorpe bragged about his driving skills, but Henry handled his team and dexterously caught the thong of his whip, proving he was far superior without the need to swagger.

Aunt Minerva was watching for us, and we joined her in the drawing room.

Aunt Minerva fairly simpered over Henry's handsome looks. "Catherine was popular today. First, Lord Baddage called for her, and then Mr. Tilney. Did Lord Baddage find you? He said he would follow you to the match."

"Yes, he found me."

Aunt Minerva's excitement dimmed when she observed how I jerkily removed my bonnet. My fingers shook when I tugged at my gloves. Henry settled me on the sofa and took the place beside me after handing off his driving cape, gloves, and hat to the housekeeper, Mrs. Hunter.

"What has happened? Catherine, your arm!"

"'Tis nothing, merely a bruise. Events transpired that I hope have led to the end of James's troubles. A brief, harrowing experience, but I am better now, I assure you."

"You have been mysterious of late, Catherine. I did not wish to press you, but there is more happening than what you have said. Lord Baddage's appearance here hints that this is so. I think it is time you told me all."

I hazarded a look at Henry, who appeared as intrigued for my story as my aunt. Mrs. Hunter provided a welcome reprieve, returning with the tea tray. I rallied as tea was poured out. My own tea was given an extra spoonful of sugar and milk. My mama was another to dose upset nerves in this fashion.

After fortifying myself, I told my sad, little tale.

"His Lordship says that James is likely safe now, because word will spread about the truth and James's reputation will no longer be in doubt. Lord Baddage said that Mr. Thorpe had the means to pay his debts all along. He let James—no, he *caused* James to suffer for his own folly."

Henry said, "There are people who cannot see their own culpability and resent those who have the stronger characters and can resist the temptations to which they succumb. They must make excuses. They must place blame elsewhere."

I considered Henry's assessment of John Thorpe. "He resented James and sought to bring him low. I believe he enacted a previous disservice to Lord Baddage from the same motivation. How dreadful! I am glad James is safe now."

Aunt Minerva stopped clutching her throat and muttering exclamations: "Poor James" and "What a scoundrel this Mr. Thorpe is" and "Goodness, Catherine!" but I did not think she meant to compliment me.

Rising, my aunt said, "We require something more fortifying than tea, I believe. I shall speak to Mrs. Hunter about opening a bottle of sherry. And I must check on my poor Jennings."

I set aside my tea and looked at Henry. His brown eyes studied me as he leaned against the arm of the couch, his hand propping up his head. His mischievous smirk was absent, but in its place grew a deeper smile, transforming his charming face. He seemed content to study me, and I felt my face grow hot under his regard.

"The injustice of my father might have seemed, on the face of matters, to have injured our felicity, but perhaps it has rather given us time to form a better knowledge of one another and strengthened the attachment."

My eyes brimmed again. "Do you really think so? You are not cross with me?"

"Not at all, dearest!"

"You appeared cross when you drove up and found us coming away from the terrible confrontation with Lady Clarissa's brutes and John Thorpe. I believed you disapproved of me."

He stood and paced to the window near Aunt Minerva's desk. He looked out for a moment then turned back to address me. "Very well. I was put out to see you on the arm of another man and looking on him like —well, like he was your champion. I ceased to disapprove when I learned how you have been the heroine all along."

My heart warmed under his handsome admission and praise but hesitated to credit it entirely.

I stood, smoothed my hands down my gown, and playfully teased. "That is good. I think His Lordship felt your coolness and took himself off."

Henry grinned.

"You do not think I was unladylike, as Aunt Minerva hinted?"

He carefully took up my hands and spoke with fervency.

"Miss Catherine Morland, you are an amazing lady. You are my lady and I am proud to own it. Can you not guess why I have come?"

I had not thought about his abrupt arrival since the first moment of seeing him. I suppose I thought he had come to assist with James. I enjoyed the feel of my hands in his and his precious face before me at last.

"I have just come from London by way of Wiltshire. My father stayed on in London after Eleanor's nuptials. He was well-pleased, and I took the opportunity to join him in the book room. We spoke candidly of the past, of the future."

Henry paused. His face clouded before he gathered himself. No doubt the conversation with the general had not been entirely amicable. I was holding my breath as I leaned closer, not to miss a single word from his lips.

"The general has given us his blessing, and Mr. Morland has added his."

The words took a moment to penetrate, as I had no such expectation. I leapt forward to hug Henry about the neck at such joyful news.

"I see that you have not had a change of mind." His hushed voice spoke near my ear, his breath warming my neck.

"You have my deepest affections, dear Henry."

I felt his lips, tender on my cheek, and I shivered. He drew back a little, only to brush his lips over my own.

"My affection for you has only grown," he whispered, listing the reasons. "Your faith through this time of waiting, your kindness and affection to my sister through her own courtship, your forbearance toward my father, and your abiding loyalty when your brother was in trouble due to Thorpe's deceit. I look forward to many years of discovering more about you to love."

He kissed me again. His breath was warm on my cheek as he murmured about the softness and sweet scent of my skin, the temptation to pull the pins from my hair and let it cascade over his hand, and the brilliance of my eyes, thus making my heart race. I leaned into Henry's embrace, my hand on his chest, lips parted, and—

"Unhand my sister!"

James was grinning with Aunt Minerva fluttering at his side.

"I think not." Henry smirked. "She has agreed to be mine. Forever."

"As it should be," James said softly, stepping forward to kiss my cheek and shake Henry's hand. "The viscount told me what a valiant and loyal defender I have in my sister. Cath, I do not know what to say."

I looked past James's shoulder to view Oxford's spires and then back.

"There is nothing to say." I paused. "John Thorpe is a wastrel and gambled away so much. And I do not just speak of money or reputation. Of course, I would defend you—as you would me—but it became something more to me. When I stood inside Mr. Roberts's parlor, I realized that Mr. Thorpe's conniving action could take so much more than your fortune or good name. The chance at higher education. Your own dreams! Please tell me he did not ruin it all—that you are not sent down?"

James's plain face was so tender as he hugged me. "No, no...a setback, perhaps, but you do not worry about my scholarship. This is a day of celebration, am I right?" He looked to Henry.

Aunt Minerva clapped her hands. "Excellent! We must toast the restoration of James and the future nuptials of a fine pair."

After a felicitous toast, Aunt Minerva pressed beef and buttered bread sandwiches on James, attempting to spoil her godson. Henry turned us aside and pointed toward Christ Church.

"You spoke of opportunity. Is it your own opportunity for scholarship which you desire?"

My eyes followed his direction and I thought of Latin, Greek, Aristotle, Plato, of heads bent over books, and stuffy lecture halls.

"Not at all. That is, my desire is to be given the choice rather than an actual desire for further scholarly pursuit."

Henry nodded his approval with no hesitation.

Boldly, I set aside my half-filled glass of sherry and met Henry's sparkling eyes. He set his own glass down as I chose to sip from his smiling lips instead.

Rather than mock my radical admission of scholarly pursuits for women, my beloved kissed me again and said, "To the ever-growing strength of our attachment."

SOPHIA ROSE is a native Californian currently residing in Michigan. A long-time Jane Austen fan, she is a contributing author in *Dangerous to Know: Jane Austen's Rakes and Gentlemen Rogues, The Darcy Monologues, Sunkissed: Effusions of Summer,* and *Then Comes Winter* anthologies, short stories inspired by Jane Austen's works. Sophia's love for writing began as a teen writing humorous stories. Writing was set aside for many years while Sophia enjoyed a rewarding career working with children and families. Reduced work hours offered an opportunity for a return to writing stories that continue to lean toward the lighter side of life and always end with a happily ever after.

A NOMINAL MISTRESS

KAREN M COX

ELEANOR TILNEY

Elegant, rational, and humble, Eleanor is the motherless daughter of a tyrannical father and has lived a lonely existence at Northanger Abbey since her brothers left home. Like a Regency Cinderella, she is a kind-hearted princess who can only hope one day to find her prince. As Miss Austen declared, *'I know no one more entitled, by unpretending merit, or better prepared by habitual suffering, to receive and enjoy felicity."* — **Chapter XXXI, *Northanger Abbey.***

A NOMINAL MISTRESS

NORTHANGER ABBEY, CHRISTMAS 1807

"Miss Tilney, may I have the pleasure of dancing the next set with you?"

I turned, surprised by a low voice at my elbow. There was no smile on the man's face, no warmth behind his eyes.

"You may, sir. I thank you."

Viscount Lynton, easily the most powerful, eligible man in attendance, strode off. Whether he expected me to follow or wait for him to summon me, I knew not. My friend Alice leaned over to whisper in my ear, her excitement palpable.

"Viscount Lynton pays you notice, Eleanor!"

"My dear, that does not make me an exception of any kind. I heard about him while I was in London, in Bath, and at the country gatherings in Gloucestershire this year. Viscount Lynton asks many"—and I leaned toward Alice, spearing her with a meaningful glance—"*many* a young woman to dance. It means nothing, except he is being polite to my father, the host of this party."

The man in question halted about ten paces from me and turned. "Are you quite ready?" he asked, impatience in his voice.

"Of course." I handed Alice my fan and raised my eyebrows as if to say to her, "I told you so."

Edward Grantham, Viscount Lynton, *was* handsome but, when I was a child, my mother had often warned me that "handsome is as handsome does."

And my mother would know.

She spent her entire adult life under my father's thumb, adapting her own wishes and needs to his every whim. He might have cared for her, but only because an honorable man *should* care about his wife. Whether he really saw the kind, intelligent woman she was, apart from being an extension of his own person...? Well, that was debatable. My brother Henry and I highly doubted it; maybe it takes a child's mind to see a mother as she truly is. My eldest brother, Frederick, and I never discuss our parents. It would seem odd to talk about my father with Frederick, a man who resembles the general in a younger, captain-like form.

Viscount Lynton said little as we took our places in the set and even less throughout the dance. It was an uncomfortable silence. If I smiled at him, he frowned and looked away. If I offered a topic of conversation, he replied with the minimal response necessary to be civil.

The dance ended, and he escorted me back to Alice. He stood in front of us, looking about as if wondering to whom he might extend his condescension next, fatigued by the entire proceedings.

Suddenly, he turned to me and spoke. "Do you like living here?"

"I beg your pardon?" Talking with the viscount was like being whipped around in a chaise and four on a bumpy road.

He gestured carelessly around the room. "This estate? Your home. Do you like it here? It looks old and provincial from the outside, but I find the interior surprisingly modern."

"My father has made improvements over the years. He cares a great deal about maintaining the estate, and his attention is visible in most every detail of its operation."

"And you serve as its mistress?"

"Since I returned from school. My mother passed on several years ago."

"Ah. A great responsibility for a young girl."

"One reason my father still oversees much of the house's keeping. You might say I am a 'nominal mistress.'"

"Yes, I see."

He executed a curt bow. "Good evening, Miss Tilney." And, as quickly as he had appeared, he disappeared into the crowd.

I chanced a look toward my father, whose eyes bore holes into mine, signaling a haughty approval that set my every sense on alert. Esteem and approbation from my father, rare as it was, usually resulted in unpleasantness for me of one kind or another.

"Come with me," I whispered to my friend. "I need some air."

Arm in arm, we exited the ballroom and, after a half-hour's turn around the quadrangle, we found the cool dark of the library. A small candelabra cast the room in long shadows.

"I still can't believe Lynton asked to dance with you. How exciting!" Alice said.

"I would not say it was exciting."

"I do not believe you, Eleanor Tilney."

"Believe me, it was just as I expected."

"How so?"

"He made no attempts at flattery or conversation. I pretended to be complimented by the privilege of dancing with him. And it was over. Like most gentlemen's attempts at courtship."

"Eleanor, for shame!" Alice laughed in spite of her misgivings about my rejection of potential suitors, then turned thoughtful. "Would you truly not consider him? Lynton, I mean. A handsome viscount? The son of an earl?"

"As I am more apt to consider the man behind the title rather than the title itself, I have to say he would be quite far down my list."

At Alice's wide-eyed expression, I continued. "In our society, the choice of husband is one of the few over which we can exert some control. It is the choice on which rides an entire life's worth of felicity."

"You make it sound so arduous a process."

"I suppose I do."

"Falling in love and getting married should be exhilarating and…and breathtaking."

"It is serious business, Alice. The sooner you accept that, the better off you will be."

I paused, taking in her fallen countenance. Alice was in her first season, brimming with the naïveté that comes with a young girl's first experience of being out.

"Besides, I am of no interest to a viscount who has an abundance of paramours, open invitations at the best gaming hells in London, and a string of hunting parties to attend all over Gloucestershire and Herefordshire."

"Some women would find those devil-may-care traits appealing."

"Some would. I, however, would not, even if he were the King himself."

Alice gazed into the fireplace. "Your father would approve of a man with the viscount's title."

"No doubt," I replied with sarcasm.

"And it is not as if you had no dowry."

"Thanks to Mother."

"You might be a better candidate than you imagine. Do not discount your qualities—or his. Viscount Lynton is so striking—tall and dark and dangerous-looking."

"He does not only look dangerous. To an inexperienced young lady, he is. Mark my words, Alice."

"Is that why you wanted to leave the ballroom?"

"I wanted to ensure Lynton had no opportunity to ask me for a second dance, although I doubt he would have. If my father got wind of any preference on the viscount's part, even if it meant nothing at all or I did not welcome it, he would pepper me with questions all day tomorrow."

Alice sighed. "There is that, I suppose. And if you really do not like him..."

"I do not know him, if I am honest. But judging from what I know about his character, the viscount is not the man for me. Too hedonistic and self-important."

"You have thought about this a great deal."

"Not until I knew Father had invited him and his family. Not until I met him in person. It is not fair to judge a man without meeting him first, no matter what the *ton* says about him. But now I have met him..."

"And?"

I considered, bringing up the viscount's image in my mind. "I cannot shake the feeling that his heart cannot be touched. His eyes are cold."

"What an odd thing to say."

"And yet, that is how I feel, and so I simply found it prudent to remove myself from the group of potential conquests. Lynton will move on to whatever pretty—whether it be animal, vegetable, or mineral—catches his eye next and give me not another minute's notice."

Alice grinned as she reached for the door. "Perchance that pretty will be me. On that note, I shall return to the ball room."

"You are lovely enough this evening to attract any gentleman's eye," I assured her.

"You should return as well."

"I will. I just want to freshen up. I shall join you shortly."

She exited the room, and I turned to the mirror, adjusting my mother's pearls, thinking of her, how her life had been pruned to fit the ideals of one arrogant, avaricious man, and vowing that I would carve out a different path for myself and my children.

A snort, followed by a little chuckle, startled me from behind. I whirled around and focused my eyes in the candlelight, dismayed as a gentleman rose from a reclining position on the settee, stood, and walked out of the shadows.

"Not even if he were the King himself?"

I was speechless, embarrassed beyond belief, and terrified of what my father might say if he heard about this. The gentleman bowed slightly, an amused smile playing about his lips. "I do not believe we have yet been introduced. Jacob Gordon Grantham, at your service."

"Pleased to meet you. Sir," I managed to reply as I bobbed a curtsy in deference to Viscount Lynton's younger brother.

"How fortuitous that it was me reclining on this couch hearing your every word instead of Edward. You might well have broken his heart. Or at least wounded his pride."

"Mr. Grantham, I must apologize. I meant no disrespect. I—"

He laughed, a sound without an iota of humor in it. "You think I would take offense? I love my brother, but I also know him well. I can almost hear his reply if he were privy to this conversation."

He pitched his voice in an uncanny caricature of the viscount. "'I care not about the opinion of a general's daughter on some bourgeois estate. I have been side-stepping avaricious parents all my adult life. I live the way I see fit and care not what a country miss might think.'"

Mr. Grantham smiled at me. It was a kind smile, but I could detect a hint of reproach in his tone.

There was nothing for it. I had to accept responsibility for my rudeness. "Nevertheless, you have my most sincere apology. What I said was unbecoming—to me and my family—and as hostess of the evening, it was inexcusable." *Although a gentleman would have made his presence known, rather than snooping like a servant girl.*

He picked up a brandy decanter, opened it, sniffed the contents, and replaced the stopper with a wrinkle of his nose.

"You are worried I will tell your father." It was not a question but a statement. Quite possibly an attempt at intimidation.

The idea dredged up a daughter's anxiety to please an un-pleaseable father, but I could not let Mr. Grantham see that. I gathered my courage and met his gaze. "I do not fear my father, but he would be as unhappy with me for being impolite as I am with myself."

Mr. Grantham stepped into the firelight, the flames giving his hair a reddish cast. "I have been intrigued by the rare opportunities on which I happen to catch females—at all levels of society—in conversation with each other, without the ominous presence of a gentleman's censorship. Quite illuminating to hear that they are rational creatures after all. I am always struck by it. At his own peril does a man underestimate a woman's mind."

I looked at him, stunned with an admission of such bare honesty. I had never heard any gentleman—except for my brother Henry—speak in such a way.

"Well, Miss Tilney, have no fear. Your secret opinion of my brother is safe."

"Thank you, sir. I appreciate your discretion."

We stood there, awkwardly, as the seconds ticked by.

"I should return to the party. I will be missed."

"Of course." He returned to the settee and lay back down upon it. "I will return after some time has passed so as not to sully your reputation."

I had been dismissed and, grateful that it had not been worse, I turned and fled the library.

~

"May I have the honor of this dance, Miss Tilney?"

For the second time that evening, I was surprised by a deep voice in my ear. Mr. Grantham stood beside me, his gloved hand at my elbow.

"You—you may, sir."

Here in the light, away from the shadows of the library, he seemed much less mysterious and threatening. His eyes, as blue as a summer sky, shone with humor. He was tan, which showed off a set of even, white teeth when he smiled, and I remembered hearing that the younger Mr. Grantham had just returned from the south of Italy.

He led me to the set, and as we met and joined hands, he spoke:

"I told my brother of our conversation in the library."

Heat crept up my cheeks. *So much for discretion.*

"I see from your expression you are unhappy with me for that, but it was too delicious a morsel to keep from him."

"You told me you would not say anything."

"To be precise, I said your secret was safe. Edward, I can assure you, will tell no one."

"You are splitting hairs, sir."

We turned away from each other, and when we met again, I could not help but inquire. "I hope the viscount is not too angry."

"On the contrary, I believe he found it rather amusing."

"Well, it is not amusing at all from my perspective."

"When you and your friend were conversing in the library, I should have made my presence known earlier, I suppose. As a gentleman."

Exactly. "Regardless, I have no excuse."

"As your friend told you, most would think Lynton quite a catch."

"Yes"—I struggled with an appropriate response—"but your brother is simply not for me."

Blue eyes caught my gaze and held it, intense and captivating. "My brother is for no one. At least no one with expectations of marital felicity."

"Not according to my father."

"Do parents do that? Coerce a child into marriage? Especially when the gentleman has my brother's roguish reputation?"

"You must not have any sisters."

"True, I do not."

"The general has no compunction about coercion, including his children's potential spouses. It would mortify me, of course, but consideration for my feelings would be nothing if he thought I could secure a future earl."

Mr. Grantham tilted his head curiously.

"I should not have said that." *What is wrong with me this evening?* "Nor should I have any more punch, apparently," I muttered.

He smiled; his blue eyes crinkling at the corners in a strangely attractive way. "Perhaps you should not. I, however, am in need of some refreshment. Would you at least accompany me to the punch table?"

"As you wish."

The dance ended, and he held out his elbow. "Maybe we can find you something else to quench your thirst?"

I took his arm, appreciating its solid warmth and the feeling of being dwarfed by his height. As a tall woman, it was pleasant to have a man beside me who did not make me feel as if I were a gawky girl.

Mr. Grantham took me to the side of the room, beckoning our footman with a gesture. He bent his head to speak to Abraham in a confidential voice and indicated me with a subtle gesture. Abraham spoke sharply to a young lad holding a tray full of precariously perched crystal. The boy nodded, undecided if he should put the tray on the punch table or the floor and finally decided to simply shoulder his way through the door into the kitchen.

I stepped over, not caring how it would look to Mr. Grantham the Younger—his opinion of me was probably ruined anyway—and held out my hands to take the tray.

"May I help you?"

The boy's eyes widened with surprise. "No, miss. I mean, yes, miss. I mean, no. No. Miss."

I could not help but smile. The boy was not a day over sixteen.

He glanced nervously at Abraham, engaged in an exchange with Mr. Grantham. The gentleman himself tossed me a little smile.

"What is your name?" I took the tray from the lad.

"Joe. No, Joseph." He stood taller. "Joseph," he repeated more firmly. "I'm newly arrived."

"Joseph, then. Quick, open the door and let me give you back this tray before Abraham observes us and barks another order at you."

"Yes, miss. Thank you, miss." His smile beamed. "You're very kind."

Taking the tray, he disappeared through the door.

Mr. Grantham joined me, punch cup in hand, gazing out at the room full of dancers and on-lookers.

"You were considerate to assist that lad. Many gentlewomen would not."

I blushed at the compliment, knowing from experience my cheeks were awash with pink.

"What prompted you to do so?"

I paused, trying to formulate a response acceptable to society, and decided that Mr. Grantham had heard the stark honesty of my opinions and was still tolerating my conversation. "I find I cannot be blind to people whom others of my station judge invisible. For I myself have lived and endured the purgatory of invisibility."

We took each other's measure for just a moment too long. He cleared his throat and looked away.

"Miss Tilney, if I may say so, you are *anything* but invisible."

I cast my eyes to the floor, wishing I could hide my smile. I considered myself reserved but not shy. Something about the younger Mr. Grantham, however, made me giddy and unsure of myself. It might have been the punch, but somehow, I did not think so.

After the ball, my father summoned me to the salon. I only wanted to retire; the evening had been exhausting. But one did not deny my father an audience when he requested it. I had no sooner shut the door than he began his intrusive barrage of questions.

"I saw your dance with Lynton. He was asking General Worther about you. I think we should consider finding out which events he will be attending in the near future. You may have a chance of attaching him if you are thrown together enough."

I shuddered at the thought I would have to face the viscount again and be continually reminded of my faux pas at every ball and house party.

My father sat back in his chair, looking at me with a new appreciation. "I know it is only the beginning of your second season, but we need to begin making plans for a successful resolution this year."

"By successful resolution, you mean a marriage." It was an obvious statement; I knew my father's avarice too well.

"Well of course, I mean a marriage, girl!" His voice was impatient. "Lynton would be an excellent match. What did he say to you?"

The interaction with the earl's younger son roared to the forefront of my thoughts. I needed to sever my father's plans for a match with Lynton before he grew to expect the idea to become a reality. My experience with my first season, as well as my observation of my brothers' supposed conquests, reinforced my resolve. The general's mind leapt rapidly from dancing to attachment to marriage, especially if the young person in question was rich or titled or, heaven forbid, both.

"Viscount Lynton said nothing of consequence, Father. He barely spoke to me and only asked me to dance out of politeness." After a thought, I added, "And out of respect for you, of course."

"Still, it is not out of the question that he would offer for you. He is over thirty, and I am certain the earl and countess expect heirs."

A vague nausea crept from my middle toward my throat. How I hated the idea that I was merely a brooding mare, born to bring my father status. I sought to change the subject.

"I also danced with the younger Mr. Grantham this evening."

The general waved away the specter of Jacob Grantham with an impatient swipe of his hand. "The one they call Jago? He is nobody. The second son, but unlike any self-respecting second son, he chose neither the army nor the church as a profession."

"What does he do?"

"He is a barrister and involves himself in trade, if you can believe that. The earl has him sailing all over—Italy for olives, India for spices, Ireland for brewing."

"I found him to be a very pleasant gentleman."

"He is little better than a steward."

I did not reply.

"Do not waste your time with Jacob Gordon Grantham."

SUMMER 1808

I sat alone under a canopy in the early morning light. My easel before me, I worked diligently, sketching the hills behind the house and trying to distract my mind. Other early risers were at work inside and on the grounds, but I had to escape the abbey for a while. My father, so mannerly when the guests were up and about, cast a grim pall over the place when only servants and family were stirring. I told Henry in what direction I was headed, secretly hoping he might let it slip when he rode out with Jacob this morning. Henry needed his time away from the abbey too.

"Good morning, Eleanor."

My heart leapt with joy, and I cursed it for wanting what it could not have.

"Good morning." I was not sure how to address him, this man who had become closer to me than a "Mr. Grantham," yet, according to the rules of society, not a beloved "Jacob" either. Society had no idea I called him "Jacob" in my mind a hundred times a day and into the nights.

"I think it symbolic that our assignations take place in the light of the morning." He ambled toward me, but I kept my eyes focused on my work. "Most lovers' clandestine meetings take place in shadows under the moonlight. But you and I? We examine our love in the bright light of day."

"And face it head on?"

"Is there any other way?" He stopped only a step behind me. "Henry said I might find you here."

I smiled as I shaded a hollow tree trunk on my drawing. "Henry approves of you."

"It is nice to have someone in your family on my side."

"Do not expect Frederick to ever care one way or another. My father may yet come around. With time."

"I have been toiling away these last six months, building the family's accounts in an attempt to persuade your father that even a man without a title is a worthy suitor." He wound a curl at the back of my neck around his finger. "A worthy husband."

I shivered.

I heard him smile before he continued. "I have been making other plans too. I have engaged an architect to begin designing our home."

"Oh?"

"Well, at first I suppose it will be my home. The earl has given me some land for my thirtieth birthday for the express purpose of building a house." He replaced his fingers on my neck with a brief brush of lips. "I want to have it ready for its mistress."

I was at once terrified of discovery and silently begging for more contact. My hand shook as I worried the image of that hollow tree on my parchment.

He straightened. "But the house will have to wait."

"It will?"

"I am soon to leave for Barbados."

My heart sank. "When?"

"Within a fortnight. I sail on the Carthage." He looked over my shoulder at my drawing, resting his large, warm hand on my arm, almost like an embrace. He leaned close again and whispered, "How lovely."

I did not turn to him, did not look at him. I was afraid of what I might say if I did so. "Thank you. I need to shade this hillside a little more."

"I did not mean the sketch."

"Such shameless flattery."

"It is not flattery if I express sincere admiration, now, is it?"

"How long will you be gone?"

He pulled the other chair I brought beside my easel so he could face me, took my pencil, and after setting it on the tray, he took my hands in his. His eyes were serious. "It will be several months, maybe even a year."

I said nothing.

"It is not as if we did not expect this."

"Yes, I know."

"I understand that we agreed to delay before approaching your father but, with this long voyage looming over me, I now find this open-ended waiting intolerable. The thought of being separated from you, an ocean away, when I have grown accustomed to being near you? It leaves me weak-willed and angry."

"I, too, regret my circumstances are such that we cannot be together."

"I hoped you would say as much. Eleanor, my love, come with me."

"Come with you? My father will not give his consent. He still believes I have a chance with the viscount."

"We do not need his approval. I can take care of you quite well. You are of age."

"Jacob…" I tried to form a sentence, but the words would not coalesce in my mind. After several seconds, I shook my head in silence.

He released my hands. "You are afraid." His voice took on a sharp edge, one that immediately roused my courage and my obstinacy. Standing firm in the face of hot temper was one of my better-practiced skills.

"I am not afraid."

"You are afraid of the journey. You care only about your own security. Your comfort."

Suddenly the words were there behind my lips, bursting forth like the sun from behind a cloud. "You are wrong, Jacob. So very wrong. Circumstances exist under which I would leave Northanger Abbey. Circumstances exist under which I would sail with you to Barbados. But not like this. Not as a misbehaving girl. When I leave my father's house, it will be as a grown woman, going toward the rest of my life, not running away from the past."

He frowned, but I could see him curb his anger—let it run through him and out into the morning air. It was a trait I admired. A trait I wished my father would learn.

"You are not like other females."

"Am I not? I rather think I am not unlike any other woman."

"Oh, but you are…most certainly, unique."

He took my hand again, matched our hands together, then engulfed my fingers with his.

"'And palm to palm is holy palmers' kiss,'" he quoted with a smile.

I squeezed his hand. "If I am an unusual woman, maybe it is because I say my thoughts aloud, at least to those I trust. I suppose growing up around men has made me think like them and, when events warrant decisiveness, I am likely to act, perhaps as a man would."

"Perhaps." He kissed my fingers. "Sometimes, though, you infuriate me."

"Because I will not do as you wish?"

He laughed. "Yes, exactly that."

"I love you too much to marry in haste and repent at leisure."

"Curse me for loving a wise woman."

"It may seem to be a curse now but, in the future, it should be a blessing, should it not?"

"Ah. She speaks truth. How can I argue?"

"You cannot."

"I still believe events would sort themselves out if we eloped."

I started to reply, but he held up his hand. "But I can accept your decision, even if I do not like it."

I caressed his cheek. "I do not expect you to wait indefinitely. I do not want a lonely life for you. I would release you, Jacob. It would break my heart, but I would do it. You have only to ask."

He held my hand in place and turned his lips to sear my palm with their heat. "I do not think I will ever be able to be free of you, dearest. As long as I shall live."

Henry approached us from the direction of the stables. "I came to walk you back, Grantham. Father is asking for Eleanor and none too pleased with the world. Something about the lack of good quality pork for tonight's dinner."

Jacob pouted like a toddler as he rose and began gathering my art supplies. "He is a tyrant." He handed me my sketch book.

Henry and I exchanged smiles.

"I had better return to the house," I said, retrieving my parchment from the easel.

~

That evening, I circled the festivities, insuring that all guests were enjoying themselves.

Henry approached me from the stairs. "Father has retired early," he informed me.

"His digestion?"

"Yes."

"The doctor has recommended he take the waters at Bath. I wish he would give that suggestion serious thought. These bouts are becoming more and more frequent."

"The stubborn old goat will not attend to his health if it means abandoning his matchmaking." Henry shook his head. "Is he an old man or an old woman? Sometimes it is hard to tell."

"Now, Henry—"

"You are the wise and prudent one, but I have become quite annoyed with his schemes. How many times must I tell him I will not offer for Felicia Higgins? She has no charms to recommend her except her dowry."

"He is trying to look out for us, I suppose."

"He is trying to elevate his own importance, I assure you." He leaned down and quietly asked me, "Where is Grantham?"

I looked around, but Jacob was nowhere in sight. "I must have lost him."

"Then you must find him." Henry's eyes twinkled with amusement. "I will tend to the guests in your absence. Hurry along, while Father has retired."

With a smile for my brother and a giddy kick to my pulse, I began my search. I checked the library, the lower salon. I looked out the gallery windows into the quadrangle. I took a turn around the gardens, glancing up at the moon as it emerged from behind a cloud, giggling as I remembered Jacob's comment about assignations in the morning light.

"What amuses you, my dear?"

My heart jumped into my throat, and I turned to see Jacob—thank goodness, it was actually him!—stepping out from behind a boxwood.

"The maze, Jacob? A lovers' meeting in a maze?"

"And under the moonlight, too. I have become a gothic novel Lothario."

A strong breeze blew across our path, and lightning flashed in the distance. I held out my hand.

"Come," I said. "The orangery is a better choice."

We ran toward the building at the edge of the gardens. Large raindrops began to pelt against the orangery's glass just as we reached the door. Laughing, Jacob yanked on the door handle and pushed me in ahead of him. I stood, looking up at the ceiling, as the deluge of a summer storm began. I turned, a delighted smile on my face at our impeccable timing, my hands instantly going to my hair and rearranging the pins and curls that had come loose. Lightning flashed once again, and my smile slipped at his expression.

Jacob, my gentleman Jacob of the ballrooms and the morning light, was gone. This man, with Jacob's face and hair and eyes, tall and broad shouldered, was dangerous, predatory, and surprisingly appealing.

We stared at each other a long second. Then he rushed into me, gathering me into his arms, his lips on mine, provoking a fevered response I had no idea I was capable of. His hands were in my hair, destroying my attempts at restoring it, and then they slid down the column of my neck, out to my shoulders and gripped my arms.

"You must not make me go to Barbados without you." He lips began a descent down my throat, ending at the delicate skin above my neckline as I arched uncontrollably toward him.

I was a creature without words, only sensations. The feel of his hair, the wavy softness of it under my fingers. The burn of his lips on my skin. The impending collapse of my knees under his tender assault on my person.

"Come with me," he growled in my ear. "Tonight."

Tears sprang into my eyes. "I cannot."

He stopped suddenly. Straightened. Righted my gown back onto my shoulder. "Bloody hell, woman!"

I began to cry. I loved him, God knows I did, but I knew not what to do in the face of his temper. I did not know him well enough. And at the moment, he frightened me.

Anger dissolved into a horrified expression that I saw when the lightning flashed again. He guided me onto a bench seat, then knelt in front of me, his arms encircling my hips, his head in my lap.

"My darling, my beloved. Can you forgive me? For these liberties I have taken? I have offended you. I beg you, Eleanor, do not cry."

"You oblivious, insensitive man! I am not offended that you want to hold me or kiss me." I covered my face with my hands and sobbed quietly, whether from shame and embarrassment or panic, I did not know.

He raised his head but remained kneeling before me, waiting. Finally, he took my hands from my face. "Then what is the reason for these tears? They tear at my heart."

"You are angry with me."

He sighed and sat beside me on the bench. "I am not. Truly." He drummed his fingers on the wrought-iron arm. "I am worried about being separated from you for so long. You are so under your father's control. I fear he will sway your judgment, and I will return to you, only to find you have accepted another man and become some Countess or Lady something."

"You think so little of my constancy?"

He sighed again, looking off into the dark shadows of the young trees. "No, it is more that I think so little of my power to keep you. I am accustomed to always being second in the eyes of the world. I would find it unbearable if I were second in yours."

I leaned my head against his arm. "I love you, Jacob. That will never change."

"And I love you enough to try and persuade you to elope. It is entirely possible I am not the rational creature I thought I was."

I turned and rested my chin on his shoulder. "You could refuse to go abroad."

"I cannot. My father insists…" He stopped suddenly and looked at me. Then he laughed.

"See?" I said gently. "It is not so easy to refuse a parent."

"No, I suppose it is not. So, here we are."

I turned my head to rest on his shoulder and took his hand in mine. "Here we are, indeed." Rain fell on the glass roof, steady, calming, cooling as we stared into the darkness, hand in hand.

OCTOBER 1808

We sat at supper as the autumn winds rattled the window panes of the abbey. This gathering of neighbors and friends was a more informal group than my father had entertained recently but, of course, the Earl and Countess Sanborn and their eldest son, Viscount Lynton, were in attendance.

Over the last few months, my father had continued to throw the viscount in my path at every opportunity, even going so far as to arrange that I sit next to him at this evening's supper. As usual, there was little conversation from Lynton, but his silence, bordering on incivility, drew my notice. He seemed pale, definitely out of sorts.

"Are you well, my lord?"

"Yes. Why?"

"You are very quiet this evening."

"I suppose I am." He leaned forward. "I would like to request an audience with you, in private, if you would be so kind."

My heart pounded in my chest.

"My lord, I do not believe..." I stopped, dread filling my soul. "Have you spoken to my father?" *Please, by all that is holy, say you have not.*

"I have not. What I have to say is between you and me. Are your servants discreet?"

"Not at all. Northanger is full of those who would inform General Tilney of any tête à tête between us."

"Then what do you suggest as far as privacy? Although I must tell you a rigorous ride out into the hills is not an option."

"My father is an early riser, but he retires early as well. Perhaps the lower salon? After eleven? That room is rarely used when we have company."

"As you wish. It matters not where I speak to you, only that I do."

As the clock struck eleven, I was strolling along the stacks of books, rearranging the few I saw were out of place and plucking my copy of *Belinda* off the shelf. I had the impression I would need a novel as a source of distraction tonight.

Lynton quietly opened and shut the door, arrogant and proud as always, but moving slowly. He sank down in a chair.

"Can we get some damned light in here?"

"Of course." I hurried to light another candle, reminding myself to exchange it in the morning for a fresh one. A used candle would alert my father that someone had been in this room. Not that he would suspect me necessarily, but I tried to spare the servants as much grief as possible. And I had no desire to explain my presence here.

Lynton watched me as I retrieved the candle. It was unsettling, and I became aware again that some might consider this meeting *very* improper. He was keeping his distance, however, and I did not sense any villainous intentions. Intentions of some kind, though, were quite apparent.

"I have watched you for some time, Miss Tilney."

"I know not what you mean."

"Pray, do not interrupt me. My spirits flag easily these days."

"Yes, sir."

"As I said, I have watched you for some time. You are a lady, well-dressed and elegant, mannerly—for the most part—and educated. Yet you have unfortunate relations: no mother living, a greedy father, a nefarious brother—what is his name again?"

"I have two brothers, my lord."

"Ah yes. The younger one is a clergyman. Not him. The soldier."

"Frederick?"

"As you say. They interest me not. You, on the other hand, do interest me a great deal."

"Again, I do not understand."

"We danced once before, do you remember?"

"I do."

"And do you remember what happened after? My brother confided the whole thing to me."

"I could never forget."

"You insulted me."

"My apology stands, sir—"

He waved my response away. "It is forgotten."

"I doubt that, or you would not have mentioned it."

Lynton laughed, a humorless bark that dissolved into a cough. "Touché, Miss Tilney. I do appreciate your forthright nature."

"Sir, if I may be so bold as to ask...why are we here?"

"I have come, hopefully, to find a wife—"

"Sir—" I was desperate to stop him.

He held up his hand to quiet me. "For my brother."

I sat, dumbfounded.

"Come, girl. I know he has offered."

"How...?"

"How did I know? He told me, of course. We are very different, but he is my brother. He manages my affairs and the family interests, and we are in each other's confidence. Always have been."

Lynton sat back in the chair, closed his eyes briefly. He really was a handsome man, but fast living was beginning to wear on him. He looked pale with dark circles under his eyes.

"If your brother has confided in you, I imagine he has also told you that our union is unlikely to take place in the near future."

"And what a fool you are for that. An affectionate heart is a rarity in our circles, and life is short. You may never again find a man like him, Miss Tilney."

"I know," I whispered, tears springing into my eyes. "He has no equal, in my opinion."

"Yet you refused his proposal."

"To be quite frank, I never received a proposal. We had discussed the future, of course, but when he finally came around to asking...well, he did not *ask*."

The viscount frowned, and I saw Jacob in his expression. "Now I do not comprehend *you*, madam."

"He wanted me to elope. He *proposed* I run off with him to Barbados."

"I see," he said, laughing.

"I fail to see the humor, sir."

"What? Oh, 'tis nothing—just amusing to hear of proper, obedient Jago suggesting something so scandalous. You have bewitched him! Who could have imagined such a thing?"

Torn between embarrassment and insult, I weighed my next words carefully. "Jacob does not—"

"Christian names. How intimate."

The viscount was laughing at me, at us, and I was not amused. It must have shown on my face, because he cleared his throat and his expression and said, "I beg your pardon. Do go on."

"Your brother does not understand what he asks of me. To acquiesce means I must leave everything and everyone I know."

"You are afraid," he accused me, just like his brother had.

I sat upright, jolted out of my sadness. "As I told your brother, I am not afraid! I do love Jacob, but I also love my family and my home. My answer was not a rejection of him. It was for the best. I did not want Jacob to ever feel guilt for severing the connections with my family, and I did not want to become resentful." Anger colored my voice. "Notice that your brother will not be giving up anything if we were to elope—not his living, his future home, his people. Jacob's only thought was for what he wanted at the moment. I must think about the likelihood of securing my best chance at happiness for a life-time—and of *his* contentment too, since he will not consider it for himself. Whom and when to marry are decisions that have far-reaching effects for ladies, much more so than for gentlemen. It could be a grave mistake to simply obey a rush of lover's emotion, no matter how strong that pull might be. To elope would be to abdicate my current life with all its benefits and struggles because my father will not approve a match with your brother."

"Your father is as much a fool as you are. My brother manages the affairs of the Earl of Sanborn. Under Jago's supervision, the family coffers have doubled, tripled perhaps, in an era when many of the great estates are being drained by the idleness and dissipation of gentlemen heirs who have no concept of stewardship. My brother has more resources at his disposal than many a viscount or marquess."

"It is not only finances. However misguided he might be, my father desires a title for his daughter. It is foolish, perhaps, but it is his wish and, due to his parental power over me, his wishes remain paramount."

"Will you grant him his wish, then? Will you give up my brother for a title from some idle peer in the future?"

"No, I would not bend to my father's wishes and marry another. And I have offered to release your brother to find his happiness elsewhere. It would not be fair to do otherwise, but…"

"Go on."

I wrung my hands in my lap. "He said *he* will not release *me*."

"I see you have discovered the obstinate side of his character," he said, amused.

"If, however, Jacob changes his mind and decides to marry someone else, I shall remain unmarried."

"The perpetual, nominal mistress of Northanger Abbey?"

"Is that so terrible a fate?"

He sighed. "I suppose not."

"To marry for title or money without affection will introduce more problems than living under my father's roof—which has its own significant set of problems, I assure you."

"And when your father dies?"

"He will probably live forever."

The viscount laughed.

"However, when that time arrives, I will go the route of many a spinster and rely upon my brothers for my care."

"And never marry?"

"I cannot imagine myself marrying another, for my heart is with Jacob. I do not foresee that ever changing. And that is my fate."

To my great surprise, the viscount leaned forward and placed a hand on mine, pressed it.

"I see the attraction. For my brother, I mean. I see why he loves you. You and he are very much alike. He would appreciate the steadfast nature you display, the real elegance, the integrity you live by. He would want, not just a wife, but a friend, a partner. That is his way. And apparently it is yours as well."

He sat back. "I am here to tell you that you should reconsider your fate and prepare yourself."

"My lord?"

"My brother will return to you and ask again—and I shall counsel him to *ask* this time. I know not when, exactly, but it will not be too terribly long. I have spoken with him at length about this. You see, Jago will be my father's heir, not me."

"Sir?"

"I am dying."

"I—I do not know what to say, my lord."

"It is a heart ailment, they tell me, brought on by a childhood illness. My brother escaped the infection, just so you know. He was at home with my mother at the time I contracted the fever. He is safe."

"I am in shock. And so, so sorry."

"Well, you may be the only one, besides Jago, to say that and mean it, which speaks well of your kindness. And I think perhaps, under the circumstances, since you are likely to be the closest thing to a sister I shall ever have, you should call me Edward."

"I could not."

"If you please, it would bring me comfort, in the absence of my brother, to have a friend with whom to converse openly about my family, my wishes. My situation is not common knowledge among society, and I would appreciate your discretion about this matter. I have no wish to hear of the *ton*'s snide comments about my imminent demise."

"You have my word."

His noble persona returned. "Very well, then. You should return to your rooms. It is late, and I am tired."

"Should I send a servant to assist you?"

"For heaven's sake, do not ruin our secret now, and do not treat me as an invalid. There will be time for that soon enough."

He rose and executed a stiff bow. "Good night, Miss Tilney." His face softened. "Eleanor."

~

CHRISTMAS NIGHT

"Eleanor! Where are you, girl? I demand to see you in my study! Now!" His voice rose with each imperative.

I hurried down the stairs and into my father's domain, quietly closing the door behind me. Over the years, I had developed the fortitude to weather the general's tirades and whims. My mother had seen to it, and Henry had encouraged it, teaching me to know my own mind and let the sharp bite of our father's words wash over me and out the door. Henry was fond of saying, "Northanger Abbey is no place for timid women." And yet, every time my father shouted for me, my stomach still leapt into my throat.

"Yes, sir?"

"You were seen conversing with Viscount Lynton at the Monforts' Christmas dinner tonight. And last month, at the Thompsons' party, Lynton escorted you into supper."

"You seem to be extremely interested in my conversation partners."

"Of course. You have been out for three seasons. I expected that you would have accepted an offer by this point, and yet no suitable gentleman has applied to me for your hand."

"Perhaps said gentleman is planning to ask me first."

The general snorted. "Whitman tells me a servant girl heard you talking with the viscount in private when he stayed here last October. What are your plans for securing him? He would be an acceptable match."

"Acceptable? To whom?"

"To me. And to you, if you have any sense at all."

"Because he is titled."

"I want my grandson to be an earl."

"Yes, I am aware."

"Eleanor! You exasperate me! Has the viscount taken an interest? Has he declared himself to you?"

I walked over to the book shelf and swiped my hand across it, rubbing the dust off my fingers and frowning. "Hannah needs to dust in here. I will remind her."

"There is no need for you to do that."

"It is my responsibility as mistress of the house."

"It is my bloody study, and I will send for the stupid servant girl when I like! Answer me about Lynton."

"I enjoy the viscount's company, but he has not declared himself."

"Well, there may still be hope. I understand he is to stay at Mount Eden for the foreseeable future. Seems he is looking to settle down, finally."

"Father, Viscount Lynton is unlikely to ask for my hand. We are friends, he and I, nothing more."

"But—"

"And even if he were to do so, I would decline."

"You would do no such thing, Daughter. Many successful marriages have been based on much less than friendship. When he proposes, you will do your duty to your family. It is for your own good as well."

I stiffened my spine. In my mind's eye, I saw my mother, pale and brittle as a sapling in the face of this man. My father was a giant oak, still imposing, even in his fifties, unmovable, unyielding. My brothers each took their respective methods of escape and planted themselves elsewhere, but I had not a gentleman's freedom. But no matter. I could not be an oak of a man like my father or a strong young tree like my beloved Jacob or my brothers. Yet I was not a delicate twig that snapped in the face of a storm either. I...

I was a willow, limber and resilient, my branches arching over my surroundings, providing shelter to myself and those under my care with the soft brush of nurturing foliage. I would not break; I would bend. And regardless of how the storm raged or the river ran, I would endure.

"Are you listening to me?" he bellowed. "You will not refuse Viscount Lynton's offer of marriage. I forbid it."

I looked my father square in the eye. "No, Father. You will not forbid it."

I turned and left the room.

~

Over the next several days, winter howled around the eaves of

Northanger Abbey, and I endured cold both outside and inside the house. My father's health continued to be a concern, as he struggled almost daily with his stomach complaints, making him even more irritable.

Three days into the new year, I stared out the window of my sitting room, pen poised above paper. Ice had formed in a crescent at the bottom of the modern windows, installed last summer at the general's insistence. Frost had visited in the night, painting a jungle of crystal leaves and swirls that put me in mind of the palms and exotic plants of the West Indies. It was flora I had never seen with my own eyes and might never see, but I felt I knew it from Jacob's letters, delivered via Edward through my friend Alice.

The imagined warmth of Caribbean sunshine faded into a brittle image in my mind's eye as a gust of freezing wind rattled the window pane. I shivered and tugged my shawl tighter around my shoulders.

I had just enough time to dash off a response to Jacob before the general rose and made whatever demands he saw fit to inflict on me that day. Since my declaration that I would not have Viscount Lynton, my father had become even more abrasive, usurping my authority with the servants, dining with me in cold silence. Henry, bless him, had made more frequent visits to the abbey, attempting to mitigate my father's increased cruelty by serving as a jovial, if rather masculine, lady's companion.

Yet I was unmoved by my father's coldness. No, I did not wait in anticipation of the viscount's passing, for that sad event might occur in months or perhaps not for years. I knew that, independent of his brother's health, Jacob was working toward our future, building his own resources as an arsenal to burn away my father's disapproval. I remained steadfast to my purpose, held onto my dreams, yet remained flexible to the circumstances that blew in from far-off places. I kept the faith that happiness would find me, in time. Until that day, I would do my best to create joy on my own.

I leaned over my paper and began to write.

3 January 1809

Dearest,

I hope this finds you in good health and good spirits. I find myself at leisure but lonely this morning. Dear Henry has been visiting with us during the

Christmas holiday and left us only day before yesterday. His company was a boost to my happiness, as it always is. Yet as I observe how winter has covered the Abbey's courtyard with a snowy blanket, I feel as if I am smothered in winter's bleakness as well. I miss my brother fiercely and long for the time that he will return to imbue this cold place with his warmth and humor. It is, as you are undoubtedly aware from the rest of my letters, a rather solitary existence for a woman here at Northanger Abbey. I understand now what my mother must have often felt living in this place, surrounded by the cool efficiency of servants and the luxury of improvements bought with her money but without her agreement.

And I descend into a place that is no good for either of us. Forgive me. You are far from home, and I should write to you of happy things.

Henry has conjured the idea of spending the winter and spring in Bath, and I have to say, his notion is a good one. Dr. Newton believes the waters would help our father's digestive ailments and his spirits and, I confess, a stay at Bath would boost my own spirits as well. To be amongst a crush at the Pump Room! To walk along the paths by the river! To meet old friends and conceivably find new ones. The notion has great appeal for a young lady whiling away the time until her dearest friend returns.

Henry plans to journey ahead to secure lodgings, so maybe I can sway the general and convince him of the merits of such a trip. I do not anticipate that will be a pleasant task, so I will save it for later today. This morning, I find my mind engaged elsewhere, in the warm seaside town of Bridgeport, perhaps? How I wish I might see it, and you, sometime soon! The isolation of Northanger this winter is hard to bear. Since I cannot be with you, I will console myself with a family venture to Bath.

Be well, my love, and return to me, hearty and hale. Until that time, rest assured that I will be forever yours,

E

~

JUNE 1809

"I have brought you a gift, Mrs. Grantham, I mean, my dear viscountess." My husband of only one fortnight executed a courtly little bow, which made me laugh.

"You know perfectly well I would have been content as Mrs. Grantham for the rest of my days."

He laid a thin, velvet box on the dresser. "Open it."

I opened the box and gasped at the contents. "Jacob, how exquisite! I've never seen anything like it."

"I found it in Bridgeport. A pink pearl is a rare thing—like a woman who will wait for a headstrong second son—so I thought it a fitting gift. I admit, when I first saw it, I thought of presenting it to you in order to send your father a message—to show him I could provide everything you might need or want, even luxuries such as this. I fancied he would immediately grant my request to marry his only daughter when he saw it."

"Well, it is lovely, and I much prefer this setting for gift-giving."

"Not a general in sight. Thank goodness." Jacob took the pearl, mounted in a gold setting, and placed it around my neck, fastening it with his large but nimble fingers. "I find, however, that I am still disgruntled."

"Why are you disgruntled, my love?"

"Because despite all my hard work to improve my standing in the world, safeguard my family's investments, and generally make myself acceptable, the reason I attained your hand in such a timely fashion was because I lived up to my namesake and took my brother's title."

I gazed in the mirror at him, this strong, capable man, a much better catch than any peer I had ever met. "Your work, a labor you took upon yourself in part for the love of a woman, has made you more desirable to me than any title, I assure you."

"You flatter me, Eleanor."

"I speak only the truth. Besides, you are not a supplanter, no matter what you think your name might mean. You are the steward and guide of your family, and you should take pride in that."

He ran a finger absently along the chain. "I miss Edward."

"As do I, although I only really knew him for a short time."

"He would have been a good brother to you, in spite of what you may have heard about him."

"While you were away, he and I became better acquainted, enough for me to know you are right. He was fond of you and kind to me because of it."

"His illness influenced his character and overshadowed the good man he could have become, had he lived."

"We will always remember his reputation in society was only part of his story."

"He was callous toward others, perhaps, but never toward me. He could have been bitter, but he chose to put events in motion that would improve my life. Near the end, he wrote me I was his legacy and I should live life to the fullest measure because he could not."

"Your brother took a tragedy and did his best to preserve the family while he could."

I paused, standing and turning to face him. "I have come to a decision."

I leaned back to take the lips that were already descending to my own. When he raised his head, I stepped away.

"Come back, wife," he growled, pulling me toward him. "I want to see how your necklace looks without your gown."

"I must tell you. I have come to a decision."

"What decision is this? And can we talk about it later?"

"We certainly will discuss it at length, but I want to tell you now."

His arms dropped to rest at his sides, amusement gathering in his expression. His eyebrow lifted. "Yes?" he said with patience.

"When we return from Ireland, I want to visit Northanger Abbey. I must speak with my father."

"Whatever for?"

"He and my brother Henry are estranged because of Father's infamous treatment of Henry's Miss Morland. I told you of Miss Catherine Morland?"

"You did."

"Henry and Catherine have formed an attachment. They would like to marry—"

"And your father does not approve. I can see how a daughter might have to bend to her father's will, but that is no excuse for an independent man with his own living. Your brother must stand up to your father, as a man should."

"Henry did stand up to him, I mean, he does. It is not the general who is preventing the marriage. It is the Morlands. They are reluctant to give their consent when they know Father is against Catherine. I am in Father's good graces, thanks to our marriage and, in honor of your brother, I want to attempt to heal the breach in my family."

"Wise and kind is the new Viscountess Lynton."

"I once told Edward I was the 'nominal mistress' of Northanger Abbey. Maybe, as a married woman, I have enough authority to affect real change for my family's happiness."

~

OCTOBER 1809

The carriage pulled into the drive and the coachman reined the horses to a halt. I playfully pushed my husband away by resting my palm against his chest and began to rearrange my hair. I had begun carrying a small mirror for just this purpose and retrieved it from my reticule. The jewels in my wedding ring, another piece selected for me in the West Indies, glinted in the sunlight as we descended the carriage.

Father greeted us stiffly like the old oak he was, and Jacob returned the formality. But I extended the gentle greeting of the willow in the wind, offering tranquility and peace. I had a mission: to soften my father's harsh opinion of Henry and Catherine and, no matter how the storm raged or the river ran, I knew I would endure.

KAREN M COX is an award-wining author of five novels accented with romance and history: *1932, Find Wonder in All Things, Undeceived, I Could Write a Book,* and *Son of a Preacher Man,* as well as a novella companion to *1932, The Journey Home.* She also contributed short stories for the anthologies *Sun-Kissed: Effusions of Summer, The Darcy Monologues,* and *Dangerous to Know: Jane Austen's Rakes & Gentlemen Rogues.* Originally from Everett, Washington, Karen now lives in Central Kentucky with her husband, works as a pediatric speech pathologist, encourages her children, and spoils her granddaughter.

THE EDIFICATION OF LADY SUSAN

JESSIE LEWIS

LADY SUSAN VERNON

As the young, unmarried daughter of an earl, she learns from those who ought to be teaching her better that one must manipulate the world to achieve one's desires. Though she later earns the reputation as a practiced seductress, her rational yet *selfish* instincts effortlessly yield success, even at this tender age. *"Lady Susan does not confine herself to that sort of honest flirtation which satisfies most people but aspires to the more delicious gratification of making a whole family miserable."* —Letter IV, *Lady Susan*.

THE EDIFICATION OF LADY SUSAN

Letter 1
LADY SUSAN BEAUMONT TO MISS ALICIA FFORDHAM

Kirkbank

My dear friend, I have ever admired your fortitude and patience, but my own, as you well know, is wanting by comparison. I urge you, therefore, to hasten your recovery and join me here directly. Claire has been insufferable company ever since she resolved to fall in love with one of her brother's dinner guests last Tuesday. You are familiar with him—your cousin's favourite playfellow Mr. Frederick Vernon—thus I shall not attempt to sketch his character except to say that he is younger and less dour than I have heard you describe him.

Of far more moment, and the foremost reason I require your immediate presence, is the astonishing alteration to be seen in Claire's brother, and his behaviour towards me. Do you recall that when we all visited last, Lord Doyle was a rather ungainly, pimpled thing, who never spoke but to complain and would certainly never deign to engage with his younger sister's friends? What a difference a few years make! He is quite the handsomest gentleman now, and more than willing to speak to me at length on whatever subject I choose. He has singled me out for several walks in the garden and two rides in his curricle thus far this week.

Would that you were here to confirm my suspicions, Alicia, for I am almost certain that he is beginning to fall in love with me. Were I the sort of girl to lose her head over such matters, I might be in some danger. Instead, I find myself almost overcome with an intoxicating sense of power, for he is uncommonly attentive to my every move. (Learning which moves to make was the work of a moment. I simply acted in a manner wholly contrary to Claire, whose attempts to entice Mr. Vernon have thus far proved fruitless at best, mortifying at worst.) I have been used to men's indifference to my company; I cannot express my intrigue at suddenly being of enough interest to one that he should go out of his way to please me. It makes me wonder what I might make him do.

I insist that you cease reading this instant and avail yourself of more spa waters to hasten your recovery and travel hither. Your assistance in my study of the matter cannot happen soon enough.

Yours ever,

S. BEAUMONT

Letter 2
THE DOWAGER COUNTESS OF WITHINGTON TO LADY SUSAN BEAUMONT

Great Mandeley

Dearest daughter, I feel justified in neglecting any enquiries as to whether you are enjoying your visit since I have been informed directly by Lady Doyle that you are. And may I say how delighted I am to hear of your blossoming intimacy with her son. It has long been our hope that you and Teddington might one day be married—increasingly so as we have watched you grow into remarkably similar characters. I daresay, a more sportive, liberal husband you will not easily find, and you will need all those qualities in a husband if he is to tolerate your perpetual disdain for the world and all its inhabitants.

Do not mistake me, my dear; I could better endure an eternity of your contempt than suffer another moment of Charlotte's lamentable docility. She inches towards her confinement with ever-increasing timidity for which I can summon no patience. This morning she verily sobbed into her toast upon receiving word that Samuel means to remain in London for another month. I might be persuaded to think it *my* company to which she objects but that her utter feeble-mindedness leaves me in no doubt of her possessing an unwholesome reliance upon her husband's society.

Were it not for your present pursuit, I might insist that you return home to dilute her company, but I shall not ask it of you. Lord knows I have tolerated worse, and you must concentrate on the task at hand. Lady Doyle has assured me she will facilitate every possible opportunity for you and her son to be together. I strongly encourage you to take advantage of her approbation. Teddington is not known for over-thinking his decisions; thus, you must act while his interest is piqued if you are to secure him.

In anticipation,

C. WITHINGTON

Letter 3

MISS ALICIA FFORDHAM TO LADY SUSAN BEAUMONT

Albermarle Gate

Dearest Susan, How I envy you! Here I am, trapped within doors, drinking foul-tasting water, and coughing myself insensible every moment, and there you are, in the very best of company and holding court over them all. Your success in that regard is of no surprise to me. Your talent for beguiling has ever exceeded the world's at large. It still amazes me that you inveigled yourself into Lady Carmarthen's soiree at the age of but thirteen. Still, I am eaten up with jealousy at forfeiting my share in such diversions on account of a glorified cold.

Since I cannot share in your fun, I insist you share yours with me. You must write to me with your every discovery: What conversation pleases him best? What charms reap the finest response? Precisely what *can* you make him do?

What a joke it would be if I set you a challenge in each letter to test your supposed power over him! Today, I dare you to make him lend you the use of his coat. I witnessed Mr. Johnson drape his about Miss Longshaft's shoulders outside the assembly rooms at home, and it positively outraged all the relics.

Bon chance, mon amie. Enjoy your flirtations and write soon with news of your success, ere I go distracted with *ennui*.

Yours ever,

ALICIA

Letter 4
LADY WITHINGTON TO LORD WITHINGTON

Great Mandeley

My lord, I beg you would come home. Or at least allow me to join you in Town. Your mother grows more detestable by the day. She takes delight in my increasing discomfort and teases me constantly for my inelegance. I should have liked to think I might receive some partiality on account of providing her first grandchild, but she treats me the same as she treats everybody else—abominably. She is uncivil to her neighbours, impatient with callers, and vile to the servants. She threatened to cast out the poor housekeeper because of a stain on the carpet that was left when she herself threw a glass of wine at the footman.

Not even Susan is exempt from her cruelty, for she is scheming to make her marry Lord Doyle. *Lord Doyle!* I would not wish that man on any woman, not even your sister. Your mother is completely devoid of compassion. You cannot truly mean to abandon me to her clutches for another month? Pray, make haste and return to me as soon as you are able.

Yours ever,

CHARLOTTE

Letter 5

LADY SUSAN BEAUMONT TO MISS ALICIA FFORDHAM

Kirkbank

Your jealousy is unfounded, Alicia. I hold court over nobody. Lord Doyle is not in love with me. My brother has written, warning me that his friend's reputation about Town is that of an incorrigible rake. I was never of any value to him, other than a means to indulge his own sense of importance. Worse still, his attentions have convinced the world that I wish to marry him! Why it should be assumed that a young woman's greatest aspiration should be marriage I shall never understand. Of course, *one day* I shall marry, else I should have to live with Samuel and his mouse of a wife for the remainder of my days—few though they would then be, for that is the best method of which I can conceive of robbing a woman of her will to live. I have no wish to shackle myself to the first single man across whom I stumble, however, and certainly not one whose credibility has been exposed as wanting.

Neither my mother nor his can suspect Lord Doyle of such dissipation as my brother describes, else they would never have encouraged the match. Yet Samuel has ever had the measure of his set and I would be a fool not to heed his warning. I am furious at my own credulity! To think I had convinced myself capable of influencing him! Nevertheless, one ought always to search for the profit in any situation; thus, I shall say this of the matter: if he *is* a rake, all the better for me, for it will relieve me of any guilt I might otherwise have felt in working on him.

Be not alarmed by this declaration. The explanation is simple. I see no reason why I should not make him love me, given that so many people deem me capable of it. It is no worse than his toying with me. Indeed, it would be fine retribution for his duplicity were I to make him love me in earnest, only to abandon him for the next man. And as fortune would have it, just such recourse has recently become a possibility. In his letter, Samuel made mention of another of his friends, Mr. Cohen. "If marriage is your design, Sister," wrote he, "might I suggest another option?" It was not my design, of course; yet what an opportunity to punish Lord Doyle and, at the same time, test the efficacy of my newly learned charms! Samuel has promised to bring Mr. Cohen to Great Mandeley when I return next month. I insist that you do whatever it is you must to hasten your recovery that you might join me there to set all the challenges you please.

Yours &c.,

S. BEAUMONT

Letter 6

MISS ALICIA FFORDHAM TO LADY SUSAN BEAUMONT

Albermarle Gate

Dear Susan, I wish it were in my power to congratulate you on your forthcoming acquaintance with Mr. Cohen, but alas, I must spoil your anticipation with unwelcome news. Your brother cannot have heard, but it will not be long before it is universally known: his friend Mr. Cohen has recently become engaged to none other than our very own dear Jennifer! They met in Surrey some weeks ago and are rumoured to be violently in love.

Pray, be not distressed by this small disappointment, for I am convinced that had he met you first, he would never have noticed Jennifer, for she has not half your wit and none of your looks, the poor dear. I daresay, with your cleverness and beauty, you could make any man love you, should you so choose. Even the incorrigible Lord Doyle.

I have felt stronger these past few mornings. If my convalescence continues thus, I might be able to join you at Kirkwood before you leave. Wish me well!

Yours ever,

ALICIA

Letter 7

LORD WITHINGTON TO LADY SUSAN BEAUMONT

Grosvenor Square

Upon my word, Sister, you concern yourself too much with idle talk. There is no formal engagement between Mr. Cohen and Miss Garrick. I grant you there was a passing rumour arising from the silliest of incidents that occurred whilst they were at Dundishead together, but nothing that could not be easily overlooked were Cohen to turn up engaged elsewhere. You are young yet—too young to comprehend the customary manoeuvrings of our set—but rest assured, it is all perfectly regular. Nobody will blink an eye.

I cannot impress upon you earnestly enough how well you would do with Cohen. Of course, you need not take my word for it, only pray do not dismiss him before you have met. Send word when you are for home. I shall send him to you, and I daresay you will thank me for it.

Yours &c.,

SAMUEL

Letter 8
THE DOWAGER COUNTESS OF WITHINGTON TO LORD WITHINGTON

Great Mandeley

Samuel, I shall not attempt to describe my vexation at the news of your officious interference. Not since you came of age have I taken the liberty of intervening in your affairs. Not when you chose to sell my dowager house to pay for your new—and, I might add, still empty—orangery. Not when you drunkenly invested half your fortune in the *West* India Trading Company. Not when you married the milksop of a woman presently polluting my home with her endless melancholy. Throughout every stupid decision you have made since your father's death, I have kept my own counsel and respected your position as the head of this family. I demand, therefore, that you do not presume to interfere in *my* affairs—particularly those that jeopardise the very future of our family.

I have had it from Charlotte that you are attempting to poison your sister's mind against a union with Lord Doyle and are instead pushing her into an alliance with the morally corrupt man you call a friend, Mr. Cohen. I scarcely dare imagine why you might be pursuing such a course of action but, whatever your motive, it cannot be as imperative as mine. Lord Doyle is on the brink of destroying his family's reputation. If Susan does not marry him and salvage what is left of it, Lady Doyle has threatened to reveal to the world how your father almost ruined our own good name. It is her favourite pastime to remind me how she saved us on that occasion. Believe me, she would have no qualms whatsoever about reversing her schemes and allowing our reputation to be dashed along with hers.

I have long since accepted that you will do nothing to preserve our good name, but not while I live to draw breath will you prevent your sister from doing *her* duty to us all. For if not her, who else is left? Lord Doyle may be something of a Lothario, but he is young, handsome, and lively—something you are quite alone in not desiring in your partner in life. And if he is rich enough to be as profligate as rumour would have him without diminishing his coffers, then he is worth having. Besides, your sister is a frightful thing, all sauce and no civility. If Lord Doyle is willing to have her, then more's the advantage, for you will not be lumbered with her for the rest of your days.

I trust this matter is now settled, and that I can expect your support in encouraging the match.

Yours in good faith,

C. WITHINGTON

Letter 9

LORD WITHINGTON TO LADY SUSAN BEAUMONT

Grosvenor Square

Sister, I write to you with the utmost urgency having this moment received the alarming news that you are persisting in encouraging Lord Doyle's attentions. I beg you would not. Indeed, I am bemused as to why you should doubt the earnestness of my caution. Lord Doyle is a rogue—a diverting enough fellow with whom to play at cards, aye, but not a man to whom I would entrust my sister. Moreover, be not fooled into believing he has duped either our mother or his own. I assure you, they are both well aware of his character. I am sorry to pain you, but in this instance, Mother has not your best interests at heart.

You will recall the troubles our family endured in the years preceding Father's death, and how they were miraculously resolved, our reputation saved and fortunes restored? Have not you ever wondered how that rescue came about? Lady Doyle was the architect of our salvation then, and now that Mother sees her friend in similar straits, she wishes to repay the favour. Her son, you see, has done more damage to his family's good name in the one year since his father passed away than our father managed in the two decades of his decline into debt. If Lord Doyle were to marry—and marry *well*—it would shore up the family's credibility ere he can do further damage. You, Susan, present the perfect solution to Lady Doyle's predicament and therefore, also, Mother's moral obligation.

Let not this revelation distress you, for there is a painless remedy available. Mother could not compel you to marry Lord Doyle were you to marry elsewhere first. In that regard, allow me to reiterate my previous recommendation: I cannot conceive of a better husband for you than Mr. Cohen. His character would complement yours in every way conceivable. Where you are amusing, he is easily amused; where you are assured of your opinions, he is in dire need of somebody to tell him what his are; where you are clever, he is obscenely rich. Send word when you return to Great Mandeley and I shall arrange for him to visit you there without delay.

Your humble servant,

SAMUEL

Letter 10

THE DOWAGER COUNTESS OF WITHINGTON TO LADY SUSAN BEAUMONT

Great Mandeley

Susan, I am wounded that you should think me capable of having any other motive than the sincerest concern for your happiness. Have not I ever been the most indulgent of mothers? You suffered none of the overbearing obtrusions to which so many parents subject their progeny.

Other children are enslaved to this master or that, forced to learn languages they will never use or embroider samplers upon which no soul will ever set eyes. You were left entirely to your own devices, to engage in whichever pursuits you chose, completely free of any intervention from your father or me—sometimes for years at a time.

Let not my allusion to your ingratitude cause you any distress— children are never appreciative of the things their parents provide, only those which they are denied. Only allow it to convince you that your happiness is my paramount concern. Of course, I shall not deny that a match between you and Lord Doyle would answer the very great debt I owe to my friend, but I would be dismayed if one happy coincidence were enough to make my dearest daughter doubt her mother's lifelong regard.

Allow me to end with a repetition of my previous endorsement. Teddington is truly an excellent match for you. Not often does one find such a mix of handsomeness, fashion, levity and wealth united in one person. That our families are on such excellent terms only enhances the prospect.

Yours affectionately,
C. WITHINGTON

Letter 11
LADY SUSAN BEAUMONT TO MISS ALICIA FFORDHAM

Kirkbank

My dearest friend, What a blow that your symptoms should have worsened, just when you believed yourself to be improving at last! Persevere with the waters, even if they do taste foul. I daresay many a less deserving person has benefitted from their restorative effects and besides, I need you here, not languishing by a smelly puddle in your bedclothes.

I cannot agree with your opinion of my mother's intentions, though I thank you for your attempts to make her behaviour appear less objectionable. Regrettably, there is no concealing her true motivation, or that she considers me fool enough to believe her prevarications. She is wrong on one account, however. I *am* grateful—eminently so—for her indifferent approach to mothering. It saved me innumerable excruciating hours in her company.

You would not credit it, but my mother is not alone in her desire for me to marry Lord Doyle. Claire has expressed a similar wish. Her purpose is no less self-seeking than my mother's, though at least she had the decency to be honest. Indeed, she could scarcely hide the truth of it for we both overheard the conversation that induced her to ask it of me. Mr. Vernon's father, it seems, does not look favourably on a match between Claire and his son.

He arrived, quite unexpectedly, two days ago, demanding an audience with Lady Doyle. Claire and I listened at the door, she, anticipating that he had come to offer his consent, and I rather surprised that she thought her consequence great enough to warrant such attention. The disappointment was hers, of course. "I am shocked to discover where my son has been spending all his time," said the gentleman, in none too gentlemanlike terms to Lady Doyle. "Though not as shocked to hear where your son has been spending all of his." (Lord Doyle, I understand, is a frequent visitor to several insalubrious establishments about Town.) "He is depraved," he went on. "My son will never marry into your family whilst it is on the brink of ruin." He concluded with a demand that Lady Doyle prevent her children inviting him to Kirkbank ever again.

One wonders that he had not the authority to simply forbid his son from accepting their invitations. He is not in good health, by the looks of him. Mayhap his influence diminishes with his health. Such delicious independence his son must possess! I confess I am rather intrigued—but I digress.

The product of these overhearings was Claire's plea that I should marry her brother to secure her family's reputation and redeem her romance. She sees no disadvantage to me in his behaviour. When I remarked upon his profligacy, she replied that it did not seem to trouble any of the other women with whom he keeps company and that she could not see why it should trouble me. It occurs to me that sentiments such as these will not please Mr. Vernon half as well as she thinks.

As you see, I am beset with other people's concerns, none of which bear any relevance to my own. Nevertheless, I shall continue to entertain Lord Doyle's flattery whilst I remain here, for it pleases me to observe his increasing interest and will please at least three of the people who would govern my heart into compliance.

Yours ever,

S. BEAUMONT

Letter 12
MISS JENNIFER GARRICK TO LADY SUSAN BEAUMONT

Crimble Hall

Susan, I am all incredulity! I have had it from Alicia that Claire has set her cap at Mr. Vernon! That she could be so heartless as to accept attentions from a man with whom she *knows* I have been in love for an *age*, the very *moment* she hears my name in conjunction with another man's—it is intolerable!

I am not in love with Mr. Cohen, violently or otherwise. Indeed, at present, my strongest sentiment towards him is vexation, for had he not been so resolutely bent on proving his mastery of shuttlecock, our exceedingly brief and perfectly insignificant little encounter would never have come about, and my father would not be insisting that we marry! I have no desire whatsoever to be his wife, Susan; he is a simpleton. He finds amusement in absolutely everything, no matter how prosaic, and has the most inane, effeminate laugh, it would drive me to distraction to hear it at every moment. He is as fickle as a weathervane in a storm, and he is only rich because he is better at cards than all his friends. It is beyond *everything* that Claire should steal my only chance of escaping such a torturous alliance by purloining the only available alternative. I beg you would speak to her on my behalf and make her desist her flirtations!

Better yet, perhaps you could turn your attentions to Mr. Cohen? You could win him over in an instant, I know! Then I would be free of him entirely (for he would be in love with you and not even my father's remonstrations could convince him to forsake you), and I could focus my efforts on securing Mr. Vernon before Claire ensnares him. Now that I think on it, I believe you would do rather well with Mr. Cohen. Notwithstanding his juvenility, he is exceedingly good looking and has a generosity of spirit that not even you could outspend. Mayhap it is not such a silly idea—you ought to give it consideration. In the meantime, pray let it be known to Claire, in that clever way you have, that I am seriously displeased.

Yours &c.,

JENNIFER

Letter 13

LADY SUSAN BEAUMONT TO MISS ALICIA FFORDHAM

Kirkbank

How I long to return to the world in which I lived but a fortnight ago, when it was only the delinquent sons of other families with no honour to their name. Seven days on and I must acknowledge there is little honour left in the world at all, and my own family have exhausted what meagre share they had of it to begin with. If my mother's schemes were not hateful enough, my brother's motivations for promoting the match with Mr. Cohen have now been exposed as equally duplicitous!

Yesterday, after dinner, the gentlemen invited Claire and me to play cards with them. My late father's near ruin has taught me better, and I declined the invitation. Thinking myself very wise, I was taken aback when my refusal drew their laughter. When asked to explain what diverted them, Lord Doyle suggested my brother ought to have learned his lesson as well. So it was that I became aware of Samuel's gambling debts, the majority of which he apparently owes to—you will never guess—Mr. Cohen!

The coincidence is too great to ignore; I cannot believe my brother's indebtedness to that man is unrelated to his desire that I should marry him. I am forced to conclude that he is as guilty as my mother of attempting to auction me off to settle his obligations. From there, reason leads me to suspect that Mr. Cohen wishes to wed me only to escape his entanglement with Jennifer—and *that* leaves me no other choice than to conclude they are all the most inconceivable imbeciles. That two grown people should inadvertently find themselves unhappily shackled to one another, quite without any deliberation on either's part, is almost as absurd as my brother's notion that I should have the slightest desire to marry one of them, or that I would not discover his attempts to trick me into doing so. Add to this both Claire and Jennifer's flagrant pleas that I sacrifice my happiness to save theirs, and I am quite done with the whole matter of marriage.

Yours in disgust,

S. BEAUMONT

Letter 14

MISS ALICIA FFORDHAM TO LADY SUSAN BEAUMONT

Albermarle Gate

Would that I were there to champion you, Susan! It is the hardest thing in the world that you should be so ill used by everyone closest to you—by everyone whose purpose in life ought to be to cherish and protect you. You ought not have to suffer it, but what can you do? We little women are powerless against our fathers, our brothers, and even our mothers, apparently. That such an intelligent, witty creature as you should be reduced to naught more than a pawn in such games is shameful. Truly you are wasted on your family, Susan, they do not deserve you.

At least at present, it is merely suggestion and cajolery. Pray another recourse presents itself before it turns into downright insistence. I regret I am wholly without any recommendation, though I hope you know I am at your disposal should you devise a way in which I may be of service.

Yours ever,

ALICIA

Letter 15

FROM SAME TO THE SAME

Albermarle Gate

I ought to have known *you* would not be powerless against anybody! Your scheme is a splendid one, and I cannot conceive of a single person more apt to engineer such an outcome. Nothing could please me more than to be of assistance. You may rely upon both my help and my utmost discretion. I have passed on your letter and will forward any response the moment I receive it.

Yours ever,

ALICIA

Letter 16
THE DOWAGER COUNTESS OF WITHINGTON TO LADY SUSAN BEAUMONT

Great Mandeley

My dear Susan, You hardly need ask if you may bring your friends home with you; they would be more than welcome. That Claire is your very particular friend is a source of great happiness to me (far better her than that frightful strumpet Miss Ffordham, with whom you insist on keeping company), and of course it makes perfect sense that Lord Doyle should accompany his sister as companion. The cleverness of such a ruse (for you ought not doubt that I perceive your true purpose of securing his affections) gives me great hope for your future felicity. A woman who can convince the world of her innocence whilst doing whatever she must to arrange it to her advantage has all the tools she will ever require to ensure her lasting comfort and happiness.

Yours proudly,

C. WITHINGTON

Letter 17
MISS JENNIFER GARRICK TO LADY SUSAN BEAUMONT

Crimble Hall

Dear Susan, I will admit to a good deal of consternation upon first reading your letter, but after further consideration have come to the very conclusion to which you wisely suggested I should. Mr. Vernon ought never to have been discouraged by something as trifling as my accidentally becoming engaged to somebody else. He evidently lacks the gumption to fight for me and therefore does not deserve me. That he is shamelessly misleading Claire despite his father's disapprobation gives me further reason to despise him. His must be a heart of stone!

I am gladdened to hear Claire will be returning with you to Great Mandeley. It will be for the best if she means to withstand his overtures. Rest assured, I am no longer angry with her. I see now it was Mr. Vernon who worked on her and not the reverse. I gladly accept your invitation to visit also, for I should dearly like to see her and commiserate over our shared misfortune. Your suggestion that I might find comfort in her loss being as great as my own is quite shocking! (Though if that should transpire to be true, then I trust my triumph will remain between you and me.)

In any case, a visit to Great Mandeley would be most welcome, for I live in hope that if I evade Mr. Cohen for long enough he might accidentally importune another, more grateful recipient.

Until next week,

JENNIFER

Letter 18

THE DOWAGER COUNTESS OF WITHINGTON TO LADY DOYLE

Great Mandeley

I received your note and am happy to report that you have absolutely no cause for alarm; Susan is working wonders on Teddington. Indeed, I should not be surprised if they were engaged within the se'nnight. Your troubles are nearly over, my dear, and what a relief to us all that will be.

I confess I am as relieved by my daughter's success as I know you must be. It has been some years now that I have despaired of what appeared to be her total want of mettle. I recognise that young girls in general are flimsy, useless things, but that *my* daughter should be so ineffectual, so *pointless*, has been inexpressively difficult to accept. These past few days I have observed ever more signs of my own resourcefulness and resolve in her, and it warms my heart to see it. She is by no means what I would call an accomplished coquette, but her activities of late have afforded me renewed faith in her chances of surviving this man's world.

Just yesterday, she contrived to turn her ankle in so convincing a manner that Teddington all but pinned her in his lap and rode with her directly to the front door. So scandalous was their attitude in the saddle that it was rather a shame the butler and I were the only witnesses, for it would have necessitated their immediate nuptials had they been observed by anyone else. One supposes, however, that with a reputation as fragile as your son's it would be best that he arrive at an alliance in a more conventional fashion.

More to the purpose, we all know Teddington has ridden in more scandalous ways with countless other women without feeling the urge to marry any of them; thus, it will please you to know how well Susan is working on his nobler sensibilities. Goodness knows how, but she is forever finding things for which to praise him, and he, being as vain as all other young men his age, puffs up further with every compliment. She may have begun late, but let it not be said that my daughter is not a fast learner.

I shall write again soon and anticipate that my next letter will contain exceedingly happy news.

Yours sincerely,

C. WITHINGTON

Letter 19
LADY WITHINGTON TO LORD WITHINGTON

Great Mandeley

My lord, I am resigned to your not soon returning home, though your absence grieves me all the same. I have been afforded some relief from your mother's tyranny at least, for Susan has returned home, and with her Lady Claire and her brother Lord Doyle, as well as Miss Garrick of Crimble Hall in Rochdale. The two young ladies are pleasanter company than their being favourites of your sister might reasonably lead one to expect. Lord Doyle is every bit as false as he was in Brighton. He showed no hint of embarrassment whatsoever when he saw me; thus, I presume he has forgotten that you and I were witness to his misadventure there.

Though he still makes love to everybody with the same brazenness as marked his character then, I must say he is exhibiting a tenderness for your sister of which I should never have believed him capable. If there is playing or singing to be done, he would have it done by her. They walk in the garden, whisper at the dinner table, and conspire in the drawing room all the day long, yet never seem in want of conversation. And do you recall how seriously it vexed him when Mr. Norris poked fun at his ridiculous hat? Yet Susan laughs at him openly for his every faux pas, sartorial or otherwise, and never once has he appeared piqued. I begin to suspect he might be in love with her.

I have tried to warn her against surrendering her heart to such an unscrupulous man, but of course she paid me no heed. "I thank you for your concern," she told me with a look that spoke more of her incredulity that I should have presumed to obtrude upon her business than of any real gratitude, "but I have no intention of surrendering my heart to him or any other man." She must know that her behaviour makes it seem as though she welcomes Lord Doyle's attentions! But if your mother has no interest in curbing her daughter's wanton coquetry, then I shall not waste my time attempting it. Neither of them will have any sympathy from me when Susan ends up shackled to the most dissipated rake in the country.

I hope you are enjoying yourself in Town. Your child grows livelier by the day, and we both grow increasingly anxious for your return.

Yours ever,

CHARLOTTE

Letter 20

LADY SUSAN BEAUMONT TO MISS ALICIA FFORDHAM

Great Mandeley

It will never cease to amaze me the stupidity of people. All I required of Lord Doyle was that he love me and, in doing so, concede that my worth was greater than his original estimation of it. Never satisfied with the abundance of what is readily available to them, it is the detestable vice of the over-indulged to always pursue more than is rightfully theirs. By which I mean, the petulant buffoon has proposed to me! Had I known he would jump from intrigue to admiration to *marriage* in less time than it takes to dance a quadrille, I should never have troubled myself with him. I could never marry a man so profoundly feeble-minded as to fall in love with me simply because I decided he should!

He has jeopardised all my carefully laid plans, Alicia! But I shall not be defeated so easily—certainly not by a man who can barely comprehend his own mind, let alone the exceedingly intricate workings of mine. Fortunately, I had already begun to work on him before this utter failure of common sense on his part. For the past week I have been drawing Jennifer more and more into our conversations, either by mention or in person. The foundations are in place; all that is required is to do away with subtlety, for it is lost on them both. They are so well suited to each other— both capricious, dissolute, and obtuse—that it cannot be long before each recognises his perfect partner in the other.

I thank you for the letter so cleverly concealed in your last. Pray pass on the enclosed reply, which I beg you would do me the very great favour of delivering in person, should you feel well enough to venture out. He is staying at the Kings Head in Bayshill. I have said all I need to in the letter to appeal to his heart but suspect his reason will be better worked on in the presence of your ever-persuasive countenance.

Yours ever,

S. BEAUMONT

Letter 21

LORD WITHINGTON TO LADY SUSAN BEAUMONT

Grosvenor Square

In the name of all that is holy, Susan, will you *for once* do what is asked of you! I could not have made it any clearer what misery would result from an alliance with Lord Doyle. Neither could I have stated more emphatically my wish that you acquaint yourself with Mr. Cohen.

Your determination to be the most contrary, disobliging young woman in the country is severely testing my will to indulge you. I have sent for Cohen; he is on his way to Great Mandeley. Do as you are bid and secure him, else you will receive not a farthing more in pin money 'til you find someone else to keep you.

LORD WITHINGTON

Letter 22

MISS ALICIA FFORDHAM TO LADY SUSAN BEAUMONT

Albermarle Gate

Of what was Mr. Cohen thinking to turn up without notice in that fashion? It would not matter if the King himself issued an invitation, common courtesy still behoves one to check with whomever is actually in residence. I must say, I think you can lay the blame at more doors than just your brother's and Mr. Cohen's. It can only have been that wretch Charlotte who informed Samuel of Lord Doyle's presence there. Has the horrid little vixen no allegiance to her fellow women? She is a disgrace. As for your brother, I am quite ashamed now of ever having considered him a good catch. He is a brute.

Describe to me, though, Jennifer's countenance when Mr. Cohen was introduced into the parlour. Did she blush terribly? Did Mr. Cohen? To come face to face so suddenly when both were at Great Mandeley to escape one another—what mortification must have been theirs! I am in awe of your talent for smoothing ruffled feathers. To have convinced each that their being under the same roof would not further imperil their chances of evading marriage to the other was quite the feat of persuasion. Your influence over everybody increases by the moment. I have no doubt whatever about your ability to enact the remainder of your scheme despite this small setback. It should not be difficult, for Claire and Mr. Cohen both appear to be operating on a similar echelon of fatuity. Your mother is a different matter; pray take care to keep her ignorant of your designs.

On a happier note, I have done as you asked, and the meeting went very well indeed. Rest assured, your letters have more than adequately achieved their purpose. He was delighted to learn of your imminent arrival and has postponed his planned departure to await you. His latest is enclosed.

All this conspiring has been far more efficacious than the gallons of revolting water I have been forced to take these past weeks. Were it not for my imperative duties to you here, I should feel perfectly well enough to join you at Great Mandeley. Instead, I shall look forward to seeing you whenever you are able to steal away.

Yours ever,

ALICIA

Letter 23
THE DOWAGER COUNTESS OF WITHINGTON TO LADY DOYLE

Great Mandeley

There is a frightful streak of rebellion in my daughter and a towering caprice in your son, neither of which I can commend, but which on this occasion have brought about a most felicitous outcome. Teddington is engaged to be married—you are saved!

You will have heard of the young lady. She is Miss Jennifer Garrick, daughter of Sir John Garrick of Crimble Hall in Rochdale. It is a family of considerable wealth and a conveniently nondescript reputation. They do not possess any great consequence, but a little anonymity might be just the thing at this juncture.

I confess the incident took me quite by surprise, for until yesterday it would have been impossible to convince me Teddy would soon forsake Susan. I dared turn my attention for but a few hours to make a house call, however, and by five o'clock, the wily baggage had managed to discourage him enough that he had invited Miss Garrick to ride out with him alone. It was Susan, the butler informs me, who then meddled with everyone's places at dinner such that Teddy was seated with Miss Garrick, of whose elaborately embroidered and exceedingly low neckline my daughter spent the entire six courses in praise. An after-dinner stroll in the gardens—and the entire twelve-hour courtship—was hastily concluded when Susan drew everybody's attention to Teddy's ungentlemanlike examination of Miss Garrick's embroidery beneath the horse chestnut.

I am furious with her, of course. She always has been a detestably wayward creature, and I have banished her from the house as punishment. She will learn to do as she is told, or she will find somebody else to put up with her! Her defiance notwithstanding, you must agree the result for Teddington could not have been happier. And since it came about under my roof, I trust you and I are now in harmony.

Yours most sincerely,

C. WITHINGTON

Letter 24

LADY CLAIRE WINTERBOTTOM TO LADY DOYLE

Great Mandeley

Dearest Mama, I write with the most wonderful news. I am engaged! His name is Mr. Cohen, and he is twice as handsome as Mr. Vernon and four times as rich. Brother has already given his consent, for he said he could think of no one he would rather have as a brother than somebody with Mr. Cohen's talent at cards.

I have quite forgotten Mr. Vernon. Susan has been a dear friend and led me gently to comprehend the dishonour of his insincere attentions. He travels often, Susan informs me; I should be forever alone while he journeyed about the country on business. I have seen loneliness thrust upon you by my father's passing, and I beg you would forgive me for saying that I do not wish such a forlorn existence for myself at such a young age. The very idea of being wife to Mr. Vernon seems anathema to me now.

Mr. Cohen is a wholly different prospect. I did not entirely approve of him when he first joined our party, for I had heard he was attached to Jennifer. But Susan explained all she knew about that and soon put my mind to rest—though what fool could mistake an innocent tumble into the bushes during a game of shuttlecock for an illicit tryst, I do not know! After that, it was the work of but a few days before I began to feel the stirrings of a deep and lasting affection for him. Indeed, how could one not love a man so content with all the world? He finds amusement in most things and, as Susan suggested, will not mind my ignorance of the classics, for he demands very little in the way of clever conversation. His smile is handsome, his fortune is great, and he has promised me a white mare as a wedding present—Mother, I am in love!

We shall travel to Kirkwood on the morrow for, notwithstanding Brother's permission, Mr. Cohen wishes to gain your blessing also. For that alone, I know you will love him as dearly as I do.

Yours affectionately,

CLAIRE

Letter 25

LORD WITHINGTON TO MR. COHEN

Grosvenor Square

My dear Cohen, May I be the first to congratulate you on your most felicitous engagement. Lady Claire is almost a sister to me, so long have our families been acquainted; thus it is with genuine pleasure that I welcome this news.

Fate evidently did not agree that you and my sister should be united, though I understand from Susan that she was instrumental in bringing you together with your future wife. I cannot express strongly enough my delight that your lasting future happiness *and* your salvation from that awkward unpleasantness with Miss Garrick occurred as a direct result of my efforts, and under my roof. I trust you agree that this settles the little matter of my debt to you.

Yours sincerely,
LORD WITHINGTON

Letter 26

LADY SUSAN VERNON TO MISS ALICIA FFORDHAM

Windermere

My dearest Alicia, If you could only see the views from my balcony! I have determined to bring you here one day, for you would create such masterpieces with your watercolours. It would be the least I could do to repay all your assistance these past weeks.

I thank you for arranging things so carefully. Mr. Vernon and I met precisely as planned. I had intended to present my concluding arguments for the alliance at that time, but it turned out to be unnecessary. He assured me I had quite bewitched him from the first moment we were introduced at Kirkbank. I own I went to some lengths whilst there to make a good impression—something Claire made infinitely easier for me by dint of being the most inept flirt in Christendom. She never was, he has since admitted, the reason for his repeated visits. Rather, it was my presence there—my "heavenly countenance" and "sublime wit"—that drew him back again and again, and only my apparent interest in Lord Doyle prevented him from declaring himself sooner. When we met, therefore, none of the methods of persuasion I had prepared to employ were necessary; he proposed to me on the spot.

We married last Tuesday and travelled here directly to honeymoon by the Lakes. Here we shall remain for a further two weeks before returning to London. His house there is not as light or airy as my previous establishment in Town, but his father is knocking stridently at death's door (of this I made certain before embarking on this venture); thus I have every reason to believe I shall be mistress of Vernon Castle by year's end. I hope it will be sooner, for there is something exceedingly spiteful about an aged relative who clings to life merely to deprive his progeny of their inheritance.

In any case, when his father does the honourable thing and dies, Frederick will inherit enough to make him richer than Mr. Cohen and Lord Doyle combined. I shall never want for pin money again—a fact that gave my brother no end of cheer, hence his hasty consent to the match. Indeed, the whole affair has worked out remarkably well, if I do say so myself. My mother will be delighted at never again having to pretend to a maternal affection she does not possess, for I cannot think of a reason for ever having to see her again. Charlotte will no doubt be vastly relieved that I will not be present to pollute her growing brood with my unfashionable independence.

I suppose my friends will not be quite so pleased. Claire will inevitably be disappointed in Mr. Cohen, for any man stupid enough to get himself accidentally engaged will not long evade further misfortune. And Jennifer will never be content with Lord Doyle, for any man who has known more women than she has had hot dinners will not long be satisfied with just one. It is of no consequence. I have as much concern for their happiness as they have shown for mine, and in any case, they ought none of them to be so effortlessly directed. I can barely think on such blind credulity without abhorrence and therefore declare that is as much thought as I am willing to give the matter.

My own circumstances could not have been more advantageously resolved. Mr. Vernon is away on business much of the time (another fact I took pains to discover early on); thus I am at liberty to do with my time what I wish. And what I wish is that you would stay with me to finish your convalescence and share the benefits of my new situation. It will be as though we are young again with no one to prevent us from doing as we please and all the money we could desire with which to do it.

Yours ever,

S. VERNON

JESSIE LEWIS enjoys words and wordplay far too much for her own good and was forced to take up writing to save her family and friends from her incessant rabbiting. She dabbled in poetry during her archetypal angst-ridden teenage years, but it was her studies in literature and philosophy at university that firmly established her admiration for the potency of the English language. She has always been particularly in awe of Jane Austen's literary cunning and has delighted in exploring Austen's regency world in her own historical fiction writing. You can check out Jessie's musings on the absurdities of language and life on her blog, **Life in Words**, or see what she's reading over at **Goodreads**. Or you can drop her a line on Twitter, **@JessieWriter** or on her Facebook page, **Jessie Lewis Author**.

ACKNOWLEDGMENTS

"There, I will stake my last like a woman of spirit. No cold prudence for me. I am not born to sit and do nothing. If I lose the game, it shall not be from not striving for it." —Mansfield Park

When assembling my dream team of authors for *Rational Creatures*, I wanted strong women, not just strong writers. Many thanks to the "**Sweet Sixteen**" who enthusiastically joined me on this adventure, wrote insightful/clever/witty/poignant stories, offered great feedback on the concept, cover, marketing, and countless particulars. Most of all, thank you for trusting me with your words. I'd go on a *Thelma & Louise* road trip with any of you!

I was not a little star struck meeting **Dr. Devoney Looser** (acclaimed author and editor, 2018 Guggenheim Fellow, professor, Stone Cold Jane Austen, et al.) at the 2017 Jane Austen Society of North America General Meeting in Huntington, California. I was awed by her spectacular vitae, sharp mind, and strength—physical and intellectual! Have you ever met someone that glows from within? That's Devoney. Turns out she has a generous heart and enjoys shining her light on talented women too. How could I not ask her to consider writing the foreword? When I told the authors she had agreed, a handful messaged me that I had amped up the pressure to deliver something wonderful, knowing she would be reading their words. Thank you, Devoney, for your time, dedication to Austen and women writers, and your thoughtful words.

Shari Ryan of Mad Hat Books created another stunning cover for The Quill Collective series. It was my first effort envisioning a cover with an image from a classical painting…so grateful for all the reassurance on her end. **Beau North** created our beautiful book interiors and hand-corrected numerous eleventh-hour edits. I am all astonishment of her many talents, patience, excellent advice, and keen eye for what is on trend.

Sub-editor **Debbie Brown** was always forthcoming with her opinions and corrections: tricky homonyms, unnecessary commas, necessary commas, plural possessive apostrophes ... all those details that need to be precise before a book is ready for the world. I was also fortunate to have **Elizabeth Adams** do a *final eyes* proof. Many thanks for catching those frustrating strays!

Because this is an anthology about several of Austen's female characters, I hoped it would be more meaningful to have bespoke products from female artisans for our promotional giveaways. If you haven't yet, do check out the gorgeous Rational Creatures creations by **Northanger Soapworks** (soap), **Paper and Slate** (candles), and **PNW Vibes** (shirts). So proud to have partnered with these inspiring entrepreneurs on this project.

My thanks to **Claudine di Muzio Pepe** for her wealth of ideas, scheduling the two-month long blog tour, and her overall munificence. I am lucky to be able to count her as a friend.

I am indebted to the indie publishers, editors, and authors who have shared their expertise with me as I make my way in this Wild West that is modern-day publishing. Thank you to the bloggers and readers who have supported *Rational Creatures*, *The Darcy Monologues,* and *Dangerous to Know: Jane Austen's Rakes & Gentlemen Rogues* by buying, reading, reviewing, and telling a friend. Your reviews are EVERYTHING. I hope you have appreciated this collection in the affectionate spirit it was created.

Special thanks to **Claudine** of Just Jane 1813, **Rita Deodato** of From Pemberley to Milton, **Meredith Esparza** of Austenesque Reviews, and

Laurel Ann Nattress of Austenprose for all the encouragement—as well as invaluable author recommendations for *Rational Creatures*.

As always, much gratitude to Mr. B, Finnegan, and Ellary for not begrudging my dreams and accepting "me being me"—a woman who can still choose for myself.

Choosing for oneself. Choice. I believe that's one of the reasons millions have loved Austen's rational creatures and their choices these last two-hundred years. I daresay, it's those little bits that will endure another two hundred.

CHRISTINA BOYD wears many hats as she is an editor under her own banner, The Quill Ink, a contributor to Austenprose, and a commercial ceramicist. A life member of Jane Austen Society of North America, Christina lives in the wilds of the Pacific Northwest with her dear Mr. B, two busy teenagers, and a retriever named BiBi. Visiting Jane Austen's England was made possible by actor Henry Cavill when she won the Omaze experience to meet him in the spring of 2017 on the London Eye. True story. You can Google it.

CPSIA information can be obtained
at www.ICGtesting.com
Printed in the USA
LVHW111616080319
609994LV00002B/459/P

RATIONAL CREATURES

"But I hate to hear you talking so, like a fine gentleman, and as if women were all fine ladies, instead of rational creatures. We none of us expect to be in smooth water all our days." —Persuasion

Jane Austen: True romantic or rational creature? Her novels transport us back to the Regency, a time when well-mannered gentlemen and finely-bred ladies fell in love as they danced at balls and rode in carriages. Yet her heroines, such as Elizabeth Bennet, Anne Elliot, and Elinor Dashwood, were no swooning, fainthearted damsels in distress. Austen's novels have become timeless classics because of their biting wit, honest social commentary, and because she wrote of strong women who were ahead of their day. True to their principles and beliefs, they fought through hypocrisy and broke social boundaries to find their happily-ever-after.

In the third romance anthology of The Quill Collective series, sixteen celebrated Austenesque authors write the untold histories of Austen's brave adventuresses, her shy maidens, her talkative spinsters, and her naughty matrons. Peek around the curtain and discover what made Lady Susan so wicked, Mary Crawford so capricious, and Hetty Bates so in need of Emma Woodhouse's pity.

Rational Creatures is a collection of humorous, poignant, and engaging short stories set in Georgian England that complement and pay homage to Austen's great works and great ladies who were, perhaps, the first feminists in an era that was not quite ready for feminism.

"Make women rational creatures, and free citizens, and they will become good wives; —that is, if men do not neglect the duties of husbands and fathers." —**Mary Wollstonecraft**

quill ink